Stalag Sunflower

by

Wes Brummer

Stalag Sunflower

Cover Art by *Jennifer Greeff*

The Wild Rose Press, Inc.
PO Box 708
Adams Basin, NY 14410-0708
Visit us at www.thewildrosepress.com

Publishing History
First Edition, 2021
Trade Paperback ISBN 978-1-5092-3489-9
Digital ISBN 978-1-5092-3490-5

Published in the United States of America

My fingers trembled as I picked up the reply card. Was it from anxiety or excitement? "I'll fill out this card and mail it tomorrow."

Horst took an expensive pen from his pocket. "I'll do it. But this doesn't mean you're going."

"That is acceptable." I inclined my head to hide my smile.

Horst began marking the postcard.

Even if he was against the trip, I intended to use any means necessary to get to America. The thought of seeing old friends again filled me with anticipation. Was Emily still alive? I'd thought of Fräulein Henning often since Della's death. The possibility of meeting her again made my heart race with anticipation. Della was my true love. But Emily was my first.

And there was the memory of my friend Brian Novak. Novak had died at Camp Conrad more than fifty years ago, but not by his own hand. I still wondered how I could have saved him. If only I had been there when it happened.

"Papa?" Horst held his pen aloft. "There is a question about medical issues. I'm listing your memory lapses."

I flicked my wrist. "Write whatever you like." My mind was already imagining my flight across the Atlantic. My second visit to America would be a chance to correct a small piece of history. My friend's death was no suicide.

Brian Novak was murdered. And I had the letter to prove it.

Praise for Wes Brummer

"*STALAG SUNFLOWER* is a well-crafted mix of intrigue, conflict, and romance as told from the point of view of "Henry" Rohling, a German prisoner. The story is set in Kansas in 1943, at Camp Conrad. During his confinement as a prisoner, he grapples with a friend's 'suicide' he believes to be a covered-up murder. Henry returns to Kansas in 1995 to attend a camp reunion where he attempts to expose the real truth of his friend's tarnished legacy. But, will anyone listen? *STALAG SUNFLOWER* is an engaging and original novel I am pleased to recommend."

~B.J. Myrick, author

Dedication

To the preservationists at Camp Concordia,
keeping a bit of Homefront history alive

Chapter One

I've always hated getting old. The specter of death didn't bother me, though. I disliked the inevitable need for assistance. Especially when my otherwise well-meaning son decided I had grown incapable of doing tasks I had always done since youth.

Around Christmastime of 1994, my eldest son Horst banned me from driving because of a few minor accidents. A trip to the eye doctor early the next year showed I needed glasses. They helped a great deal, but Horst still refused to return my license. "There's something else going on, Papa. We need to know what it is."

That meant more trips to other physicians. During each examination, Horst hovered about like an overprotective parent. Or an untrusting prison guard. Our fourth appointment landed me in a brilliantly lit examination room with three caster-wheel stools and a bed covered in butcher's paper. "This man is a neurologist," my son told me.

"My nerves are fine." I held my head up, endeavoring to look my sternest. The glaring lights made me queasy. Was I about to be interrogated?

"Quit scowling. Doctor Lehman is a native Berliner. You'll like him. Today, he will be going over your test results. We're here for answers."

"The doctor is late." My voice rose in pitch.

"Besides, there's nothing wrong with me."

"Plenty is wrong, Papa. Your auto has dents and scratches, and you forget things. That's why we're seeing this through."

"People drive too fast."

"Probably so." That was his usual response when he didn't want to argue.

Ten minutes later, the physician entered and sat on a stool facing me. Doctor Lehman was a young Deutsch, quite handsome, with sandy hair and a ruddy tan, despite the dreary spring. Beneath his lab coat, he wore a dress shirt and wide necktie printed with small medical emblems—the ones with two serpents intertwined around a cross. "*Guten tag*, Herr Rohling. I promise not to take up your day. A few questions and a short visit."

I nodded.

"Your full name, please?"

A ridiculous question. Every form I've filled out asked my name. "Heinrich Rohling."

"Do you have children, sir?

"Two sons and a daughter."

"*Gut*. And what are their names?"

"Horst, Johann, and Caroline."

"Any grandchildren?"

I held my head high. "*Ja*."

"*Bitte*. Could you give me their names?"

I frowned. This was not a question on any form. I composed a list in my mind. "Caroline has a second husband. Surely you can't expect me to name his children as well."

"Tell me the grandchildren you can remember." The doctor didn't seem fazed by my irritation.

I recited names, counting each with my fingers. "They don't come by often. Each holiday I have to relearn their ages." It was unwise to say more. This interrogator was searching for weaknesses. I could not admit I had depended on Della to help me remember which child attended what school or their favorite subjects. She was my rock. I lost her to cancer two years ago. Or was it three? Since then, Horst has noticed my small blunders, and now this doctor prodded me with his questions as well.

The physician leaned forward; his stool screeched in the confined space. "Can you tell me the birthdays of your children?"

I crossed my arms. "*Nein*, my wife kept track of dates."

"I see." The neurologist tilted his head. "How old are you, Herr Rohling?"

"Seventy."

Horst cleared his throat. "Tell the truth, Papa."

I stared at my son. He was never one to remain quiet. "I'm seventy," I said with emphasis.

"No." Horst pointed to an April 1995 wall calendar with a scenic photo of blooming yellow edelweiss. "You were born in 1921. So you're seventy-four."

"I get tired of figuring my age each time someone asks. It's easier to say seventy and leave it at that."

Horst brushed his hand aside, a gesture he often used in court. "You should know your age. It's like reciting the current year or the color of your eyes."

I wrinkled my nose. For a lawyer, Horst can fabricate the oddest arguments. "Eyes don't change color from year to year."

"You have a point." Dr. Lehman scooted his stool

back to address us. "For many growing older, yearly age diminishes in importance as do past details. Your tests show some holes in your memory, Herr Rohling. Not alarming when seen alone. Think of this as a snapshot. But it's not enough information to make a diagnosis. For this reason, I want you to retake the tests in four months. That will give us a better picture." Lehman scribbled on a pad and handed the sheet to Horst. "Give this to the admittance desk. They'll schedule the appointment."

Horst pursed his lips. For a moment, I wondered if he would protest. My son expected immediate results. Not a four-month delay. At least he was gracious, bowing slightly, taking my elbow, and helping me to my feet. "*Danke*, *Doktor*." We filed out of the office.

Horst said little on the way home. I kept quiet as well. Those probing questions revealed my trouble in recalling names and dates, and I wondered if worse would come. Was Horst thinking the same? In front of my modest bungalow, he retrieved the mail, then turned his expensive car into the drive. "I'll help you to the door." Grabbing the mail, Horst left the vehicle.

I stared at the small home I had built with my own hands. Della and I moved in the day after our wedding in June 1948. Those were turbulent times for all Berliners—the ever-present threat of hunger, power outages, and the constant drone of planes during the Airlift. By the time the Berlin Wall divided the city, our family was complete. Horst turned nine and Johann was seven, both playing soldiers with other boys. Caroline went from toddler to escape artist.

Horst opened the passenger door. "Let's go inside, Papa."

Horst unlocked the house, and we entered the front hall. While I hung my wool jacket in the closet, my son stopped by the long table to separate the mail. Once a week, he helped me with paying the bills. I suppose I never got used to doing that after Della passed.

"Papa, could you draw some of that fine *Weissbier* you've been brewing? It will take a few minutes to get these payments in order."

"Of course." Even after my retirement from running a neighborhood *Biergarten*, I still indulged in homebrewing, especially the darker styles of *Dunkel*, *Altbier*, and *Doppelbock*. My favorite is *Eisbock*, but that required cooling equipment I no longer owned.

My brewing area used to be the pantry, just off the kitchen where I milled and masked my own grains. Age has forced me to be content with buying malt extracts, a much less time-consuming way of brewing. I drew a stein of wheat ale for Horst and a small glass of *Heller Bock* for myself. Americans drank their watery beer ice cold, but a full-bodied German ale tasted better at room temperature.

With drinks in hand, I returned to the front room. Horst had already shed his suit jacket and loosened his tie. He stood by the hall table, studying a thick manila envelope.

He held the package for my inspection. "This is from America. Shall we see what it is?"

I had set the thick parcel aside a few days before, not bothering to look at it. "Perhaps the mail carrier delivered it to the wrong address."

"*Nein*. It is sent to you from the Conrad County Historical Society in Kansas." He tilted his head, frowning. "Curious."

I was intrigued as well. Conrad County was a place very familiar to me. "Let's sit down. These mugs are heavy."

"Sorry, Papa." Horst shoved the envelope under his arm and took the mugs from me.

We sat in two comfy chairs with a coffee table in front. Horst took a sip of ale, tore open the mailer, and removed copies of news clippings, a schedule of events, and a cover letter. "Shall I read the letter first?"

"*Ja.*" My hands felt clammy. Other camps had sent out letters to former soldiers my age. Now, it was happening to my group as well.

Horst donned a pair of glasses and read aloud.

"Dear Mr. Rohling:

"The Conrad County Historical Society is planning a special fifty-year reunion and cordially invites you to be a part of the celebration. Fifty years ago, Camp Conrad was the wartime home to some four thousand German servicemen. In October 1945, the last interned soldiers returned to Europe. In all, nearly eight thousand enlisted men and officers passed through the prisoner-of-war camp during its thirty months of operation.

"After the conflict, Camp Conrad was dismantled, and nearby farmers purchased the land. With World War II over, the townspeople looked to the future. New residents moved to Conrad who had no idea that a camp for interned German soldiers ever existed a few miles away. But as the camp's memory faded, the Conrad County Historical Society decided to build a museum to preserve German POW artifacts.

"And so began our project: to reconstruct a part of Camp Conrad.

"We developed a plan, raised money, and began construction. The restoration is nearly complete. On August 10, 1995, you will get a sneak peek at Camp Conrad's restored main barracks, mess hall, auditorium, and Visitors' Center. With your help, we will organize an oral history archive as a permanent part of the museum.

"While millions of American soldiers left home, you sowed and harvested our fields, raised our livestock, worked in our canneries, planted trees, and paved roads. Though you were here involuntarily, you made productive use of your stay by taking classes, learning new skills, and making lasting friendships. You left an indelible mark on this country and this community.

"Join us in celebrating this milestone.

"If you wish to attend the two-day event, complete and return the reply card enclosed. Thanks to a federal grant, we can pay air travel and lodging for ten Camp Conrad veterans. So complete and mail the enclosed reply card immediately.

"Be part of the festivities!

"Sincerely,

"Virginia Powell,

"President, Conrad County Historical Society"

Horst slowly lowered the letter, looking at me in shock and perhaps a touch of anger. "Papa, what is this all about?"

My hands trembled, for I knew what was coming. I had never told my children the particulars of what I did during the war. Oh, sure, they knew I fought in Field Marshall Rommel's Afrika Korps. But by May of 1943, Germany's desert army was *kaput*. I had never told

Horst and the others what happened afterward. I suspect many veterans avoided talking about the war, and few children pressed them for details. No child wants to know their father was a National Socialist. I never discussed my part in the conflict for one straightforward reason. "I took no part in the last two years of the war." It was hard to meet his eyes. "Because I was an American prisoner."

He drew his head back as if I slapped him. "You were captured?"

"No." I glared at him. Capture was a disgraceful word. "Our division had little petrol, and a few rounds of ammunition left. We surrendered."

Horst avoided my gaze by turning his attention to the papers. "Sorry, Papa. I didn't mean to offend. So your captors sent you to a prison camp, and this is an invitation to a reunion?"

I peered at the return postcard. "It's a chance to see old friends."

Horst leaned back, appraising me, the way he probably assessed his clients. "You never told any of us you were a prisoner of war."

A sharp retort rose to my lips, but Horst did have a point. I didn't want to anger my son. Not if it meant getting what I wanted. "It's not a subject I care to discuss."

"Why not? It happened a long time ago."

"To you, maybe. For me, the details are still vivid."

A hint of a smile crossed his lips. "Your army was defeated. You had no choice about what would happen next. There is no shame, Papa. Just history. We would have understood."

"I made that decision long before you were born." I

brushed my hand in front of me, wishing I could dismiss his questions with the same gesture. "After I married your mother, it was time to look ahead and start a family. Not dwell on the past."

Horst was forty-four with a successful practice. He attended an athletic club to stay lean. His suits were tailored, and he hired a stylist to color his hair dark brown, leaving traces of gray on the sides. Maintaining a photogenic image was part of the theatrics of being an attorney.

He raised an eyebrow. "What was it like after your capture?"

I sipped my beer, pondering what to tell. "My division surrendered in mid-May of '43, and our captors sent us to a large internment camp. There we awaited transport to England. A few weeks later, the Tommies released us to the Amis, and we crossed the Atlantic on what they called a liberty ship."

Horst frowned. "Tommies?"

"Our nickname for the British. 'Amis' was shorthand for Americans."

He nodded. "Like the Americans calling Deutsch troops Krauts or Jerries."

Along with the rest of his generation, Horst grew up on a diet of American Technicolor war epics where actors wore clean, well-fitted uniforms, and those who died did so with theatrical grace and little bloodshed.

"Every country had names for the enemy."

"But why America? The…Tommies had you in hand. Why didn't they ship you to England?"

"Britain had been fighting for two years. They already had thousands of war prisoners with no more room to spare. America, however, had lots of space.

After landing in New York, we marched to a mammoth train station and boarded a car for Kansas."

"To Camp Conrad." Horst picked up one of the copied news clippings. "What did you do there?"

I leaned back, wondering where to begin. It was amazing how easily the memories came flooding back. "I passed the time like everyone else."

"It must have been difficult."

I bit my lip, hiding a private smile. "We ate well, pursued hobbies, had our own newspaper, read library books, listened to concerts, and attended classes. Still, at times, it was boring. The worst part was not knowing how our fellow soldiers were doing during the war."

"The Americans didn't tell you?"

"Radios weren't allowed in the compound." Let him think it was the Americans' idea. "For us, news of the war came each time new prisoners came through the gate. They could give us a vivid picture of the fighting, the weaponry, and the losses."

Horst scanned the photocopied news clippings. I knew my long years of silence still bothered him. Finally, he peered at me. "You've misled us, Papa. I accept the fact that you were a prisoner. But you constantly droned into Johann and me, playing soldiers as kids, the importance of being loyal to the Fatherland. Yet you were a captive. And a comfortable one at that."

There was that annoying judgment in his voice again. Why did I stress pride and self-importance, even arrogance? I could never tell him the truth. It hurt to admit it, even to myself. I wanted my sons to be something I never was. "A soldier is still a soldier no matter which side of the fence he is on. Prisoners and guards have duties to perform, jobs to do. Both must conduct themselves with discipline and reserve."

"But you were in the enemy's camp. Aren't prisoners of war supposed to resist?"

"Like some grand war movie? It wasn't like that for me." I paused. "Other than spotting a guard in one of the towers, I seldom saw an American in camp. We were left to ourselves. Who would we resist against except fellow prisoners?"

Horst shook his head in disbelief. "What about escapes?"

"There were several attempts. But America is vast. Able-bodied young men during wartime stuck out. One man from our camp hid in a farmer's woodpile, but a thunderstorm scared him silly. He begged the farmer to turn him in."

"He could have been shot."

I shrugged. "Not likely. Most escapees returned to camp within days."

Horst drank the rest of his brew, then gathered the papers together. "I'll toss this in the trash and work on your bills."

"Wait!" I slapped his hand away. "I want to go to this reunion."

He peered at me open-mouthed. "You have a doctor's appointment in four months. Traveling anywhere—especially to America—is out of the question."

"I wish to go. Another chance to see my old comrades may never come again."

Horst rubbed his temple. "The risk of something going wrong is too great."

I glared at him. "Who gave you the right to decide what I can and cannot do?"

"I am your caretaker." He spoke the words with deliberate slowness.

"I'd like to hear what Johann and Caroline have to say about it."

He drew in a breath and blew it out. "I suppose they'll want a say in this."

"I doubt if Johann will even care," I said. My middle child had an unhealthy love for Berlin's nightlife. How he kept his job as a hospital orderly was beyond me.

"Probably so. And Caroline has a new husband and four children to manage. But I am willing to make this a family decision. If either one agrees with me, then you're staying."

"Please." I wanted to grasp his hand. "You can't deny me a chance to revisit a place that is important to me. If our roles were switched, I wouldn't stand in your way."

He sighed. "Papa, even if I agreed to this adventure, I can't go with you. I've already taken my holiday, and I have cases to prepare for. Johann or Caroline will have to accompany you."

"At least I have a chance to go." My fingers trembled as I picked up the reply card. Was it from anxiety or excitement? "I'll fill out this card and mail it tomorrow."

Horst took an expensive pen from his pocket. "I'll do it. But this doesn't mean you're going."

"That is acceptable." I inclined my head to hide my smile.

Horst began marking the postcard.

Even if he was against the trip, I intended to use any means necessary to get to America. The thought of seeing old friends again filled me with anticipation. Was Emily still alive? I'd thought of Fräulein Henning often since Della's death. The possibility of meeting her again made my heart race with anticipation. Della was my true love. But Emily was my first.

And there was the memory of my friend Brian Novak. Novak had died at Camp Conrad more than fifty years ago, but not by his own hand. I still wondered how I could have saved him. If only I had been there when it happened.

"Papa?" Horst held his pen aloft. "There is a question about medical issues. I'm listing your memory lapses."

I flicked my wrist. "Write whatever you like." My mind was already imagining my flight across the Atlantic. My second visit to America would be a chance to correct a small piece of history. My friend's death was no suicide.

Brian Novak was murdered. And I had the letter to prove it.

Chapter Two

13-14 May 1943

A violent shaking. Brian Novak shouted in English. "Henry! Wake up!"

I jerked to my feet, jumping to the edge of the slit trench. My hands threw the Mauser to my shoulder, and I sighted down the long barrel. Where was the enemy? In my mind's eye, the Tommies were preparing for a raid behind distant sand dunes.

"It's not the British," Novak said. "Look!" My friend pointed behind us. A massive armored truck with caterpillar treads exited the motor yard. I brushed the sandflies from my eyes and pulled on my tinted goggles. Thirty meters away, the half-track rumbled to a stop. An Afrika Korps officer in a high-peaked cap climbed to the turret, and a soldier handed him a long pole. More officers stood at attention, looking up to the commander who saluted with his right arm thrust forward. As one, they returned the gesture, their cries of "*Sieg Heil!*" barely audible above the roaring engine. Then the half-track rumbled from camp heading east, throwing back a stream of dust. The sound dwindled as it disappeared over a sandy hill. Why would a single armored truck drive into the Libyan Desert in blazing daylight? It was suicide. Patrolling Allied bombers would target the vehicle in no time and attack our encampment as well. The Mauser in my hands held only a few rounds. Not enough to stop any determined attack. The thought of being defenseless under a strafing aircraft left me feeling uneasy.

"Something's up." Novak was emphatic. "Did you see who climbed aboard that communications truck?"

I nodded. "The *Generalleutnant*. Had to be."

"And did you see what the other officer handed him?"

"A flag?" Then it dawned on me. "*Mein Gott*, we're surrendering!"

Novak smiled. "Not *mein Gott*. Use the English phrase, 'My God.' "

"My God," I mumbled. Since I'd learned Novak grew up in New York City, I asked him to speak to me in English and use American idioms whenever we were alone. As a joke, he called me "Henry" instead of Heinrich. I liked the nickname and enjoyed his colorful use of language and soon learned he could weave a string of foul words that would make a stable boy envious.

I pointed to the tread marks. "I hope his mission is successful. There is little petrol left. No new supplies have arrived in the past week."

"I wouldn't worry about the *Generalleutnant*. With the truce flag and the dust he's kicking up, I'm sure the Brits will be serving him tea by nightfall. In two days, we'll be guests of Mr. Churchill."

"Tommy's rations have to be better than the foul-smelling stuff the Italians have been shipping," I said.

Novak grinned. "Lieutenant Schwartz calls it 'Dead Arab.' I heard a rumor about American rations. They get canned fruit, chocolate, and even cigarettes.

Uncle Sam probably feeds the Brits as well. I'd gladly surrender just to smoke an American cigarette."

"You're nuts." I slouched below ground to avoid the scorching sun.

At the age of twenty-two, I was older than most of the other conscripts and enlisted men. Brian Novak was four years younger than me. Freckles spattered his youthful face. His eyes were a washed-out blue, and his once brown hair was now a bleached sandy-white. More handsome than my ruddy Italian features, bushy black eyebrows, and short frame. I once poked fun at him by suggesting he pose for an Aryan youth recruiting poster. "Don't ever say that!" he snapped at me. "The walls have ears!" He later told me his Jewish relatives had vanished. Thousands had disappeared from home without a trace. Even soldiers spoke of the missing in hushed tones. They called it "Night and Fog."

Brian nudged my shoulder. "Do you like jazz?"

"I've heard of it. Do the Tommies listen to such music?"

"You can bet the Brits have taken to all things American. My parents collected jazz records when they lived in the Bronx. We had a big radio in the front room. I often listened to Count Basie and swing music. Then the German government offered my father a university position in Munich. I hated to leave New York. My parents gave away those records. Jazz was banned in Germany."

"How old were you when you left America?"

"Thirteen." Brian sighed. "I still remember riding my bicycle along Long Island Sound."

"Where will we go? Britain? Canada?"

Novak brushed away a fly crawling in his ear. "Anywhere away from these vermin."

I flipped the leather cover off my wristwatch, a gift from my father. "It's nearly 1700 hours. I go on duty in ten minutes." The blasting desert heat showed no sign of diminishing. I drank metallic-tasting water from my canteen, but it still soothed my dry throat.

Novak tipped back his own canteen. "I should report to my post as well."

"See you tomorrow, Brian." I grabbed my greatcoat—nights were chilly—and climbed out of the trench. Novak followed me.

He clapped me on the back. "Take care, Henry." He waved, heading for the command tent to report for guard duty.

Our daily routine was determined by the harsh desert environment and by enemy aircraft. Many of us slept during the hot daytime temperatures. Any movement attracted sandflies to the moisture in our eyes, noses, and throats. Patrolling Allied bombers dominated the sky. If a plane came near, all activity stopped. We could not move anyway. Ammunition, petrol, engine parts, food, and medicines—all those things needed for a mobile division—no longer existed. The Tommies had seen to that. Our supplies remained aboard transports inside sealed crates, lying at the bottom of the Mediterranean.

I trudged through sand to the motor yard, reported to the sergeant on duty, and began my night of greasing engines with the few supplies I had.

All our motor vehicles bore the emblem of the Afrika Korps, a palm tree with the swastika over the trunk. The trucks were huge with large front grills and powerful, almost indestructible engines. I said almost. Fine sand driven by high winds would cripple any motor. Small granules worked their way inside every crevice, beneath gaskets, and between moving parts. A mechanic must grease every vehicle thoroughly and often. I've heard more than one military officer lament that men were expendable, but running trucks and armor were not.

The temperature chilled as night descended. I stood hunched over an engine with a hooded lamp shielded by overhead canvas to maintain blackout conditions. Tedious work, yet essential; I wiped away the tainted, sandy grease and reapplied new lubricant. Even the rags were in short supply. I mentioned this to the sergeant, who glanced around before answering. "In a few hours, it won't matter. Depending on what news the *Generalleutanant* brings back, we may set fire to the entire motor yard."

I raised my eyebrows. "Why?"

"To deny equipment to the enemy." He looked about once more. "Now, get back to work and forget everything I said." He strutted down a line of vehicles, shouting at another engineer to stay busy.

I worked for the next eight hours. At 0400 hours, the heavy clanking of the half-track returned, parking near where I worked. Voices reached my ears, but it was difficult to make out the words. Soon, a commanding tone rose in pitch. It had to be the *Generalleutnant*. "That is an order! When we move out, I want the plastique fully in place."

The air seemed void of oxygen, and I slumped to the running board of a troop carrier. For the last year, our unit had raced across the desert sand, raiding

Tommy's supply dumps and evading pursuit. I'd eaten dust, swatted flies, endured sandstorms, heat, scorpions, lice, and—occasionally—bullets. Now it might be over. The end of our fighting unit. *Look about. Pay attention. This will be a memorable day.*

We assembled at dawn. The *Generalleutant* announced the news over a hastily wired loudspeaker; we would surrender to a unit of the 2nd New Zealand Division. Our paths had crossed so often we had acquired nominal respect for each other. "Each soldier is responsible for destroying his rifle. Officers will render their sidearms useless." He spoke in clipped tones, hands behind his back. "Sappers will detonate charges in the ammunition dump and motor yard after we exit camp." He paused to brush fingers across his eyes. "It has been an honor to be your commanding officer. You are the bravest of the brave. Be proud of your victories! And face the future with that same spirit, knowing you have given your best for the Fatherland!" He thrust his right arm forward, hand extended. "*Sieg Heil!*"

"*Heil!*" As one, we returned the salute.

He dismissed us, and we soon set about fouling our weapons. Until assembly that evening, there was little to do but wait. I wandered to the mess tent and received some canned rations, then trudged back to the trench. There I found Novak nestled in what little shade the ditch provided from the rising sun. "You awake?"

He groaned as he lifted his head. Novak had acquired some fly netting, which covered his face. "I am now."

"What did you trade for this thing?" I lifted the helmet from his head with the netting attached to the brim. Practical, but a soldier wearing this would look like a beekeeper.

"Ah! That's mine!" He made a grab for it, but I kept the helmet out of reach.

"Not before you tell me how you got this."

"I traded my pocketknife. The one I found on a fallen Brit a few months back. You've seen it."

I had. An ingenious device with two blades, corkscrew, and file.

I tossed his helmet back. "You're always thinking ahead." I swatted at the flies buzzing around my head. It just irritated them more.

"That's why I'm sticking with you, old man. You've stayed alive for more than two years in this desert. You're my good-luck charm."

I shook my head. "Well, this good-luck charm needs sleep. We'll be meeting our captors this evening. Fill your canteen, grab some rations, and get some winks." I smiled, liking how I worked in the American slang.

He gave me a mock American salute. "Yes, commander!"

"Dismissed." I wave him off, shaking my head.

Novak climbed over the wall and disappeared.

Despite the flies and the rising heat, I drifted off to sleep.

At 1800 hours, we gathered without fanfare and slogged out of camp. Not a march. Imagine trying to march on a beach. With each step, we churned the sand, which worked its way into our boots. The weight was not much, but each step whittled our strength to a helpless state of fatigue. A desert army is only as fit as its vehicles and armor. We had neither.

Our unit plodded eastward in a narrow column, following the faint path the half-track had taken the previous day. On either side of us were unexploded German landmines. Eating dust stirred from the marchers ahead was preferable to stepping on a mine.

Nearly eight hundred men were making an act of faith that the New Zealanders would follow through with the surrender and then feed and give us shelter. Our lives depended on that promise. Heat bore down on our backs, sucking the sweat from us. The day waned but not fast enough. Our shadows grew longer before us, but the relentless heat failed to abate. We lumbered on, our canteens growing lighter each time we drank.

Behind us, a muffled series of thuds filled the air. I glanced behind me. Two thin columns of thick smoke rose and merged in a darkening azure sky. Our sappers had succeeded in destroying our vehicles and supplies. We had nowhere to go but forward.

Novak trudged beside me; his netting draped around him like a veil. "What if our friends from Down Under let us walk all night? What if they decide not to be bothered?"

I turned to him with raised brows. My friend seldom revealed this kind of gloom. His words reflected my thoughts. "Let's hope you're wrong," I rasped over a parched throat. Soldiers of all countries followed an ethical code, even when dealing with the enemy. Our captors would deliver us. They had to.

Twenty hundred hours. Long shadows faded as the sun dipped behind black dunes. We were two hours into our Exodus. Our enemy stood ahead, not behind us, and we had no Red Sea to cross. Just an ocean of sand sapping our strength. Few of us carried our greatcoats.

Too much weight. The night's chill would be, at best, uncomfortable.

Novak grabbed my shoulder. "We're being watched." He pointed past my shoulder. "There. To the left."

Only then did I notice dozens of dark figures standing atop the dunes. More appeared to the front and back, surrounding us. As they advanced, more shadows topped the dunes. A score of canvassed vehicles rumbled to our column. From a nearby jeep, a New Zealand captain in khakis stepped out and ambled toward us. "Any of you chaps speak English?" Like he was asking for directions.

Novak answered the officer. "I do, sir."

The officer grinned, enjoying himself. "Excellent. That makes my job a whole lot easier." The mustached captain was my age, with well-trimmed nails and an impeccable uniform.

Another officer approached and saluted. "I came to assist, sir."

"Thank you, lieutenant." The captain pointed to Novak. "This man is your interpreter. Make your way to the rear of this column. Instruct the prisoners we will transport them to a temporary camp, where they will be processed. Cramped conditions, I fear, but they'll get food and water. The less fuss they make, the sooner they can bed down for the night."

I touched Novak's sleeve. "I'll see you later." Without meaning to, I spoke in English.

The captain glanced at me. "You speak English as well?"

"Some. I'm still learning."

"You'll do. Come aboard."

I rode with the captain and two other soldiers to the front of the line, where more cargo trucks arrived. There, I explained to my comrades the captain's message. "Our host will transport us to a holding camp in the rear. As soon as they can sort things out, we will move to a more permanent encampment."

A German captive, no older than a boy, looked up, his eyes reflected defeat. "Where will we go?" he asked in German.

"I don't know," I said.

"Can you find out?"

"I'll try."

The guard behind me motioned for the boy to move on. I never saw him again.

More troop carriers surrounded us. A cargo transport halted in front of the New Zealand officer. The empty truck bed reeked of petrol.

The captain gestured with a sweep of the arm. I pointed and yelled, "Get onto the trucks!"

German soldiers boarded each vehicle to capacity. Some even climbed on the side of the canvas trucks and found a foothold. Each loaded vehicle joined a convoy heading north. I stood to one side, my role as interpreter no longer needed as the last of our column boarded the remaining troop carrier. I caught the captain's attention and motioned to the last vehicle pulling away. He nodded, and I jumped onto the running board and grabbed a support bar. We, too, joined the northbound procession.

At one time, the Afrika Korps sent Allied forces retreating across the continent, but the tide of war had shifted. We were vanquished. What would happen to us? Where would we go?

And when would we see home again?

Chapter Three

Three days after Horst sent the reply card back to America, I sat on a park bench in the English Gardens, near the center of Berlin's best-known park, the Tiergarten. Pigeons flocked around the breadcrumbs I threw from a paper sack. It was a pleasant way to spend an afternoon, listening to songbirds and watching children play in the fountains. My favorite pastime at the park was chatting with tourists and discovering where they came from, a useful way to practice my English with Britons and Americans. With strangers, it was easy to be anyone besides a dependent old man.

I chose this place to hear my children's verdict. Would any of them accompany me to America? No companion meant no trip. Holding this family meeting in a public place would give me a chance to prove I could find my way around. And give me an edge as well. Horst was always pressed for time. Johann hated parks, preferring the night clubs instead. And Caroline felt she was needed at home.

I leaned back, wondering who would attend the reunion. Some would be former officers who arrived at camp long after I left in the summer of '43. Would Novak's killer show? A whimsical question since the Americans deemed his hanging a suicide. But I knew better, and I had the proof. Another prisoner had killed him and made it look like a hanging. After fifty years, was that killer still alive? Even if he lived, I could not hope to catch him. At least I could remove the stigma of suicide from Novak's death record. Would anyone care? It didn't matter. Brian Novak was my friend. I should have vindicated him long ago.

I had to get to the reunion. Alone if necessary.

With no more breadcrumbs, I strolled to a nearby trash container to dispose of the greasy bag. To my right, five lanes of honking traffic converged at the Tiergarten's famous roundabout with the Victory Column as its hub. Della and I had toured the military monument years ago. We entered through a tunnel beneath the street and climbed some two hundred spiral steps to the observation deck. Della clung to my side as we leaned over the safety rail and watched the miniature cars pirouette below us. I never ascended those steps again. Wresting my gaze from the pillar, I walked back to my seat, fighting down a tightening in my throat.

"Papa!" Horst waved his arm as if he was hailing a taxi. Pigeons scattered before him as he approached. Despite the warm weather, he still wore his suit coat. "You could have picked an easier place to meet. I had to park the car nearly a kilometer away."

"You love your auto too much. I got here quite easily on the S-Bahm."

Horst mopped his brow. "The trains are too noisy. Why did you choose to meet here?"

"Everyone knows where the English Gardens are."

He motioned to the roundabout. "That thing is a circus with all the tourists and taxis blaring their horns. We should find a quieter place."

"I know a secluded spot. When the others arrive,

we'll go there." I gestured to a bench. "Let's sit. Standing in one spot tires me."

Horst took my arm. I wanted to shake him off, but I relented. We reached a wooden bench, and he eased me down.

"*Hallo, Vati!*" Caroline's high voice rang as she crossed Atonaer Strasse, one of the avenues that joined the roundabout. Carolyn was a petite woman with short blonde hair that followed the contours of her face. Her peach-colored blouse and dark trendy American jeans made her look like an *Amerikanisher*.

I embraced my little girl. "You're looking well. How are the children?"

"They're fine." She embraced Horst. "Good morning."

"Good morning to you, Caroline. I'm glad you came."

Caroline brushed fingers through her pampered hair. "I promised Peter I wouldn't be away long. He's with the children at the zoo." She turned to me. "Big brother tells me you have a special conference in America."

Horst blew through his nose. "Maybe we should wait for Johann to arrive before we start this discussion."

Caroline waved with her finger. "I want to know about this now. You were a prisoner, Papa? It must have been terrible."

"Not at all," I assured her. "The Americans did their best to keep us occupied. Many prisoners have gone back to revisit friends there."

"And now you wish to visit as well?"

"I hope so." Her question brought a rush of images:

my first sight of Emily, exploring the prisoner camp with Novak, singing patriotic songs as a group of us marched around the compound, the last time I saw the Henning family.

"Mama never mentioned this. I can't believe we're just now learning what happened. Were you ever going to tell us?"

I bowed my head, unable to answer.

Caroline grabbed my hand. "It's okay, Papa. I hope you get to go."

"I need a travel companion." I glanced at Horst, who averted his eyes. "Otherwise, I have to stay at home."

"I wish I could help." Caroline bit her lip for a moment. "But I have four children, a husband, and a house that needs constant attention."

"I understand."

"Johann is coming." Horst pointed to a bicycle-cart. Johann rode in the double seat behind the driver. The cart halted before us. Johann jumped to the ground, paid the driver, and produced a bottle of water. Downing half of the container, he burst with a theatrical sigh of pleasure and recapped the lid. "Hello, good people! Did I miss anything?"

Johann was in many ways the opposite of Horst. Caroline called him a free spirit. Today, Johann wore frayed jeans, a black T-shirt advertising a cabaret dance club, unkempt hair, and a day's growth of beard. Taller than Horst and rather thin, he looked much like the street musicians that frequent the Tiergarten. I also saw the similarities between my two sons: Della's bright blue eyes and the wavy hair I had in my youth. Very little of that hair remained at seventy-four.

"Hallo, Jonni!" Caroline embraced him. "Still dancing the night away?"

"Not as much these days. After I get home from my shift, I'm too tired to go out again."

My daughter's eyes grew large. "Hospital work must be exciting. Do you like it?"

Johann shrugged. "Emergency rooms are frantic. Moving patients from the OR to recovery is less frenzied."

Horst had been tapping his foot since Johann arrived. "Now that we're all here, I suggest we find a quieter spot to talk. An important decision needs to be made."

"Let's go then." Johann stretched his neck the way a boxer would. "This is my day off, and I don't want to waste it."

"There's a hideaway alcove a short distance away," I said. "We can talk there."

I led the way through a winding manicured path inside the Gardens. Soon, we were sitting in a room-sized red-brick patio bordered by wrought-iron benches at the end of a cul-de-sac. Linden trees surrounded us, creating an illusion of a fairy-tale forest. Caroline and I sat together, while Johann sat opposite from us.

Horst paced like he was in a final argument. "I've been visiting Papa at least once a week these past few months. He is forgetful, and I wonder if his memory is getting worse." His eyes met mine. "Forgive me, Papa, but I wish to be candid."

Johann leaned forward. "All of us overlook things. Is this absentmindedness or something more?"

"I missed a few questions during a doctor's exam. Nothing more," I said.

Johann rubbed his unshaven chin. "If Papa wants to go, I have no problem with that."

"The problem is more complicated than that." Horst stopped his pacing and loomed before Johann. "The doctor wishes to retest in four months, the same time as Papa's conference. I can reschedule, but if Papa goes on this trip, one of us must accompany him. I have an important case coming up, and Caroline has family obligations. How about it, Jon?"

Johann sighed heavily. "I'm on probation for missing work. I can't take any time off."

An uncomfortable pause.

"Wouldn't the Americans watch after these veterans?" Caroline asked.

"Not all the time." Horst flicked his arm in a dismissive gesture. "I'm sure the people of this small town mean well, but I fear they will not be prepared for emergencies. That leaves only two alternatives. The first is that Papa will not go to this reunion."

My heart sank. I took a lungful of air to steady my breathing.

"Or…" Horst glanced at me. "I'll go with him. My firm agreed to give me a working vacation. If I can send and receive documents and e-mail, it would work."

My breath caught. Horst had come through! Giddiness swept over me. Here was my chance to vindicate Novak's memory. I brushed tears from my eyes. "Thank you, Horst. I know this will put a burden on your workload."

He shook his head, a half smile touching his lips. "I can see you catching a plane and not telling anyone. This way, I can continue doing my job while you attend your conference." He took a seat by Johann. "How big is the town you're going to, Papa?"

I leaned back in my seat. "Probably a small town, but I really don't know. Prisoners were not allowed in Conrad."

"One of my paralegals can look into it. If there is nothing more to discuss, then we're done here."

Horst drove me home afterward and escorted me to the front door. "I won't be able to help with the mail today, Papa. This case I've been given will take a lot of preparation. I can come by early next week."

"What's it about?"

Horst sighed. "Our most important client manufactures paper. They've come up with a cheaper process for producing long-lasting acid-free paper. This product will preserve documents for well over a century."

"No more moldy paper smell?" I asked.

Horst gave me an odd look as we stepped inside. "This is serious, Papa. Licensing this process will earn this company millions of Deutschmarks. But there is a problem. An employee claims joint ownership. Normally, work-for-hire rules apply, but this employee has done some work on his own at home. His attorney has presented enough evidence for a trial, and that date will be set next month."

"An entire company and a law firm against one man? That is hardly fair."

Horst sighed heavily. "I get that a lot. Listen, the paper company offered him a generous settlement, but he turned it down. Now, it's my job to protect my client's interests. If all goes well, I may net a partnership in the firm."

I refrained from comment. "Good luck. Can I offer

you some ale?"

Horst waved a hand. "Have to run. Tonight, Gretchen is hosting a fundraiser at the Berlin Story Museum. I'm required to attend." He frowned. "It's their third fundraiser in two months. Her hobbies are forcing me to work later hours."

My son's wife adores black dress soirees. It seems like they lead two separate lives. "Perhaps this trip will be a chance to get away from the social set."

My son looked down. "There's a thought." He turned to go but stopped at the door. "I hope your old friends will lift your spirits as well. Good day, Papa." He left, closing the door behind him.

I was alone and needed to find Novak's letter.

It was a message Novak wrote to me, and I found it long after he died. Years ago, I asked Della to hide it away—but not to destroy it. I never thought to ask her about it before she died. I've searched for the letter a couple of times but never found where Della stored it. Now, his last words had gained renewed urgency. The only place left to look was a broken-down dresser in Caroline's old bedroom where Della had kept her quilt and knitting supplies.

Several screws holding the drawer runners in place had worked loose over the years. With effort, I still managed to pull each drawer out and searched beneath bundles of cloth and yarn. Only the bottom drawer left to search. A wave of hopelessness seized me. If Novak's note remained elusive, then looking further would be useless. The drawer hung crooked from a broken support, one edge brushing the carpet. The entire bureau shuddered when I yanked on the metal handles. I needed a softer touch.

By gently tugging on one side and then the other, I managed to open the heavy drawer. Boards screeched in protest with each pull of the two handles. Finally, I created enough space to wrestle a square cedar box out of its hiding place and placed it on the carpet. A flip of the catch allowed the lid to spring open.

Inside the felt-lined container was a treasure of old memories: black and white photographs of our young family and even older pictures of Della and me as newlyweds. There were baptismal certificates for our children and several yellowed newspaper clippings of the new rebuilding in Berlin. One news photo showed me wielding a hammer.

My heart grew anxious as I probed further back in time. Next came some love letters I wrote to Della while I was in Hamburg constructing new government buildings. Below that was our marriage certificate and my discharge papers from the Wehrmacht. And my prison tags! Somehow, they survived the war. Near the bottom was a bundle of fragile square envelopes wrapped with a silk ribbon. My letters from Emily. Of course, Della would have read them, but she'd kept the old notes. Bless her.

At the bottom of the box, I found a waxed envelope with a folded sheet inside. While I carefully opened the brownish paper, my mind flashed back fifty-two years ago.

Other prisoners discovered him inside the shower building. The official camp record called his death suicide by strangulation. Private Brian Novak stood on a wooden chair, hooked his belt over a shower pipe, placed his head in the noose, and stepped into eternity.

The letters were blurred to a faded gray, but I had

memorized the content years ago.

Henry,

Sgt Stecklein pulled me from the stockade today, telling me I had to be in uniform during my trial. I'm being tried in a Nazi court. Not sure where. In any case, Sgt S said if I were found guilty, the court would carry out my sentence immediately.

Sgt is standing outside now while I get my uniform. Then we will proceed to the shower building. The court wants me presentable before sentencing. If I'm to die, it will be as a soldier. Not a coward.

I'm hiding this note so only you will find it. Please know that I am proud of my country, but not of those in charge. They will destroy our land, but they won't destroy me. Not without a fight.

S is coming.

BN

I tucked the envelope in my shirt pocket. Another prisoner had killed my friend or forced him into suicide. I kept silent about the note. What if his killers came after me? The National Socialists who ran the camp could bar me from working in the Labor Program. I wouldn't be able to work outside of camp. Or see Emily again.

If I am to die, it will be as a soldier. Not a coward. Now was my chance to redeem Novak's honor. And mine as well.

Chapter Four

May-August 1943

The New Zealanders handed us over to the British, where we spent two months in a sprawling tent city ninety kilometers south of Casablanca. They, in turn, gave us to the Americans. The United States would be our home for the duration. Island Britain had no more room for war prisoners. America, however, had a vast amount of space. But in the pecking order of war, moving prisoners took low priority—and so we waited our turn to cross the treacherous Atlantic.

In early July, Novak, myself, and a thousand other men boarded the *Samuel Bell*, an oily-smelling cargo steamer converted to a troop carrier. We spent three miserable weeks confined to a steel room with cramped bunks stacked seven high. On our third day at sea, a storm slammed our convoy all the way to America. For days I could eat little due to seasickness. Often, the ship plunged deep between waves or tilted sideways at an impossible angle. During the crossing, we were never allowed on deck. Huddled below, we had no clue what was happening. "Puking my guts out or swimming with sharks," one of the men in my cabin said. "A hell of a choice."

After twenty-three days, we climbed steel ladders and arrived topside, blinking beneath the sweltering sun. We had arrived at the Port of New York. I longed to walk on anything besides steel decking or gritty sand. In little time, military police from ashore hustled us off the ship to an assembly area outside a sooty brick building with darkened windows. There, a group of army clerks took our names and examined the identification booklets that every *Wehrmacht* soldier carried, then issued us numbered prisoner tags. The processers sent us inside where we shed our filthy clothes and washed under stinging hot showers. The soap reeked of a chemical that left me sneezing, but I shampooed with it anyway. Afterward, we recovered our fumigated clothes, took a cursory medical examination, and received an injection in the backside. Upon leaving the shower building, guards reassembled our group and marched us through the bustling streets of New York. The destination, Novak discovered, would be a train depot he knew well, a fantastic cathedral-like building called Grand Central Station.

"You'll love it, Henry," he said. "It's a majestic place."

Dozens of civilians gawked at us as we strode past busy shops and vendors selling food from wheeled carts. My mouth watered from the tangy aroma of sausages, mustard, curry, and spices I could not identify. Incredibly tall buildings Novak called skyscrapers seemed to pierce the clouds, casting the streets in shadow. Younger women whistled and waved like we were soldiers returning home from war. So many cars and so much noise! German radio had assured us that terrified Americans huddled underground because *Luftwaffe* bombers had turned their cities to rubble. Didn't these people know there was a war?

The guards pushed us forward. A train was about to take us from the city.

One structure we marched past moved Novak to tears. He ran his hand along the ornate facade. "This is the Chrysler Building. One of the most beautiful skyscrapers in New York."

"I'm tired of looking up," I said, staring ahead. "This place is a forest of granite, and I, for one, will be glad to leave."

"Grand Central is just ahead." My friend pointed to a massive domed block of white stone with three huge windows. Only when we entered the atrium did the stunning dimensions of the structure dawn upon me. The soaring, impossibly high turquoise ceilings took my breath away. It was a cathedral, not to a deity but to progress. People rushed everywhere, many in uniform, and the marble floor rumbled beneath my feet. There was little time to gaze at the well-dressed travelers before we made our way through shiny brass doors and down long ramps to the train platforms below. Blaring horns and rumbling engines echoed off tunnel walls. Large clocks could be seen in any direction. We tramped across several boarding areas before stopping. The guards positioned themselves on either side of us. Silly. The thought of escaping inside a cavern full of moving trains seemed absurd.

At 1338 hours, a rapid bell signaled our attention. A bright light approached us, and the oncoming engineer announced his arrival with two taps of the great horn. The locomotive's deep rumble hit me like a physical assault.

Novak gazed in wonder as the train swept past us,

pulling a long line of elegant-looking dark-orange passenger cars. In Germany, soldiers boarded boxcars for rail travel. "Those are Pullman cars," he yelled. "We're traveling in style."

We boarded, seventy-five to eighty prisoners per car. Guards took posts at the front and rear. Ebony-skinned porters, wearing smart blue jackets, black bowties, and creased black pants, greeted us as we settled in cushioned seats. A steward rolled a beverage cart, stopping beside me. "Tea or coffee, sir?"

An American serving me? "Tea, please," I stammered.

He held out a small dainty cup which I took. "And you, sir?" he asked Novak.

"Tea as well. Thank you."

I sipped my beverage as the porter served others aboard. "I'll never understand this country," I said. "Captured prisoners, yet we're treated like paying passengers."

Novak leaned back in his seat. "Enjoy it while you can. Party ends when we arrive at our new home, wherever that may be."

With a long blast of the engine's horn, we entered an underground tunnel. Minutes later, we emerged in an area of older apartment buildings and warehouses, many blackened by chimney soot. Novak seemed mesmerized by the sights.

"Haven't you seen all this before?" I asked.

"Sure. But it's like coming home. I want to soak up as much as I can."

A few seats ahead of us, a deep, guttural voice erupted in anger. "Where are the bomb craters? The piles of rubble? Where's the *Luftwaffe*?"

Another voice spoke, this one more contemplative. "I noticed that. Perhaps the Americans are directing the train around the damage."

"That's it," the first man said. "They don't want us to see the results of our airpower."

Novak stirred in his seat. "Oh? Is that so?" He sat forward, eyes glaring.

"Of course!" the harsh voice called back. "It's the beginning of the end for the Amis. They're only now finding out."

My friend leaned close to my ear. "This guy is an idiot."

I saw no point in arguing. "He sounds like a party member. You won't change his mind. The man could be right."

"Henry." My companion frowned. "You disappoint me. Listen. I'm going to teach this joker a lesson he won't soon forget."

I gripped his arm. "You'll make a Nazi enemy. That's not what you want."

"He can't touch me. We're in America now." Novak jerked his arm from me.

"The Amis are afraid," the voice in front announced. "They're losing the war, and they know it. That's why they're good to us. They know it will go better for them after our victory."

"Have you ever heard of a bomber able to fly the Atlantic?" Novak asked.

"Zeppelins can," the man called back. "Besides, our engineers are constantly perfecting weapons that will win us the war. A long-range bomber is an ideal weapon against the Americans."

"These bombers." Novak smiled, enjoying the

banter. "They'd have to carry weapons, a crew, and fuel to cross an ocean and back. The pilots would have to make the trip without fighter escort, and somehow be able to elude defending American planes. Would you want to be that pilot?"

The voice ahead muttered an oath, then called out, "Our pilots are brave men who will not be daunted by long odds."

All other conversation stopped. The debate between Novak and this other soldier captivated the rest of us.

"It would be a fantastic weapon," said Novak. "To carry that much fuel. And a rather easy target, even for a mediocre American pilot. Too bad *der Fuehrer* didn't use it in North Africa."

I poked Brian none too gently with my elbow. "That's enough. You've made your point."

"Not yet." His eyes held cold fire.

"What are you suggesting?" The voice grew silken soft.

"A lost opportunity for Germany," Brian said in a raised voice. "Otherwise, we'd still be fighting. Too bad *der Fuehrer* didn't choose to use his secret weapons to save the Afrika Korps."

Silence.

A vague uneasiness crept over me. Insulting the National Socialists was deadly sport. A devoted party member would believe in the *Fuehrer* the way a Christian would believe in Jesus Christ. Any competing point of view was a threat to the party.

As if reading my thoughts, a prisoner in the row ahead spoke to Novak. "Watch yourself, sir. The man you argued with is Sergeant Alfred Stecklein. Very tough. Not one to have for an enemy."

His warning was clear, but my friend had to ask. "So?"

The man's jaw set in a grim line. "Stecklein is relentless. He'll find you."

As the cityscape turned to countryside, I expected the porter to return with an afternoon meal. Instead, a kitchen worker in a dirty apron and tilted paper hat delivered ham sandwiches on paper plates.

"So much for the Pullman service." Novak sighed.

I didn't care; the sandwiches were the first solid food we'd had all day. After handing out the food, the kitchen man left with his cart.

Before we finished eating, a lieutenant entered, followed by a civilian translator. "May I have your attention, please?" The young officer read from a script. "Until you reach your destination, the following rules will be in effect. One." He held up a finger. "You will remain seated until you're allowed to stand. Two." He extended another finger. "You'll raise your hand if you wish to use the head."

"Eighty men and one toilet," Novak whispered. "That'll require fortitude."

"Three." The officer read on. "Only one prisoner may leave his seat at a time."

That drew a ripple of protest.

"Four. If you need water, feel sick, or need to stand and stretch your legs—raise your hand."

Novak shifted about in his seat, distracted.

"And five," said the lieutenant. "When you're finished eating, throw the paper plates out the window. That is all." Without another word, he and the translator passed through the passenger compartment and out the other door.

I turned to my friend. "I believe our host is afraid of a mutiny."

"Never mind him. I've found a train schedule." He produced a folded map. One side covered the eastern half of the country; the other covered the west. "We can follow our route through each town we pass."

"Better than making enemies," I agreed. "Would you like the window seat? You can watch for the names of towns. Maybe we can predict our final stop."

"Do you still have your watch, Henry?"

"*Ja*, but it's hidden. Each time the Americans search us, there's always a guard looking for souvenirs. In New York, I saw a soldier giving up his Iron Cross. So I'm keeping it in my boot."

"A wise idea." Novak watched the scenery but fell asleep in minutes.

Soon my chin drooped as well. The clacking tracks lulled me into the best sleep I had in weeks.

Three days later, the novelty of riding in a Pullman car had slackened. I longed for a chance to stroll the aisle or take a shower. By this time, we no longer needed to raise our hands to stand, and the guards hardly paid attention to the line of prisoners waiting their turn for the washroom. The train car reeked of unwashed bodies, and it didn't help that we couldn't open the windows more than a few centimeters.

Rolling hills gave way to flat countryside. I didn't care where the Americans took us, provided we got there soon. But Novak seemed immune to the constant sitting, always watching outside the window. Somewhere he'd acquired a pencil and drew a line across each town we passed.

I gave him a nudge. "Are you part of the *Abwehr*?"

"Of course not." He gave me a sideways glance. "But I've noticed that all of our stops are in small towns. Other than Chicago, we've avoided the large cities."

"Where are we now?"

"In Nebraska. That's in the center of the country." He showed me places he'd marked: Fisher's Point, Fort Crook, Weeping Water, Hebron, and Alta. "At each stop, the guards marched a carload of prisoners off the train, loaded them onto trucks, and drove away. In Alta, they emptied the Pullman behind us. We're next."

All morning we passed tall grasses, immature corn, and an occasional distant barn. I couldn't escape the notion that the land was conjuring itself into existence ahead of us, and we were heading into a world apart where cattle outnumbered people.

"The train is slowing," he said.

We bumped over a coupling and turned away from the main track, decreasing speed as we entered the outskirts of another town. A water tower on scaffolding crept into view with the words CONRAD, KANSAS, POP. 6500 painted on its curved surface.

"This is our destination." Novak pointed ahead. "We have a reception waiting for us."

I peered out, drawing in a sharp breath. We approached soldiers in white helmets standing at attention. Beyond them at the train depot were men, women, and children, some waving, as the locomotive slowed. Seconds later, the engine braked, sending a shudder back to the last car. The side door slid open, and the American lieutenant we had seen earlier entered. "Form a line and exit the train! Men outside will lead you."

We stood and shuffled on unsteady legs to the exit. Ahead of me was a square-built, thick-necked bull of a man wearing a sergeant's field uniform. That had to be Stecklein. Unlike many others, he jumped to the ground without difficulty. My own knees threatened to collapse. Sitting three days with little activity had rendered me unsteady as a newborn calf. Outside the train, the clean air invigorated me. Townspeople shouted and cheered from the train platform.

"Welcome to Kansas!"

"Look at them! They look just like our boys!"

"Krauts, go home!"

"America," I groaned. "Are the guards here to protect the civilians or us?"

Novak glanced at me. "Relax, Henry. Some of these guards have German ancestors."

Further conversation was impossible as sentries marched us away from the crowded station. On the next street over, we boarded a convoy of canvassed trucks and followed a dirt road out of town. Twelve kilometers later, the guards deposited our group on a strip of new asphalt leading to a gate topped by barbed wire. Any other day, the short march would have been easy, but walking on wobbling knees took a surprising amount of stamina. At one point, I grabbed Novak's shoulder after stumbling over an unexpected bump. Ahead, green-and-white-painted barracks shone in bright afternoon sunlight behind two rows of tall fencing. Before the metal gate was a guard shack and above was a red banner with white lettering: CAMP CONRAD.

"Our new home," Novak said. "And the Americans have organized another welcome committee."

Novak was right. Another processing line. Oh, how tempting to reach for my watch, a sure way for guards to claim another prisoner trophy. How many more times were we to be searched?

In a building just left of the main gate, we again showed our soldier books, gave information to a group of clerks, and submitted to another search. Thankfully, my watch remained untouched. At our last stop, a quartermaster looked me over, then stuffed dark-blue work clothes, raincoat, shoes, socks, and underclothing into a seabag. The letters PW were stenciled on the back of the pants and shirts. "What are these initials?" I asked.

"Prisoner of War." The quartermaster thrust the long bag in my hands. "In case you escape."

I imagined an American aiming his rifle at me. At least in the desert I could hide below ground. Here, our captors expected us to act normally with a target painted on our backs. Was the war really over for us?

Ten minutes later, we gathered in the camp's mess hall, still lugging our new clothes. I found a spot at one of the long tables that filled the open room, sighing with relief to get off my shaky feet. Novak sat across from me. Conversation filled the room, and some men sniffed the air. My mouth watered from the pleasant aroma of corned beef. Was that possible?

At the far end of the room, a beefy-shouldered *Wehrmacht* colonel approached a swastika-adorned podium. His well-pressed uniform with field medals and high-peaked hat had me wondering if a staff car and attendant officers waited for him outside. Just how did he manage to keep his decorations, anyway?

Novak leaned toward me. "Get a load of that guy.

His nose could open a can of beans."

The colonel, a hawk-faced man with a perpetual sneer on his lips, thumped his fist on the stand before him. "Attention, please." Despite his smile, the hairs on the back of my neck prickled. This was an officer to be wary of.

He thumped a couple more times. "Quiet now," he said. Then a heartbeat later he slammed his fist. The wood cracked, sounding like a pistol shot.

All conversation stopped.

"Hello to the new arrivals," he began. "I am Colonel Ernst Reinhardt. Speaking for the officers in this compound, I welcome you to Camp Conrad." Reinhardt scanned the crowd, as if assessing each person in his audience. "Judging by your appearance, I can see you've had a long journey across enemy territory. But within this compound you are safe. Be yourselves. The Amis seldom come inside the wire. This is our ground. Our place away from home. As your liaison officer with the Americans, it is my duty to see that your stay here is as pleasant as possible. And now, we offer a small meal to sate your appetite." Reinhardt swept his arm to the kitchen.

Cooks in white aprons bustled through swinging doors carrying metal plates stacked with sliced beef, mashed potatoes, cooked beets, and bread pudding. A young man slid plates in front of Novak and me, then dashed back to the kitchen for more. Around us, men marveled at the food before them.

"I haven't eaten like this in ages," Novak said, digging in.

I peered at the wondrous food, reminding me of home. Could this be a test? A temptation? What was the cost of failing this challenge? I pushed the plate away and surveyed the men around me.

"This is a feast." Novak stuffed a heaping forkful of potatoes in his mouth. "My parents won't believe this. Prisoners in America, but we're eating like kings."

This seemed too good to be true. I turned my attention up front, but Reinhardt seemed oblivious to the diners. He stood at a table next to a huge man, talking and laughing like they were old friends. A chill coursed down my back. Sergeant Stecklein! They knew each other. If Camp Conrad seemed ominous before, the twin threats of Reinhardt and Stecklein would be menacing at best. And deadly if some unlucky soldier crossed them. I needed to warn Novak. But not here.

Somehow, I finished the meal. Afterward, Novak found our assigned quarters.

Barracks C held forty bunks with shelves at one end. We had electricity but no plumbing. I found empty beds for both of us. Other soldiers wandered in, tossing their seabags on empty bunks. "I'll take the bottom one." Novak set his bag down and moved his gear to the bottom shelves. I checked my sleeping place for scorpions, a habit I acquired long ago in the desert.

A refreshing shower and a clean bed. That, I couldn't pass up. Also, Novak needed to know how dangerous our new surroundings were. "Grab some clean clothes," I said. "Let's see about this bathhouse. We need to talk."

"What's up?"

"I'll tell you on the way."

With a change of clothing in hand, we exited the barracks, turning to the main gate.

"What's going on, Henry? You look like your pet

dog died."

I sighed heavily. "I'm concerned about this place. It doesn't feel right."

"Seems okay to me. We got a good dinner, got clean duds, barracks are neat. What's not to like? Other than the fact it's a prison."

"It is a prison," I agreed. "That's why we got PW on our backs. It might as well be a bullseye."

"The Americans won't shoot unless they have reason to."

"I hope you're right."

"Is that all you're worried about, Henry?"

I stopped in midstep. "I'm just starting. What did you think of Colonel Reinhardt?"

"Another full-of-himself officer, why?"

"Think he is a National Socialist?"

Novak pursed his lips. "I suppose. He can't do anything about it. We're in America now."

Heat shot to my temples. I stepped forward, keeping my voice low. "That's not what Reinhardt thinks. 'This is our ground,' he said. I suspect the colonel is used to getting his way."

Novak clenched his teeth. "We are in the heart of the United States. Our captors will not stand for a two-bit Nazi to be a cock of the walk. They won't let it get that far."

I thrust an arm toward the mess hall. "I got news for you. It's already happened. Did you see any American guards in our little rally? What about the swastika out there in plain sight? Was that just an oversight?"

Novak made to reply, but no words came immediately. "What are you getting at, Henry?"

"Your precious Americans are willing to guard their prison but don't care what happens inside. That scares the hell out of me."

"That's...impossible. I can't believe it." Novak wiped a sheen of sweat from his forehead.

"Judge for yourself. But there's one more thing, and it relates to you."

Novak smiled ruefully. "More good news? I can't wait."

"This is serious." I took in a breath, wishing I was wrong. "I've got a good idea who your sparring partner was on the train—"

"Sergeant Alfred Stecklein. I remember."

"I've seen him. Big man. Heavy, but well-muscled. Reinhardt and he are friends. Steer clear of both these men."

Novak stared off in the distance. "I see your point, Henry. But I got an ace up my sleeve. I grew up in this country. I'm practically an American. With a little luck, that could be my get-out-of-jail ticket."

I shook my head. "A risky gambit. Think twice before playing it."

He slapped my back. "Buck up, Henry. We've made it this far. And now, it's two showers in one week. Things are looking up."

I envied his optimism.

A long structure of white-painted cement, the shower building sat next to where the guards searched us earlier that day. A row of evenly spaced wooden timbers supported a detached roof that sloped over the outer walls to form eaves. The entire structure sat alongside the warning track that circled the compound.

We entered a dressing room, hung our clothes on

brass hooks, and tucked our new boots under chairs. Stacks of clean towels sat on benches with a laundry cart in the corner. After disrobing, we stepped through a narrow cement doorway into an open space with ten showerheads mounted on reinforced iron pipes. Beyond this room, a doorway led to the *toilette*. For a few minutes, I allowed the hot stinging spray to obliterate my worries.

Take care of yourself, Heinrich. Novak is an impulsive child.

Never! To the last measure, we would make our stand together.

Do you have that kind of will?

Other showers came alive, filling the room with a haze of steam.

"I can stay here till breakfast!" Novak yelled over the spray.

Occasionally, a cool draft whisked the steam away. I wondered what would keep the pipes from freezing during the winter months. That sobered my thoughts. Rinsing a final time, I turned the spigots off. "I'm heading back to the barracks."

"Be along in a bit," Novak called.

Back in Barracks C, I folded my soiled field uniform in the seabag for washing. Atop the shelves of other bunks were photographs of parents and girlfriends inside makeshift frames. A few held paintings of Rommel, desert landscapes, or hand-carved plaques of ornately designed swastikas. Why would the Americans permit these symbols to flourish on their own soil?

One carving caught my eye. Gouged into a neighboring bunk, one crude swastika looked like a pinwheel with its hub off-centre, and the arms splayed at different angles.

"Do y-you like it?"

Nearby, stood a tall, husky youth, his oily blond hair streaked with strands of brown. He weaved from side to side as if impatient for me to give an answer. I wondered if he'd tried to artificially color his hair to look Aryan. If so, he thoroughly botched the job. Was he once a soldier? Had the requirements loosened since I enlisted? "You must have spent many hours on this carving." No sense demoralizing this young man.

"I u-used a screw from the bed to dig out the w-wood. Nobody else l-likes it."

"You did well, given the tool available," I lied.

He beamed. "It's nice to find s-someone who likes it. *Heil*, Hitler!" He thrust his arm in a quick Nazi salute. "I'm Oskar Kimmel. And y-you?"

I did not return his salute. "Henry Rohling." I bowed slightly, clasping my hands behind me.

His eyes narrowed, but he continued in a friendly tone. "I c-can show you around. Introduce you to the National Socialists who run the camp. Good to know those w-who will rise to the top when Germany wins the w-war." He paused, then spoke in a lowered voice. "You should call yourself Heinrich. For obvious reasons."

I took a step back. "I prefer Henry."

The pathetic boy bobbed his head as he spoke. "Sure. Maybe later you can meet Captain Dietrich."

"Good evening, Herr Kimmel." I drifted to the door.

"I can make a carving for you. Any t-time."

The better part of me said to walk away, but I turned back to face him. "Pardon?"

51

"You said you liked it. I can carve a swastika for you. Pay me back l-later."

"I'll think about it." I turned away, seeking fresh air.

"For free! Be my f-f-friend, and I'll do it for nothing!"

Men who beg disgusted me. But this wretch seemed more like a lonely child. I sighed, not meeting his eye. "We'll talk again."

"Wonderful!" He clapped his hands.

I rushed outside to escape the man's niggling. In front of the barracks was a field of short grass large enough for soccer. Beyond that, an asphalt track ran parallel to the barbed wire from one corner tower to the other, perhaps circling the camp. Beyond the outer rim of the track, knee-high metal stakes held up a thick wire. It, too, might circle our prison. Between the track and the barbed wire lay four to five meters of weedy grass. Guards stood inside two corner towers at each end of our compound, both capped with a tin roof. I wandered closer to the nearest, curious but watchful.

Wooden rails and timbers enclosed the guard's platform, which sat atop four meters of scaffolding. The tower stood next to the inner row of barbwire fencing. Beyond it lay another row of barbed wire three meters away. Both rows stood about even with the tower platform. Two soldiers stood beneath the roof with shouldered rifles along with a mounted searchlight and machine gun. Both men smoked and paid me little attention. Below them, wild sunflowers grew along the rows of barbwire.

I considered that: how could beauty and menace coexist so closely together?

Without warning, sirens revved to an ominous wail.

Chapter Five

The reunion packet arrived in mid-June. Horst helped me examine the contents, which included a revised schedule of events, hotel information, airline tickets, and trip itinerary. "This Wheatland Hotel makes no mention of internet service. My staff told me I may need to rent a car and travel to a larger town for an e-mail connection."

I turned the brochure over. "There's a map of Kansas on the back. That may help."

Horst studied the simplified road map. "Salina is eighty kilometers south. If their city library has a computer connection, then I can work there. You can fill me in on your reunion when I return in the evening."

"Just don't try to teach me about your computers," I said.

Horst gave a rueful grin. "Not to worry, Papa. I won't try that again. But you should learn e-mail. It would make corresponding with friends much quicker."

I waved the idea away. "That doesn't interest me." To change the subject, I retrieved the airline tickets. "The Americans came through with a ticket for you as well."

Horst held out a hand. "Let's see those. Boarding agents can be fussy if the name on the ticket doesn't match the I.D." Horst donned glasses and inspected the documents, pursing his lips. "The names are fine, but we're not sitting together. Not even in the same section. My staff can correct the error. This won't be a problem."

"When does the flight leave?" Until now, the possibility of flying to America hadn't seemed real.

Horst scanned the itinerary. "We leave Tegel Airport at nine a.m. on the twenty-fifth of August and arrive in New York nearly ten hours later. Layover for an hour while we change planes, and then we fly to Chicago. The final stop is Kansas City International, where we touch down at 5:49 p.m. local time. A representative from the historical society will transport us to Conrad. We should reach the hotel by eleven o'clock."

I sighed. "It sounds exhausting."

"You'll have plenty of time to rest on the plane. And the Americans will be driving the last leg of the journey. Other than finding our gates in New York and Chicago, the trip will be easy."

"It was different in my day, three weeks aboard a rusty ship and another three days by rail."

Horst smiled. "Now, it's a matter of a few hours. Of course, we'll be traveling west across several time zones, so the day will seem longer."

"I've never been on a plane before."

"One thing about it, Papa. You won't be seasick."

Over the next month, I obtained a passport, brushed up on English phrases, and shopped with my daughter Caroline. She insisted I wear dress clothes and not look like "an *alter mann* living alone." So, in addition to my dungarees, suspenders, and comfortable shirts, I now owned a suit and tie, dress shirts, and dark slacks. Johann coached me on American culture, acquired from visits to a New York-themed nightclub near the Tiergarten. I could not imagine a small town in Kansas being anything like New York.

This reunion would be a chance to renew old friendships. Any Nazi veterans would have buried that past long, long ago. Novak's killer may already be dead. But if he still lived, and if he attended the reunion, how would I know it was him? Whatever happened, I would not allow myself to retreat again.

My last night at home was a restless one where shadows from long ago kept me in twilight wakefulness. Fragments of memory raced and spun in a kaleidoscope of events, real and imagined. Novak and I watched a soccer player run across a warning track only to be shot while retrieving a ball. A dog barked on a country road as a truck approached. My friend gasped for breath in the camp's infirmary after thugs beat him. And an unexpected exodus from the Kansas POW camp soon after Normandy left me riding a northbound train.

It was an exciting three years, Henry. Novak's commentary on my newsreel dream seemed entirely natural. *Our captors sent us to their land. But who was the real enemy? Fifty years have gone. Don't try to avenge me, Henry. If you must chase windmills, search for Emily.*

I rose from bed and trudged to the kitchen, giving up any further chance of sleep. There, I prepared a cup of strong tea. Finding Emily. My heart raced at the thought. Long ago, I promised to come back, but I never did. Was she still alive? Did she have children and grandkids? I hoped so.

****

Horst and I entered the double door at the Tegel Airport terminal and stopped at the check-in station. An attractive young woman in a tailored blue uniform smiled as we stepped to her well-polished counter. "Good morning, gentlemen. Where will you be flying with us today?" Even her voice carried a smile.

"To America." A man used to air travel, Horst had already produced our tickets and IDs and handed them to her.

"Thank you, sir." She soon gave my son two slips of heavy paper. "Here are your boarding passes, Herr Rohling. Have a good flight."

Behind the ring of airline ticket desks, we passed through security and boarded a tram that whisked us to trans-Atlantic departures. We gained speed along a curved track that tilted like a roller-coaster. The air rose to a piercing howl. Standing beside me, Horst frowned at the boarding passes in his hands. Only after we slowed could I hear him. "The airline never changed our seats," he said.

"Probably a mistake."

He slapped the slips of paper. "This is unacceptable. I'll take care of this myself."

"Please don't make a show. It's a small thing."

"Twenty rows apart is no small thing," he said.

After the tram stopped, we took a series of moving walkways to our gate. Most of the seats were already taken. In front stood a large podium where an attendant scrutinized a bulky computer screen. A hallway in a darkened corner led to where the plane would soon dock. I found two empty seats while Horst marched to the podium. Loud conversation filled the air as more passengers found seats. Rambunctious children ran squealing through the aisles, and young couples sat holding hands. Not far away, two older men were laughing with their heads bent together like schoolboys sharing a joke. One was a bearded, bald chap with a raptor nose. The other was a formidable mountain of a man with a bullet-shaped head and no discernible neck. He may have been intimidating at one time, but his muscle had now dwindled to fat. The hair on the back of my neck prickled. These travelers seemed familiar, but I could not place where I'd seen them before.

What was taking Horst so long? Passengers filled every seat in the waiting area. The clock on the wall indicated our take-off to be in twenty minutes, and a passenger jet taxied close to the expansive windows.

Horst returned as some passengers shuffled to the boarding line. "I learned what happened," he said. Before Horst could explain, a microphone screeched to life, and an announcer described preboarding procedures. He stood scowling until the spiel ended. "It seems you are a part of a group traveling together. The airline will shepherd you all the way to Kansas City." He glanced at the group of seniors, families with babies, and a few physically challenged travelers. "Let's get you in line."

My son walked with me to the line and handed me a boarding pass. Ahead of us, a young lady helped some passengers to the corridor that connected to the plane. "You're in good hands, Papa. See you in Kansas City." He gripped my arm for a second and left, merging with the crowd waiting to board.

Cool air filled the waiting area, but sweat poured down my arms. I had to journey alone.

"Boarding pass?" The petite fraülein with short red

hair held out her hand.

I handed her my slip of paper.

"Ah, one of our special guests." She flashed a bright smile. "A flight attendant will show you to your seat. Enjoy your flight, Herr Rohling."

Aboard the plane, I marveled at the long rows of seats, and the strange way voices became muted. The flight attendant showed me to a window seat next to the two lively seniors I had seen earlier. With difficulty, I squeezed past the bullet-headed fellow and sat next to the window.

"Another fellow traveler!" the goateed man exclaimed as I negotiated my seatbelt. "Are you going to Kansas as well?"

I nodded. "How did you know?"

"We're going there. So are the veterans in front. That makes eight of us all together."

I held out my hand. "I'm Henry Rohling."

"I'm Ernst Reinhardt." His grip was like that of an elderly woman. "And this is my friend, Alfred Stecklein. Alfred and I have been ruminating about the old days."

Stecklein nodded to me. With difficulty, he retrieved a plastic inhaler from his tunic pocket and took a puff. His head was a misshapen lump with thick folds of pasty flesh at the neck. Skin sagged from bluish jowls. *Oh, no.* I took two deep breaths to steady my nerves. Reinhardt was the camp's liaison officer, and Stecklein had ruled my barracks with an iron fist.

All the old fears came flooding back.

Reinhardt squinted at me. "Rohling. Why is that name so familiar? Were you an officer or an enlisted man?"

"Enlisted." I spoke through dry lips.

Reinhardt stared upward, taping his hairy chin. "I remember now." He nudged Stecklein. "Do you know who you're sitting by, Alfred?"

The big man shook his head. "No, *Oberst*."

"The *biermeister*." Reinhardt snapped his fingers. "Drosselmeyer's helper. We knew about the brewing, of course." He sighed dramatically. "Too bad, the camp received a by-the-book commander just then. Otherwise, we would have gotten to know your skills better." He smiled, showing perfect teeth. "I've always liked you, Rohling, even though you didn't join the party."

I remained quiet.

"Sergeant Drosselmeyer is aboard," said Stecklein. "Three seats ahead."

"Oh?" Reinhardt arched his brow like a Shakespearean actor. "Very good."

"I remember the sergeant," I said. Patriotic songs rang in my head. "I hated those forced marches around and around camp."

"You hated…" The colonel leaned forward, speaking to me past Stecklein. "It's a good thing I liked you. Keeping company with that delicious pretty young friend of yours could have been dangerous." He shifted to Stecklein. "Alfred, what was that boy's name who talked like an American?"

Stecklein wheezed in a breath. "The garbage collector. Don't remember."

I gritted my teeth. "His name was Brian Novak. Someone killed him."

Reinhold bowed his head in feigned sadness. "Really? Do you remember that, Alfred?"

The massive sergeant wobbled his head. "The man hanged himself."

Reinhardt cast me a pitying glance, yet his eyes were a cold shade of blue. "Examine your memory, Herr Rohling. The Americans determined young Novak took his own life. Why would you think differently?"

"I have evidence his death was involuntary." Airing my suspicions was a calculated risk, but I wanted to see his reaction.

Reinhardt shrugged, but his eyes remained alert. Age had not mellowed this cold bastard. "My dear man, I commend you for your loyalty, but Novak was a troubled soul. Instead of taking a concern to his liaison officer, he stirred the camp to frenzied anxiety with conspiracy theories. Poor man. A delusional mind and a weak mental constitution."

I wanted to smash his smiling face. I spoke impulsively. "If that was true, why was his trial a secret? What were you hiding?"

Reinhardt faced me, eyes narrowing. Even Stecklein turned his bullet head.

"So you knew about that. I'm surprised, but it changes nothing. Your friend took his own life. Even the Americans agreed. Best to leave the past alone."

"The hell I will."

Reinhardt's smile faded. His eyebrows drew together as he peered at me. "Be careful, Herr Rohling. Opening old wounds can be a painful affair."

"May I have your attention, please?" A flight attendant stood before us with microphone in hand. I sat through the emergency procedures spiel, my mind seething with unexpected anger. Reinhardt just threatened me. Why? Novak's verdict in his Nazi trial had to be guilty. A guilty verdict always meant death—a self-inflicted death the prisoner must carry out himself. But Novak's letter proved he didn't intend to die by his own hand. With regret, I realized I had spoken hastily and sacrificed the element of surprise.

The jet gained speed as we raced down the runway, and the nose tilted skyward. My next Atlantic crossing began.

Chapter Six

19-20 August 1943

The siren rose, filling the evening air with an ear-piercing scream. Around me, the compound erupted in frenzied activity. Men darted out of barracks, bumping into one another, rushing to form ranks. In less than a minute, hundreds of prisoners filled the parade area, some dressed in their desert uniforms, while others wore the blue-dyed prison clothes with the stenciled PW on the back. All stood at ease but ready to come to attention.

"What's going on?" I yelled at a man standing nearby.

"Not sure. An escape maybe." He gestured ahead. "New inmates are to stand in front. Hurry. The Americans will be here soon."

I found a place in the forward ranks, my ears ringing from the keening wail. A minute later, the siren began its long decline. Novak stumbled behind me, followed by a red-faced Sergeant Stecklein. When my friend bent over to catch his breath, the beefy sergeant knocked him to the ground. "That's for being smart on the train." Stecklein turned on me, his eyes glaring. "Teach your friend proper respect, or I'll be coming after you next." He muttered under his breath, then stalked away.

I pulled Novak to his feet. "What got him so angry?" I asked.

"I didn't jump fast enough when he rousted me from the shower building." He tied his laces. "What's the ruckus about?"

"The Amis are coming. Something's up."

"Why would the Americans stage a dramatic entrance to their own camp?"

I shrugged. "We'll know soon enough."

Five minutes later, two jeeps followed by two canvas trucks drove through the main gate and along the perimeter road, stopping in front of our assembly. Soldiers hustled to surround our group, while officers from the lead vehicles strolled forward. Judging by his stripes, I guessed the senior officer to be a captain. He approached, followed by four lieutenants, each holding clipboards.

"*Achtung!*"

We came to attention. The lieutenants milled about us, pencils in hand, making their count. Soon they conferred and compared their totals. Apparently satisfied, one of the officers approached the captain with a brisk salute. "All accounted for, sir!"

The captain thanked his men, then faced us, raising his heels for a moment.

"As you probably guessed, an incident has taken place." The captain paused while his aide-de-camp translated the message into Deutsch. "A German officer was found hanged in the officers' compound minutes ago. The unfortunate man was a victim of suicide—and he only arrived here a week ago. If any of you were under the command of Captain Gustav Dortmann, contact your liaison officer. Any information about his demeanor would be useful, should an investigation take place."

The officer observed our reaction. Did he expect anyone to step forward? Why would a highly disciplined German captain take his life soon after he arrived here?

"The time for Captain Dortmann's memorial service will be posted tomorrow. That is all!" The captain retreated to his jeep, followed by his entourage. His driver made a tight U-turn and exited the main gate, followed by the other vehicles. We remained at attention.

"*Entlassen!*"

We dispersed. I wandered toward the barracks when Novak caught up with me. "Interested in supper?"

"No. I'm still full from lunch," I said.

"Tea, then."

I agreed, and we soon found seats in the mess hall, both of us holding cups of hot tea. "Dortmann must have been homesick," Novak said, leaning over the table. "What else could it be? We're on American soil and out of the war."

I sipped some tea. "The Amis will get to the bottom of it."

"I can tell you're new." A small, wiry man with a flattop haircut and a plate of apple strudel sat nearby. He held out a hand. "I'm Rudolf Hauser."

Novak eyed the pastry while we introduced ourselves.

"The Americans don't run the inside of this camp," Hauser said. "It's controlled by a small group of German officers and their stooges in the two compounds."

I turned to Novak. "Now do you believe me?"

Novak dismissed me with a wave. "What are these compounds?" he asked.

"Independent sections of the prison camp." Hauser drew an imaginary square, then sliced the middle with his finger. "One is for officers and the other for enlisted men. Each has a liaison officer who communicates with the Americans." Hauser talked between mouthfuls of flaky pastry.

"And *Oberst* Reinhardt is the liaison for this compound?" Novak asked.

Hauser nodded. "Rumor is he's looking for a new aide to assist him."

"Is Reinhardt a party member?" I asked.

"He is a passionate National Socialist, so be careful what you say. Any perceived threat will not be taken lightly."

Novak leaned away from the table. "How can a Nazi push his beliefs under the noses of the Americans?"

"*Stille*." Hauser thrust his head close to us, his voice low but urgent. "Don't say that word. To the National Socialists, it is *verboten*. Forbidden. Never utter it. Reinhardt's stooges are listening. You could be reported to the Inner Circle."

"Inner Circle?" I asked.

"It's a group of officers controlling each compound. Reinhardt is a part of it. As bad as it is here, it is especially bad for officers who despise the party. Saying anything critical of the *Fuehrer* can get you a beating during the night. Or worse."

Novak sniffed. "We're enlisted men. That sort of thing shouldn't affect us."

Hauser's eyes narrowed. "Don't be so sure. You've met Stecklein. He's new but already assuming the role of Reinhardt's eyes and ears."

Novak thumped the table with his fist. "No Nazis will squeeze the rest of us with the Americans watching."

"The closest guards are in the towers. We're mostly left to ourselves."

Hauser's fear reflected mine as well. I tapped the tabletop with a finger. "We should be more circumspect."

Novak pushed his cup of tea away. This conversation went against everything he believed. "How did…these people take over?"

His plate empty, Hauser took a seat by Novak. "They are a well-organized group, experienced in seizing power. Be wary. The war, even behind the wire, is still very much alive."

I stared at the table. "On the battlefield, we had a common enemy. Here, we're plotting against each other."

Novak set his jaw. "And fear our own officers."

"Welcome to the Coliseum," I muttered.

I slept that night troubled and exhausted. With no direct way to contact the Americans, we were on our own with nowhere to turn.

Next morning, the Americans held an orientation meeting for new prisoners. We sat on wooden folding chairs in the auditorium while Major Roy Brunswick, the American liaison officer, reviewed rules, mail regulations, use of the prison library, canteen, plus the new Labor and Education Programs.

"Our goal is to make your stay in Camp Conrad

comfortable," he said. "Each enlisted man will receive a stipend of five cents a day in paper script, spendable at the camp's canteen. For those who wish to earn more, there are many jobs available within the compound, or you can join the Labor Program. Inside the camp, you work for eight cents an hour. Sorry, no raises. Jobs available are posted on the mess hall bulletin board. Each job has its own supervisor. Talk to that person about the job you're interested in. The supervisor has sole discretion in whom he may hire and fire."

Novak leaned against my shoulder. "That's for me. Finding a job."

Brunswick continued. "The canteen is open Monday and Thursday in the mess hall. There you can buy personal supplies, writing materials, art supplies, hobby kits, chips, and candy. Hours are posted in the mess hall.

"We have sports and leisure activities. Join a soccer team or start a new one, play baseball, check out a book from the library, or join the band. In three weeks, you can take advantage of free college-level courses. We will have both German and American instructors. Courses available will be posted on the door of the Education Building. The clerk there can help you enroll.

"Another way to earn money is to join our Farm Labor Program. As you might guess, civilian manpower is rather limited around here. Farmers need help with livestock, repairs, fieldwork, and bringing the crops in. They will pay you up to eighty-five cents a day for a job well done. There is no shortage of jobs out there. Sign up at the mess hall, and you could be working within the week."

Major Brunswick continued his speech for another twenty minutes, then concluded with some words of warning. "Pay attention to what I am about to tell you," he said. "This could save your life. This is an internment camp, and we take our duty of guarding you seriously. Guard towers stand at each corner of the camp, and each tower contains a machine-gun, spotlight, and armed men. A perimeter road runs along the fence with a wire along its outer border. You can march on the road but not over the wire. Guards will shoot to kill any prisoner who ventures beyond the wire. Be aware of the danger, and you will be safe. That is all. You are dismissed."

Few men spoke as we left the hall. Even Novak remained somber as we stepped outside. "Let's see what the Recreation Hall has to offer," I said as a palliative to liven his mood.

Instead, he pointed to the parade grounds where two teams of ten men each were playing a lively game of soccer. Chalk marked the field, and netting between two poles served as goals. A group of onlookers hurled encouragement and insults as the players worked the ball back and forth across the field.

We stepped forward to watch the competition.

Some of the players practiced good teamwork, maneuvering the ball and passing it to other mates for a better shot at the goal. Other players seemed content with kicking as hard as they could and watching the ball sail. One mid-field player lofted the ball high in the air. It sailed off the side of his foot, well over the heads of the onlookers, bounced a few times, and rolled to a stop in a stand of sunflowers by the fence.

Novak and I exchanged glances. What now?

One of the opposing players waved his arms over his head as he trotted across the warning track. I held my breath with a glance at the corner tower. A guard watched but made no move to aim his weapon. The player bent to grab the ball, returned to the field, and play resumed.

Novak blew out a breath. "Nothing happened."

"Hope the guards will warn the players if they change their minds." I rubbed the stubble on my chin. "The results will be terrible."

My friend slapped me on the back. "Nothing to worry about."

Novak's bravado sounded more like a prayer than reassurance.

We explored the library that afternoon, then walked to the Education Building. "Come on, Henry. I bet you'll find at least one class that will catch your attention."

"You go ahead," I said. "I want to know more about the Labor Program. It would be a good way to practice my English."

My friend threw an arm to his forehead in an overdramatic gesture. "You hurt me. Am I not a real American?"

I gave him a sideways glance. "You're as German as I am. Everything you know about America is five years old or more. Besides, it's more than just practicing the language. I want to view the countryside and see how Americans live."

"The countryside is so quiet it numbs the mind," Novak said.

I longed to find a place of quiet solitude, but Camp Conrad held few such places. The completion of two more barracks meant more German soldiers would be arriving soon. "Quiet countryside," I said. "Can't wait to go there."

Novak enrolled in American History and English Composition. "Last chance, Henry," he said.

"No."

"Then, let's hope a farmer will hire you."

Strolling back to the mess hall, we passed inmates mowing grass, tending gardens, and planting trees. A horse-drawn cart carried metal cans of refuse to an unknown destination. In one building, a tuba player practiced a familiar polka. The streets and sidewalks were immaculate. The internees here strived to keep the camp neat.

"You ever worked on a farm, Henry? You could be asking for a sore back."

I shook my head. "I've done my share of lifting beer barrels for Papa growing up. Hard work doesn't bother me. What kind of work are you interested in?"

Brian pondered the question. "Working with the library or teachers."

"You've got the skills for that," I agreed.

At the mess hall, we signed for the jobs we were interested in. To join the Farm Labor Program, I needed permission from *Hauptmann* Dietrich, one of Reinhardt's officers, so after supper, I made my way to the administration building, a two-story structure bordering the camp's northwest corner and across from the double row of fence that separated the two compounds. It sat next to the officers' barracks, a well-kept structure with flower planters beneath curtained windows. I hesitated before knocking. Hauser's warning about suspicious Nazi officers gave me butterflies. But why should I worry? This request was entirely routine and necessary to get the job.

I rapped twice on the door and stepped back.

Immediately, the door flew open, and a tall, broad-shouldered *Hauptmann* in field-gray uniform stared down at me. His dark, squinty eyes and a lipless mouth gave him a surly look. "What is it?" he snapped. This had to be Dietrich. Unlike Reinhardt, this man showed no pretense of cordiality.

For a full two seconds, I stood transfixed by his seething intensity. Training took over, then. I thrust out my arm in the proper salute. *"Sieg Heil!"*

Instead of returning the salute, Dietrich took his time examining me as a herdsman would his livestock. The captain circled me in a casual, disinterested manner. I remained frozen in place. For a long moment, he stood outside my line of sight, yet I felt his eyes on me. Finally, he completed his perusal. "You were slow in your salute."

I remained immobile, waiting for his returning salute.

"Perhaps I need to teach the private a lesson. Running ten laps around the compound might be a good inducement to remember. Or fifty push-ups."

My arm remained outstretched.

"You probably think you're a good soldier who made his papa proud by joining the *Wehrmacht*. But you are nothing now. A waste of my breath." He scowled, but I sensed he was tired of the game. A few seconds later, he returned a half-hearted salute. "What is your business, soldier?"

I thrust my hand out again, but Dietrich waved that aside.

"This soldier requests permission to join the Labor Program, sir!"

He smiled, showing yellowed teeth. "Really. And how bad do you want this?"

"Very much, sir."

"For ten percent of your wage, I'll put you at the bottom of the list. For twenty percent, I'll move you to the top. Which would you like?"

I snapped back with a ready answer. "At the top, sir."

"Let's see…at eighty-five cents a day, minus my fee…" He paused. "You'll be making sixty-eight cents a day. You start next Monday." He withdrew pad and pencil from his tunic. "Name, soldier. And ID number."

I gave the information to him.

"Glad to do business with you, private. We'll settle when you return to camp."

"Yes, sir."

I sighed with relief when Dietrich returned to his lair and darted back to safer territory. So ended my first brush with Reinhardt's Inner Circle. It would not be the last.

Chapter Seven

Our plane landed in Kansas City International at five forty-five local time. I couldn't have been happier. Rushing through airports and enduring ear-popping takeoffs and head-throbbing landings grew tiresome. For now, it was over, but a three-hour drive to the convention hotel still lay ahead.

After the noise and bustle of Tegel, Kennedy, and O'Hare, Kansas City's airport seemed tranquil and empty. Horst and I reunited outside the jetway, and we made quick progress to the baggage area where people milled about. Horst walked me to a bench that faced traffic passing the terminal. "Rest here, Papa. We'll be leaving after we retrieve all the luggage."

I took a seat beside another familiar face. I had seen him when we transferred planes in both New York and Chicago, but we never had time to speak. He sat hunched over, clutching a walker on wheels. Attached to it was a silver oxygen bottle. Clear plastic tubing ran from the bottle nozzle to his nostrils. "You're part of our band?" he wheezed in a high nasal voice.

I nodded assent.

"I think I know you." He squinted at me. "You're the *biermeister*."

Drosselmeyer! Time softens our judgments. This man had threatened to turn me over to Reinhardt fifty years ago. Yet here I was, grasping his hand. "Paul! A pleasant surprise. Is there anything I can do to help you?"

"Not unless you have an extra set of lungs. Doctors tell me it's too late anyway. But they still scold me for smoking." He grabbed a handkerchief and heaved up wet, bubbling phlegm.

I cringed at the sound but kept my voice conversational. "Any family traveling with you?"

"No relatives. Cancer is the only family I got. I'm seeing the old comrades again. Live it up one last time while I still have the will."

"Good man." I clapped him on the back. "We need to catch up before we leave."

"I'd like that." His fingers fiddled with the oxygen nozzle, and I realized even the short walk from the plane sapped his strength. There was a time I despised him and his endless schemes, but now, all I felt was pity. Drosselmeyer would likely die alone.

Horst soon brought our bags, and I introduced him to the old sergeant. This reunion was a time of brotherhood and fellowship. Not a time for old bitterness. That would make bringing up Novak's murder difficult at best.

A young couple met us a few minutes later. Tom and Beverly Poundstone were volunteer drivers, taking our group to the hotel. After packing the bags in the van, only eight passengers climbed aboard. Why so few?

"Eight veterans flew over here," I said to Horst as we left the airport. "But now there are five. I don't understand that."

"Friends or relatives greeted some of those *alte herren*. They're probably well on their way ahead of us.

Which reminds me, how was your flight, Papa?"

"I know now what a balloon feels like." I rubbed my temple.

Horst shook his head, chuckling. "I meant, did you visit with others during the trip?"

"I met some other veterans. Sergeant Stecklein and Colonel Reinhardt. The colonel is sitting behind the driver, and Stecklein is behind him."

Horst glanced ahead. "They look a bit unsavory," he said, keeping his voice low. "Were you friends?"

"We shared some history together. Reinhardt was the liaison officer with the Americans. And Stecklein watched over our barracks. Not men to trifle with."

My son frowned. "No doubt they intimidated others in their day. Not so much now."

"Likely not," I agreed. Still, I harbored doubts.

"At least I'm not the only son tagging along." Horst motioned in front of us. There, a young man wearing a trilby sat with his frail papa, a former lieutenant named Snyder. Occasionally, the son offered some bottled water to the elderly gentleman, but he always refused. I smiled to myself; doting children were everywhere. Next to Reinhardt sat former Lieutenant Unger and his wife. Both Unger and Snyder arrived in Camp Conrad after I had left.

"I talked to Herr Snyder during our stopover in New York." Horst gestured to the young man. "He told me some history of the POW camps in America."

I raised an eyebrow. "Really?"

Horst ignored my mocking tone. "He said there were hundreds of camps scattered across the country. Some held Italians. Others had a hodgepodge of different nationalities. Entire Japanese families were interned in a Texas camp, and they were U.S. citizens."

I sighed. "It was wartime. A whole different world then."

Horst waved his hand, impatient to get to his point. "I get that, but at the end of the war, while Germany released their POWs, American and English camps continued to operate long after the war. America sent many Germans to England and France to work as forced laborers to rebuild their countries. Did that happen to you?"

"I cut stone near Nice and repaired roads torn up by tanks."

"So the Americans took your human rights away?"

"Human rights were a luxury few enjoyed in Europe back then," I said. "At least our captors deemed us worthy of living."

"I didn't know." Horst remained silent for a moment. "Herr Snyder also said prisoners worked outside the camps for less than a dollar a day, but the army charged employers twice that amount. By the end of the war, the American War Department had created a lucrative employment agency. Did you ever feel the Americans took advantage of you?"

My neck grew warm and clammy. "It's interesting to me," I said, "how people who know the most were never there."

Horst drew back. "Didn't you work for what was essentially play money?"

"Most of us were grateful for the Labor Program. You can't imagine how confinement feels unless you've experienced it firsthand. The boredom can be stupefying." I gestured to the window. "The Labor Program gave us a chance to go outside the barbed wire, perform honest work, and feel a sense of freedom."

"And the money meant nothing?"

"Of course, it meant we could buy things we wanted." I sighed. Wasn't that obvious? "It was a bonus."

Horst sat for a moment, taking in my words. "So, while it was mixed, would you say your time in America was overall a good experience or a bad one?"

The question surprised me. I never thought about those three years as good or bad. Simply, a long moment in a world apart. I rubbed my forehead, hoping for inspiration. "I survived the war with my mind and body intact, was in a safe place overall, and met some wonderful Americans. The journey back home was long and frustrating and seeing my home devastated hurt me to the core. But that was after I left America." I nodded emphatically. "So yes, being a guest of the Americans was a positive experience."

"Anything specific you wished to have turned out differently?

Oh, if he only knew. Aloud, I cleared my throat. "I wanted to keep working for the Henning family. But around the time of the invasion, the Americans decided to intern officers only at Camp Conrad. All noncoms and enlisted men had to leave for other camps, and I had to say goodbye to the family I worked for."

"Were you close?"

Oh yes. I closed my eyes and swallowed. "I was a young man with more dreams than common sense. That all changed after the war."

"What happened, Papa?"

I had already said too much. "Every bowel

movement in the past doesn't need to be revealed." I scowled and turned away.

"You're getting cranky, Papa." Horst squeezed my arm. "It'll be close to eleven before we reach the hotel. You need some rest."

He was right. The flight had left me exhausted but agitated. Settling in my seat, I surveyed the other occupants: five veterans, two sons, one spouse, and two drivers. Outside, the setting sun touched the cornfield horizon with fiery gold, much like the view from my Pullman seat many years ago. I closed heavy eyelids and let the gentle vibrations coax me to sleep.

****

"Wake up, Papa." Horst nudged me. "We're nearly there."

I jerked in my seat. Bright streetlights and shadows chased across the van's interior. An overhead sign flashed past: WELCOME TO CONRAD. We slowed and soon turned into a concrete parking lot and followed a strip of curbed grass to a brightly lit, red brick structure trimmed in white. We stopped beneath a canopy extending before the hotel's glass doors.

"This is the Wheatland," Mr. Poundstone said as his wife exited the van. "Beverly will have your room keys at the front desk. You can then register at the conference table in the lobby. Don't worry about your luggage. We'll deliver it to your rooms shortly."

"I can help the passengers," Horst said, getting out of the vehicle.

"That would be great, Mr. Rohling. There's a step stool between the front seats. I'll get a luggage cart and unload these bags."

Horst set the stool outside the van, and the Ungers

stepped to the ground.

In short order, my son helped Drosselmeyer, the Snyders, and me down. Reinhardt shook off his help and breezed through the glass doors without a backward glance. Stecklein was the last to make his way out.

The old sergeant seemed less formidable without Reinhardt. He stood on the running board, frozen in place. "Two quick steps, sir, and you'll be on solid ground." Horst gripped his arm. "I'll keep you steady."

"My cane," the big man rumbled. "I need my cane."

"I'll get it for you in a minute. Let's get you on the ground, first."

Gingerly, Stecklein felt for the step with his foot and made it to the stool, though a bit shaky. On the final step, his massive frame wavered, one foot extended, and his arms windmilling the air. He leaned sideways, about to topple over, but Horst managed to keep him balanced enough to reach solid ground. Once down, Horst got the cane, handed it to Stecklein, and clapped the sergeant on his back. "You made it!" The sergeant still held my son's arm as we entered the lobby. After getting his room card, the sergeant hobbled to the reunion table to rejoin Reinhardt.

"*Mein Gott.*" Horst wiped his brow with shaky fingers. "That fellow just about flattened me. Not too stable on his feet, but he's got an iron grip. I'd say he's more of a threat to himself than to anyone else."

"Stay away from them," I warned. "These men. Don't let their age deceive you."

My son gave me a wry smile. "I have my own work to do. No sense getting caught up in…" He waved an arm, looking for a word. "Conspiracies. I'll get the room card. You get your conference material."

I made my way to a long white table where two casually dressed women sat with a large box of pale green folders between them. In front was a row of plastic nametags. The first lady stood and extended a hand to me. She was younger than me by a few years. Her skin wrinkled by years under the sun.

"We're glad you made it to our reunion." Her hazel eyes and bright smile caught me by surprise as we shook hands. "You will enjoy the next two days. Maryanne will get you signed in."

She wore a nametag, but I couldn't read the name when she took her seat behind the table.

"*Danke, Madam.*" I moved to the next woman in purple vest embossed with a stylized cat.

Maryanne donned glasses and grabbed a pen. "Name, please?"

"Henry Rohling."

She looked through her box of folders. "I have a Heinrich Rohling from Berlin. Is that you?"

"I prefer Henry—"

"Henry Rohling?" The first woman gazed at me. She rose to her feet and rushed around the table, smoothing her lime-colored dress. "I can't believe this. We got a message saying you weren't coming. How are you?"

Horst stared at me from across the lobby with a raised brow. I shrugged. Was I supposed to know this woman?

"I'm doing well. Thank you for asking."

"Do you know who I am?"

Was she beaming at me? "My memory is not always reliable," I said, my thoughts racing. Was it possible we've met? I held my breath, not daring to believe my heart.

"I'm Emily Henning."

My throat went dry. I never thought I would see this girl again. Of course, she was no longer eighteen. She had to be…seventy? We'd lived separate lives, yet I reminisced about her often. Once, I promised to come back for her. Why I didn't was a long story. Did I love her? Yes! But I chose to stay home. A lost opportunity. Yet, for every door that closes, a new one opens. I found Della and a new life in Berlin.

I couldn't tell her these things. They sounded both pious and lame. "I thought about you during the trip coming here." The butterflies would not go away. "I never expected to see you."

"Oh, but you would have," she said, laughing. "I'm vice-president of the Historical Society. Our group has been working on this project for nearly a year. It took three months just to track you and the other veterans down." She stepped forward, extending her arms.

I embraced her. Half-remembered memories came rushing back. Those stolen moments when we hid from the guard—and her father—inside the barn. The time we repaired the windmill after a windstorm. The day she cried on my shoulder when I buried the family dog. My lips brushed the back of her neck. Emily's skin smelled of cornstalks and peaches. To kiss her seemed like a violation. I stepped back, holding her arms for a moment. "I hope we have a chance to visit."

"We will. And I want you to meet my husband."

I bowed my head. Of course, she would be married. "I would be honored."

"You'll be sitting together in the front table. He

says you'll have much to talk about."

My mind whirled like newspapers caught in a gale. Married to another prisoner? And I know this man? Who came back for Emily? Who whisked her away? "He's a lucky man. What is his name?"

"Oh, I forgot. I shouldn't have introduced myself as Emily Henning. I wanted you to recognize me. Both of you worked on Dad's farm, and he's told me many times how you liked his wood carvings when you first met." She straightened as if coming to attention. "I'm Emily Kimmel. Oskar Kimmel is my husband."

Chapter Eight

21-31 August 1943

My remaining week before starting the Labor Program fell into a steady routine with breakfast at seven hundred hours, dinner at twelve hundred, and supper at seventeen hundred hours. Between meals, I wandered with Novak as he applied for jobs around the compound. He hoped to be a translator, but Sergeant Stecklein blocked him from that position and, we discovered, from every other position as well—except for garbage detail.

Four days after his job search begun, Novak received a terse note from Stecklein granting him the position. "The man likes to make me squirm," he muttered.

Thinking about my run-in with *Hauptmann* Dietrich, I had to agree. "We have to be humble to our superiors."

Novak blew out a heavy breath. "With Stecklein, I fear it's too late."

"You can still join the Labor Program."

"I'm staying. The courses I picked will provide a diversion."

I pushed my tin plate aside. "Stay respectful of Stecklein. The war may be over for us. But we're still part of the *Heer*."

After supper, we ambled to the horse stable, a solid red structure with an attached exercise pen. Inside the open double doors, the place smelled of straw, manure, and new paint. Daylight from the high open windows gave the interior an airy appearance. Stored inside sat a long refuse wagon with wide metal wheels. Harnesses, horse collars, bridles, and leather straps hung from the walls. Four roomy horse stalls filled half the building with a center alleyway. Each enclosure stood a meter or more high with chicken wire attached to a stout wooden framework above. Two stalls contained large draft horses, their ears flicking at flies buzzing in the warm air. The animals watched us with placid eyes. From an empty pen, a man wearing a cap whistled an off-pitch tune.

"Hello?" Novak called.

"*Ja?*" A short man with a manure fork peeked around the stall. "No one's allowed here."

"I've been assigned to the cleanup detail," Novak said.

"Oh, that's different." He set his tool aside, taking his cap off and scratching his scalp. "Sarge said someone would be coming along. I'm Private Bauer." He rubbed his pants and held out a hand.

Hesitating for only a moment, my friend clasped his palm. "I'm Novak. What's the work like?"

Bauer pulled at the bill of his cover. "The garbage route takes little time. You keep a weekly schedule and make a few stops each weekday. Most of your job will be caring for the Belgians and looking after the equipment."

"And mucking stalls." Novak eyed the manure fork ruefully.

"That's no trouble. Thank the gardeners. Today, you rake it; tomorrow, they take it." Bauer snapped his fingers. "Voilà."

Novak took the manure fork and hefted it. "Could you walk me through everything? I'm to start tomorrow."

"Tomorrow, then. Cleanup detail starts early, so be here by oh five thirty. Wear your work clothes. The Amis will replace anything too soiled to clean. I'll show you how to hitch the team and start your route. In a week, you'll have it all figured out."

"Where will you go?" Novak asked.

"My *Vater* was a baker. I'll be making bread in the kitchen."

"Good for you," I said.

Novak gave a final look around. "I'll be here," he said. We bid the man farewell and left.

Novak strolled beside me to the barracks, a despondent look on his face. "I would have been a good translator," he said.

"You could rotate out in three to six months," I said, hoping to encourage him. "By then, Stecklein will find a new target to abuse."

He gave me a sideways glance. "I wouldn't wish that kind of grief on another."

His tone of finality alarmed me. I stopped, grabbing his forearm. "Look, this is all temporary. Your job, my job, the war. Someday, this will be over, then we can go back to what we used to do. Life will be normal again."

My friend stepped back, his face growing red. "Life will never be normal again. And I'm not going back to Germany. This is my home, and I intend to stay here."

"You can't." I wanted to shake him, but that would have been a mistake. "You're German."

"No, Henry." He stared at me, his eyes defiant. "To hell with the Reich. I was born in New York. That makes me an American."

His anger unsettled me. "You better hope the Amis win. Or you'll be a man without a country."

"If I can get an audience with the camp commanders, I can show I'm just as American as they are. I can maybe get out of here."

I sucked in a breath. How would Reinhardt or Dietrich react to that? "That would be risky. Only the liaison officer can talk to the Americans."

"Don't worry. I wouldn't show my cards unless I had a good chance of success."

I sighed with relief. "Keep your head low. We can compare our pursuits when I get back after harvest."

"I'll try." Novak thumped my back. "Thanks for listening, Henry. I wish you hadn't enrolled in farmwork. It won't be the same without you."

"Two months," I said. "Three at the most."

My last night in camp, Novak told me of a discovery he made. "In the admin building, the officers throw away a lot of paper," he said. "Some of it is in English."

American papers? "Don't be poking your nose where it shouldn't be. Stick to your job." The thought of Novak poking in officer business terrified me. "Why would you be interested?"

"Curiosity—knowing what they know. There's no risk, Henry. I can browse at my leisure inside the stable and throw the papers out the next day."

"That is insane. Even if you find bothersome information, you'll have to keep it to yourself."

He shrugged. "True. Other than you, I wouldn't tell anyone else. But the intrigue is exciting."

"Intrigue is for spies. You'll get yourself killed."

"Don't be a mother hen. I'll be careful."

We turned in early that night. Tomorrow, our paths would separate.

I awoke early at oh six hundred, but Novak's bunk was already empty. I left the main gate soon afterward in a canvas truck carrying nineteen other prisoners—including Kimmel—five guards, and two noncoms. Following the back roads, we came to a wooded area some twenty-five kilometers from camp.

Under the guard's direction, we built our temporary work camp: clearing trees and brush, digging trenches for a latrine, and constructing a wooden shelter strong enough to withstand the elements, short of a tornado. By dusk the next day, we were at ease around a fire eating rations without any worry about an aerial assault. Tomorrow, we would meet the American civilians who hired us. I turned in at twenty-one hundred, thrilled to be away from the main camp, but anxious if our new employers would accept us.

****

"Civilians approaching!" Sergeant Wilkins stood and pointed to the east with his tin cup as a set of headlights approached from the predawn horizon. The vehicle dipped in a depression but soon reappeared, its engine straining up the incline. "Could be Henning or Swope. They're the only two farms east of here. Corporal, ready the prisoners."

Corporal Gray, a burly man with a double chin,

climbed to his feet. "East teams. Atten-hut!"

Gray had drilled us numerous times on falling into formation. I lined up shoulder to shoulder with Adler, Kimmel, and Goetz. We were picked to work for Mr. Efren Henning on his one-hundred-sixty-acre farm. Four other men working for the Swope farm came to attention as well.

The pickup honked as it jerked to a halt before us. In the lantern's light, it was hard to discern the vehicle's color. Blue, maybe? And small compared to military trucks. A female's voice called from the driver's window. "I'm Mildred Henning. It'll be a bumpy ride going back. My husband threw in some wooden crates for your men to sit on. Safer than sitting on the sidewalls."

"Much obliged, Mrs. Henning." Wilkins motioned for us to jump aboard. He gestured to a guard. "Nichols, you take this crew."

"Yessir!" Nichols, a small man of at least forty, walked with a slight limp. He saluted the sergeant and clambered in the back with the rest of us.

The journey to the Henning farm was as rough as Frau Henning promised. "Wouldn't she think it dangerous to pick up a truckload of war prisoners?" I asked Nichols.

He shrugged. "I'm sure she feels safe enough. Her doors are locked, and she probably has a deer rifle stashed under the front seat."

That startled me. "A civilian with a gun?"

He chuckled. "Don't worry. Do your job, and no one will shoot you. If you hear gunshots, it's probably boys hunting rabbit or squirrel—a favorite pastime around here."

"Children carry firearms?"

"It keeps them out of trouble."

I shook my head. "In Germany, no civilian, especially children, could own a gun. Only with special permission from the Party."

"That's why no dictator will take over this country. People won't give up their guns without a fight."

I wondered about that, but further conversation was impossible as we lumbered over dips and potholes. Occasionally, a tree branch caught the cab and whipped over our heads. With a startling lurch, we climbed onto a gravel path. Gears shifted, and we gained speed. I breathed a sigh of relief. No more rocking about.

Nichols took off his cap, wiping his forehead. "That's the worst of it. We should arrive at the farm in five minutes."

I translated the news to the three other men. Adler, a slight man and an art teacher who joined the *Wehrmacht* to avoid scrutiny by the Nazis, never complained of any assignment, no matter how taxing. Goetz, on the other hand, enjoyed showing his strength. As stout as a circus strongman, he loved a good joke, but could be arrogant as well. And there was Kimmel, who kept to himself the most.

The pickup made a sharp turn, and I grabbed the side of the truck. Headlights illuminated a rutted driveway and wooden fencing. "Look alive," said Nichols. "We're about there."

Ahead of us, a dog barked. The headlights caught a collie racing toward us, then he circled the vehicle as we neared a large barn. The dog stayed a safe distance away, his tail twitching, as we came to a stop. Outside the barn's wide doors, a broad-shouldered man in overalls and western hat stooped to attach a harrow to the tractor. Beside him, a young woman held high a kerosene lantern. As we fell into line, Frau Henning parked the pickup by the farmhouse a short distance away.

Our guard watched Henning for a moment, then cleared his throat. "I'm Private Nichols. Your crew is ready to work, sir."

Henning lifted his eyes as if he'd just noticed our presence. He wiped his hands on a rag hanging from a belt and extended it to the guard. "Glad to meet you, Private. Friends call me Efren but probably best to keep it formal. Mr. Henning will do."

Nichols nodded. "What can we do for you?"

"Well, sir." Henning waved to rows of plants in the predawn light. "I hope your men have strong backs. After I turn over the potatoes, your crew will follow behind to sack and load them in the pickup. Can any of your group speak English?"

I stepped forward. "I can, sir."

He gave me a quick glance. "All right then, I'll need a head start. In five minutes or so, you can start digging. Give me plenty of room when I come back on the next pass." He scrutinized the four of us again, lingering on Goetz's muscular build. "Private, are these Jerries…you know…safe to be around?"

"Yessir." Nichols smiled. "Safe enough."

"And you'll be with them all the time?"

"That's my job."

Henning bit his lip. "I'm thinking about my wife and my daughter, Emily. Well, no time like the present." He climbed aboard his tractor and kicked on the engine. With a grinding roar, the machine lurched toward the rows, pulling the harrow behind it.

The plow dug in, flipping the leafy plants bottom side up, leaving a ridge of dirt clods, roots, and potatoes. The hairs on the back of my neck prickled. I glanced around; Emily peered at me. "Fräulein?"

She cast her eyes downward for a moment, her cheeks reddening. "Don't worry about Daddy. He doesn't like the prison camp, but he knows the four of you can do the job."

I couldn't help but notice how the dawning sun brought out freckles on her cheeks and the sheen of her auburn hair. "Glad we can help, Miss Henning."

Nichols cleared his throat. "It's not five minutes, but that tractor is plenty far ahead. We should get to work."

"What other crops does your father grow, fräulein?" I asked.

"Can it, Rohling," the guard snapped. "No fraternizing." He tipped his cap to the young woman. "Ma'am, it might be best if you talk directly to me."

She hung her head, not quite hiding mischievous eyes. "Sorry, sir. I didn't mean to break any rules, sir."

"It's okay." Nichols took a deep breath. "Seems like rules are changing all the time. Prisoners working for civilians. No guard towers. No barbed wire. You wonder who came up with Krauts working outside the gates."

"My father thought the government would build an airfield instead of a prison camp. Now, he's changed his mind. Daddy says if the war keeps up, the country will have to feed more prisoners."

Nichols grunted. "Well, civilians are grumbling now, calling us the 'Fritz Ritz.' It's embarrassing."

That made no sense to me. I sauntered to where Adler sat. "I wonder what the dog's name is," he said, rubbing the collie's ears.

I knelt on the grass next to the dog, who'd readily accepted another hand scratching its back. "I don't know." I glanced around, looking for the other two members of our crew. Kimmel stood by the field's edge, examining a stack of burlap bags. Goetz stood at the double doors of the barn; his attention fixed inside.

Nichols whistled for our attention. "Gather 'round!" He ambled to Kimmel's pile of bags and retrieved a couple. He thrust one in my hands as I approached. Goetz came forward but frowned and crossed his arms when the guard held a sack out to him. "Tell him what he needs to do, Rohling. Maybe he doesn't understand."

I suspected Goetz did understand, but Fräulein Henning waved to us.

"Bring some bags to the field. You need to learn how to dig for potatoes." The four of us followed her into the dirt, where she donned a pair of work gloves and held a garden rake. "All of you stand on the opposite side of the row while I show you how to work the ground."

We stood in the soft earth while Nichols watched from the grass. Frau Henning raked back and forth through the dirt, exposing roots and tubers. "Don't be afraid to dig with your fingers and sack everything. We'll load the bags in the pickup and later, onto Big Nellie. She's the truck in the barn." The young woman handed the rake to me. "Now, you try it."

I accepted the garden tool and raked through the mound. Adler plucked the exposed potatoes and placed them in a sack. I moved down the row to uncover more roots, but the finicky girl grabbed my rake and broke open more dirt clods, exposing new tubers. "Get all the small and split potatoes as well. Chickens will eat them." As I resumed work, she retrieved another rake for Goetz. "Start at the other end of the row and work your way back. Two people rake. The other two dig and sack. Every twenty minutes, you should switch, so no one is stooping all day."

Goetz stepped back, crossing his arms. "I'm not digging with my hands. Not for anyone. Any job but that." He marched back to stand by the barn.

"Goetz refuses to dig," I called to Nichols.

The guard shot a finger at me. "Tell him he's out if he doesn't work."

"I'm sure he's aware of that."

"No. You convince him to start digging, or I'm sending all of you back. No work for anyone. Period." His voice rose as Henning approached atop his tractor.

Emily Henning stood in the tractor's path, waving her father to stop. The noisy machine settled to a loud idle as father and daughter conferred a short distance away. Finally, Henning silenced the engine, and the two walked to the edge of the field. Nichols strode to meet them while Adler, Kimmel, and I stood in a huddled group near the barn. I tried to reason with Goetz, but he remained adamant. He would not stoop or dig.

Henning approached us with Nichols. "Who's the stubborn one, Private?"

Nichols pointed to Goetz. "I told them I'm getting a new crew if he doesn't work."

I stepped forward. "Goetz says he'll do anything else."

Nichols broke in. "Mr. Henning, I'll have a new crew out here first thing tomorrow."

Henning pulled his hat low. "I need the job done now. To hell with the army. I'll hire kids if I have to."

A small intake of breath barely disturbed the quiet that followed. Henning's daughter peered at Goetz for a long moment, her lips pressed together.

Nichols paced about before returning. "How about we do what we can today, and tomorrow I return with a new crew?"

"Fine, but I'm only paying for three workers." Henning kicked a rock with a worn boot.

Emily Henning touched my arm. "You said your friend will do any other job?"

I nodded, "*Ja*, fräulein."

"Emily." Henning jerked a thumb to the field. "Get these Krauts working. I'm turning the next row."

Emily gazed at Goetz. Her eyes brightened. "A mule!" she called, but Henning was already halfway to the tractor.

Nichols motioned for us to remain seated. Fräulein Henning raised her voice, calling to me. "Talk to Mr. Goetz. Would he be willing to carry full bags of produce to the pickup? He could even drive the pickup to the barn and load Big Nellie. The man looks strong enough. It will be heavy lifting all day. But it will keep everyone busy, especially if he can drive. Might even move the work along quicker."

I relayed the information to Goetz.

The big fellow smiled, showing a chipped tooth. "I hauled and loaded artillery in the desert. Driving a toy truck is nothing."

"He'll do it." I held my fingers in a Churchill

victory sign.

"Great! Tell your guard while I give Daddy the news."

A few minutes later, Henning came off the field, scrutinizing Goetz. "Looks tough enough," he said to Nichols. "If he can pull it off, we can still put in a full day's work."

Nichols jerked a thumb up, and I conveyed the good news to the crew.

"The Americans will let us keep our j-jobs?" Kimmel gave me a sideways glance.

"Yes. Goetz loads all day. The rest of us rake, dig, and sack."

Adler broke into a rare smile. "We'll make Goetz hurry to keep up."

"*Wunderbar.*" I breathed a sigh of relief.

After a good bit of whooping and cheering, it was time to get to work. Henning ambled back to his tractor. Nichols rode with Goetz, who drove the pickup to the field. Fräulein Henning caught my eye and gave me a theatrical wink. I gasped, not quite sure how to respond and stumbled, nearly falling on my face.

Eyes bright and biting her lip, she made a *V* sign as well.

For the rest of that day, I found myself often looking to see if she was still with us, my excitement tempered by grim reality. I was the enemy.

Chapter Nine

I followed Horst into our hotel room but was surprised when he whirled to face me. "What just happened out there, Papa? Why do I feel there's yet another secret you're not telling me?"

"The hour is late." I yawned. "Let's talk about this in the morning."

Horst found a seat on the nearest bed. "Now, Papa. I'm your son, and I deserve some answers."

Our plane trip and the long drive here left me tired and irritable. And now, I discovered Emily alive and married to my old rival. How could such a needy man have won her over? Answers would come in time. As sleepy as I was, it was clear that Horst would not be satisfied until I provided some explanation. I blew a heavy breath, hoping he wouldn't probe too deep. "I knew Emily Henning many years ago. Back then, she was eighteen. I worked on her father's farm during the war as a laborer along with other men. We became close."

Horst massaged a wrinkled forehead. "So you met her while working for the Americans? Wasn't that against the rules?"

An honest question. I eased into a swivel chair by the writing desk. "A unique situation that could only happen in America. The Americans worried about civilians mixing with enemy prisoners, so they established a strict set of rules we were to follow. Of course, from the start, those who made the rules were seldom around to enforce them. Over time, we became comfortable with each other. The guards watched us casually at best, and sometimes not at all, and the Hennings became friendly as well."

"More than friendly, Papa. You mean involved."

I saw where this was going. "You could say that."

"How did this happen?"

I stifled another yawn. "Since I knew English, I got to know each member of the family. The youngest boy, Billie—twelve when I first saw him—wanted to know all about General Rommel. Frau Henning liked to watch us eat. And Efren Henning worried about each decision he made about the farm. Emily hoped to see the world. I saw her as a feisty, yet vulnerable, farm girl—as much a prisoner as I was."

"Did you love her?" Horst asked.

His question struck a spark. I jumped to my feet and glared at my successful, yet clueless son. How dare he ask such a question! "Yes. Be thankful we never married, because you would not be alive today."

Horst bit his lip, rubbing his chin. "Sorry, Papa. I deserved that. I feel odd for asking, but you're right. You'd be an American now. So what kept you from marrying her?"

I fell into my chair again. "When I got back home, I realized I could not leave my country again. And now Emily is married to another prisoner I knew back then."

Horst leaned forward. "So you pined for this American girl, but stayed home, allowing a countryman to marry her?"

Couldn't he understand? Swallowing hard, I forced

the words out. "Of course, I wanted to see her again. But I'd been away from home for six years. Foreigners had invaded our country and claimed our women. Getting material to rebuild and finding food was a daily struggle. Before I met your mother, my only ties were Mum and Papa. Many of us wanted to take back our country. Some fled to America. To me, that reeked of cowardice."

"Even if it meant finding happiness?"

"I did find happiness. I married your mother."

"Did Mama know about this American?"

I stared at the floor. "I never told her directly. But I know your mother found Emily's letters. It was just like her to keep them safe."

"I know you're tired, Papa. One last question, and we can both get some sleep. This fellow prisoner who married your first love. Can you accept that? Because you'll have to. They've been married a long time."

I gave him a sidelong glance. "I know my place in the world. Intruding on another man's wife would be shameful."

"I'm glad to hear that, Papa." My son stood and offered me his arm. "I can sleep better now."

Later, as I lay huddled under stiff sheets, my wandering thoughts turned to words in Emily's final letter to me. "No matter what happens, you'll always be in my heart."

****

The next morning, Horst and I had a quick breakfast, then he walked with me down a wide hallway with comfortable chairs and tables along the wall. Outside the conference room marked VETERANS' REUNION, a young volunteer greeted me. "You'll be sitting at Table Three, Mr. Rohling. The program will start shortly."

Horst squeezed my shoulder. "Have a good time, Papa. I'll be at the Salina Public Library all day. They have reliable dial-up service. See you this evening."

"I'll see you then," I said.

With a final wave, he retraced his steps up the corridor, turned a corner, and disappeared.

I entered a brightly lit conference room buzzing with activity. Gold tablecloths draped six tables with a long VIP table, podium, and microphone front and center. Conversation filled the air. Some of the veterans wore suits and ties, but most, like me, dressed casually. Most of the women were wives who accompanied their husbands, and two young women could only be granddaughters.

Table three sat to the front of the speaker's stand. I found my name on a small blue table tent, took my seat, and sipped from a water glass.

"*Guten morgen*, Herr Rohling." A hand reached out in greeting. "*Ich bin Oskar Kimmel.*"

Beside me sat an impeccably dressed man wearing a dark blue shirt and striped tie. His black hair showed only a hint of gray at the temples, much like those men's hair-coloring commercials.

I nodded without extending a hand. "Herr Kimmel. *Es ist lange her—*"

"Fifty years, Heinrich," he said in English. "And we meet again. This time as guests of honor instead of pawns of war. Don't you find that ironic?"

"That was long ago."

"True. I've always wanted to see the old country again, but never did. Got a dozen travel books about

Bavaria. You came from Berlin, correct? How is it today?"

I gazed at this man pretending to be German. "It's a beautiful city with many museums. You can still speak Deutsch, though your accent is distinctly American."

He chuckled. "What can I say? Came here in '47. Straight to Conrad and renewed my ties with the Henning family. Poor Emily. You left her heartbroken. It was fortunate I could console her."

My teeth clenched for a moment. "Unlike some, I wanted to help the Fatherland."

"Ah, Heinrich, still playing the good German." He chuckled with false bravado. "To tell you the truth, I couldn't wait to leave that sad country."

"Germany's loss," I said.

A shadow fell across our table.

"Look up, you two, and say 'Cheese!' " A silver-haired woman held a camera. Her nametag read VIRGINIA POWELL. "Come on, Mr. Rohling. Give me a big smile."

Kimmel leaned against my shoulder like we were old friends. An instant later, the world flashed before my eyes. Mrs. Powell thanked us and hurried on to the next table. Kimmel pushed away. "Better get used to the pictures," he said. "Cameras will be snapping all day."

"Understandable." I stared at this stranger. "You're looking fit, and the stuttering is almost completely gone. That must have taken a lot of work."

His eyes narrowed. "Only you would have noticed. It took effort, but that was not my only conquest."

His meaning could not have been clearer, but I

didn't rise to the bait. "Was sharing this table your idea?"

"Virginia—Mrs. Powell—arranged it. We worked on the same work crew, so of course we'd be seated together. Your reply card suggested medical issues, though. Virginia wrote you off, but I suspected you'd find a way to come, so I insisted your name remain on the arrival list."

"My son tends to be overprotective. He came with me but isn't attending the reunion."

"Why not?" he asked.

I sighed. "Horst is a busy attorney. His office demanded a working vacation."

"I'd like to meet him sometime."

"My son needs an e-mail connection for his work, so he is driving to Salina. Horst should return by evening."

"How about drinks tonight? We can meet at the hotel bar at nine."

I did not intend to socialize with Kimmel. Before I could answer, a familiar voice called to us.

"Look up, everybody!" Emily Kimmel stood three meters from our table with her own camera poised. "Smile!" The camera flashed and whirred.

"Sweetheart!" Kimmel waved her over. "You're doing a marvelous job." He rose and gave her a lingering kiss while watching me from the corner of his eye.

Turning away meant weakness. My eyes remained locked on Kimmel's.

Emily gasped and pulled away. "Honey, you're embarrassing me. I really need to take more pictures before we start." Her voice was low and urgent.

Kimmel pointed at me. "Henry here told me how glad he was to come to our little reunion. He said if it weren't for you, he'd never have made the trip."

Emily stared at me, wide-eyed for a moment, then dashed from the conference room. Slowly, Kimmel regained his seat, oblivious to the shocked faces from our table. "I apologize for my wife. The stress of organizing this gathering has been a strain on her. But she has fortitude and will be back in a few minutes."

I leaned toward Kimmel, keeping my anger in check. "What the hell are you trying to pull? I had no idea I'd see her."

He patted me on the wrist. "It's quite all right, Heinrich. It's all over your face. We don't forget the past, do we? Not when the mind still yearns. Now admit it. You still long for her."

I grabbed for my water glass and gulped all of it. "That was years ago. I married and had three children since then, and I still love my wife."

Kimmel glanced about. "Other wives came. Where's yours?"

"She's dead."

"Sorry to hear that. I truly am." Kimmel could sound sincere when it suited him. "All the more reason for you to see your missed opportunity."

I held my tongue, refusing to take the bait. Kimmel's naked resentment bothered me. And two long days remained ahead.

Chapter Ten

2 September to 28 October 1943

In the following days, we settled into a routine: waking at 0400, boarding the pickup an hour later, and receiving our assignments from Mr. Henning, usually by dawn. We worked until an hour before sunset, when Frau Henning gave us cookies or a slice of pie. Afterward, Emily drove us back to camp. There, we relaxed until lights out. Most of the noncoms returned to main camp, replaced by draftees and one corporal. Nichols took little interest in us, dozing beneath a tree or talking to the family. At night, the guards kept to themselves. Away from the overbearing atmosphere of the prison, we maintained self-discipline. No one talked seriously about escape. Why should we? While the world was at war, we camped at peace under the stars.

My joy at seeing Emily as our driver turned to chagrin when Nichols chose to ride in the cab with her rather than ride in back with us. Sass, Emily's dog, often rode as well. Watching a restless collie looking out the side window over our unhappy guard made for some amusement as we drove back to camp.

Gathering potatoes soon gave way to other jobs. We dug a cellar to store turnips, onions, beets, and carrots. Goetz replaced rotted boards while the rest of us painted the barn a dazzling cherry red. We even relieved Billie, the youngest boy, of his milking chores.

Each of us found work we enjoyed doing. Goetz liked showing off his strength. Adler preferred working with livestock. He modified the hog pen so the farm's two mean-tempered sows wouldn't gobble the hens that passed too close. Kimmel, the most solitary of our group, split timber for the barn's wood-burning stove.

One job I became adept at was keeping "Big Nellie," Mr. Henning's delivery truck, running. Three weeks after we began work, the rusty old beast refused to start. That day I laid new planks in the barn loft while Henning attempted to turn the engine over. With some muttering, he retrieved tools from a workbench and clanged about beneath the hood. Once, he grunted in pain and backed away, grasping a bloody hand. I clambered down a ladder. "Can I be of help, sir?"

"I'm no good with engines," he said grimacing. "Josh is the mechanic of the family, but he's in Guadalcanal." He pursed his lips like he just revealed some vital strategic information.

"Trucks were my specialty," I assured him. "You take care of your hand. I'll see what I can do."

"Much obliged." He rushed out the double doors, leaving me alone.

I tried the ignition to get a feel for the problem, then gave the engine a cursory examination. Not in the best of condition. Checking the filters, belts, and electrical revealed several areas of concern, the biggest being spark plugs and wiring.

With some adjustments, I managed to get the vehicle running when Mr. Henning returned, his right hand wrapped in bandages.

"Hey! Nellie's alive. Good job!"

I wiped my hands on a rag. "For now. Plugs and wiring need replacing. My fix today is only temporary."

Mr. Henning removed his tattered hat, running fingers over thinning hair. "Hate to tie up the truck with a mechanic. I've got work to do."

"You won't have to," I said. "I kept trucks like this running in the desert. Get me the right parts, and I can do the job tomorrow morning."

Mr. Henning reached in the cab, turned off the ignition, and searched in his pockets for pencil and paper. "Give me that list. I can run into town this afternoon."

I recited the list. "Some of those parts will prevent future trouble."

"Sounds good." He stuck out a hand, and we shook. "An unexpected bonus to have a mechanic. Thanks for the help."

"My pleasure, Herr Henning."

A shadow crossed his face. "For a second, I forgot you were a prisoner. Too bad it has to be that way." He looked up to the loft. "Finish reinforcing the flooring. Baling will start soon, and those boards will need to take the weight. Do good with the truck, then I'll have you take a look-see at the tractor."

I headed back to the ladder. "Any time, sir."

The next morning, our crew set about weeding the garden. Emily was there as well, filling a basket with produce. After giving instructions to the others, Mr. Henning gestured for me to follow him to the barn. As I approached the newly painted building, "Big Nellie" emerged seemingly without a driver. The vehicle stopped outside, and twelve-year-old Billie in patched overalls hopped to the ground. He was a stout youth like his father while Emily took after her slight mother.

"I figured you could work better out in the sun," Henning said before facing Billie. "Fetch the toolbox from the barn."

"Yeah, Pa."

As the boy raced away, Henning brought out the box of parts. "I found most of what you listed. All used. No new parts for a truck this old."

It was a marvel he could find them at all. In Germany, the needs of civilians were of small priority. Only a well-connected Party member could drive an auto—if they could obtain the petrol. Replacement parts were impossible to find. All scrap metal went to the war effort. "These will do," I said.

The first thing was to crack the hood and loosen wiring. Billie disappeared for a second time, returning with a fruit crate. He deposited the box by the front tire, clambered on top, and thrust his head close to mine. "Pa says you fought with General Rommel. Did you see him?"

I smiled at the musings of a child. "The Libyan Desert is a big place. I never saw the field marshal in person."

"What was it like being a desert fighter?" he asked.

I removed the last of the old wiring before answering. "It was mostly boring and uncomfortable with occasional periods of sheer terror."

Mr. Henning cleared his throat. "Be careful what you say. He's just a boy."

I gathered the new wires, framing an answer that would satisfy the notions of a young boy. "Weather was hot during the day. Cold at night. Sand constantly bogged down trucks and artillery. Winds stirred up massive sandstorms. On calm days, sand flies would buzz around your nose and mouth. We were constantly finding ways to distract ourselves from our discomforts."

"But what about the fighting?" Billie asked.

With a screwdriver, I tightened the first wire in place before answering. "Mostly defensive. Our job was to protect the panzer supply lines. That meant a lot of moving around. While we tended to avoid battles, we were open to air attacks from the British. Staying still under camouflage netting lessened our chances of pilots spotting us."

Billie glowered, disappointed with my answer. He studied me as I completed the new wiring. "So you never fought in battle? Ever?"

The boy was persistent. I had work to do, but my continued employment depended on how well I got along with all members of the Henning family. "There were attacks. Supply raids. Since we had no heavy armor, the Allies may have thought we were an easy target." I could not suppress a smile. "At least until the end, we proved them wrong."

"Did you kill anyone?" the boy asked.

My tool nearly slipped from my grasp. I glanced at Billie's father, hoping for intervention. But Mr. Henning seemed more interested in his pipe. With some uneasiness, I realized he was as interested in the answer as his son. "I have no idea," I said. "With gunfire all around, it would be impossible to know whose bullet felled an enemy. The smoke and blowing sand made details murky at best. And the noise." I winced at the memory. "I could feel the sound with my gut, and it bent my eardrums. Any sane man who valued his hearing would huddle in his trench. But our job was to keep the supplies moving. Once the enemy probed our defenses, they often fell back and radioed for aircraft to strafe us. British warships sank most of our supplies at sea. In the end, we had nothing left to fight with."

I wanted to say more: how the Reich abandoned us and then demanded that we fight to the last man. Or why our generals let a housepainter determine war strategy. But I remained quiet, attaching the new spark plugs. "She should start a lot easier now."

Mr. Henning put a match to his pipe, coaxing it to life. "Billie, fire up the engine."

"Sure, Pa." The boy jumped from the crate and scrambled inside the cab. Moments later, Big Nellie roared to life.

"Stay there for a minute!" the farmer called to his son.

Henning continued to indulge his pipe as I checked the connections. Finally, he withdrew the odorous thing from his mouth. "Thanks!" he yelled.

"For what?"

"The things you didn't say."

"I don't understand."

"Billie sent a letter to his brother Josh last winter. 'How many Japanese have you killed?' He wrote that. It took four months for him to get an answer. Josh wrote, 'I don't know, and I don't want to.' " Henning peered at me. "You and my oldest have a lot in common."

I shrugged. "We're both soldiers."

He shook his head. "It's more than that. You're the same age. Similar experiences, but worlds apart. You two share a common bond. A brotherhood."

"Maybe," I said. "When news spread of our coming surrender, many of us wondered who we'd face. A division of New Zealanders had hounded us for months. Pesky bastards. Yet we wanted to surrender to them."

"I can see you and Josh sharing stories," he said, his eyes growing bright.

The truck still ran a bit rough. I had more parts to replace and had no desire to meet an American combat soldier. "Better cut the engine. We're not finished yet."

He puffed on his pipe. "I know that doesn't appeal to you. Best to leave it alone, I suppose. You're taking his place, after all."

What did he mean by that?

Henning left me alone with young Billie and his persistent questions. On days like these, I wondered what living free in America would be like. How would it feel to call on Fräulein Henning without the PW brand on my back?

Best to keep these fantasies to myself. Stay quiet. Go with the flow, as Novak would say.

All that changed the day Emily's dog died. The death of a collie foreshadowed everything that was to come.

Late in October, I painted the rail fence that ran along the main road while the rest of the crew harvested corn. "Finish as soon as possible, and get back to the cornfield," he told me. Redbirds sang in the maples overhead as I applied the first coat. Behind me, grass rustled; Sass bounded toward me, hoping I'd scratch his neck. He seldom strayed from the children, but the dog did enjoy attention from Adler and I.

Emily strolled down the driveway, singing a soft

tune.

"Good afternoon, fräulein," I called.

"*Guten tag*, Herr Rohling. Great day, isn't it?" Emily often greeted us in German. I found it delightful.

"Yes, it is. Out for a walk?" I asked, rubbing the dog's shoulder. Sass bounded away to follow his master.

"I'm getting the mail." She waved to where four mailboxes stood at an intersection some distance away. She turned the corner and ambled along the shoulder of the road. At times, the dog lunged ahead and circled back. Other times, he fell behind, rooting in the grass.

Each morning we drove past those dented gray metal boxes leaning together like drunken singers. Did Emily get personal letters? Who from?

I dismissed the thought and focused on brushing the wood. With the steady breeze, I could add a second coat in an hour or two. Just a matter of retrieving more paint from the tool shed. Brushing back and forth relaxed me. I imagined myself conducting a stirring version of "The Blue Danube." Close by, a squirrel scolded me for disturbing her territory.

My reverie shattered with the long blast of a vehicle horn. A farm truck, the size of Big Nellie, blared as it passed Emily. Sass pawed at a spot in the road, oblivious to the danger bearing down on him. The massive vehicle swerved. Brakes screeched. Tires threw up dust, but it was too late.

Much too late for Sass.

I dropped my brush and hustled to the scene. Emily screamed and ran to the grass by the road. There, she knelt over her companion. I reached her moments later.

The collie lay in a twisted heap, its head caved-in

111

on one side. The farm truck sat still, its engine knocking and sputtering. The driver's door squawked open, and a pair of bare feet landed on the dirt road.

The boy wore faded pants with holes worn through the patches. He peeked at Emily, one hand shading blue eyes beneath a mop of blond hair. "Sorry, ma'am, I didn't mean to hurt the dog."

That did it. I stepped in his line of sight, advancing. "You idiot." I spat the words.

He jumped back, his eyes widening. "Are you one of those Krauts? The ones the Jerry-lovers got working?"

"I am."

He scrambled to the truck, grabbing for the steering wheel to pull himself inside. Fearful he would get away, I pulled him roughly to the ground. Twisting him around, I pointed to the dead creature. "Look what you've done."

He sniveled. "Look, mister, I didn't do it on purpose. Honest!" Tears rolled down his cheeks.

That wasn't good enough. The boy should atone for his actions. I pushed him between the shoulders. "Apologize."

"I already did!" The boy sniffled but didn't try to run away.

"Again!" I gave him another stiff push that sent him staggering. His shadow fell across Sass's body. "Ma'am, I'm sorry."

Emily looked up, eyes rimmed in red, her breath catching in her throat.

Oh, how I wanted to throttle the boy, but I knew this to be an accident. With some relief, I noted the Henning pickup approaching; its horn tooted several times. Upon reaching us, it pulled over. Henning and Nichols jumped out. Emily's father knelt beside her, shaking his head. The guard leveled his rifle at me. "Move away from the kid."

I stepped back, my arms raised in surrender. Nichols sauntered over to the farm boy and bent close to glare into the youth's upturned face. "Listen up. Get your butt out of here. Now."

He jumped in the seat, revved the engine, and spun his wheels, shooting away with the driver's side door still open.

The world grew quiet, except for Emily's quiet sobbing. Mail lay scattered about the road. I retrieved letters as Henning bundled his daughter in the pickup.

"We can't leave the dog here," I told Nichols.

"Put the carcass in back."

I did as ordered, then the guard and I jumped in the pickup bed. Henning drove to the rear of the farmhouse and walked Emily through the backdoor. "Bury Sass behind the barn," he called.

Nichols fixed me with the same glare he gave the child. "You just volunteered. I've got to check on the others." Without another word, he jumped to the ground and ambled to a distant field.

I stared at the lifeless dog for a moment, surprised that the guard hadn't reprimanded me for handling the boy. Resigned to whatever happened, I dropped to the ground and headed to the tool shed. There, I found a stack of burlap bags and a shovel. Going back to the truck, I placed the corpse in the coarse bag and tightened the drawstring. Now to find a suitable resting place.

Behind the barn lay stacks of split wood, a tall

stone smokehouse with a tapered chimney, and a pile of rusted metal. The best place for Sass was some twenty meters away, along the pasture fence line. Finding a spot between two posts, I broke ground for a grave.

Working alone gave me a quiet sense of freedom. I could be anywhere, bound only by imagination. Digging the foundation for a great memorial or a cellar to store Papa's beer barrels. The mournful wail of a train whistle drifted from the north. If a sound could reflect my own heart, that was it. Emily's loss was mine as well. Sass had accepted me as a friend. He deserved a fitting marker for his name. One that stood the test of time.

Under the warm autumn sun, sweat collected beneath my cap, so I tossed it aside. Sandy soil and a wet spring made the shoveling easy. A half meter more should do it. I glanced at the bag, flashing back to Emily weeping by the road. I wanted to hold her hand, stroke her sun-dazzled curls, and wipe the tears from her eyes. I smiled at the fantasy. No way to tell her how I felt. And if I did, what would happen to me? I was the enemy.

Feet shuffled behind me. I turned to see Henning and Emily peering at me from a few meters away. "You picked a good spot, sir," Henning said. "Out of the way, but still…" He glanced at his daughter. "A fine resting place."

"Thank you, Mr. Rohling." Emily wiped her cheek. "You're most considerate."

"You're welcome, Miss Henning." I averted my eyes in deference to her father and continued with my work.

"One of the other men can take over and let you

rest." Henning shoved his hands in his pockets. Clearly, he wanted no part of doing the job himself.

"I can do this." Sweat tickled the back of my neck, but I resisted the urge to wipe it away. "The paint can out front is still open. The fence needs another coat."

Henning stomped his feet a bit more. Standing still was not in his nature. "No sense letting good paint dry out. I'll take care of it." He ambled a short distance away before glancing back at Emily. "I know you wanted to see Sass one last time. Mom will be making supper soon, and it's your job to help."

"I will, Daddy."

Henning was about to say more but sighed and trudged to the back barn door and disappeared inside. I bent to complete the pit.

"What is your first name?" Emily asked. "I only know you by Mr. Rohling."

"I was born Heinrich. But I prefer Henry."

"That sounds much friendlier." Emily settled to the ground, her hands wrapped around her knees. "What did you do before you were a soldier?"

I loosened more dirt. "Served customers in my father's tavern. And helped him with the brewing."

"Oh, how fun."

"It seemed more like work with all the cleaning involved."

"Not always fun, I'm sure. At least you got to see new faces every day." She plucked a blade of grass and blew it between her lips, mimicking a startled goose.

"How did you do that?"

"It's easy. I can show you."

"Later." I hid my excitement as I shoveled. To keep Emily from asking me more questions, I ask her one. "What do you do for fun?"

"On Saturdays, I go into town with friends. There's a drugstore where we order fountain sodas or ice cream sundaes. And then we'll all go to the afternoon movies."

Nearly finished with the grave. "I watched a western the first week I arrived at camp."

Emily's eyes brightened. "What was the title?"

"I don't remember the name. It was about a cowboy who played guitar. Only you never saw the guitar when he rode his horse."

She giggled. It made her seem much younger. "Most people wouldn't notice that. Did you leave any girlfriends back in Germany?"

The question caught me by surprise. I leaned on my shovel, thinking of an answer. "No one serious. I wrote to a young lady when I first joined the *Wehrmacht*. She never answered my letters."

"That's sad. Do you get letters from family?"

"Not often enough. The war is taking a toll on daily life at home."

"Why is that?"

"Food is scarce." I didn't want to tell her any more. With the hole finished, I tossed the shovel aside and climbed out. Time to bury Sass.

I lifted the sack and walked to the edge of the pit. New tears formed in Emily's eyes. "Perhaps, you shouldn't look," I said.

"No." She bit her lip. "I want to see this finished. Just...be gentle with him."

"I will." I knelt and lowered the bundle as far as I could before dropping it. It seemed so small at the bottom of the pit. On my feet, again, I retrieved the shovel and began filling the grave.

"Wait!" Emily looked around and grabbed some wildflowers. She stepped beside me and tossed in the blooms. "I took care of Sass since I was eight years old. I'll miss him."

We stood so close together. I reached out and held her hand. She didn't resist. "Sass wouldn't want you to be so sad."

For just a few seconds, we stood linked together, her head leaned against my shoulder. A slight breeze blew her soft curls across my cheek. Her lips were so close. It would be easy to turn her head up to mine and steal a kiss.

But that would be taking advantage. Emily was so vulnerable now. I couldn't allow myself to do that. A kiss deserved the proper moment, and I hoped soon to find the opportunity.

I filled the hole, and Emily left to help her mother.

After supper, Mrs. Henning brought out warm oatmeal cookies. Later, we piled into the pickup, and Mr. Henning drove us back to camp. Emily stayed home.

On the way, we wondered what tasty confections Mrs. Henning would bake next. Some apple strudel? Linzer torte? A batch of delicious gingerbread cookies? As the others talked of cherry-filled tortes and cream puffs, my mind could only picture Emily and me kissing over a dog's grave.

Lanterns shone as we drew to a halt in front of our makeshift barracks. Two guards I'd never seen before flanked our vehicle. Nearby sat the large troop carrier we'd arrived in two months ago. Workers from other crews climbed in the back. "Gentlemen, get aboard," a sergeant said. "We have orders to take everyone back to Camp Conrad."

"What happened?" I ask one of the guards, a military policeman. Not a good sign.

"You'll know soon enough. Now haul ass."

We had arrived last. Goetz had no more than sat down before the big truck jerked to life and headed into the twilight.

"All this seems so strange," I said to the prisoner jammed against me, a small fellow with a billed cap like mine. "The Amis didn't tell us a thing."

"Didn't you hear?" The man seemed incredulous. "The Americans have gone and done it."

"Done what?"

"They shot one of ours."

Chapter Eleven

An hour into the reunion conference, and I already wished for a break. The morning session began with much fanfare but little substance. After the welcome message from Virginia Powell, the reunion's head coordinator, the town's mayor spoke a few self-congratulatory words, then a state politician praised the international guests and the state of Kansas. I drank water to hide my smirk at the irony. He kept calling us "the guardians of our wheat and corn." Outside of Kimmel, I knew of no other attendee who worked in the Labor Program.

Thankfully, Emily had returned, sitting at the head table next to the podium, her demeanor much improved. I wondered if being humiliated by Kimmel occurred often. That would explain her ability to recover so quickly from his snide comments. I watched for signs of distress as she faced the convention room. She smiled at all the speaker's lame jokes and led the audience in applause when he punctuated a point. Sometimes our eyes met, but she showed no reaction. Emily was either a resilient woman or a practiced actress. How could I break her from her bonds? Or should I? These were scandalous, daring thoughts, but they would not go away.

The congressman droned on about German culture in the heartland. "And so, we come together, not to relive a long-ago war, but to celebrate our common ties." The Americans gave him a standing ovation. With some effort, I rose to applaud as well.

Emily next stepped to the microphone. "We're going to take a fifteen-minute break. Congressman Walters would like to meet all our international guests. Afterward, we will gather back here to begin an important project. One of the goals of this convention is to create a permanent historical record of your memories of Camp Conrad. History students from nearby universities will tape interviews of you and compile these sessions in an audio archive. The recordings will be a part of the Oral History Exhibit within the Camp Conrad Museum. I'll have more information about that later. So stretch your legs. We have some work ahead of us."

As I got to my feet, a hand grabbed my wrist, nearly pulling me back to my seat.

"I'd appreciate it if you made no mention about my wife in your interview," Kimmel hissed in my ear, the menace in his voice unmistakable. "The only person you'd hurt would be Emily."

In truth, I thought more about my friend Brian Novak. The interview gave me a chance to talk about the events leading to his murder. And to reveal his letter. Novak's note would be a part of the historical record as well.

"Don't worry," I said in measured English. "No harm will come to Emily's reputation. I have other priorities."

"What's that supposed to mean?"

"It's not your affair."

At that moment, the Congressman approached with

a hand extended to Kimmel. Turning away, I made my escape.

Mrs. Powell held a mobile phone to her ear, a bulky device that looked like a transistor radio with a keypad. Emily gave the mayor a brief update on the reconstruction before he left the conference room. As much as I wanted to talk to Emily, my interest lay with the conference director. I stepped in front of Mrs. Powell as she finished her call. "I must speak with you, madam. I have evidence about a murder that took place inside Camp Conrad."

The director scribbled information on a small pad. She finished her notes and tucked away her material, peering at my nametag. "Slow down, Mr. Rohling. Evidence of what? Murder?"

"Yes." I swallowed to catch my breath. "It happened during my internment at Camp Conrad. To a comrade, Brian Novak, in 1943."

Mrs. Powell brought up a hand as if warding off my words. "Emily, you know more of the camp's history than I do. Ever heard of such a thing?"

She nodded. "Brian Novak was one of at least five prisoners who died during the camp's first year of operation. All prisoners reportedly took their own lives. Camp administration called Mr. Novak's death 'self-inflicted.' "

I set my jaw. "It was murder."

Powell scrutinized me. Dismissive, but still curious. "Why do you say that, Mr. Rohling?"

"Mr. Novak wrote a letter just before his death. I have it." My voice trembled as I spoke. The old stirrings of dread and anger came hurtling back. Fearing reprisals from former Nazis at a hotel convention seemed ludicrous, but I could not dispel the lump in my throat as I forced the words out. "I didn't find it until long after his burial. He stated he would not willingly take his own life. Someone else forced his hanging."

Virginia Powell was an elegant woman with silver hair, tasteful pearls, and matching red skirt and jacket that exemplified power. I could imagine her being on the board of a local business group. "Interesting." She gave me a stern look, an expression she had no doubt practiced many times. "Feel free to tell your interviewer the story. But do not accuse other guests of foul play. That will not be tolerated."

"I was hoping for an investigation. I want to live long enough to see the results."

The director scowled. "You must be joking, Mr. Rohling. Who would investigate? The army? They've already made a decision fifty years ago."

Emily reached for my hand but drew back. "Why are you waiting until now to tell your story, Mr. Rohling?" she asked. *Mr. Rohling.* In our secret moments long ago, she called me Henry.

Why did I wait? During my time in America, I feared to say anything. Zealous Nazis excelled at revenge—and often served it cold. After I went back to Germany and married, I had no wish to be haunted by the past. So I said nothing. But that had changed. "Until I received the reunion letter, I had no wish to come to America. Now that I'm here, I want to set the record straight."

"You and Mr. Novak must have been close," Emily said.

"We were comrades. I'd like to see his grave before I return home."

The two women exchanged looks. Mrs. Powell looked uncomfortable, probably a rare state for her. "The Army moved the Camp Conrad POW graves to Fort Riley Army Base," Powell said.

"But the van could stop there on the way back to the airport," Emily said, her eyes brightening.

Powell tapped her chin. "It's possible. We need to know if that part of the base is open to the public."

I bowed slightly. "You're most kind. Both of you."

"Nothing's for sure, yet." Powell brushed the thought aside. "I assume you have this note with you?"

"Yes, madam."

"Bring it this afternoon. Your interviewer will certainly wish to see it. My German is rusty. Emily, could you examine the letter as well?"

Emily smiled. "Sure, I'd be happy to."

"It's in my room. I'll retrieve it during the noon break."

"This should be interesting." The coordinator looked at her watch. "Break is over. Emily, call the group together and start your presentation. I have some details to iron out with the hotel staff. Enjoy the conference, Mr. Rohling." With that, the coordinator strolled to the nearest exit and disappeared.

I stepped toward my seat but nearly collided with the massive bulk of Alfred Stecklein.

"Pardon me." His voice rumbled. "I have a message for you."

A wave of revulsion washed over me at the sight of him. "A message?"

"Herr Reinhardt wishes to share company with you over dinner." His words were like an articulated growl. "Noon sharp. Room 162."

The camp's liaison officer wanted to see me? I glanced around me. Reinhardt wasn't in the room. "Why didn't he ask me himself? We can eat in the restaurant."

"The colonel likes his conversations private. He instructed me to deliver the following message: you will be interested in the subject of discussion."

"And what is that?"

"The trial of Private Novak."

As the group ambled back to their seats, Emily began the next session. Volunteers passed out pens and writing paper while she outlined an exercise to prepare ourselves for the afternoon's interviews.

"Let's rekindle those buried feelings and recollections from fifty years ago. I'm going to read a series of questions to guide you through your war experiences. From the time you entered service to your journey back home. Jot down the first thing you remember. Turn off your internal editor and let the memories flow but stop and move on when you hear the next question. We want to uncover as many memories as possible. So pick up your pens, and let's begin."

With a few short breaks, I filled page after page with veiled memories that became clear again: my awe at seeing the Statue of Liberty, the surreal tranquility of rural America, how untouched American cities were by the war. I wrote about the flood of new POW arrivals in the summer of '44 and the awe in their voices about the enemies' weapons. I scribbled about leaving Kansas in a boxcar and sleeping under misty stars in the snow-covered hills of Wisconsin.

Some thoughts felt too personal to share: my growing fondness for Emily and the forces that separated us. And now her bondage to Kimmel. What should I do about that? The answers disturbed me. But to leave her with this ogre would be wrong. She deserved better.

We broke at eleven forty-five for lunch. I followed the hallway to Room 162, checking my watch before rapping on the door. A muffled voice bid me to enter.

Reinhardt greeted me in a maroon-colored bathrobe and slippers. He seemed more bird-like and less hawkish in his bedclothes. The aroma of grilled fowl filled the room, and near the window sat a table for two with a large stainless-steel dome in the center. "I see no reason to wear uncomfortable garb unless I go out," he explained.

"You haven't been to the conference all morning?" I asked. "It seems strange you'd come all the way here and not attend."

"I care little about celebrating with the Americans."

I raised an eyebrow. "So you're not interested in the reunion?"

"Who said I wasn't interested? I came as a companion with Alfred. And to see some of the old comrades. You, I must say, were a surprise."

I took note of the room's exit. Standing alone near Reinhardt gave me chills.

The old Nazi regarded me with his penetrating eyes. "You needn't be wary, Herr Rohling. I don't wish us to be enemies. Sit down." He waved to the table. "Let's eat before our food gets cold."

My host served with a flourish, rivaling a French waiter in a five-star restaurant. He plated wafer-thin strips of white meat in a row with sprigs of parsley, then used tongs to add a medley of asparagus, squash, and carrots in an eye-pleasing crescent around the meat. "Bon appétit," he said, raising a small bit of carrot to his lips.

The lemon-peppered meat tasted like game fowl. I asked what it was.

"It's pheasant. Some associates I know prepared the dish as I instructed and delivered it. Please. Try the vegetables."

The heavily peppered side dish took my breath away. I gulped down half my ice water and wiped watery eyes. "It's spicy," I said, gasping.

Reinhardt chuckled, refilling my glass from a carafe. "It's Cajun. A regional cuisine. Like it?"

"It takes some getting used to."

"Try it with a little wine." He poured from a large bottle nestled in a silver bucket. "You'll like this. It's *Maitrank*, fruity and aromatic. Very enjoyable to the palate."

We ate our meal in silence, topping it off with more glasses of wine. Finally, my host leaned back in his chair and regarded me gravely. "You're a persistent man, Herr Rohling. Alfred tells me you intend to present this mystery letter of yours to the conference this afternoon."

The old sergeant must have heard my discussion with Powell and Emily. Bad enough Stecklein overheard our talk but relaying the conversation to Reinhardt struck me as a personal violation.

I leaned forward with narrowed eyes. "The Americans wish to create a wartime oral history. I intend to set the record straight for Private Novak."

"Americans like to paint a comfortable picture of

126

their history. They will reject irritating facts that would spoil the nostalgia. I wouldn't piss on their parade."

"That's not your concern."

"I only wish to protect you from anguish, my friend. I trust you have this vital document locked away in the hotel's safe?" He shrugged. "Assuming they have one. You wouldn't want anything to happen to it."

The thought never occurred to me. I sought to hide my surprise, but Reinhardt gave me a knowing nod. "You should be more careful, my friend. Precious documents are irreplaceable."

"I'm taking the letter with me to the afternoon session. My interviewer will want to see it. After that, I'll put it in a safe place."

"Of course." He inclined his head. "I hope you made copies—in case you misplaced the original."

I crossed my arms before I realized the giveaway. "I'll do that as well."

"These are mere precautions, comrade. To guard against the unthinkable. Have you written an account of how you came into possession of this document? What if you met an accident? Would anyone know the meaning of the letter?"

The wily old Nazi struck again. I kept an account of my war years, but I hadn't seen those pages in decades. "I've written a few things a long time ago."

"That is good to hear. Have you told your children? Do they know of this letter?"

Of course I hadn't! No point in hiding secrets from this man. I suspected that in his day, he could pluck information from American prisoners like a dentist would a tooth. "My oldest knows a little about my internment years. But until the reunion letter arrived, my children had no clue."

"You're a lucky man, Herr Rohling. Any number of chance events could have prevented you from sharing your story." Reinhardt refilled both wine glasses and held his up. "To revelations. New knowledge and new beginnings."

Go with the flow. Tasty wine. We clinked glasses and drank. It warmed me. The more I drank, the easier it went down.

Reinhardt set his glass on a napkin. "We should get to the purpose of this discussion."

I nodded. "The fate of my friend," I agreed.

"Poor Novak," the colonel said, tilting his head to the ceiling. "Of all the guests at Camp Conrad, he would have offered the keenest insights on this reunion. German parents raised him in America, but he fought for the Fatherland. Captured and sent to Kansas, he became a prisoner in a country he called home. Had he lived, his assessment of the war would have rankled both sides."

How did my wine glass become empty again? "You're spot on," I agreed. "Brian Novak had a knack for cutting to the truth."

He refilled my glass. "An insightful man. A genuine person." Reinhardt held up a finger. "And tormented, but being an honorable man, he realized his transgressions and found the courage to complete his last noble act."

That angered me. I slammed my fist, sloshing wine over the tablecloth. "Brian Novak tried to save lives, even against the wishes of your clique of officers. He was the better man."

"Silence! You're here to learn." Reinhardt's voice

had an ominous edge. He stepped to the bathroom. "I'll get some towels. Feel free to leave if you wish."

He was right. "I'll curb my tongue," I said.

Reinhardt returned with dry towels. Even though the wine had seeped into the fabric, he did an admirable job of cleaning the spill. "And now, back to business," he said, regaining his seat. "You were working for the Americans before the trial. What did you know about Novak's job?"

"He removed rubbish from the camp. I don't know much else. The Americans recalled us back to the main camp the evening after the shooting."

Reinhardt sipped his drink. "The Americans feared a riot. The commander recalled every garrisoned soldier back to duty that night."

"I remembered guards standing outside the wire, all holding rifles. After we got back, I managed to see Private Novak in the infirmary. Thugs had beaten him. He said a few words before I had to leave."

"What did he say?" Reinhardt leaned forward.

This, I refused to divulge. "Gibberish. He had a concussion."

The colonel set his glass aside. "You're holding back, Herr Rohling. I'm sure you suspect more and—from a circumstantial point of view—it may be accurate."

I jumped to my feet. "So you did murder him! The show trial was a sham."

"*Setz dich!*" Reinhardt grabbed a silver fork and held it to my throat. "Any more outbursts and our dialogue ends."

I sank back to my seat, heart pounding in my ears.

"Are you prepared for the truth, Herr Rohling?"

I could only nod.

"My staff learned of growing turmoil among the American officer ranks. Most of the anxiety came from the sloppy, indifferent leadership of Lieutenant Colonel Beard, who commanded Camp Conrad. This indifference trickled down to the lowest officer ranks. The result was contradictory, vague orders often ignored by subordinates. Line officers drank before coming on duty. No inspections. No discipline. This left the guards with virtually no command structure."

"What did this have to do with Private Novak?"

"I'm getting to that." Reinhardt sipped again and replenished my glass. "With little supervision, the camp guards became opportunistic. Some were angry about guard duty and abandoned their posts. Others chose to quietly profit from it. Guards began pilfering our food during the summer with no way for us to stop it. Brunswick, the American liaison officer, even got involved, selling our meat supplies to civilians in town. The theft increased and was becoming intolerable. Commander Beard ignored our complaints. Then, an opportunity came when we learned of the new guard-tower rules of engagement. We formed a plan."

A cold wave, like ice water, cascaded down my back. I saw Reinhardt's stone-cold solution to the Americans' stealing.

"Camp Conrad didn't operate in a vacuum," Reinhardt continued. "Army inspectors made unexpected visits and evaluated the leadership. With a bold move, we could force the resignation of Lieutenant Colonel Beard. Hopefully, his replacement would be an officer demanding discipline from his men."

"You wanted the guards to kill one of our

soldiers," I said, my throat dry. "With a full-blown crisis, the army would have no choice but to install a new commander."

"Exactly." Reinhardt smiled. "One casualty, and the entire prison population benefits in the end. With a by-the-book commander, the lower ranks would fall in line, and the pilfering would stop. We called the plan Cornucopia."

"And you didn't want Private Novak spoiling your party." I kept my fists hidden beneath the table. Sadness touched me. My friend never had a chance.

Reinhardt shrugged. "We didn't want the new orders to be common knowledge."

"So you put him in the infirmary?"

"I never ordered that. We demanded Novak's silence but nothing further. Many of the prisoners saw Novak as being a collaborator with the Americans, especially when he talked to the American liaison officer."

That shook me. Did Novak make direct contact with the Americans? I swallowed fear but kept my thoughts focused. "That was your excuse. The reason for his mock trial was to guarantee his silence, even though your plan succeeded."

Reinhardt shook his head. "You have it wrong, my friend. The change in camp command didn't occur until nearly six weeks later. During that time, Commander Beard seemed untouchable. Private Novak had to stand trial for violating orders not to speak out. I had to maintain discipline within the compound. The trial would have been a mere formality. But in Novak's case the unforeseen happened."

My head spun with the twists and turns of the

colonel's story. I knew of the kangaroo courts the Nazis conducted within American POW camps, including Camp Conrad. The hapless soldier—usually a low-ranking anti-Nazi officer—is tried, found guilty, and coerced into hanging himself. No surprises ever occurred.

I rubbed my temple, trying to piece Reinhardt's story together. "What happened?"

"Some of the jurors were young officers who didn't know about Cornucopia but heeded Novak's warnings. They were sympathetic to his motives. Others knew of the operation but were concerned how allowing a man's death would reflect on their command. One solution stood out: give Novak a commuted sentence. Even that failed. In the end, we acquitted him."

My head reeled. Was it the wine or Reinhardt's fantastic story? I gulped down some ice water. "That's impossible. Those trials were a foregone conclusion."

"Believe what you like. I presided over the court. You can call it a mistrial. No one wished anything further to do with the case. A retrial could leak to the general population, who may have come to Novak's defense."

My thoughts whirled down a yawning hole. I still did not know why Novak died, and who had a hand in it. "Private Novak wrote me a note saying he would not willingly hang himself. You haven't addressed that."

Reinhardt bowed his head. "I don't have an answer for you. We assigned a noncom to escort Novak from the stockade to the shower building. We wanted him to be presentable in court before receiving his verdict. Or lack of one. You know the rest of the story."

"Not all of it. Who was the escort?"

"Sergeant Stecklein."

I shoved myself away from the table and staggered to the exit. The air in the room seemed thin, making it difficult to breathe. The door swayed before me, but I managed to grab the knob and flung it open.

"Herr Rohling!"

I whirled around, fists clenched, ready for anything. What I saw was Reinhardt pouring himself more wine. He raised the glass in salute. "Be careful, my friend."

The hallway tilted slightly as I ran one hand along the wall, making careful progress to my room. If only my son were here. He could help me decipher these new facts. Even if Stecklein murdered my friend, I still had no definitive proof of a crime. What if Novak did take his own life? If that was true, I spent fifty years deluding myself, chasing a mirage. I might as well go home and accept my old age. Quit tilting at windmills. Sit in my rocking chair and nitpick old war movies until my own shabby end. Waiting to die was worse than death itself.

Was it even worth going back to the conference? As much as I wanted to see Emily again, I didn't want to admit my folly. I wished to sleep, go home, and lay Novak's memory to rest.

I found a corner and turned, going a few rooms down before discovering I went the wrong direction. Turning around, I leaned forward and propelled myself forward. Why were the fluorescent lights shimmering so bright?

The numbers grew smaller. Confident I'd picked the right path, I ambled with deliberate care. Shouldn't let anyone think I was tipsy. With delight, I read my room number, reciting each digit aloud. How nice! The door was in the same spot I left it this morning. A nap would do me good. Those interviews weren't that important. Couldn't do anything about history when it had already happened!

Now, how do I get inside?

Horst opened the door last night. Which way do I put the card in the slot? I found an arrow on one side, rammed the card in the slot, and yanked it out. The lock made a satisfying click, and the door swung open before me.

I stared at the room spellbound. Trashed.

Suitcases lay tossed on the bed. Clothing scattered on the floor. Hangers knocked off the rack. Dresser drawers hung open. Even the Gideon Bible lay face down near the hallway door. I rushed to my satchel, sitting next to one of the queen-sized beds. Empty. I didn't care. The case contained a hidden compartment. I pulled the bottom fastener back and felt underneath the backing.

Be with me, my friend.

Oh, no.

Novak's letter—gone.

Chapter Twelve

28 October 1943

With an alarming lurch that shook several of us off our seats, the troop carrier rocked onto the road that led back to Camp Conrad. Twenty men sat crammed in the back, all of us smelling of sweat and dirt. It was dark inside that enclosure, but the rolled-up canvas allowed us to see behind us. A guard sat with his weapon resting across his knees. He needn't have bothered. None of us cared to worsen the situation.

I nudged the small man beside me. "Was it an escape attempt?" I asked.

"The guards aren't talking," he said.

"They have to know something," I scoffed, then called to the American sitting in the rear. "Sir, will we be returning to work soon?"

The gun-wielding silhouette shrugged. "No idea. Hope so. Otherwise, we'll have a lot of angry farmers calling the prison."

"Why take us away from work?" another prisoner asked. "We haven't caused any trouble."

The shadowy figure shifted his position. "Just the army's way of doing things. You'll get your answers once we're back at camp."

"What about the things left behind?" a third voice called. The guard lowered his head, refusing to answer any further questions.

We drove on, the interior of our enclosure now lit by the harsh glare of headlights behind us. If we should stop abruptly, this vehicle could crash into us. It made no sense. For weeks, the Americans seemed uninterested in watching us. Now, they were taking risks with their own lives on the slim chance one of us would dare to escape. What caused the shooting? A riot? A mass escape? Were any guards injured or killed? Would there be reprisals? We wondered about a camp out of control, and the American garrison coming down on the prisoners like the wrath of Gideon.

By the time we rolled inside the inner perimeter, we had imagined every scenario possible. Or thought we did. Lights atop the barbwire glared to fullest intensity. Armed soldiers stood outside the fences, about twenty meters apart with rifles at the ready. Mounted spotlights moved about the interior of the prison. And the air was filled with singing.

A group of twenty prisoners marched along the warning track toward us. Many wore work clothes and carried rakes or shovels over their shoulders like weapons. They strode with arms swinging in unison singing "*Wacht am Rhein*," a patriotic song among soldiers. The group passed by us, their feet thumping on the asphalt. As the marchers drew away, another formation approached, singing the words to "*Drei Lilien*."

"Return to your barracks, and don't join the protesters if you know what's good for you," one guard said. "Stay inside." He jumped on a running board, and the truck backed out of the gate.

There was still a half hour before curfew. Most of

our befuddled group meandered back to their old sleeping quarters. I had just buried Emily's dog that day. A shower called my name. After that, I'd find my old bed. Would it be occupied by another prisoner? Sorting out the craziness could wait until tomorrow.

I ambled toward the shower building. A third group of perhaps fifty men, including two officers, marched by singing "*Horst Wessel Lied,*" a National Socialist anthem. Without conscious thought, I stood at full attention, my arm thrust out as they marched past. Seconds later, I hurried on.

Since I had left camp, prisoners had built a barbershop and bakery. Several men milled about, but no one I recognized. Camp Conrad had grown in my absence. Just outside the bathhouse door, I saw Hauser. I waved a hand in greeting as he neared.

"Hello, Henry," he said. "You look like you've been rolling in a riverbed."

"I've just come back from outside of camp. What's going on?"

"The entire camp is in an uproar since this afternoon."

Another marching group thumped by. We waited until their noise died away.

"The only thing I've heard," I said, "is that a German had been shot."

Hauser glanced around. "More like murdered. Tower guards shot a soccer player while he retrieved a ball by the fence."

"No warning?" I remembered watching a game with Novak the day after we arrived.

My companion sucked in a breath. "Depends on what you would call a warning. Let's sit." He pointed to a nearby bench. "I'll tell you what happened. Part of it concerns your friend."

"Novak?" A creeping unease spread over me as I sat.

Hauser took in his surroundings before continuing. "Be wary. Conflicting stories abound. The National Socialists will tell you what they want you to know soon enough. Just nod when they do. What I will explain is the whispered version."

"No one will hear it from me."

"Novak learned that the American brass had issued new firing orders for the guards. Shoot to kill any prisoners crossing the wire."

"That's always been a standing order," I said. "But the guards have never fired a shot."

"Don't interrupt." Hauser made a chopping motion with his hand. "It's how Novak discovered these orders and what happened afterward that has many of us worried."

"I'm listening." No one stood near us, yet Hauser kept his voice low.

"We don't really know what he found when he was collecting the refuse. Many think it was a copy of the American orders given to Reinhardt's staff. Three days ago, Novak told everyone he could the new orders. If the guards failed to shoot, they would be court-martialed."

"Did anyone believe him?"

"That's the thing." Hauser emphasized the words. "We did believe him. Few played on the soccer field after that. But yesterday, Sergeant Stecklein posted a notice saying the Americans would not fire upon a prisoner. To prove the rumor false, officers in this compound would challenge any team of enlisted men on the parade grounds. Best two out of three."

"How could anyone fall for such a shallow lie?" I asked.

"Think for a minute. It behooves the rank and file to take part."

I sighed. "Of course."

Hauser watched a searchlight pan across the empty field. "The second game this afternoon was in its fourth quarter, the enlisted men ahead, four to three. Reinhardt's team about to go down again. In the final minute, one of the officers made a long kick for the goal, then fell, holding his knee. The ball sailed high and bounced over the wire."

I rubbed my temple, not really wanting to hear the rest of his account. "Did the officer retrieve it?"

Hauser smiled. "Here's where the story gets dicey. One of the unwritten rules is that whoever sends the ball to the fence has to retrieve it. The lieutenant limped toward the track, but a player on the other team, Hans Tannenbaum, waved him off. He ran across the wire. A guard from Tower B shot him in the head before he could stoop to retrieve the ball."

"*Mein Gott.*" I couldn't shake the image of a young man executed in cold blood.

"Since then, the officers have organized groups of men in both compounds to march and sing patriotic anthems. They plan to keep protesting until the Americans acknowledge what they did was wrong."

"What about curfew? It's nearly nine o'clock."

"The officers have made it clear—no rioting, but the marches will continue twenty-four hours a day. If we get through this without more bloodshed, it will be a miracle."

I rose from the bench. "Where's Novak?"

"He's in the infirmary." Hauser regained his feet as well.

"How can this get any worse? What happened to him?"

"Last night, a couple of thugs beat him while he slept. Cracked some ribs at least. Two more held shovels and threatened anyone who tried to interfere."

The infirmary sat across the compound. "I'm seeing him tonight."

Hauser grabbed my arm. "Stecklein warned us. No visitors."

"To hell with that. Novak's my friend."

Hauser released me. "Be careful, Henry. There are forces at work here. Don't get in over your head. Like Novak."

"Too late for that," I said, running for the infirmary.

"It's probably locked for the night!" Hauser called.

It didn't matter to me. I'd find a way in.

"One more thing." Hauser's voice grew fainter. "Watch out for rovers. They'll be out tonight. Be careful!"

The guards did not have to worry about prisoners stalking around at night. Not when a pack of former brownshirts pounced on any prisoner outside after curfew. They were a rough lot who curried favor with the officers by catching whoever they could. Personally, I thought they hunted for sport.

I glanced at my watch while mounting the steps to the door. Ten minutes to nine. Visiting hours were over at eight, but I had to see my friend. How badly was he hurt? Why did our officers issue orders to shun him? Did Reinhardt's men have plans for him?

An electric lamp lit the front office. I jiggled the knob, but the lanky clerk, wearing the familiar Red Cross patch on his shoulder paid no attention to me and continued to file papers. Behind the clerk, a closed door led to the patient ward. I pounded on the door. The clerk jerked his head my way, then pointed to a wall clock—seven minutes until nine. I didn't come this far only to be stopped by a civilian pointing out the time. I balled my fist and slammed it against the glass. Not hard enough to break it, but enough to get his attention. Instead, he grabbed the phone and dialed a number. Wonderful. A call for help.

Along the well-lit fences, marchers shouted in German. In the darkness behind buildings, a prisoner banged on a garbage can. In the distance, a group sang an old drinking song I remembered from my father's tavern. At least the Afrikaners were facing the tension with a lively spirit. More ominously, I could sense a quiet presence stirring in the darkness. Voiceless men preparing to prowl the night. It reminded me of the early days of the party when dangerous men roamed the streets like wolves looking for victims to pummel. Sweat prickled my brow. I should take cover before the rovers organized. Find safety inside.

I brushed an arm across my forehead. The medic tried two more times to summon help but wasn't getting through. It dawned on me that no operators were minding the camp switchboard. No guards would be coming.

I took off my jacket and rolled it around my left hand and arm, motioning for him to unlock the door. He shook his head. Fine by me. I raised my arm to smash my way in. Frantically waving his arms, the clerk rushed to the door, unlocking it. I stepped into the room.

"It's almost curfew," he said, barring my way. "Go back to your barracks."

"I came to see Brian Novak. As to the curfew—it's canceled."

The Red Cross clerk stepped back. "That's impossible."

"You tried to call for help but didn't get it. Right?"

He blinked, glancing at the phone. "They must be busy."

This man knew nothing. "Damn right, they're busy. A prisoner's been shot, and now the entire camp is protesting." Familiar heat spread across my face. "The only thing keeping this powder keg from blowing is German discipline. That could fall apart if the Americans decide to enforce the curfew."

"Shhh! Quiet." He pointed to the inner door. "You can't upset the patients."

"One of your patients is the man I need to see," I said, lowering my voice. "He's a patient who knows something about this."

"Do you think he can help defuse this blowup?"

"It's possible." I had no idea if Novak could make a difference. Any half-truth would do if it meant getting past this man.

"Let me get his file. Novak, you said?"

Finally making progress. "Yes, sir."

He slid out a drawer from a gray file cabinet, fingered through several files, then lifted a folder. "Mr. Novak came in early this morning. Multiple abrasions and bruises about the head and chest, two cracked ribs, and a hairline skull fracture. His assailants beat him good, but he'll recover in a few weeks."

"Can I see him? Just for a few minutes?"

The clerk frowned, rubbing his chin. "File says he's been given morphine for pain. Novak is probably asleep."

I clenched my hands. "I want to see his condition for myself."

"I have rules to follow." The clerk crossed his arms.

I bowed my head. Begging was not in my nature, but I had no other recourse. "Please. We've been through a lot together. Two minutes. That's all I ask."

For several seconds, the clerk peered at me. Judging how genuine my intentions were, no doubt. I remained silent. I could think of nothing more to say. A spotlight flashed across the room. The clerk let out a breath. "Don't arouse the other patients. Two minutes. Then you're back outside."

"Thank you, sir."

Sirens wound to life, announcing the nine o'clock curfew. Any other time, this would be a normal part of camp life. But on this night, it only heightened the tension and palpable danger. Would the Americans assault the prison? How soon will the rovers begin their hunt? What will I learn from Novak?

Outside the patient ward, the clerk introduced me to the medic on duty. "This man has two minutes to observe Private Novak in bed sixteen." He pointed a thumb at me. "Then he's to be escorted out."

The medic was a bookish man in silver glasses and close-cropped brown hair. His gaze followed the clerk returning to his desk. "This is a new one," he drawled. Motioning me to follow, the medic strolled down a row of beds.

In the darkness, it was difficult to see how many beds there were. My guess was two dozen. The air smelled of rubbing alcohol, bleach, and urine. We walked a third of the way across the room when he stopped and gestured to the left. "He's asleep. Don't disturb him. I'll be back soon." The man retreated, and I stepped to Novak's bedside.

In the dim light, I could barely discern tightly-wrapped bandages around his forehead. One eye had the beginnings of a shiner. He lay on his back, breathing quietly. Who could have done this? And why? At least he could rest safely here. Tomorrow, we could talk. I found a paper-wrapped candy in my pocket Emily had given me. I slipped it beneath his pillow. He'll be wondering where the sweet came from. Behind me, the door to the infirmary clicked shut. That would be the medic returning to escort me out.

"Henry? Is that you?"

I jumped. Faint and groggy, Novak's voice held urgency. I bent over him to keep my voice low. "Heard you lost a fight. I had to come see for myself."

"I got clobbered." Novak drew in a breath and groaned with pain.

"Easy. You can tell me about it tomorrow."

His eyes shifted, although I wasn't sure. "What are you doing here?" he asked.

"Guards brought us back tonight. Wanted all their eggs in one basket, I suppose. Hauser told me about the shooting. Rumor is you tried to stop it."

"I'm accused of causing a panic. Reinhardt is

trying me in a Nazi court." He swallowed hard. I wondered if his morphine was wearing off. "I don't know why."

I sensed the medic behind me. "I see you've managed to wake my patient," he said. "You need to leave."

"Brian, I'll see you tomorrow."

His hand grabbed my wrist with surprising firmness. His words came out in a rush. "The Nazis are building a case against me. They say I talk to the Americans. But I never did. What am I going to do? I'm as good as guilty."

Around us, beds squeaked. Patients stirred awake.

"I'll do what I can to help," I said, wondering what it could possibly be.

"Thanks, Henry. I knew I could count on you."

I couldn't say anything further. The clerk hustled me outside the building. "Don't pull this stunt again, or I'll report you," he said.

"Yessir."

On the steps, I surveyed the night. Along the illuminated fence, silent marchers strode by. The Americans made little noise as well. Each side seemed poised for action. The smallest provocation could create a riot.

I scurried to the shadows cast by the nearest building, making my way across the back of the darkened structure. I needed to go west, but a brilliant pool of light blocked my way. With the mounted spotlights, the well-lit fences, and the occasional sodium vapor lamps, the compound was awash in artificial brilliance. Should I detour around the lights or sprint for cover and hope the rovers weren't in place? I took two deep breaths, crouched, and made a straight run for my sleeping quarters,

Yells erupted. One of the hunters spotted me. Whoops and howls pierced the night, sounding like hounds discovering a scent. Speed was not my best trait, but I could stay the course. If only that were enough.

Finding the bakery, I nestled within its recessed doorway. Only two shadows ran past. Did the pack split? My chances of evading them just got smaller. With my heart in my throat, I took off again, this time taking a dogleg to the rear of the next building and hunkering beneath a set of steps. Evade. Stick to the shadows. Wait them out. A quick dash to the next building. And then the next. Sighing with relief, I decided to stay quiet and wait. Be patient. The hounds might go away.

But time was not on my side. The rovers could look for me at their leisure all night. And they were savvy. Two men poked around the warehouse north of me, shining a lamp around corners and thrusting a long stick beneath steps. I sensed others behind me. No more howls and whooping. The hounds knew I stood within their tightening noose.

A thought struck me. I didn't have to reach my barracks. Any building will do. Find an unlocked door. Once inside, the game would be over. Another barn-sized warehouse stood next, its rear door in shadow. Run to the doorway and slip inside unseen. Breathe easy. I crawled out from beneath the steps, partially blocked by steel refuse cans. If only my boot hadn't brushed the lid. It hit a step and rolled for two meters. A small sound, yet it might as well have been a gunshot.

A dark form rushed at me. He must have been close. I feinted to the left and then cut right, hoping to sweep around him. He fell short, but his foot caught my leg, tripping me. I tried rolling away, but he slammed into my back, pinning me to the ground. "Got him!" a voice yelled over my head.

"Take him to the soccer field," a voice called back.

"Let's go." The rover wrenched me to my feet.

"I was going back to my bunk," I protested.

"Not tonight," he said. "You're new meat for Reinhardt's circus."

Chapter Thirteen

I dropped the empty travel bag and slumped on the side of my bed. Novak's letter stolen; the hotel room trashed. What was I going to do? A bolt of energy coursed through my head, leaving me light-headed and fidgety. Dresser drawers demanded attention; clothing needed to be folded and put away; the room shouted to be restored to order. I had to produce that note. Or confess it was gone.

An idea teased at me, but I had to let it gel while tending to the mess around me.

Getting the drawers back in the bureau and refolding clothing made an immediate difference. Then I rehung slacks and shirts inside the closet. Finally, I repacked Horst's scattered papers in his document pouch.

While remaking the beds, my watch chimed one o'clock. Fifteen minutes until the afternoon session. Not enough time for what I wanted to do, but I had no choice.

A drip coffeepot sat atop the microwave with packets of ground coffee. I set about making a pot of the horrid stuff. While the pot gurgled to life, I brushed Horst's extra suit jacket with the fabric brush he always carried and straightened the creases on his dress shirts. My son must not notice anything amiss. Restoring the room to order took only another minute.

The pot gurgled one last time, and the thick stream of black liquid slowed to a few drops.

Inside a bedside stand, next to the replaced Bible, I found hotel stationery and a pen. With meticulous care, I tore the advertising away, using the holy book's edge. This left me with a blank sheet. Letter by letter, I forged Novak's note, remembering every nuance of his penmanship from fifty years of reading and rereading his words. Easy enough to finish the note and oh, so satisfying. Of course, Novak's killer would know it to be a fake, but he couldn't reveal it without exposing himself. And it could drive him to reckless action, though I had no clue what that would be.

The forgery looked good to my less-than-perfect eyes. Now, I needed to age a sheet of paper fifty years in as little time as possible. Cringing at what I was about to do, I wadded the note into a ball and grabbed the glass pot.

Smoothing out the paper gave me time to think about how to make the aging look authentic. Soaking the paper in strong coffee would destroy the message. Could I place the wadded paper on a towel and then lay a washcloth soaked with coffee on top? That seemed like the best plan. The result, however, turned out to be a messy, wet document I feared to move. Somehow, I had to move that delicate sheet to the microwave without ripping it apart. Once inside the oven, I could boil off the water, hopefully without catching the paper on fire.

Using a dry cloth, I blotted away the excess liquid, carried the towel with the note to the microwave, slid the whole thing in, closed the door, and set the timer for thirty seconds.

As the numbers counted down, I wondered who could have done this. Did Reinhardt order the robbery? The timing of our conversation seemed more than coincidental. Sergeant Stecklein delivered the colonel's invitation to me, and he heard my discussion with Virginia Powell. He had an opportunity to search this room. How could the old sergeant have broken in? By picking the lock? Stecklein had nearly fallen out of the van when we arrived last night. I couldn't imagine how he managed the burglary alone.

The microwave bell dinged. I popped the door and withdrew the hot towel. Stiff, almost parchment-like paper crackled as I folded and refolded creases. Soon, they split in several places. I smiled. Not bad for an amateur counterfeiter.

Carrying the letter to the conference presented a final vexing detail. I no longer had the wax envelope, and I needed a substitute. Looking through my travel kit, I found a plastic bag containing medicines. I dumped the pill bottles in a drawer, slipped the note inside the bag, and resealed it. At 1345 hours, I would be more than a half hour late to the afternoon session. It couldn't be helped. I surveyed the room a final time: it looked presentable enough. With the letter tucked in a folder, I hustled back to the reunion.

****

As I neared the closed doors of the conference room, a strained voice called from the glass exit doors leading to the parking lot. "Henry! Wait for me." I glanced over my shoulder. The grizzled stooped figure of Paul Drosselmeyer pushed his walker forward.

As he drew closer, I noticed a pack of cigarettes in his basket. The reek of smoke wafted from his clothing.

"I'm glad I'm not...the only one...who bailed...from this sideshow. How you doing, old man?" He gasped for air between words.

"Still breathing." I cringed at my thoughtless remark. "Sorry, I didn't..."

But Drosselmeyer was already laughing, a wet, wheezy cackle that ended in hacking up phlegm. "That's what I like about you, Rohling," he said, clearing his throat. "Always quick on your feet."

"The session has started. Maybe we should go inside."

"The show can wait. Introducing kids...a bunch of students...all like to talk. I left to smoke."

I took a step back. "You lit a flame with that canister spewing oxygen?"

"Take it easy...I haven't blown up yet. Besides, why quit? If I can't die fit...I can die happy." He gestured to some chairs along the hallway. "Let's catch up."

"Only for a few minutes. I didn't fly here to miss the reunion."

"I think you might...be interested in...what I got to say."

Intrigued, I followed him to a set of overstuffed chairs surrounding a coffee table. Drosselmeyer drew closer, I made room for his walker. He flopped on a cushion, gulping for air, but he soon leaned forward and cleared his throat, an unpleasant loud rasping he often made during the conference.

I squirmed in my seat. "Would you like some water?"

He shrugged. "I'm fine. Now...show it to me."

"Show what?"

"This treasure. The dead man's letter."

My secret seemed to be common knowledge. "How'd you know about that?"

"You're not quiet. Everyone heard you…talking. Old men gossip…more than old women…Who wrote the letter? Some think…you want to…embarrass the Amis."

"It was from a comrade at camp. He wrote it minutes before his hanging."

"Ah." The old sergeant smiled and bobbed his head, showing blackened teeth. "Novak…three or four others…died at the camp…a record, I think…But Novak…only enlisted man."

I glanced at the conference room door. "We're wasting time. Tell me what you have to say. Or I'm leaving."

He gasped more oxygen. His bluish face looked like a man close to death. "You can trust me…I can help."

I rose to my feet. "I'm going back inside."

Drosselmeyer grabbed my wrist. "Not finished!" He hissed the word.

I regained my chair and managed to wrest my hand from his grasp. "Make it quick."

"Secret orders…most noncoms didn't know…But I heard it."

"Did Reinhardt draft these orders?"

"No written orders…The colonel…had a job…but couldn't find…."

The conference door opened, and Virginia Powell stood in the entryway, peering at us. She hustled to where we sat. "What are you two doing out here? We're about to pair students with camp veterans for the interviews. We need you at your tables. Now." Her last words sounded like a schoolteacher scolding her errant students.

I helped Drosselmeyer to his feet.

"Meet me," he said, "…back of the parking lot…near the dumpsters…eighteen hundred tonight. Tell you more."

I nodded. The thought of Drosselmeyer lighting a flame near his air tank chilled me. But his knowledge could be vital.

Mrs. Powell held the door open as the old sergeant and I rejoined the other veterans.

Chapter Fourteen

29 October 1943

"Stay in step!" For the third time in as many minutes, Sergeant Paul Drosselmeyer drove his hand in the middle of my back, propelling me forward. A square-build man with wide shoulders, close-cropped hair, and a cartoonish widow's peak. I hustled forward, hoping he wouldn't push me off my feet. In the back of my mind, an errant thought: where had I seen Drosselmeyer before?

"Keep moving!" he barked, reminding me of the drill sergeants during my training days. "And I want to hear you sing!"

I marched in the back row near the deadly wire. We numbered fifteen demonstrators and so far had circled the compound half a dozen times. Some of us were caught by rovers, but most were simply drafted into service. We stepped in unison singing "Soldaten sind Soldaten" for the third time since midnight. As I glanced at the cloudless sky overhead, I wondered about the futility of this protest. Still marching in the day's heat? We never squandered this type of activity in the desert. Fatigue nagged at me. How much longer would we continue?

The armed guards outside the fence had disappeared at first light. Off-duty, I supposed. Even the tower guards paid us little attention as we turned each corner of the camp.

"Louder!" Drosselmeyer rushed to the head of our column. "Let the civilians in town hear you!"

Our voices rang out under the afternoon sun, singing a popular song honoring the German soldier, but Nazi ideology had inserted their own twisted words. Their reach even extended to the books in the prison library. During my first week in camp, Novak showed me a copy of a Thomas Mann novel, *Der Zauberberg*. "This story was written in 1924, yet the narrator is comforted with thoughts of racial purity, even though he suffers from physical afflictions."

"Do you suppose other books have been altered?" I asked.

"I wouldn't be surprised." He flipped to the front of the volume. "See here?" His finger moved to the fine print behind the title page. "Published by the Reich Ministry of Culture. I asked the librarian about it. He said the books came from the German mission in New York. I wonder if an American translator ever looked at these pages."

My thoughts returned to the present when the song ended, and we halted. More than sleep, I wanted to get back to the infirmary. How was Novak doing? Was he already being tried for not staying quiet about the guard orders? Where was this court to take place? Until I could get away, there was nothing I could do to help him. Discipline kept me silent. But we couldn't march for much longer. "At ease, men," he said. "Mess hall is still open. Get some sleep after you eat. Report here at twenty-one hundred hours to resume the protest."

"How much longer are we protesting?" one of the

men asked.

"Until our commanders decide the action is no longer necessary. Now, I suggest you get moving, or you won't get an early spot in line for your midday meal."

"Yessir," we chorused.

"Dismissed," he rumbled. "Except for Rohling. A word with you, private."

The other men scattered. Sergeant watched me beneath his cloth cap but gave no indication of his thoughts. I shifted my feet in the sandy track. Marching was not an effort for me, but I didn't like standing still. And that cold stare made me antsy. His jaw moved around in a circle as if he pondered a grand but elusive thought. Finally, I had to ask. "Yes, sir?"

"Your soldier book, please."

I handed the fourteen-page booklet to him. He scanned the first few pages, which contained my personal information, parents' names, and preservice history. He handed the worn volume back to me.

"Thank you, sir."

"I am also a Berliner," he said. "Your papa's beer cellar was a favorite haunt during my youth. I have fond memories of his Oktoberfest and winter ale."

I spent much of my childhood in that hole in the ground, helping Papa prepare the brew for patrons. "There wasn't much customer space," I said. "We only used it in the cold weather. The tables were never empty."

"My papa grew potatoes and cabbage." Drosselmeyer looked to the guard tower and back to me. "I had more free time after the frost." He chuckled. "Truth be told, I spent more time bicycling to and from the tavern than staying there."

I remembered him then. A stocky farm boy trying to keep pace with the more-experienced drinkers. "The things we did during our younger years," I said. "How many of us would jump for a second chance?"

"I have no regrets. Excellent beer and pleasant company. A person could do worse."

"Indeed." Novak's plight loomed in my mind. The sooner I understood his situation, the better I could help him. But until the sergeant dismissed me, I wasn't going anywhere.

"Have you thought about starting your own brewery?" He gave me a sidelong glance.

"I supposed I'll help Papa after the war is over."

He gave me a terse look. "I mean here. The camp has plenty of resources. As long as we make no escape attempts, the Americans care little about what we do. It would be a good morale booster for the men."

I took a step back. "Good beer takes weeks to brew. Even if I could get started tomorrow."

The sergeant worked his jaw some more. "Maybe not tomorrow. But in a month or so. Give me a list of the equipment you need to get started—and don't think small. There are thousands of thirsty men in this camp. That's a lot of brewing."

"I'll make the list and even help get you started. But I'd rather not take part in the brewing."

"There's plenty of profit to go around. You sure you want to turn it down?"

"I've got other things to think about."

Drosselmeyer scowled. "You'd walk away from an easy way to reap in cash? Men would pay ten, twenty, maybe thirty cents for a glass of fine ale."

"I have my reasons."

He sighed heavily. "Whatever it is will have to wait. I expect you to march most of tomorrow."

"Yes, sergeant."

"That's all. You're a strange one, Rohling. Now get out of here before I decide you're insubordinate."

I dashed for the infirmary where visiting hours had just started. I hoped Novak would be alert enough to answer questions. Whatever his troubles, I intended to help. Novak was not going to face this ordeal alone.

I sprinted up the wooden steps but slowed as I entered the front office. A blond clerk wearing a corporal's uniform hunched over his desk, typing a report. "Can I help you, sir?"

"I'm here to see Private Brian Novak. Bed sixteen."

The young clerk retrieved a sheet from a tray and glanced at a list of names. "Novak is crossed off my inpatient list. He's not here."

I set my jaw, impatient with this key-tapper. "Sir, is that all the information you have?"

"One of the medics may know more."

"Any help would be appreciated," I said.

He picked up a telephone and pressed a button. The tinny voice coming through the receiver sounded irritated.

"I know you told me not to disturb the patients…Well, if you'd explained the reason for discharge on the patient list, I wouldn't have to call you." He paused. "I agree. The form is no good." He leaned back for a moment, scowling. "It's not my job to fix it. It has to come from your end. Justify the problem, recommend changes, and send it to me for authorization…Of course, I'd approve it. I'm on your side."

A man's life was at stake, and this clerk sat discussing paperwork. I rapped on the metal desk. "Patient Novak. What happened to him?"

The clerk held up a finger. "Listen. Forget the form. I'll take care of it. But I need a favor…a small favor, dammit. You had a patient, Brian Novak, discharged today. Any information on him?" He leaned forward, scratching his chin. "You don't say?" He listened a few more seconds, thanked the medic for his trouble, and hung up, shrugging his shoulders.

"Yes, corporal?" It was all I could do to keep my hands at my side.

"Medics discharged Novak against medical advice this morning. A couple of men escorted him out of the infirmary. They talked about the stockade."

I retreated a step, biting my lip. Reinhardt's men— had to be. If they locked him in the camp's prison-within-a-prison, I could not help him. "Thank you, sir." I don't remember leaving the office. Novak's plight alarmed me. Hidden hands were at work.

I needed approval to visit the stockade. Or I could wait until the cover of darkness and take my chances.

****

The limestone structure could barely accommodate a man standing. It sat in the compound's northeast corner, clearly visible from the guard tower. Storage buildings and stacks of scrap lumber stood out amidst the brightness from the brilliant north and east-side fence lights. Unlike the interior of the camp, there were few shadows to hide in for safety. The mounted spotlight panned the area in irregular patterns.

Crouching behind the limestone block, I peeked through the slit that served as a window but couldn't see Novak. A German guard slouched in a chair leaning against the jail entrance on the other side of the stockade. He looked to be dozing. Hard to believe in this much light.

Dismissing the guard, I turned my attention to Novak. We could whisper through the small slit window, but I would not be able to watch the guard. If he awoke and investigated, I would be caught. But if he continued to nap, I could get a few words with Novak. From his vantage point, the tower sentry faced me and lit a cigarette. With a start, I realized I had become this American's evening entertainment.

I swallowed hard, hoping to push my heart back into place. Not for the first time, I thought about returning to the barracks and wait for my time to march. But a soldier does not abandon his comrade.

"Brian." The sound of my words was lost amid the chirping of crickets. "Do you hear me?"

A surprised whisper came from the dark. "Henry. You can't be here."

"Never mind that. Sorry I couldn't see you earlier. Long story."

"I wondered what happened."

"You've seen the marchers passing by here all day. I was one of them. Drafted for the cause. How are you holding up?"

"Could be better. Still dizzy. Side hurts. On the mend, though."

"Good to hear. What's happening—?"

"Wait. The guard is stirring."

I rushed to a different vantage point. The guard

stretched but leaned back in his chair, his feet outstretched. I watched for a full minute. Our watchful friend seemed to be settling in for the evening. Satisfied, I hustled to the rear of the stone prison. "I'm back."

"I thought you left." Relief shown in his voice.

"Not until I get some answers. Earlier, you mentioned a trial."

"I did?" Novak paused. "What is today?"

"October twenty-ninth." I stifled a yawn. "Our labor group got back to camp just before curfew last night."

"Only a day since the shooting? It feels longer."

I rubbed my temple. "Prisoners have been marching nonstop. I don't know when it will end."

"I can guess. On October thirty-first, I'm facing trial for insubordination and sedition. Every officer in this compound will attend. I expect it to be quite a show."

"I should pass the word to the Americans."

"No!" His voice was low, but the fear and urgency came through. "They said if I didn't cooperate, life for my parents would be unbearable after the war. They would destroy their reputations. Force them to live on the streets. I can't let that happen."

"It's a bluff. Who threatened this?"

"A lieutenant appointed to be my lawyer. Can you believe it?"

"They're prisoners just like you. It's all bark."

"I can't take the chance. Nothing must happen to *Mutta und Papa*."

It pained me to hear him like this. "I want to be there. Speak in your defense."

"Don't, Henry. They will target you."

I bit my lip. It would be risky. Foolhardy, even to speak out. "There's got to be a way to stop this trial. I could start a rumor. Conspirators are planning an escape. That should get the attention of the Amis. Where is this trial to take place?"

"I don't know. It's a secret."

"Damn." I stomped my foot. Beneath my heel, a twig snapped.

The spotlight swung about, splashing the area in dazzling brilliance.

"What's happening?" I asked, not daring to move outside the shadow of the stockade.

Novak's voice came back seconds later. "The guard is fumbling about and holding his hands over his eyes. The light must have blinded him. Get out of here, Henry. Go—before he recovers his senses."

There was nothing more I could do. "Take care, Brian." I dashed for the relative darkness of the camp's interior. I wondered if Novak's trial would take place in the officers' barracks. Could I stop it? Would the Americans intervene? No answers came as I marched in Drosselmeyer's band of men that night. Until the protest marches ended, I could do little.

Still, the seed of an idea took root. The game wasn't over yet.

Chapter Fifteen

30-31 October 1943

I marched in Drosselmeyer's group all that night and well into the next day, circling the compound and singing patriotic songs, but my thoughts pursued the idea of getting a secretive message to the Americans. The contents of the message would be vague since I had little information to offer. Brian Novak's trial was tomorrow, most likely within the officers' barracks. But could it take place elsewhere, such as the officers' compound? Enlisted men are quick to pass rumors, especially about their superiors. Only two rows of barbwire and four meters of no-man's-land separated the two compounds. One rumor suggested that the officers had breached the barriers by tunneling underground. So was it possible Novak could be taken to the other compound for his trial?

Impossible. The trial had to be here. The Americans entered our camp at least once a day to conduct a physical headcount. Men grouped according to their barracks. Novak's absence would be noticed. Except now, the Americans hadn't entered the camp in two days, and they would not likely return until the crisis ended.

At nine hundred hours, Drosselmeyer dismissed our group. "We reassemble at twenty-two hundred to resume the march," he said. As the men headed to the mess hall or back to their quarters, the sergeant caught my attention. "You have that list for me?"

"No, sir, but I know what I need."

"You were supposed to write it down. Well, bring it tonight. No excuses."

"Yessir." A twelve-hour break gave me time to complete my plan to save Novak. I headed to the quartermaster's hut where a German corporal outfitted me with two changes of clothing since my gear hadn't returned from outside. I showered, ate an early lunch, and slept for a good six hours.

It was nearly sunset. A few other prisoners dozed as well. The constant marching played havoc with everyday routine. I rose from my bunk, keeping as quiet as possible. Since I had nothing to write with, I peeked inside Novak's kit and found a pencil and stationery. Folding one of the blue sheets in my pocket, I ambled to the mess hall to compose my list of brewing supplies.

The mess hall operated twenty-four hours a day because of the crisis. Two dozen prisoners ate a late supper or drank coffee or tea. I filled a tin with hot water from a kettle and surveyed the choices for tea, hoping for a loose-leaf blend, but ground tea packed in small sacks remained my only choice. Convenient though, and the attached string made the tea easy to prepare.

While allowing the beverage to steep, I composed my list. A shadow fell over me. Hauser held a book and a plate of sausage and sauerkraut. He took a seat across from me.

"What are you working on, Henry?" He took a bite of savory sausage. The title of his book was *The Red*

Pony. Probably a western.

"I've been approached to start a brewery. But I can't stop thinking about Novak. He's in trouble with the Deutsch command."

"Did you see him the other night?" he asked. When it came to gossiping about German officers, soldiers leaned their heads and talked in whispers.

"Only for a couple of minutes."

"What did he tell you?"

"He's facing trial soon for warning prisoners about the guard tower. Yesterday, I learned the officers moved him to the stockade. I talked to him there last night but had to leave in a hurry. His guard heard me."

Hauser's jaw dropped. "You saw him twice?"

"I had to know what happened to him. This so-called trial sounds ominous. With a group of Nazi officers in charge, anything can happen."

Hauser gave the room a quick survey. "The Geneva Convention has rules about the treatment of prisoners. Just two weeks ago, a Red Cross inspector asked how the Americans treated us. Of course, most of us said they were doing well."

"That may be true," I said. "But no one is wondering how officers treat their own men."

"They wouldn't do anything during a crisis. Wouldn't the Americans think it suspicious?"

I set my jaw. "That sounds like wishful thinking." I wondered if Hauser could be trusted with my idea. "What would happen if the Americans learned of an escape attempt? They would have to invade the camp and search for the planners."

He shook his head. "Be careful, Henry. If a disturbance erupts, you could be their next target.

They're not stupid. Word will reach them you saw Novak. Don't do anything else. Or you'll never be safe here."

"I don't want to leave."

"Then stick to brewing. It's a lot safer." Hauser rose, retrieved his book and food tray, and left. I still had a decision to make. Risk the future to stop a Nazi trial or do nothing. Novak was a comrade in arms. And Emily? I longed to see those hazel eyes and the red handkerchief tied over her auburn hair. No denying it. I'd fallen for Emily Henning.

I got to my feet, pocketed the list, and stepped outside. I had no choice. Seeing Emily was impossible now. Novak came first.

Tonight, I would put my plan into action.

****

Two hours before my march, I returned to Novak's shelf to retrieve several more sheets of paper. With pencil in hand, I sat on my bunk and wrote three identical messages describing a meeting of the officers to discuss escape options. Location unknown, but all of the higher ranks planned to attend. The date of the gathering could be as early as tomorrow.

Stuffing the blue stationery in my tunic pocket, I then searched for some string or twine. This proved hard to find. Some twenty minutes later, I stumbled over a metal bucket in a closet and found a mop. With some difficulty, I yanked off some strings. Now, how was I going to deliver my message?

Not far from the barracks, a storage shed contained recreation equipment donated by the YMCA. Inside the door stood a rucksack filled with baseballs. The Americans tried to interest us in the game but to no avail. Germans much preferred soccer. I hefted a ball in my hand. Perfect. Tying the notes in place proved easy. Now, to whom do I deliver the message? Only one choice.

The watchtower guards.

As night settled across camp, spotlight beams danced about. Getting close enough to lob my note into the guards' nest would be tricky. My best chance for success would be near the stockade. Would Novak still be there?

At 2130 hours, I stood out of the guards' view behind a storage shed. No guard sat outside the stone building. A group of marchers turned the corner and disappeared. All was quiet except for the murmur of conversation inside the tower. The spotlight shifted and skittered north to the neighboring compound. Time for my first pitch.

I took measure of the distance to throw. Twenty meters. With the spotlights swung away, I jumped to the open but still hesitated. I threw, but my hand refused to release the ball—and the beam skittered along the ground, sweeping closer. No more time. I threw back my arm, aiming for the mounted spotlight lens. Perfect height, but the ball missed the tower by a meter and landed in the knee-high grass beyond the fences. Cursing my luck, I raced back to the corner of the building as the brilliance shot by.

Incredibly, the guards didn't notice the ball hurtling past their post. Vowing to do better, I emerged from the warehouse. Still in the game with two more pitches. I hopped to my imaginary mound and threw the ball again, this time underhanded. I hoped the ball would land inside the tower.

The sphere sailed over the tin roof and landed in the tall grass between the fence rows with an audible thump. Both guards stirred, peering into the darkness beyond. "Did you hear something?" one sentry asked.

"Probably a rabbit or a raccoon," said his partner.

"Maybe one of us should check it out."

"I'm not looking for a raccoon in the dark," said the second guard.

They examined the ground around the tower, then, by mutual consent, found packs of cigarettes and lit up. For a minute more, the spotlight remained stationary before it meandered north again.

I had to correct my pitch. One last ring toss, and the ball had to land perfectly within the tower. As I readied to throw, marching feet approached from the west. A group of singing protesters paraded along the northern fence toward the guards. One sentry swung the searchlight around, pinning the prisoners in brilliance, but they kept advancing. Now was my chance. I jumped out of hiding, loped forward as close as I dared, took a deep breath, and flung the ball.

It sailed straight and true in a graceful, lazy arc. I watched mesmerized, standing there in the open, heedless of the danger. *Come in. A little bit farther...Now drop.* As if on command, the ball fell inside the walls—bouncing off the spotlight, flying passed a guard's ear, smacking the corner post—and disappearing from sight.

Both men reached for their rifles, sighting down their barrels to the protesters below.

The sergeant walking point halted his group. The marchers fell silent. For a long moment, guards and prisoners regarded each other without moving. My foot nudged a stone. I could toss it against a building, drawing attention away from the prisoners. Or the added sound could trigger a shot. The thought left me shivering.

My plan had failed, and I had to rejoin Drosselmeyer's group, but I stood transfixed. How would this standoff end?

The two guards muttered between themselves. Finally, one of the rifleman pointed his carbine to the sky. "Get moving!" he yelled. "And no more rocks!"

Nearly 2200. I loped to the parade grounds, wondering if the guards might find any of my notes. The plan may yet succeed. Three messages lay in the weeds. A single discovery would set off a search within the prison. *Please. Make it soon.*

On the parade grounds, Drosselmeyer yelled at the men to form ranks. I ran to join them, finding a place in the back. The bullish sergeant paced along the column, getting in the faces of several men. "Stand straight!…Quit your gawking!" Reaching me, he leaned forward, pushing me off my feet. "Glad you could join us, Rohling. A minute later, you'd have been running laps while the rest of us took our stroll."

"Yessir." I thrust a paper in his hand. "Here is the list you requested, sir."

Drosselmeyer glanced at the contents before thrusting it in his pocket. "Scroungers can ferret out most of these supplies." He stepped to the side and raised his voice. "Fall in, ladies! We'll be on parade until nine hundred hours tomorrow."

For the next eleven hours, we strutted about the compound with little shouting or singing this time. For the enlisted men at least, protesting had lost its charm.

Our progress around the compound wasn't so much a march but a slog. And for all our sweat and strained voices, few officers marched with us. Still, one of our own had died, killed by second-rate American soldiers. Honor and duty demanded we press on.

Sometime that morning, a corporal ran to intercept our column, saluted the sergeant, and handed him a sheet of paper. Drosselmeyer halted our group and scrutinized the note, then drew the messenger aside, leaving us at attention. They talked—and at times argued—in hushed tones. At one point, the sergeant rubbed his jowl, working those chops, pondering an issue. The corporal shook his head and gestured in our direction, but the sergeant would have none of it. Finally, the other man pocketed his document, saluted, and disappeared.

Drosselmeyer returned with a General Patton swagger. "At ease, men," he said. "Good news, soldiers. The protest is over. The Americans and our officers have come to an agreement. The shooting of Private Tenenbaum was a grievous mistake and a violation of the rules for prisoner treatment as set by the Geneva Convention. Camp commanders have apologized and will take due action to determine the guilt or innocence of the soldier responsible for the murder of our countryman. Our officers have issued a response: prisoners will cease all protest actions. Camp will return to normal activities by seventeen hundred hours. We've triumphed. *Sieg Heil!*"

"*Sieg Heil!*" we shouted in unison.

"You are dismissed."

We cheered, several of us throwing our caps in the air. I was elated but apprehensive as well. Did anyone find my messages? What if they rejected it? A third, even darker possibility came to mind. Suppose the camp commanders sent the contents of the note to the liaison officers? German officers could smooth over any concerns of our captors and proceed unhindered with Novak's trial. Despite the risks, I still needed to search for my friend.

A hand clamped onto my shoulder. "Hold it, Rohling," Drosselmeyer said. "We need to talk about our brewing partnership."

"Yessir," I responded. "But I'm not interested."

"Oh, but you will be." He retrieved my list from his pocket. "Where were you before last night's march?"

"Preparing your supplies list," I said. The timing was off, but accurate enough.

"You better hope that is true." He rolled his jaws for a moment. "You're in sheep dung up to your neck, Rohling. Our officers are looking for an *agent provocateur*, who is driving a wedge between the Americans and us. They're looking for the author of a certain note." He held up my list between two fingers. "The document they found is the same color as this."

An unseen hand squeezed my throat, and for a moment, I found it difficult to breathe.

The sergeant watched me tight-lipped. "You'd sing like a bird under interrogation. But don't worry. Your name came up, but I weaved a convincing story about you and me discussing the craft of brewing. In case anyone questions you, these will be the answers you provide." He then went into detail about our upcoming brewing business. "I boasted about how your lager was the best I ever tasted. I know these officers. They love

171

their beer. Even if Reinhard's men suspect you of…indiscretion, the promise of a brewery will keep them from taking any action. So what do you say? Partners?"

I let out a long breath. "When do we start?"

"That's the spirit." He stuck out a hand. "No more rooting in the dirt for some farmer. You've got a job to do here."

I imagined a steel gate closing, separating me from the countryside beyond. "Thank you, sir."

I jogged across the parade grounds to my quarters, feeling some relief in getting away from Drosselmeyer. For a day or two, I had time to myself. After the sergeant found his supplies, I would become his servant. At least brewing would provide a service and might even improve morale. After some rest, a warm shower, and a change of clothes, I would search for my friend.

A yell erupted from the shower building, and several prisoners rushed to the dressing room side. Seconds later, one young man, hardly more than a boy, staggered out, dropped to his knees, and puked. Another man, his tunic unbuttoned, sprinted toward the main gate, waving his arms. "*Achtung!* We need help!"

Was there an accident? A freezing chasm opened within me, and I felt myself falling in its icy center. *Please tell me I'm wrong.* I don't remember rushing into the building. One man told me later how I thrust onlookers standing in the doorway aside and stormed into the showers. What I do remember was wondering about the dank smell of mildew as I viewed the body of Brian Novak suspended above the floor.

He hung from a belt loop tied to the water pipe.

The showerhead above him still dribbled water over his naked frame. A chair from the dressing room lay on its side beneath him. The whites of his eyes peeked from under half-closed lids; the left eye had blossomed into a shiner. Dried blood from a long scrape matted his right temple, and his right cheek looked puffy. My mind hovered over the thought of my friend taking his own life.

Outside, the camp siren rose to a full wail and stayed there.

"Get out of there," a voice called behind me. "Guards are coming!"

I retreated from the concrete death vault to the changing room. There, a field uniform hung from a hook with a pair of shined shoes beneath. A set of smelly work clothes lay folded nearby. Other hooks and chairs were empty. The uniform and folded work clothes had to be Novak's. I wiped a stray tear; even in the face of death, my friend showed dignity.

"Hurry, they're almost here." Another prisoner shoved me out the door.

I scrambled from the building and stood with a growing crowd to watch the approaching Americans. Numbed by the events of the past two days and crushed by the futility of trying to save my friend from a faceless enemy, I wanted to withdraw from the chaos around me. Fade away to a quieter place. Find peace in a land where the loudest sounds were raucous calls from blue jays and crows. I rubbed my temples, clearing away the fantasies. An unwilling spectator, I noted the events around me as if they already happened.

A sergeant led five guards in single file to the building. The noncom and three others entered, while the remaining soldiers stood in front of the doorways. Soon, one of the guards exited and sprinted to the gate. Five minutes later, a canopied ambulance bearing a Red Cross emblem entered the camp and halted in front of the shower building. Two men in brown khakis jumped to the rear doors and unloaded a gurney. Around me, prisoners asked questions, and others guessed the answers.

"Did either of them look like a medic to you?" a man beside me asked.

"I don't think so. No insignia," a deep voice boomed in front.

"Someone get hurt?" asked a newcomer.

"Novak," I said.

"Is he dead?"

"Who's dead?" A voice behind me.

"Novak. The troublemaker." Who said that?

"Didn't he warn us about the guard tower?"

"More like the officers tried to warn us. Novak said it was a hoax." Meddlers were turning the conversation.

"How'd he die?"

"Don't know."

"Suicide."

"No!"

"That's right. Novak couldn't take the guilt."

"For what?"

"For hiding the truth."

"What truth?"

"Novak let the soccer player die."

"That's not it." Hauser's voice. Had to be. "I saw it happen. They shot Tenenbaum while he picked up a ball in the weeds."

"Terrible."

"Wasn't Novak in the infirmary?"

"No. He stayed away on purpose. He knew what would happen."

"Wasn't he beaten?"

"A ruse. He planned his own alibi."

"That's hard to believe."

"All true. He's in with the Americans."

"Novak was a soldier."

"He was a traitor!"

"Impossible!"

"Death for the traitor."

"Trai-tor!" The chant caught fire.

"*Verrä-ter! Verrä-ter!*"

Clenched hands rose. Prisoners shouted as one, pumping their fists like a living dynamo. In a few short minutes, curiosity changed to rage. Provocateurs turned Novak's mission into a crime. His own comrades cursed him with only a suggestion. How could the truth die so easily? The disgust that weighed on me tasted like bile. I despised these sheep who let themselves be led.

And I stayed quiet, letting it happen.

The prisoners still chanted when the sergeant and remaining guards came out and stood by the doorway while those who handled the gurney loaded Novak's shrouded body onto the truck. The ambulance gunned its engine and left along with the guards, heading back to the American garrison.

With nothing to hold their collective attention, the crowd around me dispersed. A few disgruntled prisoners muttered about Novak getting his due, but most seemed drained by their own fury or dazed, like they just awakened from a stupor. I stood alone staring at the cement building, trying to make sense of what happened.

With so little time between finding the body and wheeling it to the ambulance, the Americans could well have taken it for granted that Novak committed suicide. He did voice concerns about his parents' well-being after the war. Would he bargain his own life to save them? Impossible to say. Novak prided himself for being an obnoxious gadfly to the Nazi believers, but he was a soldier first. A soldier would sacrifice himself for a greater cause. Did that include suicide?

Still, one detail bothered me. Why bring a clean uniform when he didn't intend to wear it?

I entered the dressing room. Both the uniform and work clothes remained undisturbed. A search of the pockets produced nothing. No suicide note. The work clothes were tightly folded like he was preparing for inspection. Despite the sadness that filled me, I couldn't help but smile. Being neat with dirty clothes was pure Novak. No. The thought struck me like a physical blow. Novak had intended to wear his clean uniform. He had no thoughts of killing himself.

Novak had discovered a change in the guard's rules for firing on prisoners, a change that our officers already knew. Yet they remained silent. He told everyone he knew even after the officers ordered him to silence. For this, they beat the man and ordered a show trial—to make him an example. Despite his warnings, a prisoner died, propelling the camp into a confrontation with the Americans. How interesting that his death coincided with the end of that crisis. Now, Novak was considered a traitor—a tidy way to tie the final knot in a neatly executed plan.

Could they rely on Novak to take his own life? Or did those responsible get insurance—an angel to intercede in case the convicted man changed his mind? There was also the bleeding wound to his temple. An old wound maybe, or did this dark angel subdue Novak to complete the hanging?

The Americans were not about to investigate. It was my duty to find this killer. If he existed. With no suicide note, I could never be sure. *Novak, if you could only speak to me, I would act.*

I slumped onto a dressing room chair. Drosselmeyer owned me with a blue sheet of stationery filled with my handwriting. He could turn me over to the officers at any time. And what then? My death would change nothing. I had to let go of Novak. A scornful voice stirred within me.

Avenge Novak. Do the noble thing.

I have no proof. Then there's Emily. And home.

Emily is out of reach. Home may be years away.

I want to hope. To live.

Hope is a prayer. You live for duty. Take the final step.

I can't.

Heinrich Rohling—

I'm Henry.

You're a coward.

Chapter Sixteen

Applause greeted me with shouts of "*Du bist spät!*" when I reentered the reunion conference room that Saturday afternoon. I bowed to the gentle chiding and took my seat next to Kimmel. "Half hour late, Rohling. You and Drosselmeyer must have had quite a conversation."

I shrugged. No point denying it. Mrs. Powell had seen us talking. "He enjoys reminiscing about the old days."

The director stepped to the microphone. "You will soon begin your oral histories with one of these students. During your interviews, be aware that the information you provide will become public knowledge. Any talk about undocumented crimes or criminal activity, even fifty years ago, will have to be reported to the proper authorities. You may have to submit to further questioning. So consider your answers carefully."

Kimmel chuckled close to my ear. "Powell doesn't want her children to hear anything scandalous."

I waved him off. "I want to hear this."

The director gestured to the young people sitting in a row of folding chairs behind her. "It's time for our historians to meet you. When I call your name, please raise your hand. Your interviewer will greet and introduce themselves at your table. After that, feel free to find a quiet spot to conduct your talk. At four thirty, we will reconvene in this room for banquet announcements and tomorrow's activities." From a list of names, she then began pairing university students with former prisoners.

Couples soon shuffled into hallways or remained at their tables. Kimmel pointed to Drosselmeyer where he remained seated, shaking the hand of a young man with glasses. "You know, my wife considered barring that raspy old sergeant from coming here. 'Too frail,' she said. 'What if he should get worse?' I told her 'What if he does? He still deserves to come. Let him see his old comrades one last time.' I convinced her in the end. She always gives in to me."

I balled my fists so tight, the nails dug into my flesh. "You must be a persuasive man." I managed to say without sarcasm.

"I can be."

Mrs. Powell called my name then, ending our conversation. A petite young woman with long blonde hair and a flower-printed dress approached me hoisting a large shoulder bag. "I'm Kathy Zoeller. So glad to meet you, Mr. Rohling."

I bowed, grasping her small hand with both my palms. Shaking hands is a custom Germans practice with gusto. "At your service, fräulein. Shall we find a place to sit?"

"There are chairs near the hotel coffee shop. Would you like a cappuccino?"

"Hot tea would be fine."

"Great!" Her eyes brightened. "I'll buy. And please, call me Kathy."

****

An hour later, Miss Zoeller—Kathy—laid the shriveled letter in its plastic bag on the table, well away from her strong-smelling brew. "An intriguing letter. I'm surprised it's written in English. It doesn't read like a suicide note, yet you say your friend was found hanged in the camp bathhouse?"

I pursed my lips, impatient to get on to my point. "Novak stated he would not hang himself, but he had an inkling it could happen." I held my breath, hoping she would reach the same conclusion I did.

She rubbed her brow before speaking into the microphone. "What did the camp authorities do after the hanging? Did officers conduct an inquiry?"

"The Americans? An ambulance retrieved Novak's body in minutes and then disappeared. No investigation."

"Not even after you produced the letter?"

The interview had gone off its rails—not going how I hoped. "I, uh…never revealed it. You're the first person I've shown the note to in fifty years."

"No one?" Her eyes grew large. "Why not?"

"Let me explain. I discovered the letter while I was packing the following spring for field work. Back to working for the Henning family. Five months after his death, Brian Novak's name was *verboten*. Saying anything would have changed nothing."

Kathy leaned forward, careful not to bump her microphone. "So help me understand. From what you say, Brian Novak wasn't popular with the German officers for discovering the guard tower orders and telling the enlisted prisoners. They considered him a whistleblower?"

I considered. "That would be the right term."

She moved her finger across the small table. "But after five months, when emotions settled down and with the letter in hand—you still didn't attempt to convince anyone of your suspicions? Can you explain that to me?"

I closed my eyes for a moment, aware of the twist in my gut. There was no getting around it. To exorcise my demons, I could no longer evade the truth. "I didn't want to jeopardize my chance to enjoy the small freedom of working on an American farm. And I feared reprisals by National Socialist officers for trying to clear Private Novak's name. I've been living with that act of cowardice since the war." I grasped my teacup. Ripples in the liquid betrayed my trembling fingers.

She reached out, touching my arm. "We'll get through this, Mr. Rohling. Thank you for being so genuine. Your story deserves to be heard."

"Right now, I feel rather small."

"Is it possible your friend felt rejected because fellow prisoners didn't believe him? Many prisoners took their own lives due to homesickness, hopelessness, and depression, despite amenable conditions inside the camps."

"I was able to talk to Novak twice before I found him in the shower house. He showed no signs of depression."

"But you were away during those weeks before the shooting brought you back. You couldn't know what Mr. Novak felt in his heart."

I closed my eyes, remembering his distress in the stockade. That wasn't the picture I wanted Kathy to see. "Novak was a fighter—what you would call scrappy. He grew up in New York before his family returned to

Germany. While he spoke fluent German, he thought like an American. That's why Novak wrote his last message in English. He knew what could happen, yet he resisted to the end."

"Resisted what?"

"Do I have to draw you a picture?" My voice rose louder than I intended. "Another prisoner killed him. Brian Novak was murdered." And the man responsible was here. I knew it in my gut, but I dared not speak that thought aloud. I had no proof—only a growing certainty.

"Hush!" Kathy Zoeller surveyed the coffee shop, but we were the only customers. "Be careful what you say. That is a powerful accusation. I'll have to inform Mrs. Powell, and she'll have to tell the police, or the army, or the U.S. Marshall's office. I'm not sure who it would be. One thing is for sure. You'll have a gazillion questions to answer. By itself, this letter doesn't prove murder. Only that Private Novak may have had conflicting thoughts before his suicide."

I swallowed the last of the coppery tea. With difficulty, I pushed the words past the dryness in my throat. "That's not how I see it."

"But that's what people will think. Most of the attendees here are ex-officers who arrived at Camp Conrad after you left. You won't get any support from them. Maybe the best thing you can do for your friend is to let him rest in peace."

"I came here to tell Novak's story. He was a man of honor. A better man than the thug who silenced him. I intend for the world to know it." I leaned forward to make sure the microphone caught my next words. "The only way I can be stopped is if the man who killed my friend silences me as well."

Kathy shook her head, wondering, I imagined, about my reasoning. She popped the cassette from the machine and replaced it with a new tape. She may have heard my words, but she couldn't know the depth of my resolve. I wouldn't have at her age. Before she pressed the record button, she gave me a small grin. "I intend to do my part as well, Mr. Rohling. You remind me a lot of Grandad. He guarded POWs at Fort Leavenworth prison and told me about his time there during World War Two. He's one reason why I'm here today. Good luck with getting your story out."

"Thank you."

She pushed RECORD on her tape deck. "This is tape number three of my interview with Heinrich Rohling of Berlin." She gave me another one of her bright smiles. I wondered how many hearts this child had broken during her high school years. "Tell me how the Labor Program worked."

With Kimmel's warning in mind, I told about working at the Henning farm, omitting my contacts with Emily and Billie.

"What were your thoughts about working for a farm family?"

"I found it fascinating." I closed my eyes, inviting the memories. "Practicing my English, working for a wage—even if it was camp script—was a privilege. Weeding the field or painting the barn gave me a sense of freedom I never felt at the main camp."

"What did you think of your employer?"

"I got along well with Mr. Henning. He trusted me to work on his crops unsupervised. The guard who accompanied us often stayed out of sight. We—the four of us—joked about the guard taking a nap after eating Mrs. Henning's pies."

"Did the Hennings have any children?"

How to answer? "An eighteen-year-old daughter and a twelve-year-old boy."

"And their names?"

"I…don't remember."

Kathy paused, pursing her lips. "Okay. So, the family accepted you. How did they show that?"

I leaned back, framing an answer. "Mr. Henning often left us unsupervised, even when his son watched us work. He constantly asked questions—always curious about desert fighting and combat. He wanted to know if I ever killed anyone."

"Did you?"

"I'll never know. War is loud, intense, and chaotic. I probably spent more time huddled in my trench than pulling the trigger."

"You paint broad strokes of the war, but I can still see it."

"Scary times. I loved the camaraderie and the pride of being part of a fighting unit, but being a PW was a lot safer."

"You remember the boy. No memories about the older daughter?"

I stifled a sigh. "Mrs. Henning kept her busy with chores during the day. I hardly saw her."

"A man named Bill Henning gave our group a tour of the museum grounds. You'll be seeing it tomorrow. I wonder if he could have been the boy you described."

Billie! "Hard to say." I scratched my brows, hoping my eyes didn't give my thoughts away.

"I'd like to arrange a meeting between you two. It

could add to my oral history. Would you be willing to see him?" She bent across the table and grasped my hands. A heartbreaker for sure. Her grandad may have handled the worst kind of criminals in his day, but I suspected he was no match for his granddaughter.

"I'd be happy to meet Mr. Henning." Hell, yes, I'd see Billie. He might be able to answer my questions about Kimmel's treatment of Emily. Was he the monster I believed him to be?

By 1630 hours, Kathy changed cassettes two more times, taping on one side only. "Why not both sides?" I asked. "It seems like a waste of tape."

"Cassettes are cheap, but the content is priceless. If a tape breaks, I can repair it and lose little of the conversation."

"Do you interview many people? Your recorder looks expensive." Her player had a needle that danced about each time I spoke, and she used two microphones. Mine dangled from a rod that hung at eye level.

"My aunt does genealogy—looking up family trees. She got me started with interviewing aunts and uncles. I learned early that quality equipment makes a difference."

"Is this what you want to do for a living?"

"I do. Aunt Toni doesn't like e-mail. She says it takes all the fun out of letter writing. She still corresponds with relatives who like getting personal letters."

My gaze wandered to the little lights in the ceiling. "Mail call was always a vital part of camp life. During the last year of the war, letters slowed to a trickle. Those lucky enough to receive a note from home had to share it with everyone. That's how we learned of the bombings. I had no idea how bad the destruction was until I arrived home."

"How did that affect you?"

"Anger. For a time, I hated the British and the Americans. The conquerors took over Germany, and yet we had to act the Good German, begging for materials to rebuild our country. In the middle of it all were the swaggering Americans."

"Many of the German POWs came back to America to visit those they befriended during the war. Did you ever consider this?"

The question hit with tangible force; I gasped for air that wasn't there. "Water."

Kathy rushed from the table, bringing back a cup of cool water.

I gulped, sloshing liquid on the front of my shirt. She dashed off again, this time for napkins. I dabbed my front as best I could.

"Are you all right?" she asked.

"Yes," I lied. "There was a time when I longed to return and live the American life—marry, have children, and own a repair shop to fix trucks and tractors. It all crumbled like dead leaves when I saw my parents living in a hole beneath the rubble."

Her mouth formed a little *O*. "Did you want to come back to the dairy farmer in Wisconsin or the Henning family in Kansas?"

I swallowed, knowing I had prattled too much. "Whoever would help me get settled, but it never went beyond idle thinking and daydreams."

"It sounds like you put a lot of thought into it."

"I might have talked with the lad on the dairy farm.

We filled many evenings with chatter between the milkings." I sipped more water. Old longings gnawed at me. I wished we moved to a new subject.

"No thoughts of coming back to Kansas?"

"The welfare of my parents came first and seeing to my neighborhood. A year later, I met a girl handing out water and pastries to my work gang. We married just before the Berlin Airlift. What a glorious, giddy time that was." In my mind's eye, huge cargo planes descended on the city, missing the tops of some buildings by just a few meters. "Whatever happened, I would never leave my country. To me, any man who left was a traitor."

Kathy tilted her head. "Considering the number of German ex-soldiers who became U.S. citizens, that's a strong statement."

I set my jaw. "That is my point—they gave up on their homeland."

We soon ended our session. "Tomorrow, after our talk with Mr. Henning, I can give you a lift back to the hotel."

"That's very kind of you."

She placed the microphones in her bag. "Wait for me, Mr. Rohling. I'll walk back with you. Mrs. Powell needs to see this letter."

We returned to the conference room, my steps hurrying to keep up with Kathy's fast pace. I returned to my seat. Emily stood at the podium, making notes. My interviewer and Mrs. Powell huddled by the exit door. As most of the attendees took their seats, Emily gathered her papers. "I have a few words about the banquet tonight and announcements concerning the tour tomorrow."

A tap on my shoulder. I glanced up. From my angle, Mrs. Powell towered over me.

"A moment, please, Mr. Rohling."

I rose to my feet. The director was ten years my junior, yet I felt like a delinquent schoolboy around her. Kimmel raised his brows but said nothing.

"Let's step into the hall. We have matters to discuss."

I followed her halfway to the lobby before she spun around, her eyes steel slits. "Sir, I thought we had an agreement. No unreported crimes."

I straightened, holding my chin up. This woman would not intimidate me. "I made no agreement. The events I explained to the young lady happened. This truth has been with me for over fifty years. Brian Novak died at the hand of another prisoner. Camp authorities did nothing about it. The world should know that."

Her expression did not waver. "A little late in the telling, don't you think? You could have revealed this matter years ago. Why wait so long?"

"There is no statute of limitations on murder. I want another investigation."

The director peered downward for a moment; her brows furrowed. Looking up, she seemed almost friendly. "Would an apology satisfy you?"

An apology? A cheap way to dismiss the matter. I shook my head. "Either the authorities will re-examine the facts, or they can deny my request. Either way, they must provide an answer or shirk their responsibility."

"You realize this could well be a fruitless endeavor? Not to mention an almighty inconvenience for yourself?"

"I'm prepared for questions."

"Old crimes, real or imagined, are precisely what I intended to avoid. But you leave me no choice, Mr. Rohling. I'll do this on one condition—you discontinue this talk of murder. I won't have it."

"I don't think I can do that."

"Comply, or you will be barred from the rest of the conference."

I retreated a step. In two hours, I would meet with Drosselmeyer and see Billie tomorrow. The wily coordinator gave me no choice. "I won't discuss the matter unless another person brings up the subject."

The director glowered. "If this story creates a disturbance with other attendees, you are off the reunion roster, and your recordings will be excluded from the archive."

"That wouldn't be fair to Miss Zoeller."

Mrs. Powell tapped her foot, giving me a sideways glance. "Point taken. At least be discreet. I will need your letter to show the local police if you wish to press this matter any further."

The bag containing my letter crinkled as I clutched the conference folder to my side. "Is that necessary?"

"Of course. It must be analyzed and authenticated. Whatever clues are buried in the words or paper must be teased out."

"I assure you, Novak's letter is real."

"Well, I can guarantee you, nothing will happen until you release the letter." She held out her hand.

Lab testing would reveal the note to be a fake. With painful reluctance, I handed over the letter.

Chapter Seventeen

3 November to 4 December 1943

Brian Novak's burial took place three days after his death. The German officers decreed he could not have a military funeral, and no officers would attend. Rumors suggested that enlisted men should steer clear as well. The Americans, of course, failed to notice or take action. This left me to wonder; if camp commanders were allowing the National Socialists to practice their creed on American soil, then why were they fighting Germany?

I stood by Novak's unadorned pine box, my head bowed, while the American chaplain read from a book of prayers. His black fedora hid his face, making him look more like a Hollywood gangster than a man of God. From the west, threatening clouds shot jagged bolts of lightning to the ground. A Midwest thunderstorm would soon roll over us. Perfect. Even the elements would wreak their displeasure at Brian Novak's memorial.

The chaplain flipped two pages ahead, giving me a quick glance. I could tell he skipped entire paragraphs. Maybe, the storm worried him and presumed I wouldn't notice his disjointed words. "In His mercy, Almighty God has taken the soul of Brian Novak," he read. "We, therefore, commit his body to the ground. Earth to earth, ashes to ashes, dust to dust." With a peal of thunder, the rain broke, turning swiftly into a downpour. The clergyman shoved the small volume in his pocket. He would have run for shelter, but I grabbed his arm and motioned to the grave. "Grab the ropes. Help me lower the coffin!" I had to yell over the storm.

"Later." He tugged to free his arm, but I had a firm grip.

"Now!"

He did as I demanded, muttering under his breath. A rising wind made further conversation impossible. Water splashed off the lid as the coffin sank beneath the ground. A flash of lightning illuminated the depths that would entomb my friend's body. We worked fast, and within two minutes, Novak's coffin came to rest on the floor of the pit. His gravesite lay behind the horse barn, the only ground where the officers would allow for his burial to take place. I scrutinized the stable. Novak would not have minded this spot. He had the stable to himself during the short time he worked there.

Next day, a cold northern wind brought on an unexpected frost, dooming any further thoughts of returning to farm work until next spring. In this flat land of endless grass and scraggly trees, the wind blew for days. I never realized until then what a desolate place Kansas could be.

With nothing to do, I threw myself into establishing a brewery. Drosselmeyer's foragers brought me a couple of camp stoves, three ten-gallon copper pots, and a dozen wooden barrels of different sizes. We designated an enlarged storm cellar as the *Bierwerks*. By the middle of November, we'd cooked our first batch of wheat and barley malt, cooled the mixture with well water, added yeast, and poured the wort into barrels for fermenting. "Do you think the cereal smell will have the guards investigating?" I asked Drosselmeyer during that intensive day of boiling grains.

"We'll tell them we're making porridge," he said.

As much as I disliked Drosselmeyer, he complained little of the lifting, straining, and pouring liters of unfermented brew. At the end of the day, the cellar smelled of wet earth, pine barrels, and cooked horse feed.

"How long will these barrels need to set?" the sergeant asked.

"Ten weeks before the first batch will be drinkable," I said. "The yeast needs time to do its work, and more barrels will be needed for the second fermentation."

He scowled. "The waiting time is too long."

I stared at him beneath the single bulb that lit the cellar. "You can't hurry good beer. Each step takes a certain amount of time."

"That may be true, but for our first batch, we're cutting the brewing time in half. By Christmas, we should be selling our first pitchers of beer."

Drosselmeyer ran the business. I could do nothing but shrug. "As you wish, sir. Five weeks."

In time, more barrels turned up, better stoves, and three bags of apples. The entire camp settled into the colder weather with fewer soccer games. Those who watched stayed near the track to catch any errant kicks from going beyond the wire. Late in November, a group of American officers formally presented a large uncooked bird to our barracks. This creature, we learned, formed the central part of a national day of feasting. None of us really knew what to do with it, so I took the dressed fowl to the mess hall. The cooks had already received other birds from around the camp. "They look like a goose," the kitchen chief told me. "And goose has a strong, gamey taste. Half the men won't eat it. And the other half will complain because it wasn't prepared the way they liked it. I'm throwing these things out with the rest of the garbage." That Thursday, we had beef and cabbage.

Starting early on December fourth, Drosselmeyer and I worked in the cramped cellar, now filled with more equipment. We hoisted a heavy cask filled with partially fermented beer with block and tackle. I tied the container in place, so the tap hung suspended over the smooth-bore hole of another barrel. Drosselmeyer released the tap, and the un-carbonated beer trickled into the empty cask. In the nearby music hall, the band practiced "Stille Nacht, Heilige Nacht" for an upcoming Christmas program. I couldn't help longing for home when I hear that song.

"This is a lot of effort," Drosselmeyer grumbled. "Why couldn't we let the beer finish brewing in the same barrels?"

"It's all the things that make beer so enjoyable," I explained, "the foamy head, the fizz, the sweet combination of hops and malt, and the satisfying finish as it rolls down the palate. All this happens in the crucial final weeks of brewing." I gently rocked the suspended barrel to unclog the tap. "Plus, we get rid of the impurities that settle during the first fermentation."

"As long as it's ready by the twenty-fifth." He pulled a flat-sided bottle from his hip pocket and drank from it. A sharp whiff of alcohol filled the room. "We can start a batch of winter ale next time." His voice had a raw edge after swallowing the hooch.

My partner's drinking left me uneasy. I grabbed two paring knives from a tray of utensils. "Help me peel some of these apples. Hard cider would be a refreshing drink on Christmas day."

For the next hour or so we peeled and cut apples while the fermenting barrel emptied. With the new cask nearly full, I poured a measured amount of sugar inside for the live yeast to carbonate and finish the beer.

Drosselmeyer shook the fermenting barrel. "There still a fair amount of brew left in here. Seems like we're losing product with each step in the process." He took another nip from his bottle.

I rolled the carbonating barrel aside. It would keep until ready to serve. "Is that whiskey I smelled?"

The sergeant smirked, his eyes small pinpoints in the half-light. "I've got a distillery going. The whiskey has a rough kick, but it's drinkable. Care for a sip?"

"No, thank you." I readied the second barrel to drain for finishing, keeping busy to hide my revulsion. Papa never drank while he brewed.

"I can't believe brewing takes so long. It's not even beer yet, and we're constantly pouring it from barrel to barrel." He tugged at his bottle again.

I turned to face him hand on hips. "We've been over this. Brewing demands patience."

"Well—" He let out a croaking belch. "I'm not a patient man. At least we'll have whiskey until the beer is ready."

His impatience smacked of sloppy craftsmanship. Still, I wanted to pacify him. "You're a practical man, sir. The waiting will be worth it when you taste the final product."

"It can't be fast enough. With the cider and the whisky, the customers won't care if the beer tastes a little green."

"We have a captive audience," I agreed.

"True, but a competitor could try to take over the market. I could offer the officers our drink at cost if they convince competitors to find another hobby."

I retreated a step. "I don't want any part of that."

Drosselmeyer smiled at my discomfort and tipped his flask again. "You've been on my mind, Rohling. I've got you figured out."

I eyed him carefully. What was he talking about?

"It started with that note you tried to pass to the Americans. You were trying to cause a diversion. Trying to protect that traitor Novak."

"Help me with emptying this barrel. We're wasting time."

"In a minute. You put your life on the line for him. And for what? Nothing."

"He'd have done the same for me."

"Loyalty. A good trait in a soldier," Drosselmeyer said. "What division were you in?"

"The 90th Light Armor. And yours?" Get the sergeant to talk about himself.

"12th Panzers." He thumped his chest. "We were always in the thick of it, covering the field marshal's rear. Every Allied general wanted a crack at Rommel, but few got the chance. Thanks to us. Our unit did well until the ammo ran out."

"Supplies were always a problem. Desert fighting never made sense to me."

"We would never have gone there if the Italians had managed their end of the war."

I thought it prudent to change the subject. "What will you do after the war?"

"After our liberation? I'm going to march in a victory parade down Fifth Avenue in New York, then tour the world. Walk the streets of Moscow. Climb the Rocky Mountains. Smoke one of Churchill's cigars. See the sights in every country and watch people bow to the Reich."

I bit my lip to hide my distaste. "I'd be happy to go home and see my parents."

Drosselmeyer upended his bottle but got little for his effort. He shook the container, frowning, then shoved it back in his pocket. "Surely you want more than that? The world will be our playground. Think of the power you'll have simply for being German. You can go anywhere. Do anything."

My thoughts wandered to Emily. "I wouldn't mind coming back to visit. The Kansas countryside is quiet and peaceful. Working there, I forgot I was a prisoner."

The sergeant wiped his nose. "When our conquering armies arrive, the Americans will likely flee, leaving the land deserted and ripe for the picking."

Drosselmeyer's assessment sent a shiver down my spine, but I remembered the gun in the Hennings' truck. "You underestimate the civilians. Families here own firearms. These people would fight for their land."

"Rohling, you're talking like a defeatist. These Americans are used to the easy life. They are no match for our army." His voice held a warning. "You would do best to remember that."

"Yes, sergeant."

Silence from outside. The Christmas band must have quit for the day.

"You met someone," he said.

"Sir?" A bolt of energy left me alert.

"This American farm. A civilian has captured your heart." He peered at me over the top of the suspended barrel. "A sheepherder's daughter, perhaps?"

The comment startled me. "I don't know what you're talking about."

"Ho! Ho!" He thumped the barrel. "Rohling, don't ever play poker. You'll lose every time. Who is she?"

My only refuge was the truth. I hoped Drosselmeyer's joviality would win over his predatory nature. "The daughter of the farmer I worked for. I ask for your discretion on this."

"My dear boy, I am the embodiment of discretion. That's why you are free to help in this modest venture. That's why I'm distilling whiskey and brewing beer under the noses of the Americans. That's why I'm going to forget about your little romantic tryst." His smile faded, and he leveled his eyes at me. "You're playing with fire, my friend. It cannot end well. Remember, this is the land of the enemy. After our victory, there will be an accounting. If word spread that you consorted with this fräulein, it could destroy you."

I drew back. "I ask this remain unspoken."

"You have my word. Besides, we'll both be busy expanding the brewery. You won't be going back to the farm."

Before I could answer, the watchtower sirens wound to its familiar wail. "*Mein Gott*," Drosselmeyer grumbled. "What are the Americans up to now? They completed their headcount this morning."

"We'd better shut down. No telling how long the delay will be." The whistle faded for a few seconds, only to rise again. I left the cask suspended and doused the light. We clambered outdoors, and Drosselmeyer slammed shut the cellar door behind us. This sent him staggering. I helped him to the soccer field where we separated.

"We'll meet back at the cellar after this is over," he said.

Prisoners assembled in the usual chaotic way. As I fell in line with my group, Sergeant Stecklein barked an order, and we came to attention, facing the fence. Some forty guards rushed down the track, rifles on their backs. These men were leaner and alert. Their uniforms were clean and pressed, shoes well-polished, and they stood at full attention. No sloppiness here. A high-ranking officer must be coming.

Tension and expectancy hung in the air. A cargo truck arrived, and the guards assembled a platform with a power supply and a podium wired for sound. At least the siren had died. Five jeeps rushed toward us, cutting across the grass. The lead vehicle bore a stylized silver oak leaf on its side. The driver stopped short of the stage. The passenger door opened, and an officer stepped out.

I had never seen an American colonel before. With frosty eyes and a trim figure in his well-pressed but surprisingly unadorned uniform, he exuded a sense of quiet control. Every American present saluted as the colonel mounted the stage and stepped behind the podium, followed by an entourage of four low-ranking officers. One man adjusted the microphone, making the boxy speaker facing us pop and hiss. An army major stood to the side with his own microphone, acting as interpreter.

"At ease," he said. "I am Lieutenant-Colonel William Vogel. At oh one hundred hours, I took command of Camp Conrad. Everything that happens, both here and in the American garrison, comes under my watch, and I take my duties seriously. For that reason, there will be a few rule changes affecting your daily routine. All these changes meet with the standards of the Geneva Convention and are in effect in all other internment camps on American soil."

New rules? I watched for any reaction from my comrades, but most seemed as baffled as I was. Probably, this colonel felt the need to exert his newfound authority. In all likelihood, he would retreat to his officer's club to celebrate within the hour.

"Guards will continue to observe from outside the fence. In addition to headcounts, there will be regular barracks inspections and periodic examinations of all structures inside the camp. Security is a priority. It has come to my attention that rules have not always been followed. Contraband has found its way into the compounds. And some prisoners have achieved powerful positions affecting the well-being of others. This will no longer be tolerated."

"Why the big change?" a man nearby shouted.

"Make the barracks warmer," another called.

Vogel swept his gray eyes over two thousand former soldiers. He seemed confident in his intent and uninterested in the surly comments yelled at him.

"A list of contraband will be posted in all sleeping quarters. Guards will remove forbidden items immediately upon discovery without punishment. My office will also post rules for your safety. The United States Army will continue to make your stay here as comfortable as possible. But this is a prisoner of war camp, and my office will follow all procedures to the letter."

"Will we get back anything taken?"

"How often will the inspections be?"

Other prisoners shouted questions.

Vogel held up a hand. "All inquiries will be answered in due time. There is one more point I wish to make concerning the power structure that has arisen within both compounds. This is important."

Guards blew whistles to quiet our ranks. "*Achtung!*" a voice ordered.

"I am now addressing those who have made themselves the authorities within this compound. This includes liaison officers." Vogel's tone became harsh. His eyes no longer surveyed the ranks but looked to the back where Reinhardt and his Inner Circle stood.

"All German officers. Let there be no mistake. No matter what your rank is, it will be lower than any American guard. You will follow guards' orders immediately, without comment, and to the letter. And you will be responsible for the safety of your men. If any prisoner causes harm or threatens another prisoner, that action will rest on your shoulders. Military police will investigate all reports of violence or threats of violence. We will treat any loss of life as suspicious and will transfer those found guilty to higher security facilities. Finally, National Socialist symbols, such as swastikas or portraits of Adolph Hitler will be considered contraband."

This last comment drew considerable comment.

"*Nein!*" one voice yelled, adding a curse. I recognized it as Drosselmeyer. "You can't come in here. I forbid it!" The sergeant emphasized his last words with a string of foul language. The guards close to Drosselmeyer brought him forward. The sergeant breathed heavily; his face contorted into an angry mask. "Fat Yankee pigs!" He tried to shake off the men holding him, but they held him fast. A third soldier hustled up the platform steps, saluted, and spoke to the lieutenant-colonel. The microphone, however, broadcasted his words for all to hear. "The man smells of whiskey."

Whiskey is the same word in German as it is in English. "Is there liquor in the camp?" a man beside me asked.

"The sergeant has been hinting at a surprise for weeks," another prisoner said.

Vogel raised his brows but otherwise showed no expression. "Put the prisoner in irons," he said. "And find that still." Realizing his words carried to the crowd, the colonel held his arms high. "Quiet, everyone."

But the crowd of disappointed men grew angrier. A rock sailed past the commander's head, missing him by centimeters. Several prisoners advanced to the stage. Vogel made a gesture to the tower—a staccato burst of automatic fire ripped through the air. Prisoners kissed the ground. I, too, threw myself to the earth. The nearest watchtower guard swung his machine gun around, pointing its barrel at us. A prisoner lying by me prayed. I held my breath, waiting for the final act.

Vogel strolled to the microphone. "On your feet. Now that I have your attention, these will be your instructions: you will remain standing while the guards conduct a search of the compound. They will seize any alcohol and destroy the equipment used in its production. All other contraband will be seized. As soon as the inspection is completed, you can resume your usual activities."

There were only a few good hiding places large enough to accommodate the stove, containers, and lengths of pipe for a distillery: the back of a kitchen, behind the false wall of a warehouse, a large root cellar. All of these would be easy to find. Twenty minutes later, a lieutenant jogged to the stage, saluted the colonel, and presented him with a note. Vogel covered the microphone with his hand to keep any remarks from reaching us. Finally, he dismissed the young officer. His interpreter stepped to the microphone. "Before I release you, I repeat—you are expected to follow all posted rules. The better you cooperate, the less intrusion you will feel from guard inspections. It means your clothing will remain folded and not tossed on the floor, and hours of labor on art projects won't go to waste. It's up to you. Carry on." Vogel exited the stage, climbed into his jeep and left the camp. Behind him, officers and a group of guards began to dismantle the stage.

The huge crowd scattered. I meandered back to the music building and stared down the open cellar door to our brewery, sniffing the heavy malt. Drosselmeyer had closed that door during the siren.

I descended. Beneath the single bulb, now lit again, lay the remains of the brewery. Barrels sat broken, jagged holes punched in their sides. Undrinkable brew shimmered under the dim light. Pieces of wood floated about, like toy boats on a dark pond along with pieces of apple. Even the copper pots and the stoves were dented beyond use. Eight weeks of work—erased.

No winter ale. No hard cider. No brewing at all.

I smiled.

Spring couldn't come fast enough.

Chapter Eighteen

Now that Virginia Powell held my forged letter, it would only be a matter of time before my plan to reclaim Novak's place in history and possibly find his killer would unravel. When I returned to the reunion, Emily had already dismissed the group. I tried to catch Drosselmeyer's attention without being obvious, but the old sergeant refused to glance in my direction. I did catch up to Stecklein, who trudged down the hall, making slow progress with his heavy walking stick. Had he ever used it as a weapon? "Sergeant, may I speak with you?" I asked, keeping a wary eye on his cane.

The big man swiveled his bull neck, giving me a one-eyed stare. "I'm listening."

"I want to ask you about an incident that took place after the soccer field shooting. You were escorting a prisoner to his trial—Private Brian Novak."

"I remember. The insubordinate one."

I let that pass. Of the men surrounding Novak, Stecklein had the means and opportunity to kill him. A dangerous man in his time, but slow and lumbering today. "You knew he and I were comrades?"

"I've seen you together. We can talk in my room." His throaty rumble filled me with unease.

"I'd rather talk in the hall."

He gave me an accusatory glare. "Still afraid,

Rohling? That time is long gone."

"Maybe for some. Tell me about Novak's last minutes. You would be the one to know."

"Hard to remember."

I grabbed his cane hand. His thick wrist reminded me of a tree limb. "Try."

"Not while I'm standing." He motioned to a couple of chairs facing each other. We took our seats. Stecklein hooked his walking stick over a chair within easy reach. He took a puff off his inhaler, giving me a hooded gaze. "Where do I start?"

"When you retrieved Novak. Was that at the stockade?"

"An officer told me I'd find him there."

"Which officer was that?"

"I don't remember. Does it matter?"

It did, but I let it pass. "What happened next?"

"I marched him to his barracks to get his field uniform. The man smelled and needed a shower. My superiors demanded he be presentable for his court sentencing."

"Were you with him the whole time?"

His eyes narrowed as if I offended him. "I didn't watch him every minute. Stood guard at the entrance. That was sufficient. Novak did take his time getting his uniform, so I rousted him out and escorted him to the bathhouse."

"What then?"

"I stood outside, waiting. The private gave me his word he would not escape. His court wouldn't start for another thirty minutes, so we had ample time."

"Were there others inside the shower building beside Novak?"

His focus on me sharpened. "I gave the building a cursory inspection. Easy enough to do with no stalls between the showers and no doors for the toilets. Novak was the only occupant."

"Did anyone enter while you stood guard?"

"Two men entered the *toilette* side and left by the same door."

I rubbed my temple, wondering how to proceed. Stecklein's story sounded reasonable, so far. "When did you suspect something amiss?"

"Twenty minutes after he entered, I heard water still running. I ran inside and found a belt around the private's neck."

A vivid picture of my friend flared in my mind. "What did you do?"

"My orders were to report anything unusual to my superiors. I double-timed it to the officer's building. By the time I returned with two other men to retrieve the body, the Americans had taken him aboard a truck."

"You left Novak unattended?"

"The man was dead. I despised him, but a man's death under my watch would be a stain on my record. You think I killed him?" Stecklein's hand inched toward the cane.

I tensed, ready to bolt outside his reach. "*Nein, mein Herr*. I'm trying to understand what happened." I didn't want to believe Stecklein, but his story remained solid. If Stecklein wasn't guilty, then I had no clue who his killer might be. Either the old sergeant held some secret, or I wasn't asking the right questions. What could I be missing? The killer had to be waiting for him inside the shower building. I leaned forward. "If a man chose to hide in the bathhouse, how could he do it?"

"Why would—" His brows raised; the sergeant was a lumbering, slow-talking fat man, but he knew the intent of my question. "Looking for bogeymen?"

"Humor me."

He crossed his massive arms. "No idea. You tell me."

I bent my head in consternation. "With no obvious hiding places inside the building, my mystery person must have discovered a way to blend with the background. Was that possible?"

Stecklein reached for his cane. "Specters cannot kill, Rohling. I hope you find your answer." He heaved to his feet. I accompanied him, keeping pace with his slow hobble. I pictured the old shower building in my mind with its stark white walls and wooden roof slanting down past the concrete walls. Narrow passageways separated the dressing room, showers, and lavatory. Each room could be inspected with a glance. I kept circling that image, searching for hidden places but found none. We halted at Stecklein's door, and he pulled a card from his pocket. "Good day, Herr Rohling," he said.

"Thank you for your time, Herr Stecklein." I turned to head back to my room.

"There is one place your phantom could have escaped my notice," he said.

I faced him, startled by his words. "Where is that?"

"A man could lie atop the concrete wall. The best spot would be in the corners where the rooms meet. He could have worn brown instead of the usual blue. Like hiding in plain sight."

"Wouldn't the PV lettering give him away?"

"A simple matter of covering it with mud."

"How could he escape without exiting the doors?"

"It may have been a tight squeeze, but he could have dropped outside, between ceiling and wall. If he slipped out the back side, chances were other prisoners wouldn't have noticed."

"Wouldn't the tower guards see him?"

"Possibly. But if he didn't stray past the wire, the guards would do nothing."

"That makes a lot of sense. Why are you telling me this? I kept coming up empty."

"I could have fallen off the van. Your son helped me." He opened his room door. "I don't remember looking up when I made my inspection. Your man could have been there."

"Thank you," I said.

"It is no proof. You're wasting your time."

"It's my time to waste."

"I feel sorry for you." He shuffled inside and closed the door.

I hurried back to my room, finding it open a few centimeters. Worried that the thief returned, I peeked inside.

Horst sat at the room desk, rearranging papers in his portable file. On the bed lay his laptop. "Hello, Papa. How did your reunion go?"

I told him about the day's events, omitting any reference to Novak or the letter. "Tomorrow, we will view the old prison grounds and the construction of the new museum. They are even building an authentic-looking guard tower, complete with spotlight and phony machine gun," I said.

"I'd like to see that." My son continued poking through his papers. Did he hear anything I said? "Papa, were you looking in my files? These pages are out of order."

"Oh, that." I hung my head, hoping to look convincing. "The papers spilled out when I moved your case earlier today."

"Some managed to slip under the bed. But it's all here, I think. Keep the case upright if you need to move it again. A lot of work has gone into these reports."

I assured him I would. "And how was your day?"

"Fruitful. I sent some emails and received some updated documents. The librarian knew German. She said it wasn't uncommon to hear German in restaurants around town. We talked a lot about food when I should have been working. I need to make up the time this evening."

"Be careful. Americans have a way of working into your thoughts," I teased him.

He clapped me on the back. "You should know."

"Will you be coming to the banquet tonight?"

"Not tonight," he said. "But I promise to go tomorrow."

"We can share a pint before the hotel tavern closes tonight if you wish. I can introduce you to a few of the old comrades."

"I'd like that." Horst glanced at his watch. "You better freshen up. It's after five thirty."

I showered and changed into a dark brown sports coat and white dress shirt. To Horst's consternation, I wore a pair of loose-fitting dungarees with suspenders. "You're not wearing the slacks Caroline got for you?" Horst asked.

"I'll be sitting at a table with a bunch of near-sighted old men. No one will care. Besides, I want to be comfortable."

"*Mutta* would have had something to say about that."

Della most certainly would have. "Call me an eccentric old widower."

"More like a stubborn old man." At least Horst said that with a smile.

"Same thing." I slipped on a pair of broken-in Hush Puppies and combed back my still damp gray hair. "I'm leaving early to meet a friend. Don't work too late."

"I hope you're not stirring up old romances." This time Horst didn't smile.

"He's an old comrade."

Horst plugged his computer to an adapter. "Have a good visit."

I strolled out the hotel's back exit, followed the parking lot, and soon found a row of metal dumpsters in the corner of a crumbling section of cement. "Drosselmeyer?" I called.

No answer.

I stepped around a jagged depression and peered behind the smelly metal boxes. A pack of his brand of cigarettes lay crumpled on the ground. "Paul?" A cold prickle of worry touched the base of my neck.

"Sergeant!"

He was supposed to be here.

What happened?

Chapter Nineteen

17 March to 21 April 1944

Our first trip back to the Henning farm in 1944 occurred on Saint Patrick's day. Oskar Kimmel needled me that morning as we climbed onto the gravel road a kilometer away from the family farm. "Can't wait to see Fräulein Henning again," he said, casting an eye in my direction. "A fine-looking filly with inviting hips. Capable of squeezing out many fine children." The cold turned my breath into mist, but it could easily have been smoke, due to the heat rising inside me. Emily drove the truck that morning with Private Nichols in the passenger seat. I gritted my teeth, wanting to lash back.

"Keep those thoughts to yourself," I said. "If Nichols hears any talk like that, you'll be out of work."

"Nichols doesn't know German."

"Don't be so sure. The Americans know a phrase or two. They don't have to know every word to understand your meaning."

Kimmel leaned back, his voice loud. "Rohling is jealous. I saw him staring at fräulein last fall. I think he's got eyes for her."

"Believe what you want, but don't ruin this job for the rest of us."

"Same to you, friend. She is a comely one. Would probably roll in the hay with anyone who wants to take her."

Both Adler and Goetz remained quiet as we drove. Kimmel's words stirred old feelings I tried to keep hidden all winter. I'd been looking forward to this day for weeks, but now that it arrived, all I could think of was the discovery I made just twelve hours ago. A revelation about Brian Novak.

Since his death, five months ago, no one had ever found Novak's suicide note. But I found his last message while packing for the work camp last night.

Before lights out, I stuffed my seabag with work clothes, shoes, and a blanket. Not much room remained when I found a German-English dictionary tucked in my bedroll. A paper from the book slipped to the floor.

Jagged and bunched together, Novak's words would haunt me for years.

Henry,

Sgt Stecklein pulled me from the stockade today, telling me I had to be in uniform during my trial. I'm being tried in a Nazi court. Not sure where. In any case, Sgt S said if I were found guilty, the court would carry out my sentence immediately.

Sgt is standing outside now while I get my uniform. Then we will proceed to the shower building. The court wants me presentable before sentencing. If I'm to die, it will be as a soldier. Not a coward.

I'm hiding this note so only you will find it. Please know that I am proud of my country, but not of those in charge. They will destroy our land, but they won't destroy me. Not without a fight.

S is coming.

BN

Most of the other prisoners had already settled in

their bunks. With trembling fingers, I stuffed the letter down the side of the bag. My friend's final words echoed my worst fears. *They will destroy our land, but they won't destroy me. Not without a fight.* My thoughts flashed to his body hanging—and to his head wound. Though he failed to survive, Novak did not succumb quietly to his fate.

Who could I show this note to? Who would see the conclusion I saw? The letter held the key to an inconvenient crime, yet I could do nothing. All the old fears of forfeiting my chance to see Emily came back. A stomach-wrenching spasm of fear and self-loathing hit me as the realization struck. I would remain silent, but I would not destroy the letter.

Tires turning onto the Henning's driveway brought me back to the present. Emily drove to the side of the barn where Mr. Henning stood over his harrow. He straightened, stretching his back as the truck came to a halt, and we jumped to the ground. Kimmel stayed with the pickup, talking with Nichols, probably wondering what we were doing today. I approached Emily who sat with her mother. Both cut wedges from seed potatoes and threw the pieces into a laundry tub in front of them.

Nichols conferred with Henning. I whipped off my cap before the two ladies and nodded a greeting. "*Guten morgen*, Mrs. Henning, Miss Emily. It's good to be working this spring, again. I hope the crops will do well this year."

Emily gave me a shy smile, but Mrs. Henning intervened. "We're pleased you came back this spring, Mr. Rohling. Check with my husband as I think you'll be helping him today." She turned to her daughter. "We've got to finish this bag. Your father wants them planted before the end of the day."

I backed away, getting the hint.

"Rohling. Over here," Nichols called me.

"Yes, sir." I hustled to the tractor where the guard, Mr. Henning, and the other stood by the tractor.

"Rohling, Adler, and Goetz will plant potatoes," the guard said. "Kimmel will help the women finish the cutting. Any questions?"

"Yes, sir," I said. "What makes Kimmel so special that he gets to work with the women?"

"Luck of the draw." The guard gave me a sidelong glance. "Got a problem with that?"

"No, sir," I said.

"Don't worry, my friend," Kimmel said in German. "I'll see the young one is well-protected." Adler and Goetz gave me an uneasy look, but I refused to react to Kimmel's taunt.

The guard tossed a rake to Adler. "You cover the potatoes, Rohling plants, and Goetz carries the tub. We clear?"

"How far apart do I plant?" I asked.

Henning held his palms out. "Space the slices about eight inches with the eyes pointing up."

"Get started then." Nichols backed away as Henning got in his seat, revved the engine, and guided the tractor and harrow toward the untouched field. There, he lowered the blades and drove on. Behind him the ground turned over, leaving a shallow trench.

And so began a grueling day of bending and stretching my back. By noon, I became practiced in dropping the pieces into the five-inch depression, shuffling down the rows at a slow, but steady pace. Adler had to make quick use of the rake to keep up with me. After a short midday meal of cold sandwiches, Adler and I switched jobs to complete the planting that day.

I hoped for a cool glass of Frau Henning's tea and her oatmeal cookies after work, but Nichols ordered us to board the Henning pickup. Emily already sat behind the wheel, and we journeyed back to the field camp. That evening, we ate canned rations, washed ourselves with heated water from camp stoves, and retired before lights out. A full day with little leisure. What happened to the camaraderie we had last year?

For the next five weeks, I worked on land Henning rented from a neighbor, more than two kilometers from the family farm. Each morning, Mrs. Henning gave either Adler or I a paper bag containing sandwiches, and Henning drove us there, outlining what we needed to do. For the rest of the day we weeded, removed stones, brush, and trees, or whatever the job required to prepare the ground for corn planting. In the evening, Mrs. Henning retrieved us and drove back to the family farm where we drank a glass of tea or lemonade before we headed back to camp.

Compared to last fall, I hardly saw Emily—only during the drives to and from camp. Was there stricter enforcement of the "no fraternizing" rule? If so, why did Nichols allow Kimmel to worm his way into the family? Would I ever be able to talk with her again? To hold her hand? To place a gentle kiss on her lips? None of those things seemed possible.

One spring evening at field camp, I joined Adler and Klaus Berger, a corporal who worked on the Swope farm, for a few hands of poker. We used chocolate bars in our camp rations as money. To my consternation,

Kimmel joined the game as well. I won an early round with a full house, but lost the next three hands, forfeiting my winnings. I cared little for candy, but it came in handy as a form of currency. Kimmel had a sweet tooth, and this gave me an idea.

We each anted with a chocolate bar. Berger passed five cards to each player and placed the deck aside. "Your bet, Kimmel."

Kimmel glanced at his hand, then shoved a wrapped bar to the center. "Bet one."

I fanned out my cards, making a show of studying my hand. Nothing but garbage. I would lose this round, but I wasn't about to let Kimmel win. "I'm in. And raise you by two." I added three candies to the pot. At this rate, I'd have to fold soon.

Adler pushed one bar back to me. "We agreed to limit raises to one each round."

"Of course," I said. "I forgot."

Adler and Kimmel met the bet, and Berger threw down his cards. "I'll let you gentlemen fight this hand out." He retrieved the deck and turned to Kimmel. "How many cards do you wish to draw?"

Kimmel pondered his hand, licking his bottom lip, then tossed a couple of cards. "Two."

I slid one card to the table. It didn't matter which. Berger passed my drawcard. "Thank you."

Adler took four. Berger nodded to Kimmel. "It's your bet."

"I pass." Kimmel glanced at me. "Well, go on. Bet."

"I will. Betting one."

Adler stirred in his seat. "Oh my," he sighed. "I'll meet your bet, Henry, and raise one more."

The table went silent for a moment. I didn't expect Adler to come out swinging. Kimmel leaned back on his stool, holding his cards close to his chest.

Berger snapped his fingers. "It's two to stay in, Kimmel. What's your poison?"

He hesitated. That gave him away. I was not good at poker, but Kimmel was worse. "I'm in." He pushed his two remaining chocolates to the center.

"I'm out," I said.

Berger gave me an odd look. "Show your cards," he said.

Adler flipped his cards over. "A straight."

Kimmel lowered his hand. "Two pair. Kings and aces." He shook his head in disbelief.

"Looks like Adler takes the pot." I pushed my cards facedown to the deck and rose from my seat. "I'm turning in."

Kimmel also stood, flipping over my cards. "*Mist*. You had nothing!"

"I bluffed, and I lost." I walked away from the table to seek my cot, but Kimmel followed me, yanking me around to face him.

"You deliberately raised the betting just to run me out of the game."

"Don't play if it bothers you to lose," I said.

"Oh, we'll see how you feel about losing. You're probably wondering why the old man has you working so far away. A little hint planted in the guard's ear was all it took—how infatuated you were with the young fräulein, and then Nichols told that straw-sucking buffoon. Why you're still here is beyond me."

I took a step toward Kimmel, imagining him writhing on the ground. "Why, you conniving jackal!"

He backed away from me. "You hit me, and you will never see that tasty morsel again. But don't worry, friend. I'll give you progress reports of my conquest. Especially the noises she makes when I poke her in the barn."

I took two deep breaths and lowered my fists. Kimmel knew how to provoke me. "What is your point?"

"Who says there has to be a point? Maybe I just like to see you twist in the wind." He gave me a self-satisfied grin.

"Why are you so angry?" I peered at him, trying to assess his motives. "The first time we met, you wanted to be friends. And now you're obsessed with taunts and backstabbing."

"What d-did become of that friendship?" Kimmel's words took on a mocking tone. "An empty p-promise. You shunned me like all the rest. Well, I've ch-changed all that now."

That stutter again. I had avoided him since that first encounter, spending my time with Novak until I came to work for the Hennings. Kimmel came as well. Though I disliked him, he kept appearing around me like a bad *pfennig*. I could only conclude he reveled in being a nuisance.

"I'm sorry we couldn't find common interests. I've never been interested in becoming a party member. I suspect you wish to be."

"You think you know me with your little insights." He stepped forward, thrusting a finger in my chest. "You have no idea."

"I probably don't," I said, stifling thoughts of breaking his forefinger. "But now that the worst of the

National Socialists have been transferred away, tensions inside camp have eased considerably."

"Think so? You live in a shell, Rohling. A few of the true believers are still there. They are content to wait for our day of liberation. It's you, and the other doubters, who will pay the price in the end."

I knocked aside his finger. He stood taller than me by four or five centimeters, but I refused to bow to his intimidation. "Stay away from me. Stay out of my life. Or you and I will have a reckoning. I promise you."

With that, I stalked back to my cot. The echo of his laughter haunted me well into the night.

My exile continued, but knowing that Kimmel's half-baked plan didn't fully succeed made it endurable. Complaining about my treatment could backfire against me. Someday, I would prove myself trustworthy again. At least Henning still allowed me to work. I had to keep showing the Americans it didn't bother me. Acting indifferent nearly cost me an opportunity to see Emily.

On April twenty-first, Mrs. Henning retrieved Adler and me at the end of the workday and brought us back, as usual. She stopped the pickup close to the farmhouse, jumped from the cab, and bustled through the back door. The aroma of baked bread hung in the air. "Mr. Adler," she called through the screen door, "have my husband bring Mr. Kimmel and Mr. Goetz out to the truck. Mr. Rohling, clean the tools and put them away in the barn."

"I'll be glad to get the other men," I said.

She came outside again. "Do as I say, Mr. Rohling. There's a jar of oil, some rags, and a wire brush on top of the tool rack. The brush is for scraping rust spots. Make sure the job gets done. We'll be leaving in twenty minutes. Don't let me have to honk twice."

I gathered an armload of shovels, garden rakes, and hoes and headed for the hand pump. It took little time to wash off the dirt, then slip inside the barn. A wire brush set on the shelf, but I saw no spots on the equipment. I set the tools aside and retrieved the oily rag.

"Can I help you with that?" a voice teased behind me.

I jumped. Emily giggled holding a hand to her mouth. "I thought you German soldiers had nerves of steel."

"I—we do—in combat. I'm a bit outside my element." Emily stood in overalls, grinning at me, her auburn hair tied in a ponytail and partially hidden by a bandana, she held a manure fork. Dirt smudged her cheeks. At least I hoped it was dirt. She looked a mess, but I didn't care.

"What are you doing here?" I stammered.

"I've been working, silly." She leaned the fork against the barn wall. "And waiting. Mom said you'd be along."

"Did she plan this?" My thoughts flashed to Mrs. Henning's instructions about the tools.

"Partly. I asked her for help." Emily looked downcast for a moment, then peered at me with a serious expression, her eyes glistening. "Henry," she said in a small voice. "I missed you."

I rushed forward to embrace her. Holding her lithe frame filled me with joy and excitement. Our mouths crept closer to one another. The anticipation of touching her lips filled me with fear and longing. Dread and desire. Her smudged skin smelled faintly of scented soap and sweet earth. And when our lips met, Emily tasted of fine red wine. I pressed her to me, surprised at my boldness, wanting more, but not wishing to appear eager. I strove to remain the gentleman, yet an urgency seized me that begged for release.

Take her. Now.

I must remain responsible.

She waited for you.

That would be selfish.

This time may never come again. Don't hesitate.

I kissed where her neck and shoulder met. She surrendered a small moan. Strong hands gripped the back of my head. Our lips parted, and her scorching tongue ignited me.

Oh, what a sweet invasion that was.

I wanted to remember every sensation of this moment, the delectable bond of our lips, the beating of her heart against mine, her fingers caressing my neck, the breathless yearning for more.

I tore my lips from hers and squeezed her shoulders, trying to control the heat building inside me. Emily gasped as well, hugging me so tight I could feel her nails digging in my back. I held her, reluctant to give ground, yet knowing I had to. "I'm glad your mother allowed this to happen."

She glanced at the barn's closed doors and stepped back. "Last winter my parents found a letter I tried to send to you. It didn't bother Mom, but Daddy grew angry. 'You're a grown woman,' he told me. 'But you're still under my roof. Don't get any romantic notions about this soldier. He may be likable enough, but he is still the enemy.' "

I released her. "He only wants to protect you," I said.

"There's more, Henry. On your first day of work, Private Nichols pulled Daddy aside to talk."

Kimmel's whispers to Nichols. "I know about that."

"But do you know all of it?"

I didn't know for sure. "Tell me."

Emily drew a hand to her mouth, biting a knuckle. "Private Nichols told Daddy that you wanted to…" A look of horror shadowed her face. "I can't say the word. He offered to replace you with another prisoner."

I let out a sigh. I wanted to touch her again but knew I couldn't. "I'd never do such a thing." A hollowness opened inside my gut. Oh yes, I could have. Only minutes ago, fleeting thoughts filled me with Emily and me falling to the ground and making love. But now, a shadow swept over my fantasy, leaving me ashamed.

"I wish I could prove to your father I'm better than that."

"I know you are. Even Daddy knows you wouldn't. That's why he kept you on, though he's stubborn about keeping us apart."

"But not your mother?"

"She guessed the truth. 'You're in love with that boy,' she told me after she read my letter. I couldn't deny it."

I imagined the two women talking. "Your mother knows you well."

"She surprises me. She said that as long as I acted properly, she would arrange these meetings. Daddy is not big on feelings, and all my little brother thinks about is hunting. There's no one to talk to but you."

I smiled at the thought. "Thank you. That's nice to

hear."

"Mom told me one more thing, but I don't believe her. Maybe you know." Her eyes grew large and fearful, like seeing a horrible event.

"Tell me." What could frighten this young woman?

"When this war ends, what happens to you? Do you really have to go back home?"

Every prisoner in camp wondered what would happen when the war ended. Opinions ranged from a quiet trip back home to firing squads should the Allies lose. I could not tell her that. "If the Americans win, we will likely return home."

Emily narrowed her eyes. "There is no 'if.' We will win the war. We have the best equipment and manpower. Nothing else is acceptable."

Her response stunned me. "Manpower? Like the soldiers at the prisoner camp?" I knew I could be making a mistake, but this uninformed girl needed to be taught a lesson. Apologies will come later. "Your home is isolated, protected by untrained, middle-aged men pretending to be soldiers. They'd be a menace to their own side on the battlefield. Imagine what would happen if a full German brigade—four thousand resourceful, determined commandos—could land in this part of the country. They could raid small towns for supplies and use civilian vehicles to stay mobile. Terror would sweep across the Midwest. The population would panic. Politicians would wet themselves, demanding that the military protect the interior. Thousands of GIs would be redeployed to fight on their own land. Generals would have to delay overseas operations, throwing off timetables. Britain would question the caliber of American leadership. Morale would falter. And

Germany would gleefully strike back—all because of a brigade of fighting Deutsch soldiers are willing to forfeit their lives. That is the true meaning of manpower."

"We would stop you in the end."

I passed a hand across my brow. The mental image of soldiers mowing down civilians left me shaken. "Of course, your soldiers will prevail. But the point is how a minimum of men could disrupt and challenge, requiring a major force to stop it."

Emily gave me a watchful look. "Would you fight to the death?"

I lowered my head, thankful she still talked to me. "I fight to survive. Nothing more."

"I don't understand you, Henry Rohling. At times, you seem hard and calculating. And other times you're thoughtful and sensitive. Which one is really you?"

Outside, a truck horn blared.

"Both, I suppose. Your mother said I should listen for the horn." I moved to the side door with my hand on the knob.

"Wait!"

I shook my head. "I can't stay."

"Answer one more question. When you do go back home. Would you come back—for me?"

I smiled, imagining Emily as a shining beacon, my lighthouse in a stormy world.

"Of course I would."

Chapter Twenty

22 April to 6 June 1944

My rendezvous with Emily were few and far between. Mr. Henning's work assignments kept me on his rented land most of the time. We lost a week of work during late May when a wave of thunderstorms rolled across the country. During those rainy days, we passed the time in camp. Other days, we did odd jobs around the farm, waiting for the fields to dry. During those days, Mrs. Henning still found clever ways for Emily and me to see each other for a few precious minutes at a time.

By the first of June, the fields dried enough for us to return to work. That first week we began the weeding of sweet corn. The plants stood a meter tall or more. I got used to the scratchy stalks and the ladybugs, but the larger beetles and ticks gave me that creepy-crawly feeling. On Tuesday evening—the sixth—Mrs. Henning sent me to the barn to clean and oil hand tools. I learned later what a momentous day it was for the world. It was a fateful day for Emily and me as well.

She stood just inside the double doors, waiting for my arrival.

I embraced her and nibbled around a small birthmark on her neck I hadn't noticed before. She pushed on my chest. "Stop, Henry. I want to talk."

Surprised, I stepped back. "Have I offended you?"

"It's not that." She looked down, squashing an unfortunate bug. "We need to decide about the future."

Her statement baffled me. "What's to decide? I work and wait for the next time we meet. What else is there?"

"I mean after the war."

"That could be years from now."

She bit her lip like a small child keeping a juicy secret. "Just listen to me. When it's all over, you should come here. As soon as possible. We can marry. Live in town. Or a city farther away like Abilene or Junction City." Her words tumbled out. Quick and fast. She had contemplated this for a while, but I could barely keep pace with her thoughts. "You can get work teaching German at the high school. Once you've learned about sports, you could be a coach. Teaching the basics of basketball or football to students is a prestigious job in a small town."

I hardly understood a word she said. Not wishing for her to see my look of consternation, I drew her to me. "Wouldn't you want to live close to your parents?"

"No..." She tapped my shoulder. "That would be awkward. Even living in Conrad could be uncomfortable. I can fit in wherever we go. For you, teaching and coaching sports is the best way to make a living."

"Wouldn't I need to attend a university to become a teacher?"

Emily shrugged. At least I think she did. Her head lay on my shoulders. "I suppose so. Living in a college town would be exciting."

"And expensive. How would we pay for this?"

Again, that dismissive shrug. "I could work, too. It won't be easy, but we should try."

"I'm good with my hands, and I know brewing. Best to start with that."

She pulled back, regarding me. "Kansas is a dry state. No one brews beer around here."

"You can't buy beer?"

"You can, but Daddy says it's not very strong on purpose. Still, people drink it."

"I suppose brewing is out then." Big Nellie sat in its spot not far away. "I can still fix a truck or a tractor."

"That would get us by." She seemed distracted, her eyes straying to the small-paned windows of the side door. "Daddy's coming! He can't see us here together!"

I looked about for a place to hide. If Mr. Henning discovered me, I'd never see Emily again.

"Go out the back door." She pointed to the exit that opened to the woodpile and Sassy's grave. "Hurry. He's almost here."

I dashed to the rear exit she indicated, but the massive delivery truck stood in the way. I ducked around the vehicle and reached for the back door when Henning rolled open the double doors and entered. Escaping without detection seemed impossible. Fearing the worst, I peered around the big truck to watch the exchange between father and daughter.

"Hello, Daddy," Emily said, oiling the shovel I used that day.

Henning stepped back, surprised. "I expected to see one of the workers here."

"Which worker is that?"

He stared hard at Emily. "You know perfectly well which worker I'm talking about."

"I can't help it if I have feelings for him."

"You better end this schoolgirl crush, or I'll end this affair myself."

"Why haven't you?" A hint of defiance edged her voice. I bit my lip. Be careful, young lady.

"I don't need you smarting back…" Henning took a step forward. The side of his neck pulsed in the shadowy light. Was he going to strike his daughter? I tensed, feeling a surge of giddiness radiating through me, the same feeling I got before battle.

Wait.

Henning looked around, then grabbed a couple of wooden crates near the milking stalls and dropped them in front of the truck. He motioned for Emily to sit while he seated himself. The farmer took out his pipe, patting his pockets. "Can't believe the government is rationing tobacco."

Emily looked about as well, perhaps wondering if I still remained inside the barn. "What's wrong, Daddy?"

"Nothing's wrong. Probably me." He peered at her. "Until last summer, it was easy to convince myself you were still a little girl that needed protecting. Then I hired those boys from the camp. Now I'm seeing you through their eyes. Your mother's right. You're a grown woman now, able to make your own decisions. She says I need to accept that."

Emily touched his arm. "I'll always be your little girl, Daddy. No matter how old I am."

"I should have talked to you about young men a long time ago." He rubbed his temple, clearly uncomfortable. "I suspect you've seen this Rohling boy even though I told you not to."

Emily didn't hesitate. "Three or four times."

"You have no idea what that boy's intentions are. He—all of them—don't belong here. He could turn you against us."

"Henry's a good man, Daddy. He's a soldier, but that doesn't mean he's the enemy."

Henning pursed his lips, swaying oh-so-slightly where he sat. "You may have a point. I've talked to him. Seen his work. The man never complains about anything I throw at him. A steady hand and a natural-born grease monkey to boot. So—for now—I'm still keeping him on, though I came close that first day he came back."

"Why didn't you?"

"I go by what I see. Not what a guard tells me."

"I understand, Daddy."

"I don't believe you do. Don't fall for him. Rohling will have to go home after the war. And it may be sooner than later. You've heard the news bulletins. Our boys are storming the French coast right now. Think about it, American GIs are in the Germans' backyard. Soon, they'll advance to Paris. Anything can happen after that. Roosevelt is set to talk about it tonight."

France invaded? I sank to my knees, dazed by the news. Our officers had always told us the Americans could never invade the French coast. The navy had mined every beach and heavy timbers would rip the belly off any ship reckless enough to land troops. Trained radio operators were constantly monitoring signal traffic from British bases. Yet despite these precautions, the Amis and Tommies were gathering outside our borders.

"Does anyone know how soon the war will end?" Emily asked.

"Too early to tell. The Germans are putting up a fight. Announcers are positive our soldiers will succeed, but the gains are slow. The same news is repeated over and over. I can't help but think about Josh in times like these."

"I miss Josh. What if he became a prisoner?"

Henning grunted. "Don't think about that. It's not going to happen."

They remained silent for a few moments. Henning rose to his feet. "Josh will come home. We'll go crazy if we think anything different. Now, go help your mother with supper. I'll drive these boys back to their camp. And one more thing."

Emily stopped in the doorway. "Yes, Daddy?"

"Henry Rohling will break your heart. He may not mean to. But he will. If he has family, they might not let him come back. Even if he wanted to, our government could disallow it."

"You're wrong, Daddy. Henry promised to come back, and he will." She dashed out the door, her running footsteps diminishing outside. Henning watched her from the doorway. After the screen door slammed, he faced where I hid.

"You can come out now, Rohling. Time to call it a day. Sit in the cab. I want to talk to you on the way back."

We boarded the truck a few minutes later. Private Nichols rode in back. I imagined the topic would be Emily. If circumstances were different, we could have resolved our differences, or even become friends. As it were, the gulf between us spanned as wide as the Atlantic.

I remained silent on the trip, listening to the push-button radio. The sound was low but discernible. After a puzzling advertisement about dish soap, trumpets and horns blared for a couple of minutes, then an announcer cut in. "We hope you enjoyed *The Leiber Brothers Variety Show*. And now, we present the President of the United States." I leaned forward to catch every word, but Henning punched a button, turning the radio off.

"No reason for you to know more than you already do. Though, I'm sure every shortwave radio in Europe is listening."

"Is Mr. Roosevelt talking about the invasion?"

"Every network on the dial is talking about the invasion. I won't be missing anything, though. Millie will tell me what the president said when I get back home."

"You're fortunate to have few worries, sir."

"You think so? I'm banking every dollar I've got on that land you've been working. I need you and the others to come through for me."

"We'll do our best, sir."

"I know you will, son. Dammit, if you weren't German, I wouldn't care at all if you saw Emily."

He called me *son* and then cursed me. "Are we related?"

Henning stared straight ahead. "Sorry. Figure of speech. Means I care. Don't take it literally."

"Yessir."

"One more thing. Drop the 'sir.' It's just the two of us talking here. No one else needs to know about this conversation."

"Fair enough."

His fingers drummed on the steering wheel. "I got a headstrong daughter. If she thinks you're coming back, there's nothing I can do to change her mind. She's a lot like Millie. I love them both, but often, I'm more comfortable looking after the farm than being in the house. Point is, there is nothing I won't do to keep my family safe and intact. You get my drift?"

"Loud and clear. You defend the family."

He glanced at me before focusing on the road again. "You're a good joe. Probably wouldn't intentionally hurt my daughter. But that doesn't take away from what I said."

"I believe we're much alike, Mr. Henning."

Without warning, his fist slammed on the steering wheel, causing the truck to skitter across the road. "Quit being so agreeable! We're nothing alike. Before Josh joined the army, I tried to talk him out of it. Be a conscientious objector, I told him. Break a trigger finger. Find a way to flunk the physical. Once, I came close to cracking his kneecap with the back of an ax but couldn't bring myself to do it. Memories of rat-infested trenches and the mustard gas from the last war still haunt me at night. And even though you come back, part of you is still there. You probably know that. And so will Josh." As an afterthought, he eased the truck back to the center of the road. "Thank God, this thing will end before Billie comes of age."

"No one despises war more than a soldier," I said.

The big man sank in his seat. "Hell with it. Arguing with you is taking the wind out of me. You should have been a chaplain."

"Not many chaplains in the Afrika Corps."

"I suppose not. No room for God when Hitler takes center stage. You a Christian man, Mr. Rohling?"

"Catholic, though I haven't practiced since joining

the *Wehrmacht*."

"No one's perfect. You should pray more."

I remained silent. Henning tapped into a subject that left me at times ambivalent and confused. Beyond asking for my own salvation, I didn't think my prayers counted for anything else. Men and women die each day at home for showing too much religion.

"Can't raise your dander, can I?" Henning shifted in his seat. "Let's try this one. Emily said you'll come back after the war, assuming the government will allow German immigrants to become American citizens. Any thoughts on that?"

"I hope to try, Mr. Henning. Though the war isn't over, I'm hoping your government will open its doors again in the future."

"And if those doors don't open?"

Could that happen? "Then I suppose I'll write. Urge Emily to move on."

"You'll hurt her. She thinks you're a savior and a way to escape the farm. Her mother tells me about these romantic notions, and I have no idea what to do. So I'm passing this problem to you. You need to prepare her for the truth—all this is a passing romance. Are you man enough to do that?"

My throat went dry. An impossible task. And I'm to deliver the blow? "I keep my promises."

"It's not going to be up to you. Our boys will come back, and they'll be looking for companionship. Once you get home, you'll face a hundred distractions keeping you there."

Heat rose up the back of my neck. "I will marry her when I return to this country. As a soldier, I've already given you my word."

Henning stared ahead. "Wrong answer."

We drove in silence for a couple of minutes. I tried to think of a way to salvage our conversation. "The sweet corn is coming along well," I said. Mr. Henning worked his jaw muscles but said nothing. I tried again. "The other day I found some pointed stones. They could be arrowheads. Billie might like them." The farmer shifted gears and turned onto the rutted path that led to the field camp. "I'd like to remain friends," I said.

His stillness frustrated me. My uneasiness grew as we drew closer to camp. How could I get his attention? "Sir, if any delay occurs, and I don't come back, then Emily is free to live out her life however she chooses. I cannot expect her to wait for me."

Henning followed the curving path around a stand of cottonwoods. "That is the least you can do," he said. "I'd appreciate it if you tell her yourself."

"Yessir." Voicing the possibility of separate lives forced me to realize how fragile our plans were. We depended on faith and an uncertain future.

Henning slowed the truck. Ahead, our camp stood ablaze in light with a dozen lanterns hanging from poles. Other pickups sat with their workers in back. "What's going on here?" Henning asked another driver who shook his head in bewilderment. Behind us, brakes squeaked as another pickup halted.

A lieutenant approached along the line of vehicles. I jumped out, but Nichols stood in the truck bed and saluted.

The officer ignored the salute. "Assemble the prisoners, private. We have new orders. Straight from the top. And I'm only going to read them once."

"Yessir!" Nichols jumped to the ground. "You heard the man. Fall in!"

What could be happening? No troop carriers sat ready, so we weren't going back to the main camp.

Henning leaned his head out of the window. "I'm heading back home, Private Nichols. My daughter will be by at the usual time tomorrow."

The lieutenant stepped to Henning's vehicle. "You'll want to stick around, sir. These orders will affect your work contract."

Henning killed the engine and got out. Leaning against the hood of the truck, he drew his pipe from his pocket, tapping nonexistent tobacco from it.

We fell in line and jogged to camp. Other crews double-timed it to camp as well. Within twenty minutes, all workers assembled before a few officers, including Captain Brunswick, and five civilians. Brunswick nodded to the lieutenant who retrieved a folded sheet of paper from his tunic pocket. "These are orders from the Provost Marshall's Office passed down to Command Headquarters, Camp Conrad, and will comprise three phases.

"Phase One: Commencing in fourteen days, the Provost Marshall's Office will decrease the enlisted population and noncommissioned officers of Camp Conrad by eighty percent. The PMO will then transfer these prisoners to other regional camps.

"Phase Two: The remaining prisoner population will assist in the reconstruction of barracks, shower buildings, and other structures for preparation of the final phase.

"Phase Three: On 15 October 1944, Camp Conrad will accept up to two thousand commissioned German officers, exclusively. The single compound will retain four to five hundred enlisted prisoners to provide maintenance and caretaking duties." The lieutenant folded the sheet and replaced it in his pocket.

Brunswick turned his back to us, facing Henning and the other civilians. They had crept closer to hear the lieutenant's words. "Do you folks have any questions?" he asked.

Henning stepped forward, waving his pipe in the air. "You moving these boys out to make room for Kraut officers? That's the stupidest thing I ever heard of. We hired these men. Who's going to do our work?"

Brunswick scuffed his feet for a moment. "I'm not at liberty to discuss the particulars, but I can take down your name."

"The name is Henning. With the invasion coming along, it looks like the army is shuffling all the officers here. Where does that leave us?" That drew grumbling from his group.

I bit my lip to hide a growing smirk. Henning was a pigheaded dirt farmer, but he was my pigheaded dirt farmer.

"You make a point, Mr. Henning. But I still cannot answer your question."

"I'm not finished yet." Henning pointed his pipe at the captain like it was a weapon. "With all these new officers coming here, will they be working for us?"

"German officers are not required to work," Brunswick said. "The Labor Program, for this camp at least, will need to be re-evaluated."

"You mean stopped," Henning said.

That brought a gasp from the civilians. Men behind me muttered to each other. The American jeep drivers glanced nervously at one another.

"We've got crops to tend to, sir. We've signed contracts for these boys to work the entire season." Henning wasn't going to let this go.

"That's where you're wrong, sir," Brunswick shot back. "If you look in Section H, 'Circumstances for Termination of Contract,' you will come to Number 11. This refers to unforeseen events that would require prisoners to be removed from the Labor Program. The PMO will issue a voucher for any paid work not completed."

Henning tugged on the brim of his hat. "This isn't the last you'll hear from me. I'll take this to whoever I need to, the sheriff or county attorney—even my congressman. I'll see this gets taken care of."

"Yes, sir," said Brunswick. "In the meantime, work these prisoners as hard as you like, but after June 21, they will be transferred."

A hand slapped my back.

"Make your farewells, my friend," Kimmel said.

Chapter Twenty-One

7-21 June 1944

On our trip to the Henning farm next morning, I sat with Adler near the tailgate. "What do you suppose will happen now?" he asked.

"We'll be split up," I said. "We'll be sent to different places. Camp Conrad will become unrecognizable."

"Transferred to other camps?" Adler asked. "I don't like being uprooted and forced to move."

The days were getting longer. Already, the sun sat on the eastern horizon. "I don't understand why the Amis would create a prisoner program that benefits both the civilians and us, then blow it to bits."

"Too many cooks," Adler said. "Where do you suppose we'll go?"

"Impossible to say." I imagined a game where a blindfolded American general picked a POW tag from one pile and a destination from another. "There are hundreds of camps here."

"As long as it's not in the desert," he said. "I've had enough of that."

For the last two weeks, I tended the sweet corn on Henning's rented land. From morning to early evening, I walked the field, seldom seeing another person all day. Winds whispered through nearby trees along the

Republican River to the north. I well understood Henning's affinity for the land. The corn would not be ready until October. What a grand event that would be—to take part in the harvest. If only we could still be here.

The river meandered along the northern border of the cornfield. One day during that second week of June, I slid down the tree-lined banks and watched the herons fish in the water. Songbirds filled the air with their calls. Cottonwoods spread their limbs high overhead. And the mixed scent of water and vegetation brought back memories of boyhood fishing trips.

A shot rang out, and the heron flew downstream.

I hit the ground and scrambled behind a fallen tree, watching for movement. Being caught away from the cornfield could endanger my chances of working outside any prison ever again.

A minute passed and another shot shattered the air, closer this time, followed by the excited whoop of a young boy. Was it Billie? I climbed to my feet and stepped out of hiding. "Hello!" I called, drawing out the word.

No answer.

"Billie?" I called.

A small figure came loping through the undergrowth carrying a rifle in one hand and a dead rat-like creature in the other. Billie dropped the carcass at my feet and bent over catching his breath.

"You've been busy," I said

"I've been watching a mother eagle teaching her young how to fish, then I saw this guy."

I peered down at the corpse. "What is it?"

"A 'possum. They mostly come out at night eating

anything that wriggles."

I nudged the corpse with my boot. The small-caliber shell Billie used passed through the body without mangling it. "Probably not for the supper table. You should hunt for rabbits, instead. Better to eat than this…scavenger."

Billie scratched his sun-bleached hair. "Rabbits are fast. Harder to hit. Shooting 'possums are a lot more fun."

"Shooting old cans can be just as enjoyable."

"You can't tell me what to do. Besides, my dad sets traps around his garden and kills lots of skunks and 'possums. Even 'coons."

I never fired a rifle until I joined the army and never killed for sport. It seemed unwholesome. "You know, life along the river has always been here. You, on the other hand, are the invader." The boy gave me a baffled look. How could I explain my thinking to this child, so young and from a world where firing a gun was considered play.

"Well, I got to go." He ran upriver, leaving the carcass where it lay.

"Wait!" I called after him. "Aren't you taking your prize?"

He came back a short way, but still restless to leave. "Leave it for the coyotes."

Best not to press the matter. "Before you go, I have one last question. I haven't seen your father in the last few days. Is he ill?"

"Dad's been talking to neighbors. Last Thursday, they went to Topeka and spent the whole day there. They're going back again tomorrow."

"What is he doing?"

"He says you and the other camp people are going away, and he wants to stop it. Why do you want to leave?"

I was about to retort but realized Billie didn't deserve that. Only a child, but he lived to full measure the adventurous life of a twelve-year-old boy. "Adults in charge make many decisions that affect you and me. Some choices are better than others. But we must still obey, whether we like it or not."

Billie shrugged his shoulders. "Mom says they're talking to the high-ups."

"High-ups?"

"You know." He frowned, tapping his head. "The ones with their pictures in the paper. Anyway, Mom calls them senators."

Once, Novak explained to me how American government worked. I wondered how such a system with so many tiers of officials could function. "Is that good?"

Billie shuffled his feet. "Dad seemed happy enough. That's all I know. Can I go now, Mr. Henry?"

I flicked my hand to the trees. "Have fun. Show me a rabbit next time."

"You got a deal!" He scampered behind some brush and disappeared.

I made my way back to the field, pondering the boy's words. Henning and his neighbors were stirring the pot. I wished them luck. Upriver, another gunshot echoed. That Billie—all boy. Grinning to myself, I retrieved my shovel and went back to walking the field, digging weeds.

June 21—our last day of work—came all too soon. Another long day of minding the fields. Henning arrived an hour early that afternoon. I didn't realize he arrived until he blew the horn twice. I dashed to his truck. "Anything wrong, Mr. Henning?"

"No more than usual. Get in. Millie has a surprise for us. She's keeping it a secret, but it smells like apple pie."

"Sounds wonderful."

"Jump in, then." With a startling jerk, we drove back to the farm.

"Have you talked to my daughter about the things we discussed?" Henning stared ahead, both hands on the wheel.

"No, sir. I haven't had a chance." Since the news about the camp changeover to officers only, Mrs. Henning drove us to the farm in the morning, dropped off Goetz, Adler, and Kimmel at the barn, and took me to the rented field. In the last fortnight, I never strayed far on Henning's farm.

He cast me a quick glance. "It's been hectic, I know. Neighbors and I talked to a dozen lawmakers about saving the Labor Program. Senator Capper and Senator Carlson understood our message. It's up to them now."

I remained silent, thinking more of Emily. "I could talk to her before we go back to camp."

"You'll have a chance after we eat."

"It's been a privilege working for you, Mr. Henning," I said, wondering how Emily would react when I dashed her dreams of marriage, making myself the cold Deutsch soldier.

Henning grunted. "Don't see you as much different from our own boys. Polite and respectful all around. I've been telling the story of that big fella, Goetz, for months now. How he wouldn't dig potatoes but would do the heavy lifting all day. Gets a laugh every time."

"He's a good soccer player as well."

"Wouldn't surprise me."

We drove the rest of the way in silence and arrived as Mrs. Henning finished setting the picnic table under a sprawling sycamore in front of the house. Atop a checked tablecloth sat glasses of tea, bowls, utensils, and a large covered pot. I washed my hands at the water pump and joined the others at the table.

"Since today is special, I wanted to cook a treat we don't often have," said Mrs. Henning.

"It's not apple pie?" Henning eyed the large pot a bit dubiously.

Emily handed her mother a kitchen towel and a soup ladle.

"You've had this before, dear." Steam rose as the older woman removed the lid, and dished plump, dripping pastries into small bowls, then poured cinnamon sauce on top. Emily passed the dessert to each of us, including Nichols. "Have any of you boys had apple dumplings? My friend Trisha says they came from Germany."

"My mother baked them when I was a child," I said. The sight of those wonderful, juicy pastries made me think of home. How were my parents doing now? Were they safe? What will happen to them when a relentless war draws closer to home?

Adler and Kimmel poked at their desserts. Goetz popped a big chunk of steaming apple in his mouth. His eyes grew large as saucers. "Hot!" was all he managed to say before gulping most of his tea. That brought on a chorus of laughter.

Mrs. Henning waggled her finger, smiling. "Didn't your mother teach you to take small bites?"

Goetz bowed in mock humility. "*Ja, Mutter.*" That brought another round of friendly jeers.

The conversation soon ebbed as we ate. I savored the cinnamon sweetness. Today marked our final day with the Hennings, yet no one voiced aloud that fact. I marveled at the quiet solitude here, the rustle of wind in the treetops, the calls of redbirds, and a whiff of sweet cinnamon in the air. Recent rains brought a healthy green to the farmyard and to the fields. A slight breeze from the west carried the hint of clover. A variety of flowers clustered about the house. A stand of tall lilies around the porch drew my attention. I'd told Henning I would talk to his daughter, and I steeled myself for what I would say. "Miss Emily, what are those plants in front of the house?" I asked.

"They're daylilies. Daddy got the bulbs from the farm store last winter."

"Could you show them to me?" I asked.

"Daddy, is it okay?"

Henning never looked my way. "That's fine. In a few minutes, I'll have a few words to say before taking these boys back to camp."

"Thank you," she said.

"Can I be excused?" Billie asked. "My show is about to come on."

With a nod from his mother, Billie sprinted to the house.

As Emily and I drew closer to the plants, I could appreciate the exquisite detail of the trumpeting blooms. Three large lemon-colored petals formed the crown, turning to orange-red deep inside the throat.

Many other pod-like buds had yet to open while some blooms hung down withered and spent. "Very nice," I said.

"They're called daylilies because the flowers bloom and die the same day." She gazed at me for a moment. "I didn't know you were interested in flowers."

"Just curious." I touched the thin fibers that poked from the center of the already dying bloom. "So sad. A plant that took months to blossom dies on the same day."

"They come back year after year. There will always be new daylilies." Her hands rubbed the side of her apron. "Henry, our time together is all but over. What are we going to do?"

My eyes met hers. "I have something to say, and it will sound harsh."

"I know. You could be gone for a long time. But Daddy and our neighbors have been working hard to keep that from happening. Newspaper editorials are against the changes at the prison camp. Everyone wants the workers to stay." She made to grab my hand, but I stepped back. "Henry, don't give up," she said. Her voice broke.

"We must be prepared for the worst possibility. The war may end, and I can't return for months. Even years. Life for you will move on. Young men will return and want to start families." I meant to be reassuring, but my voice sounded reserved. Even severe. "You should celebrate their homecoming. Get out. Enjoy life. Don't squander your youth by waiting for me."

She gasped. "You can't mean that."

I was only following her father's orders. But they were my words. "Grow up, Emily. This is bigger than us. We're like leaves in the wind. We have no hope of controlling anything. You live in a safe world, far from war. But I have no idea where I'll be in a month. Or when I get home. Or if home will still exist when I get there."

"You said you'd come back, no matter what."

It was hard to meet her gaze. "I spoke in haste."

"Liar!" She delivered a stinging slap to my jaw, then rushed to the house, slamming the screen door behind her.

You've gone too far, Heinrich. She didn't deserve that.

I fulfilled my duty. I had no choice.

You could have given her hope.

I had no hope to give.

Moments later, Mrs. Henning rushed into the house, giving me a sideways glance. Emily's father studied me when I sank to my seat at the table. Adler pushed pieces of apple around his plate while Goetz gave Henning a curt nod and walked to the pickup. Kimmel helped himself to another dumpling. I wished I could undo the damage I had inflicted. Fighting a real enemy seemed much easier.

Henning never gave his speech. He rose and, without a word, sauntered to the truck and climbed in. No seat in the cab this time for me. Nichols ambled to the passenger door while the rest of us took our seats in back. Henning started the vehicle, and we sped out of the driveway.

Goetz leaned back with his hands behind his head. "I don't like wondering what will happen next."

"It might not be so bad," Adler said. "We could find work on another farm."

I sat near the tailgate, my mood as dark as a cloudy winter night. "Or we could remain inside the camp and run countless errands for the incoming officers."

Kimmel stirred from his position behind the cab. "That would be a privilege. We would earn merit for service to the party. We will be among the elite when we return to Greater Germany."

"You still think Germany will win the war?" I didn't put much effort in taunting him. A new start in a different camp couldn't be any worse than the mess I made here. I only wished that one day I could make it up to Emily.

Kimmel gave me a disdainful look. "Germany will emerge the victor. Don't let the American talk mislead you."

Adler took a piece of gum from his pocket. "An elaborate ruse—rebuilding the camp for officers who aren't coming."

"Oh, they're coming," I said. "And Kimmel will have a thousand feet to kiss."

He leaned toward me. "Be careful comrade, or your fate will be no better than Novak's."

Fire coursed up my spine. At that moment, I didn't care what happened to me as long as that bootlicking swine got his first. I lunged for his throat, yelling an incoherent curse. Kimmel threw an arm across his stricken face, but my attack never reached him. Goetz's bulging arms tossed me to the back of the truck; my head rang when it connected with the tailgate. With gentle fingers, I probed the back of my scalp. There was no bleeding, but a tender area promised to be a goose egg.

Nichols poked his head out of the passenger window. "What's going on back there?"

Adler put a finger to his lips, gesturing for silence. "Just releasing a little tension, sir. All is well."

"Keep the roughhousing down," he called back. "Or I'll put you on report and send the four of you to the Alva prison camp."

"Yessir!" Adler called back. Last January, Colonel Vogel transferred the bulk of Camp Conrad's hardcore Nazis to the high-security prison in Alva, Oklahoma.

For the rest of the trip, I sat against the closed tailgate, and Kimmel leaned against the cab. Goetz kept a watchful eye on both of us. He needn't have bothered. I didn't move until we halted at the camp.

Pickups, jeeps, and a troop carrier filled the rutted path leading to our barracks. Captain Brunswick sat in his jeep and scanned pages on a clipboard. His lieutenant conferred with camp guards. Nichols jumped to the ground. "Everyone out!" he shouted, pounding the side of the pickup. "*Zu him springen!*" A terrible accent, but the meaning came across. Jump to it.

We fell in rank with the other workers. Nichols saluted. "All prisoners present, sir!" The lieutenant, in turn, ran to the jeep and informed the captain. Brunswick gestured for the farmers to approach him. "Folks!" he called. "A word, please! This news will be of interest." It took some coaxing, but Mr. Henning and the other civilians soon gathered around the army captain. I couldn't hear his words, but several farmers seemed pleased by what they heard. One by one, they bent to write on the captain's clipboard and received a sheet of paper in return. Henning stood back, glowering at the uniformed man. Finally, the officer approached him, extending the clipboard.

"You're not getting my John Hancock," Henning said, loud enough for all to hear. "I need my full crew."

Brunswick raised his voice as well. "It's a compromise. You sign this contract, or our business is finished."

The farmer hesitated for a moment, then grabbed the clipboard and signed his name. Brunswick gave him a sheet of paper. Most of the civilians edged toward their vehicles. "Not so fast," the captain called after them. "I need two volunteers to complete the conditions of the contract."

Minutes later, Henning and Mrs. Settle, a neighbor who drove her crew to her farm on the other side of the Republican River, followed the captain to our group.

Brunswick twirled fingers in a hurry-up motion, a tight smile on his face. "Proceed with the lottery, Lieutenant Lam."

Lam retrieved a cap from a camp table, took several measured steps, and stood facing us. "After much consideration, Command will continue with the Prisoner Labor Program, though in a smaller capacity while Camp Conrad converts to officers only. Five crews of two men will service the contracted farms. We can only keep ten of you. Therefore, the way chosen to resolve this exercise is through random drawing. Each of you will pick a numbered ticket from this cap. The civilians will draw ten tickets. If your number turns up, you stay."

I whistled under my breath. "Our future hinges on a lottery?"

Adler whispered behind me. "You have to wonder

who is conducting this war."

My ticket ended in twelve. We fell in line again to await the final drawing.

The lieutenant poured another set of tickets into the cap and handed it to Mrs. Settle. "Prisoners step forward when your number is called," he said. "You will remain in the program."

Mrs. Settle retrieved three tickets from the cap, and handed them to Henning, who read the numbers aloud. "Zero-two…eleven…seventeen."

One man from the Swope farm and two others stepped forward.

"Zero-nine…twenty…twenty-three."

Goetz clapped his hands and swaggered to the front with Steinhaus and Wagner.

"Zero-four…thirteen…twenty-five."

Butcher, Guida, and Danler joined the six other laborers.

One slot remained.

"Fifteen."

My heart sank.

Kimmel whooped with joy and brushed past me to stand with the other nine workers.

Lam took back his cap. "These ten prisoners will comprise the Labor Program for Camp Conrad. The rest of you—we're leaving in ten minutes."

I stared at my now worthless ticket—a passport to nowhere. With deliberate care, I tore the slip to shreds, letting the breeze take the pieces away. Kimmel watched me, a smirk on his face. Did he hope to see a reaction? Let him look. Resigned to a bleak future, I trudged back to my bunk to pack.

Chapter Twenty-Two

Barracks F, Camp McCoy, Wisconsin
August 2, 1944
My Dearest Emily,

I'm writing because I miss seeing your bright smile, your laugh, and the way you brush those curls back from your eyes. The time we shared together was so short, and I strive to recall every detail since leaving Camp Conrad. I sincerely apologize for the hurt I inflicted on you. It was thoughtless and selfish of me. I have no defense except to say it was my imperfect attempt to control the events surrounding me. I feared losing you. Instead of stating this, I turned it into a rebuke. Please forgive me.

Fritz Adler and I returned to the main camp the same day I last saw you. A week later, three hundred of us boarded boxcars with straw bales as seats. None of us knew where the train would take us. When I first came to this country, I drank tea on a Pullman car. Of course, that is not likely to happen now. A lot more prisoners have come to this country in the past year.

We rode for two weeks, often shuttled to sidetracks, waiting for other trains to pass. For inexplicable reasons, our train sat for hours not moving at all. Nothing to look at but telegraph poles and an occasional railyard. Often, our long train traveled through the night, only to stop at a depot where guards hustled prisoners onto trucks and drove away. Adler rode with me until we halted in a small Michigan town. There, three men entered our car and chose eight prisoners at random—including Adler. "Where are you taking me?" he asked in broken English.

One of the guards cocked an eyebrow. "Camp Freedman."

What a strange name for a prisoner of war camp.

I will miss Adler and his braying laugh, my last contact with Camp Conrad.

Three days later, I arrived at Fort McCoy, Wisconsin. The prisoner camp covers more area than Camp Conrad. In addition to Germans, the prison houses Japanese, Koreans, Poles, and Formosans, each in their own compounds. Unlike the camp in Kansas, officers and enlisted men live in the same confined area. The Asian compounds also housed "alien civilians." The American Army brought these families to America and imprisoned them here. Why? Because these people dared to disagree with US authorities in their own country. Each week I find fewer things that separate the Americans from the Nazis.

There is more to tell. Tomorrow is "tryouts" for soccer. Four of the German teams have organized to play monthly tournaments—the next competition will be in two weeks. A cook from the mess hall tells me both officers and enlisted men make bets on the winners using cigarettes and money issued by the camp. But I plan to pursue a different course.

Camp McCoy also has a Labor Program with the surrounding dairy farmers, a local cannery, and the forestry department. I've already signed to join.

Thinking of you,

Henry

****

Conrad, Kansas
August 10, 1944
Dear Henry,

I'm so glad you wrote to me! When you left, I feared you would never speak to me again, and I'd lost you forever. I cried myself to sleep that night and stayed in my room for days afterward. Mother encouraged me to get outside and enjoy the zinnias and cardinals with their different calls. The daylily stalks are bare, the last bloom wilted two weeks ago. I miss watching the buds grow and burst open in yellow, pink, or white. But now, I have your letters to look forward to.

Please be patient with me. Parts of your letter left me more confused than relieved. When you left, you were so definite to end our time together—like you wanted to slam the door and lock it behind you. It felt so final. As much as I wished to deny it, I came to believe you grew tired of me. Is that true?

As to the farm, Daddy has a different pair of workers each week. Some are friendly, like Mr. Kimmel and Mr. Goetz. Others are formal and silent. Daddy says not as much work is getting done, and he worries how this will affect the harvest. The guard who accompanies the workers constantly warns us not to fraternize, but he is always the first to get churned ice cream or a sugar cookie at the end of the week. I, too, miss the four of you working for us. And I especially miss you, Henry. Please, write back soon.

With all my love,
Emily

****

Barracks F, Camp McCoy, Wisconsin
August 21, 1944
Dearest Emily,

I understand your confusion, and I regret how I brazenly pierced your heart. You were right to call me a liar. More than you'll ever know. Please don't ask me to explain. I accept the label and hope to atone for it. After this war is over, I'll endeavor to explain my actions. Please know, I will not mislead you again.

Camp McCoy has a prison chaplain, a Catholic priest whose ancestors came from Hamburg. I have shrugged off his attention in the past, but when loneliness for home strikes me, I do seek his company. He tells me I should share my feelings with a person I trust. I've made few friends here, so I hope you don't mind if I share my thoughts with you. I hope what I'm about to say will put you at ease. Still, expressing my feelings on paper is not easy.

Chaplain Reid tells me I'm feeling guilty about past sins, and I'm awaiting punishment. I must have looked shocked, because the priest laughed and said all Catholics tend to feel guilty. "Maybe we're doing too good a job of putting fear in our flocks." He chuckled, but then grew serious. "For you, it may be a real issue. Do an examination of conscience and come see me for confession."

"You wish me to take a test?" I asked.

"Heavens, no. It's a list of questions about the sins you committed and your worthiness before God. Do you serve the One True God and only Him alone? Have you broken with any of your sacred beliefs? Harbor any hidden transgressions? Harmed your parents? Taken undue pleasure in killing or hurting your enemies? Have thoughts of suicide or of taking revenge on your brothers?"

"That's enough," I told him. "Follow the Commandments. I get the idea."

"There's more. Confession will ease your soul."

"Let me think about it." I soon dismissed the talkative priest. His questions brought back memories of an incident in Camp Conrad that affected a friend. It is said he took his own life, but I am unwilling to believe it.

I feel like the Confederate soldier in one of your country's past wars who discovers history will render his side a harsh judgement. Learned men will one day ridicule my country in the war. I wish I can do more than be a distant spectator to the calamity that will befall my homeland—to my city, Berlin. Here, the camp leaders allow us to listen to American radio. If the news is correct, the maelstrom is getting closer by the week, scorching the land and crushing the lives of my countrymen. Who will put our communities back together in peacetime? And will the world allow it?

Apologies, my dear, for my frightening comments. I'm worried about my parents.

Sincerely yours,
Henry

****

Conrad, Kansas
September 24, 1944
Dear Henry,

You poor man! The despair you must be going through—I didn't know. You needn't feel that way. You were caught up in events like thousands—no, millions—of others. You fought because you had to, and you could not do anything different. Don't tear yourself down thinking this way. You'll only hurt yourself. Find an activity, like working in the cannery or for a farmer nearby. Taking action is better than letting your thoughts overwhelm you.

Harvest will begin soon. We've had a good year; the stalks are tall and heavy with corn. The rented field you worked on is flourishing. A two-man crew is not enough. We need more men. Daddy has put a help-wanted ad in the paper, but so have a dozen other farmers. Billie and I will do what we can. Long hours of hard work lie ahead for all of us.

Daddy mentioned we should get another dog. I've already asked some of the neighbors if any pups are available.

Write soon. I enjoy your letters, though your last note tugged at my heart. The good news is the war may soon be over.

Sincerely,
Emily

****

Barracks F, Camp McCoy, Wisconsin
October 4, 1944
Dear Emily,

I wished I could have stayed long enough to help your papa with the harvest. Seeing the job completed would have been satisfying. Wisconsin, I've learned, also raises sweet corn.

Dairy farms abound here. The American in charge of farm contracts talked to a group of us interested in work. While there were no more openings for crop labor, there is a year-round need for dairy stockmen. I jumped at the chance. If all goes well, I will be riding out with a livestock crew in two weeks. Laborers must commit for three months with a pay raise after the first extension. I'm looking forward for a chance to try my hand with livestock.

It won't be too soon for me. The tension between Asian and European prisoners in Camp McCoy is palpable. While prisoners from each country sleep behind their own fenced enclosures at night, all must eat and spend their days together in the main compound. The Japanese taunt the Germans with insults. But they vent their greatest hatred against other Asian groups. At least three fights have erupted in the mess hall with Japanese prisoners hurtling chairs and food trays at the Koreans or Formosans. All day, their staccato shouts and screams echo throughout the camp. Sirens blow, and guards lock the warring factions in their separate areas, but they still yell and taunt each other behind fences.

And new German prisoners arrive every few days. Many come from France and Belgium and tell stories of fighting against shiny American tanks, rocket launchers, and raining shells. "No matter how secure our positions were," one machine-gunner said, "their sappers found a way to kill us in our bunkers. We could surrender or die." The new German PWs already outnumber us Afrikaner veterans. I can't wait to tend to a barn full of tranquil milk cows.

I should be able to get another letter to you before we start work. After that, I'm not sure when I can next post a message. Emily, you are always in my dreams. Both of us must remain patient until we can see each other again. Patience is all we have.

Good-bye for now,
Henry

****

The Wheatland hotel clerk stared at me with disapproval, perhaps justified in his thinking. I had already shoved my way past several waiting guests to the check-in counter. With apologies to the well-suited travelers, Horst stepped to my side.

"Can I help you, gentlemen?" The desk clerk's voice dripped with sarcasm.

Horst answered in full attorney mode. "You have a guest, Paul Drosselmeyer. We think he needs medical help. He doesn't answer his phone, and we can't get into his room. Seconds matter. We need to get in there now."

The hotel man seemed unfazed by our request. "Room number?"

My son glanced at me. I shook my head. "No idea."

He typed on a computer keyboard. "Spell the last name, please."

I began spelling. "D-R-O-S-S-E—"

"I'm sorry, sir. It's your accent. Was that an 'E'?"

Horst grabbed a nearby hotel brochure and printed the name. "Does that help?"

"Yes, sir. Thank you." He tapped more keys, peering at a bulky computer monitor. "He's in Room 124. Wait a moment. I'll call an associate."

"Can't wait." I thumped the counter. "Give us a key. We'll check for ourselves."

The counterman straightened, adopting a formal tone. "Hotel policy forbids keys to be given freely."

Horst leaned forward. "Mr. Drosselmeyer requires

oxygen. He could be dying."

"I see." The clerk rubbed his chin, then tapped more keys. In seconds, he produced an unlabeled key card and gave it to Horst. "One of our staff will be with you soon. Better hurry."

I hustled to a hallway lit by bright ceiling lights. Horst grabbed my shoulder, pointing to a different passageway showing an arrow, *Rooms 101 to 139.* "Down this way."

I hated to be corrected in public, but now wasn't the time to make my point. Horst led the way to the room, a dozen doors from the lobby and slid the card in the slot. "I hope you're wrong, Papa. He's probably at the banquet, wondering why you're late."

"I pray that is so," I said.

The lock clicked, and the door opened to a hotel room with two queen beds and a brightly lit desk lamp. Horst shrugged. "He's not here."

I stepped inside, opening the front closet. Two modest-sized bags sat in a corner. Several garments hung on a wooden rod, including a wrinkled suit. The lit bathroom contained some personal items around the lavatory. The closest bed remained untouched, but covers in the second bed were yanked at the bottom corner. I rushed to the far side of the room but nearly stepped on an outstretched hand grasping the bedsheets. A wave of dizziness hit me. Behind me, Horst let out a gasp. "*Scheisse.*"

The old sergeant lay sprawled on his side between the bed and desk, one hand on the covers and the other hand clutching his throat. An oxygen canister peeked out beneath the bed. The needle on the attached gauge hovered over zero. Drosselmeyer's blueish features, gaping mouth, and wide staring eyes suggested only one thing: death from lack of oxygen.

Horst sidled past me. "I'll check his pulse. He may still be alive."

"I don't see how that's possible."

He knelt by the body, finger resting on Drosselmeyer's neck. A long moment past before Horst rose to his feet. "You're right. Poor man. We better tell the front desk." My son hustled to the exit while I stared at the body. "Papa, we can't stay here."

It was a betrayal to leave my old comrade like this, yet I had no choice. What secret did he wish to tell me? His death seemed too much like a coincidence. Did Drosselmeyer's knowledge demand his silence? I said a silent prayer over his body. We had our differences, but I still respected the man and his rank as a soldier. He deserved a gesture of honor. I came to attention, clicked my heels, and saluted in the old way before leaving the room.

My son gave me an odd look when I rejoined him. "What was that all about?"

"A farewell."

"Was he a friend?"

"Comrade in arms. Not quite the same thing." I followed Horst to the counter where we reported the old sergeant's death.

Ten minutes later, an ambulance and police car arrived without siren. Horst and I stood by as the clerk led two medics and a blue-uniformed woman to Drosselmeyer's room. Some of the other guests lingered and asked what happened. With their curiosity satisfied, they soon moved on. But I wanted to stay. Would the old sergeant be placed in a soon-to-be-forgotten grave here, or could he be transported back home for a proper burial? Who will visit his resting place? At least some of his memories will be preserved in the POW museum. What did he wish to tell me? Was this an accident? Or a deliberate act?

"What are you thinking about, Papa?"

"I don't think Drosselmeyer's death was an accident." With some hesitation, I told Horst about Novak's death, his last letter, and my conclusion he was murdered. I even admitted someone had entered our hotel room and stolen the letter. Skipping the forgery, I explained Drosselmeyer's suspicion about secret orders fifty years ago and our meeting where he would tell me what those orders could have been. "It is my belief that Novak's and Drosselmeyer's killer is the same person."

"Oh, Papa." Horst shook his head, his eyes downcast. "These thoughts of yours are disturbing. They border on the paranoid."

"Scoff all you want," I said. "I'm positive I'm right."

"When we get back home, I'm going to find you a specialist. You may have more than memory problems going on."

"I'm not crazy. I know I have no proof, but I see no other explanation."

"You're stringing together a series of unrelated events. Drop this obsession immediately. I can't imagine where this thinking will lead."

I turned away from this stranger before me. My own son thought I should be locked away like a demented old coot conjuring stories. He would throw me in an old soldiers' home for the rest of my life. I would be a prisoner again. "Okay," I said. Anything to keep my freedom. "I won't change my mind, but I promise to remain silent."

He let out a sigh. "I thought you spilled my papers by accident. You really think an intruder stole this letter of yours? Maybe you misplaced it."

"I hid it in my satchel. A safe place. No, a thief took it."

"Did you report the theft to the hotel?"

"No. Nothing would come of it. I forged a new letter to see what would happen."

He gazed at me, incredulous. "You've got to be joking."

"I hoped for the thief to make a mistake and reveal himself."

"Did this scheme work?"

"No. But there is still another day before we go back."

Horst spoke urgently. "Papa, I want you to give me this forgery before you get into deeper trouble."

"I...can't." Why did my son have to make this more difficult? "Mrs. Powell, the director of the reunion, has it."

"Why would she take it?"

"I didn't mean to give it to her. She wanted to check its validity. I had no choice." I cringed at my own words. I really had botched saving Novak's honor.

Horst drew back like he'd been smacked in the head. "*Mein Gott, Papa.* I'm at a loss on how to get you out of this pit. You should explain to the director what happened. Tell her the truth."

As long as Kathy believed me, I wouldn't do that. "Later, this evening, I can find a chance to talk to her," I said. "Right now, Drosselmeyer is more important."

Horst glanced to the hallway. "I hope you do. So, what is planned for the rest of the reunion?"

Would the reunion carry on? Should it? "There's a short assembly in the morning, then we meet with our oral history interviewers for any follow-up questions. In the afternoon, we're going to the prison restoration. It's only a few buildings, a section of fence, and a guard tower."

"Where is this prison museum?" Horst asked. "I might be able to meet you there after I come back from Salina."

"I supposed it's at the original camp. North of the Republican River and east of Conrad by four or five kilometers."

"The historical society is restoring a museum that far from town?"

I shrugged; since drivers were taking us to the museum, I never asked about the location. "I have no idea. To tell you the truth, even if the museum wasn't there, I'd be more curious to see the old prison than some sanitized version of a POW camp."

"Maybe you'll get the chance." Horst rose to his feet and stretched his back. "Another day and we'll have this business behind us. I need to get back to work. If the authorities wish to see me, send them to the room. Are you going to the banquet?"

I shook my head. "I'll stay here in case the police want to question me, although I'm not sure if they will believe anything I say."

Horst grew firm. "Promise you'll only say what you've heard and seen. No stories. No theories. No conjecture."

My son held my future in his hands. "I will do

that."

"Sorry, Papa, for sounding harsh. We can have a late dinner and talk this out reasonably." Horst pulled me to my feet, and we embraced. He left, glancing back with a worried look as he retreated to our room.

I resumed my vigil in the lobby. Some twenty minutes later, the police officer, a brunette who'd seen time in a gym, emerged from the hallway, strode to the front desk, and conferred with the clerk who pointed to me. She approached, taking out a notebook, and I stepped forward to greet her.

"Hello, sir." She noted my reunion name tag. "Mr. Rohling, I'm Officer Jan Patton. The hotel clerk told me you and another gentleman discovered the body?"

"Yes, Madam."

"Where are you from, sir?"

"Berlin, Germany. I'm here for a fifty-year gathering with other former soldiers. We were interned at Camp Conrad during the war."

"Former POWs? Interesting. Was Mr. Drosselmeyer part of your group?"

"Yes. We were comrades back then. Both of us stayed at the camp during its first year."

"Do you know if the deceased has any close friends or relatives?"

"Mr. Drosselmeyer told me he has no living relatives."

"Were you aware of the extent of his breathing trouble?"

"More than breathing. He had bad lung cancer."

"He smelled of cigarettes. Did Mr. Drosselmeyer smoke often?"

"Drosselmeyer said it was one of his few

pleasures."

Officer Patton jotted notes as we talked. "Who accompanied you to Mr. Drosselmeyer's room?"

"My son Horst came with me."

"I'll interview him later. What room are you staying?"

I told her. She flipped to an earlier page. "The desk clerk said you insisted on checking his room. Did you know he was there?"

"We were to meet before the banquet this evening, but he didn't show. I decided to check on him, but I didn't know his room number."

"What was the nature of your meeting?"

My thoughts churned. "He wanted to talk about our time together at the camp. He was a sergeant while I was an enlisted soldier. As a noncommissioned officer, Drosselmeyer heard whisperings and rumors enlisted men would not be privy to. He wanted to talk about some of the inner workings of the camp. About secret orders not issued through the normal channels among German officers. I think he knew what those orders were, but he died before we had a chance to talk."

The officer stared at me, perplexed. "Do you have any ideas what his suspicions were? Did he mentioned any evidence backing up his allegations?"

"No." I spread my arms in consternation. "I wish I knew."

She flipped her notebook shut. "That's all the questions I have for now. Feel free to join your friends, but stay available at the hotel in case I have more questions. I'll talk to some of the other attendees and your son before I leave. Sorry for your loss, Mr. Rohling." Patton sauntered down the corridor to the conference rooms.

I regained my seat, wondering how long it would take before Drosselmeyer got a proper burial. I hoped he died from natural causes, but I could not dismiss the timing. Just a few hours after the theft of Novak's letter and minutes before our meeting outside the hotel, Drosselmeyer's death was too convenient to dismiss as an accident. I rubbed my temple with unsteady fingers. My penned letter was now in the hands of Mrs. Powell. I cared little about the harm to my reputation, but I wondered what she would do when she learned the note was a fraud.

There was also the small matter of Novak's and Drosselmeyer's killer walking among us. Watching. Listening. Ready to strike again. Soon, the killer would have to deal with me. This deadly business would end with his unmasking or my elimination as a threat.

A thickset man in an ill-fitting lab coat lumbered through the glass doors, crossed the lobby, and entered the corridor. This was the second act of what promised to be a long evening. Not wishing to attend the banquet, I decided to go back to rejoin my son. As I rose to my feet, the last person I expected to see approached me.

Emily.

Chapter Twenty-Three

Conrad, Kansas
October 9, 1944
Dear Henry,

Corn harvest began a week ago, but I fear we may not get the crops all in. Daddy and his two men are working long hours, but thunderstorms have slowed down work. The fields are too muddy for Big Nellie, and the men must wait until the ground dries. Even after presenting his problem to the commander at the prison camp, Daddy could not secure the extra help he needed. Even the *Farmer's Almanac* is predicting more rain or, at best, cloudy weather. "I'm holding the army responsible if I lose my crop," Daddy said yesterday when the clouds parted, and we saw a little sun. Today, it is raining again.

We need a dry spell. Otherwise, the cornstalks will fall over and fill the air with rot.

I'm sure you'll do well on that dairy farm, Henry. You are a very capable man.

Love always,
Emily

****

Barracks F, Fort McCoy, Wisconsin
October 13, 1944
Dear Emily,

I wish to get this letter off today. Tomorrow some

forty-five of us will be leaving for Camp Galesville, eighty kilometers away. From this smaller camp, some of us will go out each day and work on nearby dairy farms. Others will stay for three months at a time on larger farms farther away. The German sergeant who watches over our barracks heard I wanted to tend the bigger herds. "You'll be tramping around some rugged hills here. Ranchers ought to be raising goats instead of those spotted gasbags."

I will post another note to you once I get situated. By then, I will know more about the people I'm working for and the job I'm to do. It will be an adventure.

I hope your father completed his harvest.

Truly yours,

Henry

****

Conrad, Kansas

October 19, 1944

Dear Henry,

Harvest is still going slow. The rains continued for the next eight days with only a cloudy day or two in between. Granted, much of it was only sprinkling. Still, the ground became saturated. Between corn rows, the water came up past my ankles. By the time Daddy could get Big Nellie in the field, many of the stalks were drooping to the ground. Daddy thinks he may lose a third of his crop. Even if he gets a good price, some of our bills will carry over to next year. Our neighbors know we're good for it, but we can't have another year like this one.

Henry, I don't want you to feel guilty for not being here, because it would not have made any difference since the army held Daddy to the new contract. I'm only telling you this because I have no one else to talk to. I hope you are doing well. What is your job like?

Next week, Daddy is taking me to the Swope farm. Their dog had puppies. "Now, don't think you have to pick one," he told me. "You know what Sadie looks like—half bull terrier and half bloodhound. Those pups will be just as ugly as their mother."

Daddy's right. Sadie is brown and white, wide in the shoulders, and has a tremendous nose. She is protective but will moan and yowl for attention from the PWs if they don't scratch her. I can't wait to see those pups.

Good luck with your new job, Henry.

With love,

Emily

****

Lindahl Farm, Galesville, Wisconsin

October 29, 1944

What an incredible place! Two weeks ago, I started working for the Lindahl family, and I am still enthralled. This is more like a factory than a dairy farm. Since my arrival, I've been working with Sven Johansson, a husky lad of seventeen, on the finer points of milking thirty cows using a portable milk shed. The flat-roofed building consists of three stalls sitting on a four-wheel trailer chassis. Ramps on each end allow cows to enter the stalls and exit the other side. We can move the trailer to any location with a tractor.

Last night, I camped with the big Swede on a small rise overlooking the Guernsey and Holstein stock. Bright stars filled the dome of sky, and a cool breeze nipped at the back of my neck. The down-filled sleeping bag wrapped me in warm comfort. Sven and I camped alone with no one near. What if the engine that powered our milking machine caught fire, or a milking cup broke? What if a cow sickened? I hoped I could meet the challenges ahead.

Each day before dawn, Sven's border collie is already herding the cattle to our milk station. The cows, of course, have done this scores of times and need little urging. They stroll in single file and line back to the woods behind us.

"Good dog, Gypsy!" Sven sits on top of the roof, dropping a load of feed into a compartment built into the exit door. I stand ready inside the shed with a wet cleaning sponge in one hand and a steel chain in the other as my first three customers lumber up the ramp and enter through the canvas openings. Time to do my stuff.

"Hello, ladies!"

I secure the chain behind the cows' rumps, scrub the udder of the nearest beast, and fit the rubber-coated cups over the teats, repeat the operation with the other two animals, and then flip the engine switch. The pump hisses and pops, milking the cows the same way you would by hand. While the cows munch feed, I check the flow tubes that snake to the holding tanks. Even on warm days, the milk stays cool inside the collectors. Every two or three days, a tractor driver comes by to take our holding tanks and leave us with empty ones.

After the cows finish eating, Sven raises the front door to let the them wander out, and I set up for the next group. If all goes well, we finish milking some three hours after we start. Then, we scrub all the equipment and fill the engine with oil for the afternoon milking. As the herd drifts farther away in search of fresh grass, we ready the milk shed for moving. The driver hitches the shed and hauls it to the new grazing spot. With the hills, streams, and tall forests, it is tempting to think we are pioneers, but George Lindahl has five other milk sheds wandering about his big ranch.

I'm signed up to do this work until January—and beyond if I choose to. By the end of this year, I'll have around sixty-five dollars. Staying outside Camp Galesville means more to me than the money.

Emily, did you get your dog? What did you name it? I'm saddened to hear about your father losing part of his crop. He is a practical man. I'm sure he'll figure a way to make next year a bountiful one.

You are always in my thoughts,

Henry

****

Conrad, Kansas

November 5, 1944

Dearest Henry,

Milking thirty head of cattle twice a day, by itself, is six hours of work. A tough job for two people. And you seem so isolated, but I know the tractor driver would have to take the milk to market, keep you supplied, and follow the herd. I asked Daddy about the idea of a portable milk barn. He said the county agent mentioned this at a recent co-op meeting, but the dairymen here showed little interest. I'm glad to hear it works. And you are not passing the time within a prison.

Last week, my friends and I went to a Saturday matinee at the theater in town, mainly to escape our parents. So few young men were there, but I saw a soldier slouched in the back row. He wore regular clothes, but I knew he was a serviceman because he wore notched tags around his neck. He sat alone, and no one paid him any heed. He looked dazed and didn't answer when I said hello. I feel terrible about it now. One of my friends told me this young man survived hours of mortar fire without a scratch, but it destroyed his hearing. Poor man, his life is ruined. Can anyone help him? Will he have anything to live for? What if Josh returned home a broken man? I worry about this more than of him dying on the battlefield.

Time to turn to a happier subject.

Yesterday, I rode with Daddy to the Swope farm to look at their two-month-old pups. Sadie bounded out to greet us, running along the side of the truck. The Swopes' nine-year-old daughter Cindy introduced me to the five pups sleeping in a busted apple crate. The other three wandered outside the barn. Cindy pointed to the largest, a gray-spotted pup with floppy hound ears and a too-long nose. He stood near the chicken coop with his gangly legs braced wide, refusing to retreat from an irritated rooster.

"What's his name?" Billie asked.

"He's a her." Cindy shook her head, acting annoyed that a boy didn't pay attention to such things. "And *her* name is Mitzi."

I'd already made up my mind. "She's got spunk. We'll take her."

"Thought you would." Cindy stuck her nose up, proud that she knew my choice.

Billie cast me a sideways glance. "You want a girl dog?"

"She'll make a good companion." I gathered Mitzi in my arms, her wet nose sniffing my face. Cindy slapped Billie on the back and raced down the driveway, leaving me alone with my prize. I ambled to the big cottonwood where Daddy and Mr. Swope were talking shop and told them the news. We took Mitzi home that day, and she's been following me around since.

I'd love to hear more about your daily work. Hope you won't have any trouble during the coming winter. Daddy says cows can take the cold.

With love and concern,

Emily

****

Lindahl Farm, Galesville, Wisconsin

November 27, 1944

Dear Emily,

It is colder now, and we are not moving the shed as much. Our tractor driver is bringing more feed now before hauling away the milk collectors. Often we catch up on news while handing the sacks of feed up to Sven atop the shed roof. All work is done on a fixed schedule. So when we're not milking, we may be checking the engine or washing flow tubes. Mr. Lindahl likes his machines kept clean. We now sleep inside the shed. With only a month left to work, I'm thinking about signing on for the rest of the winter. The hills and starry sky are a magnificent backdrop, and I've grown attached to these passive beasts.

The antics of your new companion with the rooster brought a smile to my face. You two should make a good pair.

Sincerely,

Henry

****

Conrad, Kansas
December 18, 1944
Dear Henry,

Mitzi is growing fast. I keep her in at nights because coyotes come close to the house. She chases the chickens sometimes for fun. I'm trying to break her of this habit with swats from a newspaper. She hasn't quit yet, but she's learning. She'd better. Daddy told me he wouldn't put up with a dog that kills chickens—even accidentally—by chasing them.

Be safe, Henry. With love, as always,
Emily

****

Lindahl Farm, Galesville, Wisconsin
December 21, 1944
Dear Emily,

It's official. I'm working another three months in these hushed Wisconsin hills. Milking the herd is relentless work, but there are no barbed wire fences, no guard towers, and no prisoners quarreling with one another. The only complaint I have is a lack of anything to read. I mentioned this to the fellow who drives the tractor. Last week, he arrived with six old farm magazines. Some of the articles were interesting, but the advertisements are the most intriguing. "Our parts will keep your tractor running and win us victory in Europe!" "McCloughan Feed Corn is good for your poultry—and your wife will love the new daisy pattern on our fifty-pound bags!" Is the feed that much better, or is keeping the farmer's wife from buying a new dress more important?

274

I'm glad you are making progress with your new friend. Maintain discipline. Let the animal know when she disobeys.

Gypsy is bringing the herd in. Time for another milking.

Henry

****

For a fleeting instant in that hotel hallway, I saw Emily more with my heart than with my aging eyes. At that moment, she was the same farm girl I left behind. Curly auburn hair and sparkling hazel eyes. As she came closer, her silver-gray hair framed eyes dimmed only slightly by time. Her once flawless complexion was now weathered by years of sun and wind. We had lived our lives apart, but she never strayed far from my thoughts.

I rushed forward and drew her into my arms, holding her close. Her slender frame shuddered, and her eyes brimmed with tears. As we embraced, her tremors dwindled. She stepped away, taking a tissue from her handbag. "That poor man, dying so far from home. It'll be hard to continue with the reunion."

I drew as straight as I could, my back protesting. "Paul would want you to. So would every man here. He is only the latest soldier to cross that final bridge. Someday, each one of us must make the journey, and Paul will be there to greet us on the other side."

"I suppose you're right." She dabbed at her cheeks. "Still, it'll be hard. The police said you found his body."

I nodded. An old memory struck me, and I could not help but smile.

"Henry, this isn't funny."

"When we were prisoners, Drosselmeyer and I were making homebrew in the camp. We never sold a drop, because the guards destroyed the barrels. Today, Paul and I were to meet before the banquet, but that, too, didn't happen. It seems like nothing we did together worked out."

"Is he still in the hotel?"

"Two medics and I'm guessing the coroner are with him." I gave her a sidelong glance. "Is there anything I can help you with?"

Her face reddened with embarrassment. "I forgot. Virginia asked me to retrieve Mr. Drosselmeyer's reunion packet. The police wish to examine it."

"Care if I tag along? This day has been a roller-coaster, and I haven't had a chance to speak with you."

"We can talk on the way to the room." She grabbed my hand, and we strolled to the hotel suites by the indoor pool.

"How is Oskar taking the news of…me being here?" I asked.

She was silent for a moment. "I know what you're really asking. What would my husband do if he saw us like this?"

"It crossed my mind."

"Knowing Oskar, he'd pound home the fact he owns me, and you would have to return home to your empty house. I don't know why, but since he learned you were coming, he has been giddy with excitement, but also nasty and sarcastic. Even more than usual."

"Has he always been like that?"

Emily bit her lip. Her silence confirmed my suspicions.

Fearing I had overreached, I changed the subject.

"I never thought I'd see you again. Last night brought back all the old memories. It felt like my life had come full circle, and I'm twenty-three all over again."

"Be careful, Henry Rohling. I dare not think what Oskar would do if he heard you right now."

"Is he still at the banquet?"

"Probably drinking at the cash bar now that Virginia cut short the keynote speaker. The officer came to the head table and told us about Mr. Drosselmeyer. She wanted all the information we had on him. That's when Virginia sent me to get the packet."

"Oskar told me Drosselmeyer had no close relatives."

"None. He has been living in a veterans' care home in Munich for the past ten years."

"If only I'd known. I could have visited him."

She bowed her head for a moment. "Wouldn't it be nice to go back and correct all the mistakes we ever made?"

I sighed, thinking about Della's first visit to the oncologist. "I still wonder if my wife would have survived if we'd discovered the cancer earlier."

She squeezed my hand gently. "I'm sorry for your loss."

"It's old news. Sometimes I forget how long it's been since I lost her. Was it two years or three? It was the day after Easter, but at times, the calendar date is fuzzy. I recall the year. 1991. I count up from there."

She gave me a sad smile. "That's four years ago."

"That long?" The world tilted for a moment. "I still remember every detail of the day she died."

"Did you have a good marriage? No regrets?"

The question surprised me, and I wondered at her frankness. "We had our differences. She was more interested in American culture than I. She took the children and grandchildren to all the latest kid movies. When we argued, Della often left me scratching my head." I smiled at the time-worn memories, rubbed and polished like fine silver. "Still, we were inseparable."

"You've had children, grandkids, and a good life. I envy you."

Before I could answer, Emily stopped at a door, inserted her key card, and we entered. The lock clicked behind us.

The suite consisted of a small front room with three comfy chairs, couch, and minibar. A bathroom divided the foyer from the larger back room with two queen beds, dressers, and a small conference table with chairs. Several open boxes of folders, large envelopes, and printed paper sat on the table. Emily pulled a manila envelope with DROSSELMEYER in block letters across the top. "This should help the police." She handed the packet to me. "I need some water. Want to come back to the conference room with me?"

"I want to talk with the medical examiner before he leaves. I worry about what's going to happen to Drosselmeyer. His body, I mean. Also, my son wants to keep an eye on me. He thinks his old man is losing his mind."

"I'm staying at the hotel tonight. Oskar will be going home later this evening. We can still find time to talk." She entered the bathroom, ran the faucet, and returned with a plastic cup of water. "Henry, I hope you're not feeling responsible for Mr. Drosselmeyer's death. Otherwise, I'll have to take Della's place and give you a talking-to."

"Please. Anything but that." I stepped back in mock horror. "Cherishing old disagreements is one thing, but reliving them is another."

"Fraidy cat." She said it with a smile. "You're still the man I remembered. So very different from Oskar." Her smirk faded to an unhappy frown.

"Emily, it's clear you've been suffering for years. Leave Kimmel. He's tearing you apart."

"You're gracious. My friends say, 'Why stay married to that blustering idiot? He's killing you. Get away while you have the chance. Live your own life.' "

"I'm sure you've got your reasons for staying with him."

She set the water on the dresser and slumped to the foot of the bed, her hands covering her face. Her sobs came quietly at first, but as she leaned against me, her heart broke, and she cried like a child who lost everything. I pulled her close, my head bowed next to hers as if in silent prayer. Why would she stay married to such a man? Religious convictions? Pride? Fear? Or was there a darker reason? Whatever the cause, she chose to bear her burden alone.

Thoughts of lost opportunities surfaced, teasing me with a what-if alternate past: I return to vanquish Kimmel, propose to Emily, and marry her on the Henning farm. A few years later, our children play cops and robbers with the neighbor's kids. In my tractor workshop, my oldest son learns the repair trade. Emily and I grow old together, and she doesn't die in relentless pain. Fleeting thoughts. Wayward fantasies. Life was a shifting tapestry of images and experiences we continually reimagined. For Emily, remembrance was a minefield. There, I would not tread without her permission. I hoped she would confide in me.

The silence between us seemed to extend forever but was probably three or four minutes. She drew a sleeve across her cheek. "You should have come back, Henry," she said. "I would have waited for you."

"I couldn't. My parents needed me." To talk about the rebuilding felt selfish. I touched her chin, drawing her attention. "Now tell me. What happened here."

"It's a sordid tale. You'd hate me if I told you."

"That's not possible."

She sighed. "Even when I went along with the idea, I knew it was wrong. No going back though, after the wedding. That made me as guilty as Billie. And Oskar held control over both of us."

"Kimmel told me he came back to America and soon married you."

"He did, huh?" She drew back, incredulous. "He spent months courting me, but I didn't love him. If it weren't for Billie's hunting accident, Oskar would have tired of me eventually and moved on."

"But he found a way...to worm his way to your heart?"

She huffed then. "More like a frame to keep us under his thumb."

A prickling at the nape of my neck. "What do you mean?"

"It's easiest to start from the beginning. Oskar entered this country two years after the war ended, posing as an eastern German refugee. He showed up at the farm in the early summer, working in Conrad and doing odd jobs for Daddy. We dated, but not on a steady basis."

"Tell me about the accident."

"You're right. I should cut to what happened." She swallowed before continuing. "In mid-October, we hit a cold snap, but that didn't stop Billie from taking his rifle and hunting by the river. There, he saw a large animal lumbering through the trees, blackish with spots of brown and white. At one point, the creature headed straight for him. That's when he fired and brought it down. The beast turned out to be a man wearing animal hides."

That shocked me. "Like one of your American Indians?"

"Hard to say. I never saw him. Billie ran home. I found him out of breath gulping down water in the kitchen. Finally, he told me what happened. The folks had gone to town. If only they stayed home. I called Oskar for help but didn't give details because we were on a party line. He arrived in a borrowed truck and Billie described where he left the wounded man. 'I know where he's at. I can go with you.' "

"But Kimmel said no?" I asked.

"Oskar wanted Billie to stay home and keep off the phone until he returned. 'Everything will be all right,' he said."

"You didn't call the neighbors or the authorities?"

"Oskar said not to. Billie could go to jail and stand trial. He could be looking at years of prison—and become another man's wife."

The dryness in my mouth made it hard to speak. "So Kimmel scared you into silence and took control."

"He returned covered in mud and said the tramp had died from a wound in the neck. He hid the body in the river and disposed of Billie's gun as well. He even swept the ground with a tree branch, leaving no traces of footprints or blood."

I could imagine what came next. "He demanded a price."

"Oskar proposed to me the next day. I didn't want to marry him. You were still very much in my thoughts. I wondered about going to Berlin and finding you. So, I told Oskar I'd think about his proposal. That's when he dropped his bombshell. 'I know where the body is, and I still have your brother's gun that killed him. Deny me this wedding, and you'll be talking to your brother through steel mesh for the rest of his life.' A county judge married us the day before Thanksgiving."

I leaned back, pieces snapping together in my mind. "Murder seems to follow Mr. Kimmel wherever he goes."

"Do you think Oskar has anything to do with Mr. Drosselmeyer's death?"

"There's a good possibility."

Emily's eyes widened. "Now you're scaring me."

"Try to be strong. I'm not sure how to bring him down. But whatever happens, you and Billie should seek out an attorney, present your case, and take your chances with the authorities. At least you'll be free of Kimmel's control."

"You don't think that has crossed my mind? I can't count the times I've picked up the phone, ready to take a chance. Each time the thought of Billie in prison froze my blood. Oskar says that all the new lab tests available can place Billie's DNA at the scene of the crime."

"Confessing is the most prudent course," I said, a new urgency pressed upon me. "Meanwhile, I'll push him until he reacts and makes a mistake. No way to predict what will happen after that."

Emily touched my cheek. Her eyes bored into mine. "I'm frightened, Henry."

I rose to my feet, drawing her close to me. Both of us had crossed a threshold with no turning back. Tempting enough to dismiss Kimmel as a jealous, spiteful weakling, but I had underestimated the man. He had qualities I didn't believe possible: patience, cunning, and an ability to take decisive action— including cold-blooded murder. Provoking him invited disaster. I needed to proceed carefully. At least Horst remained uninvolved. I was, after all, an old man imagining killers. I couldn't ask him for help.

So be it.

Here was my chance to silence my fearful past, to be the soldier I should have been. Achieving this could demand a high price.

I gazed upon the girl I left behind. "Kimmel won't hurt you or anyone else again."

She looked to me, her eyes pleading for that to be true. I bent forward, her breath on my cheek. Our lips touched, as gentle as starlight on water and as brief as the call of a songbird. That was my silent promise and my hope for the future.

"I've always loved you, Henry Rohling."

My cheek rested against hers. "I won't leave you again."

Chapter Twenty-Four

Conrad, Kansas
January 8, 1945
Dear Henry,
I did something terrible today.

Mitzi must have caught a hen and killed it. I found her sniffing at some blood and feathers. I scolded her good, so much so the poor dog flopped on her side with one paw up—she knew she did wrong—but now she would have to go, and I couldn't let that happen. I covered the blood and feathers, then went to a tree to cut a switch. Mitzi followed me at a distance with her head down, but I couldn't help but wonder—would she do this again? She needed to learn a hard lesson.

I found a length of rope and tied it around her neck. I led her to a flock of hens and gave her the switch, backing her away and shouting. "No!" The third time I pulled her by the neck to the coop, my eyes grew blurry with tears.

Mom came rushing out then. "What are you doing, child?"

"Giving Mitzi a lesson."

She squinted at me the way she does when she's angry. "Untie that dog right now. You're coming inside."

Mom sat me down at the kitchen table while she poured us some tea. "Why were you beating your dog?"

"Mitzi is still chasing the chickens. I don't want Daddy to take her away." I couldn't tell her about the blood and feathers.

"Whipping won't help. She won't know what you're doing. Use a rolled newspaper and slap your hands with it when she disobeys. That will get your point across."

I swallowed hard. "I'll try that. Thanks, Mom."

"Good. Now finish your tea and take Mitzi for a walk. You two need to make up."

Dogs are so forgiving. Before long, we played tug-of-war and scurried up the trail that led to the north windbreak, now a leafless grove of maples and cottonwoods. Since that day, Mitzi hasn't bothered any of the chickens.

Since it is my job to feed the hens, no one has noticed any missing. My deception worked. But I feel dirty. Should I tell Daddy? 1 would gladly take any punishment to keep my dog. What should I do?

Emily

****

Lindahl Farm, Galesville, Wisconsin

January 17, 1945

Dear Emily,

First, the past is unchangeable. Don't conceal any more crimes. I'm not even sure your dog killed anything. There is no mention of a carcass. But she will have to take the consequences for any future actions. Don't break your parents' trust by hiding the truth. You can always find a meeker dog.

Snow has fallen all day. The tractor can still deliver supplies, but the milk will have to wait a day before getting to market. Now, I'm wearing two pairs of gloves and ski visors when I'm outside the shed.

Keep me posted about Mitzi.

Sincerely,

Henry

****

Conrad, Kansas

January 27, 1945

Dear Henry,

Daddy and I argued today. He found a hen dead behind the coop, its side gashed and feathers scattered about. Mitzi could not have done it, because she would have snapped its neck. But I couldn't say that to Daddy.

"Could it have been coyotes?" I asked him.

Daddy shook his head. "It had to be Mitzi. You'll need to find a new home for your dog, or I'll have to put her down."

A crushing weight fell on my heart. I held back tears, but my words were barely more than a gasp. "Please, Daddy. I've trained her. I know she didn't do it. But if I'm wrong—if another hen dies—then I will do the shooting. She's my dog. I'm responsible."

He gave me a level stare. "Okay, this time, but be careful what you say."

"I'll keep my word." Another creature had to be out there, and Mitzi's life depended on me finding it.

I'm worried. What if I'm wrong?

Emily

****

Lindahl Farm, Camp Galesville, Wisconsin

February 9, 1945

Dear Emily,

Too bad you couldn't post a sentry, set a trap, or rig bright lights around your chicken yard. Has Mitzi reacted to any new scent? It may be a stray dog.

We sit beside a frozen brook between snow-covered hills. The cows are now completely dependent on the feed we give them. Somehow, they know this, because the herd stays close by. At night, the sky is a misty river of stars. There is no need to move the shed until the snow melts. That may not be until spring. With the cold, the milking machine has become balky, and we coddle it like a baby. Otherwise, we're doing well in our quiet winter world.

Wishing you and your companion well,
Henry

****

Conrad, Kansas
February 16, 1945
Dear Henry,

That's it! Thank you, Henry. I'll set a trap! Daddy has one large live trap he's not using. I can set it behind the chicken coop, catch the culprit, and save Mitzi. Oh, I hope this works. You were right—Mitzi has been sniffing and growling about the farm. Daddy thinks it's a raccoon, but I have my doubts. It has to be another predator.

Wish me luck. I'm hoping to solve the mystery.
Emily

****

Lindahl Farm, Camp Galesville, Wisconsin
March 27, 1945

I'm sorry for not writing sooner. Sven turned eighteen and joined the army. I've been training a young man to operate the engine and work the feed chute. Greg Newell is from Galesville and lost his right hand in a hay bailer two summers ago. This slight, tousled-haired nineteen-year-old has found ways to work one-handed that has left me amazed. He's even rigged a way to climb atop the milk shed to operate the feeder.

He is inquisitive, though, reminding me of your younger brother. (How is Billie doing? Still shooting everything in sight?) I enjoy answering George's questions, but often, he seems disappointed by my well-rehearsed answers. "That's not very exciting," he would say, and then he would tell me about the latest private-eye story he's been reading.

I've renewed my work contract until June 30th. Camp officials told the Lindahls I should return to the camp at Fort McCoy, but my boss protested. Mr. Lindahl said he needed experienced dairymen. But someday, my freedom will end, and I will become a prisoner of war once again. A reality I'm not looking forward to.

I hope Mitzi has been vindicated.

Henry

****

Emily returned to the banquet with Drosselmeyer's papers. I remained in the lobby, hoping to talk to the coroner. An hour after arriving, the medics rolled the covered body across the hotel's reception area to a waiting ambulance. The vehicle left the hotel, lights flashing but no siren. With the lobby empty, the desk attendant retreated to a back room.

I centered my thoughts on Kimmel as a suspect for Drosselmeyer's death, but I had no evidence against him. What would be his motive? He hardly knew the sergeant. For that matter, Kimmel hardly knew Novak fifty years ago. My only clue was the last thing

Drosselmeyer said before Virginia Powell sent us back to the reunion. Secret orders. Kimmel knew Drosselmeyer and I talked outside the conference room. Did he squeeze the old sergeant for information by starving him of oxygen? Was a fifty-year-old secret worth killing a man?

I needed to pay another visit to Liaison Officer Ernst Reinhardt. Not likely to be a cordial meeting like last time; I may have to push for answers.

The medical examiner waddled out of the hallway, crossed to the hotel desk, and said a few words to the clerk. I approached him as he started for the exit. "Your attention, please, Doctor." I reached to shake his hands but dropped them instead. The coroner still wore his rubber gloves.

"Yes, sir?" he asked.

"I'm a friend of the man you saw." I motioned to the hallway. "Where will the ambulance take Mr. Drosselmeyer?"

"Your friend's remains will be transported to Topeka for postmortem."

"You mean an autopsy?" I asked.

He gave me a faint smile. "That's correct."

"Was his death an accident?"

The big man let out a sigh. "Your friend chronic pulmonary disease, his oh-two cannister depleted, and all indicators suggests asphyxiation. Most likely an accident, but unattended deaths always demand scrutiny. We'll have more answers in a few days." He moved to step around me, but I blocked his path.

"I fear my friend died by design."

His eyes narrowed. "Duly noted, sir." He pulled a

notepad from his lab coat and peered at my nametag. "I've seen this form of death numerous times, Mr. Rohling. The patient doesn't monitor his oxygen supply and runs out when he needs it the most. I'm betting this is an accident. Otherwise, a suspicious death would make you a person of interest." The coroner brushed past me and out the door.

The ominous tone of the medical examiner didn't bother me. This affair would be settled long before any written autopsy report. How could I use Drosselmeyer's death to get Kimmel's attention? I could say the coroner considered the old sergeant's death suspicious. If Kimmel was guilty, the stress could force him to make a mistake.

Not tonight, though. Too tired to think. Best to let the idea ferment. My stomach growled. Reinhardt's noon meal seemed like ages ago. I left the lobby to find Horst for a much-needed late-night dinner.

We were in luck. The kitchen remained open, and we ordered a light meal from our room. Horst told me about his frustrating efforts to turn chemical formulas and manufacturing jargon into common speech. "I'm going to need more pictures and graphs. Hard to do an ocean away."

I listened out of courtesy. I know I nodded off a few times. At the end of the meal, he talked about questions from the police. "Did you learn what happened to your friend?"

"Only that his body will undergo an autopsy."

He nodded to himself. "That would make sense. He died alone."

No, he didn't die alone, but I didn't care to voice my doubts. "I hope he will be buried in Germany. He has no family. Who would be responsible for the body?"

Horst considered. "Since your friend served his country, a responsible group will step forward to claim the body. A veterans' group, a church, even the German Ministry."

"Our group should help him. At least get his body back home."

"There's always cremation. It would simplify the transportation problem."

My thoughts drifted to a quiet place. I jerked when Horst touched my elbow.

"It's bedtime for you, Papa."

"You're right." I yawned. "Tomorrow will come soon enough."

"I've got more work to do tonight. Will a desk light bother you?"

"No, I don't think anything will keep me awake."

"I'll keep it quiet." Horst placed the dish trays outside the door while I changed into bedclothes.

"Good night, Papa."

"Don't stay up late," I said, slipping beneath the sheets and turning away from the light.

I slept until a shadowy dream of being pursued startled me. Red numbers blinked in the darkness. The bedside alarm read 4:17. The firm pillows no longer felt comfortable, and my son's snoring didn't help. I imagined hearing the telltale sounds of Kimmel picking the door lock. Should I get up and check? Horst would call me paranoid. I would call it prudent to peek in the hall.

The hall, of course, was empty.

At six thirty the phone rang. Horst groaned, picked

up the receiver, and let it fall. "Wake up call," he said, then rolled over and pulled the covers to his neck.

I stood and shuffled into the shower. The stinging spray eased the nagging ache between my shoulder blades and gave me a chance to think about exposing Kimmel. It would have to be a pivoting plan with deliberate risk-taking and watchfulness. I had to do more than make Kimmel uneasy. He needed to feel threatened enough to take action. I could say the coroner had found hair and fibers in the room. Kimmel could come after me anyway, but a threat might force him to be reckless. I shivered at the thought; there had to be a better way. But I had no clue what it could be.

Protecting myself and limiting my exposure to danger were essential, like getting out of this blasted shower and staying close to others. It would be so much easier if I could trick Kimmel into a confession. But that meant nothing if no one else heard it.

I considered again asking Horst for help. Another pair of eyes to watch my back would lessen the strain of watching the shadows alone. But I couldn't risk his life, and Kimmel could merely wait for my son to leave for Salina. Better for Horst to think I was paranoid than put him in harm's way.

A knock at the bathroom door jarred me from my thoughts. "Papa, you've been in there quite a while. Need help?"

"I'm fine," I shouted above the water. "Be out in a minute."

"The coffee shop is open. I'm going down there. Want me to bring you back a cup of tea?"

Icy fingers caressed my neck. I did not want to be alone. "You can make coffee in the room."

"That stuff is terrible. I'd rather have a fresh cup."

"Wait. I'll go with you." I turned off the water and grabbed a bath towel.

"No need to hurry, Papa. I'll be back before you're dressed."

A cold embrace. *Don't go. Please.* I thought I'd conquered my cowardice when I learned of Emily's plight, but its coils ensnared me like frosty tentacles.

"Papa?"

"I...I'm feeling dizzy."

The doorknob jiggled. His voice became urgent. "It's locked. Did you fall?"

"No. Feeling better now. Be right out."

"Could you unlock the door? I'd feel better."

"Of course." And I did—after I dressed. Three minutes later, I peeked around the corner. Horst sat fully dressed at the end of his bed flipping through a tourist magazine. He rose to his feet. "You took your time. What's going on?"

I gave him an offended look. "I wanted to go with you. Is that too much to ask?"

He tossed the periodical to the dresser. "Why didn't you say so?"

Admitting fear to my son would only convince him I needed more assistance when we returned home. "We haven't seen much of each other since yesterday. It's good that we should talk more. I need your opinion about a certain matter."

Horst grunted. "We talked last night at dinner, but you practically slept through the entire meal. Besides, I don't think you always welcome my opinions."

I shrugged off a rising irritation. "It's true, we do see things differently. But today...a few things trouble me. I'd like your advice."

He looked at his watch. "It's past seven. The hotel restaurant is open. We can talk over breakfast."

A few minutes later, I cradled a mug of strong tea, while Horst stirred his concoction of coffee, cocoa, cinnamon, and whipped cream with a skinny straw. I ordered a poached egg and toast, while Horst asked for a plate of buttermilk pancakes and bacon. "Listen." Horst bent forward. "I'm sorry for suggesting you needed a care home." He sighed heavily. Even from where I sat, the sweet cinnamon made my nose twitch. "I do worry about you living alone."

"I don't want to give up my home."

"Papa, there are some excellent senior living centers for veterans. Very clean and well run. All funded by the government. You'll be around comrades who have served, just as you did." He took a sip from his spiced drink.

"I have a better idea."

"I'm not sure I like the sound of that."

It was hard to stifle a grin. "It's Emily Henning. She needs my help."

"Oh, no." He held up a palm as if warding off a blow. "Don't tell me you've fallen for her."

"Don't be so dramatic. Her husband is abusive. I intend to protect her."

Horst rubbed his forehead. "I'd expect this conversation coming from my son. Not from my father. Papa, you're being hasty."

I met his eye. "This is serious. Oskar Kimmel manipulated Emily into marriage by framing her brother for a crime." I didn't dare skate any closer to the truth.

Horst stared at me, wondering, I suspected, if I lost another piece of my mind. He shook his head. "This sounds dangerous. Even if the allegations are true, you should stay away from her and leave the matter to local authorities."

"I've told her that. But—"

"But nothing. If it's true, she could be like a drowning victim grasping for a lifesaver. She'll pull you under, too."

"It's not like that."

"Oh, no? You're getting intimately involved with a married woman. No one will see you as the rescuer. Do you plan on stopping a crime while committing another?"

I gave him a sidelong glance. "You watch too many American movies."

"Papa." He regarded me like an obstinate child. "You always say that when I get too close to the truth."

"I think her husband may have killed Drosselmeyer. I plan to expose him."

"There is no evidence foul play is involved. Yesterday, you thought the same killer dispatched your friend. If this man is so dangerous, you are no match for him. Stay away from him. And stay away from his wife as well. No good will come of it." He looked at me incredulously. "Is this how you expect me to help?"

I gave him a half-hearted smile. "Any ideas?"

"On concocting a scheme to make this man confess?"

"I was thinking of a way to draw him out. To give himself away through his own actions."

Horst muttered under his breath. "Now who's watching detective movies? At least you haven't suggested something crazy like telling him you knew of his actions, and you were turning him in. That would be like painting a target on your back."

I held my tea mug tighter, hoping the small ripples inside the cup would diminish. "You're right," I admitted. "That would be an insane notion."

Horst let out a sigh of relief. "By this time tomorrow, we will be on our way home. Give your imagination a rest. Let the Americans pamper you for the rest of the day. Mrs. Kimmel has stirred some old feelings that seem exciting. Let it pass. She's trouble, and you know it. In a month, all this will be a distant memory."

"I don't think so." I sipped the now-cold tea.

"Here comes our breakfast," Horst said, moving his silverware to one side. My toast and eggs arrived on a smaller plate, while my son's order came with a container of syrup and small paper cups of butter. I nibbled a corner of toast without enthusiasm, thinking about the day ahead. What would I learn from Billie Henning? The tousle-headed twelve-year-old I remembered would now be around sixty years old. I smiled, anticipating our meeting on the old prison grounds, a much more pleasant encounter than with Kimmel and Reinhardt later today.

"You didn't have much to eat, Papa. Would you like some pancakes?"

I smeared some jam on the remaining slice of toast. "I'll be fine until noon. Our group will have lunch before we tour the restoration."

"You seem distracted. I hope you're not thinking any more about crime-fighting or seeking revenge."

"I was thinking about meeting another man I

hadn't seen in fifty years. He was a kid then, but is now a foreman on the restoration project. I wondered what kind of man he grew into."

"He must be someone who cares about history. You two will hit it off great." He glanced down for a moment in a feeble attempt to hide a smile, then met my eye. "Just don't nitpick his work if the buildings don't look accurate."

"I'm aware of that. The Americans are calling it a living museum, hoping to cater to tourists. So I wouldn't be surprised if the auditorium chairs had padded seats."

My son's eyes widened. "No leather upholstery in your time?"

"Of course not." Was he kidding?

"Imagine the possibilities, Papa," Horst said. "Cushiony seats for paying tourists could be just one of the amenities. Your auditorium could be a cabaret in the evening with live music and stage acts. Women dressed as male singers, some naughty bits, and good draft beer. It could be a big entertainment venue. Not just a stale old museum. What else is being built?"

I thought back to Virginia Powell's speech yesterday. "There's a mess hall, a sleeping barracks, a guard tower, and a gift shop."

Horst tapped the table with his fork, the remains of his meal forgotten. "No clue about what to do with the barracks. But you could turn the mess hall into a tavern when the auditorium is not in use. Or a family-friendly eatery with the help dressed in prisoner garb serving guests. Your planners could promote their museum into a destination for weddings and family reunions."

I surveyed the décor of the hotel restaurant. Black

and white pictures of old harvesting machines adorned the walls, and mounted hand tools formed a naturalistic pattern around the room. "I don't think this town is ready for a 1920's-style Berlin cabaret. And I find servers dressed as war prisoners…disturbing."

Horst waved away my concerns. "You could have POW reenactors marching about and singing patriotic songs." He took a drink of water, warming to his subject. "Nothing offensive. Most tourists wouldn't understand German anyway. There could be a prison escape attempt and a skirmish with the prison guards who rush to stop it. One prisoner knocks down a guard and grabs his weapon."

"This sounds like a western."

Horst rubbed his hands. "Good suggestion." He held up both thumbs and forefinger like the bottom corners of a movie screen. "Camp Conrad meets Dodge City. After the finale, stay for the currywurst and schnitzel served in the mess hall."

I cradled my head in mock agony. "I'm so glad you didn't go into marketing."

He scrunched his face in an exaggerated pout. "I'm wounded, Papa. Practicing law is selling under a different license."

Despite my anxiety, I chuckled, imagining Horst pitching his POW escape as a Wild West melee to the Cloud County Historical Society. "Please exit through the gift shop," I said.

But Horst had to add the crowning touch. "Be sure to see our Signature Deluxe Expanded 1995 Collector's Limited-Edition Camp Conrad playset. Five dollars off when you fill out our survey card." Both of us pounded the table chortling at the sheer absurdity. I wiped my eyes, ready to add another rejoinder, but Horst's expression changed to a serious demeanor. "We have visitors, Papa. Neither looks very happy."

Staccato heels approached from behind. Virginia Powell glared down at me. Emily stood to one side, her eyes downcast. "Mr. Rohling, yesterday I gave your letter to the police for a cursory examination. This morning, I received a call from an officer with the results."

She was about to give me a dressing down in front of the two people I most cared about. I had to seize the moment to blunt her attack. "Mrs. Powell, allow me to introduce my eldest son, Horst." I extended my hand across the table. "Horst, this is Mrs. Virginia Powell and Mrs. Emily Kimmel."

Horst jumped to his feet, grasping Mrs. Powell's hand, pumping it as any good German would. "This is a great pleasure." He stepped forward to shake Emily's hand as well. "Mrs. Kimmel, an honor to meet you. Papa says you keep the old soldiers awake and the meetings on schedule."

"Both Mrs. Powell and Mrs. Kimmel head the oral history project as well as the prison ground restoration. They made the conference possible," I said.

Emily gave Mrs. Powell a furtive glance.

The director cleared her throat. "Please sit, both of you. What I have to say will not be pleasant."

We sank to our seats.

"The police told me your document is most likely a forgery, artificially aged. The ink came from a mass-produced ballpoint pen. Modern pens were not common until after World War Two. Also, the paper shows no sign of yellowing or browning that comes with time.

The brownish spots most likely came from coffee. Can you explain this?"

I wetted my lips and swallowed. "Someone stole the original note. I had to fabricate another letter. But Novak's words are true."

Mrs. Powell gave Horst a piercing look. "Do you have any knowledge of this?"

My son blew through his nose, tapping a forefinger on the table. "Papa told me about the letter last night."

She centered her attention on me. "So no one has seen the original?"

I swallowed. "No."

"That's unfortunate." A ghost of a smile on her face.

"I've held this letter for fifty years. Now Novak's killer has it." I willed her to believe me. "He's here and has murdered again."

"That is ridiculous. I'm sorry, Mr. Rohling, but I can't allow you to attend this morning's conference or accompany the rest of the group to the restoration site this afternoon. The same goes for finishing your interview and attending the luncheon and banquet this evening." She stepped back, already dismissing me.

"So you'll be punishing Miss Zoeller as well?" I asked.

"Nice try, sir. That won't work a second time."

"Maybe he should continue with his interview." Emily spoke, striding forward. "Mr. Rohling's history is still vital to the project. These are his words. His perceptions. His perspective. That is the point of oral history. Editing his thoughts would be tantamount to censorship."

The director gave me a steely-eyed frown. "Fine.

But that will be the extent of your participation in this conference."

"What about tomorrow?" Horst asked. "How will we get back home, Mrs. Powell?"

"Of course, you'll be taken back to the airport. I'm not heartless, sir."

With that, the director stalked out. I wondered if those pounding heels would damage the restaurant's ceramic tile. Emily followed behind her. At the entrance, she flashed a quick V for Victory sign, then hurried from sight.

Chapter Twenty-Five

Conrad, Kansas
April 3, 1945
Dear Henry,
I'm so glad you wrote back!

Good news! We caught the predator the first night Daddy set the trap in mid-February. The next morning, Mitzi sprinted to the cage and circled it, barking up a storm. As I drew near, the creature inside the wire mesh hissed. I know they kill hens, but a red fox trapped with her kits huddled outside broke my heart. Daddy said she had to be destroyed. "If I released her, the fox would become a neighbor's problem. Now fetch my rifle, then go help your mother. I'll come in when this business is done."

I helped Mom dust and sweep the front room. Afterward, Mom suggested we make sugar cookies. I know she was trying to distract me. We baked a second batch when I saw Daddy get in his pickup and leave. I never heard a shot.

An hour later, he came in the house, taking off his heavy shoes behind the back door, drew a glass of water from the sink, and sat at the oaken kitchen table looking glum. I sat with him, aching to know what happened, but I dared not ask the question.

He drew a second glass and settled in his chair again. "I must be getting soft," he said. "The foxes were panting from thirst, and I gave them water. After that, I told myself, 'Well, you can't shoot the mother now.' So I let them loose by the river."

"Thank you, Daddy."

He shrugged. "I doubt if they'll show up here again. But if I see another one, I'll shoot it."

I hugged him and realized then why I love you, Henry. You remind me of Daddy.

The Camp Conrad prisoners are working for us again this year, planting potatoes and expanding our garden with more cabbage. Like last year, we have a different two-man crew each week. Some of the same men are back, including Mr. Goetz and Mr. Kimmel. Isn't that great?

Emily

****

Lindahl Farm, Wisconsin

May 13, 1945

Dear Emily,

I'm still working for the Lindahls. The owner delivered the feed yesterday by tractor. He told me Germany has surrendered, and the war in Europe is over. "I haven't heard from the army yet, but Uncle Sam will likely send you home soon. Thing is, son, I don't want you to go, not till our boys get back."

I kept a solemn face, not wishing to show my excitement. "Life here will go back to normal."

"Not likely." Lindahl spat a stream of tobacco from puffed cheeks. "Our guys will head off to Japan to fight Hirohito. As far as I'm concerned, you're staying."

After unloading the feed, Lindahl drove away, leaving me to wonder, am I still a prisoner of war or merely a useful captive? I'm hoping the journey home will not be as rocky as I fear.

    With love,
    Henry

****

Conrad, Kansas
May 22, 1945
Dear Henry,

Many of the farmers here feel much like your boss. They do not want to lose the prison workers. For the last three years, they've become an important part of our lives. Daddy's already wrote to Senator Carlson to delay the departure of his crew. "Good riddance to the Kraut officers," he said over supper one night. "They're no good to me. But we should keep the workers."

How the army will handle the enlisted men is anyone's guess. I hope they treat you fairly. You and many others provided a service to this country, and the army should recognize that. Getting our boys back home will take time. But I hope you will be able to leave soon.

    Be patient.
    Emily

****

Lindahl Farm, Camp Galesville, Wisconsin
September 23, 1945
Dear Em,

It's been four months since the war in Europe ended. I am not a free man, but I'm happy to earn a steady wage, which will put American dollars in my pocket when I leave this country. I can make good use of this money when I return home.

In a week, I'll return to Camp McCoy to await a train east. As glad as I am to end my time as a prisoner,

I will miss working for the Lindahls and your family. With any luck, I should be back in Berlin by the end of the year. Our dream of reuniting may still come true.

With hope in my heart,
Henry

****

Conrad, Kansas
October 15, 1945
That is terrific news. Your journey back home will go quicker than you think.

The workers here finished their jobs and left by train a few days ago. The whole town turned out for their farewell. Girls from a nearby college threw kisses, and a group of farmers parked their trucks along the rails and honked as the train passed them out of town. Camp Conrad officially shut down today without much fanfare. Since the Japanese surrender, a few of our boys are arriving back home each week. We haven't heard word from Josh when he will return. I hope it will be soon.

Let me know when you are leaving for home.
Emily

****

Camp McCoy, Wisconsin
October 27, 1945
Dear Emily,
I arrived back at Camp McCoy a month ago. We are still waiting for word on when we depart for home. There are a thousand Germans here, and they are as restless as I am. The Asians are already gone. Their compound is closed off, but we still have plenty of space to move about. There is, however, much tension here, due to how the Americans are treating us. It is

baffling and disturbing.

First, the Americans are feeding us bland food and in smaller portions. Meat is limited to one meal per day and always canned—never fresh. The timing is suspicious. Now that American PWs have returned home, this stinginess feels like a reprisal. If the Americans wish us to be gone, why don't they send us home?

Second, the guards are forcing us to watch ghastly and repulsive films each evening. They are movies of prisoners liberated from what the Americans call "death camps." Mounds of naked, shriveled bodies lay stacked on the ground. Gaunt, skeletal men hobbled on misshapen limbs. Piles of eyeglasses and shoes sit with no one to claim them. No human being should be treated in that manner. One brave prisoner rose to his feet during the film, his shadow blocking the screen. "Why are we forced to watch this horror? We didn't know about this. How could we? And we didn't cause this to happen!"

The rest of us cheered his boldness, but the American sergeant in charge ordered the man to sit. He turned off the projector, and the lights came on. "Listen up!" the sergeant said. "Maybe none of you marched these civilians into the gas chambers, but you were there at *Kristallnacht*. You could have stopped the murder and the terror then, but you didn't. And that is why you're watching your handiwork now."

And so, we sat until it was over.

Blaming an entire nation for what a few Nazi officers have done seems to be the intent of the Americans. They want all Germans to take the blame for the death camps. But I wonder. Can Lady Liberty's treatment of her own citizens bear such scrutiny?

Sorry to burden you with these questions.

Henry

****

"Virginia Powell makes a commanding performance," Horst mused. "A lioness. But your friend came through for you. I'm sorry you won't be seeing the construction. I know you've had your heart set on it." Horst sipped the last of his coffee brew.

Words failed me. I could only stare at my clenched fingers.

The waitress arrived then to clear our plates. Horst paid with a traveler's check, and we withdrew to our room. I brushed my teeth and shaved, while my son packed his computer bag with papers, throwing in a scribble pad and pen. "Since today is Sunday, the library in Salina will be closing at two. I should get back in time for us to enjoy an early dinner. I hope you won't be too bored while I'm gone."

"I'll find things to do," I said, splashing on some cologne. "There is still the interview, and I can find a way to see the old prison grounds."

Horst froze, one hand still on his bag. "I'm not sure if that's a good idea. Better keep a low profile. Try not to antagonize Mrs. Powell, and stay clear of Mr. Kimmel. You're too old for these cowboy antics."

"If the grounds are open to the conference, then anyone can observe the construction. I'm only curious. It would be a shame to travel back home and not see it."

"I suppose." Horst muttered the words. He fished around in his bag and brought out a business card, handing it to me. "Here is the telephone number to the library. Call me if you need to. The staff can page me."

I placed the card in my pocket. "Not likely to need it."

"All right then. I'll see you when I return." Horst and I strolled to the lobby where we said our goodbyes and went our separate ways, Horst to his rental car and me to sit outside the conference room. I soon found a seat in the same lounge pit where Drosselmeyer and I talked the day before.

Muffled voices filtered from the closed doors with an occasional rumble of applause. I wished I could have been inside. How did I get ostracized? By not listening to good advice. Even Reinhardt warned me about speaking up during the plane trip. I did not listen to Mrs. Powell or even to my son. Still, I had no regrets in vindicating Novak's honor. I would have done it again.

To fill the time until the morning session ended, I read a copy of the tourism magazine Horst perused earlier. It soon captured my attention.

Germans were the largest European group to settle within the state, especially during the 1800s. Many were devout Catholics, Quakers, and Mennonites oppressed in their native countries and made the trek to America looking for cheap land. These religious settlers wanted no part of slavery, and they fought to keep Kansas a free state. German food, festivals, and culture still thrived in many smaller communities. An old Deutschlander could become comfortable here.

The doors opened. Several attendees and students strolled down the hallway, looking for a spot to finish their oral histories. Kimmel passed by me, following a well-dressed man of Asian descent, carrying a knapsack—as did all the students. I caught up with Kimmel, tapping him on the shoulder. "A minute of your time, sir."

He kept walking. "I'm busy."

"It's about Emily."

"Couldn't care less."

"And a certain hunting accident."

He stopped, turning to his student. "Tuan, find a place to set up your gear. I'll be along in a few minutes." The young man nodded and hustled ahead, moving with ease between others in the hall. "This better be good, Rohling."

"I want some honest answers before I go to the police."

"So you want to play hardball. Okay. Let's talk over there." He pointed to the exit doors. "No one will hear us if we keep our voices down." He led the way out and stood between the sliding panes of glass. I trailed behind. "Move to the wall," he said, "so you don't trip the electric eye."

I followed his example, and the glass door remained closed.

"Why so secretive?" I asked. "What is there to hide?"

"You know why." He regarded me with expressionless eyes. "Call it quits, Rohling. You're washed up. Virginia Powell has called you a fraud, barred you from the conference, and grounded you. I'm willing to bet your little cutie is wishing she drew someone else for her assignment. My advice is to go back to your room and stay there. You might make it home."

His humiliation game wasn't going to work with me. "Not until I've completed what I came here to do."

Kimmel grinned, showing perfect teeth. "Showing

off Novak's latter? Ashes now. You won't get anywhere that way."

"At least I'll have my words on the record."

"Accusations from a forgetful old man backed by a forgery will never be taken seriously. You're nothing but background noise."

I stepped back, causing the outside door to open. Losing the letter, creating an easily recognized fake, and now ostracized from the group—all this was a fruitless mission. I saw that now. I sensed a yawning emptiness in my gut, an abyss to fall into and hide from the shame I inflicted on myself. In saving Novak's legacy, I hoped to save my own.

I licked dry lips. It was hard to form the words. "Admit to me you killed Novak, and I'll leave you alone."

He smirked. "Better you die an old man, still wondering."

"You must still have been worried. Otherwise, you wouldn't have silenced Drosselmeyer."

"He died from his own neglect. Besides, I was at the conference all afternoon. Or at the hotel bar. The police have verified my story."

"That can't be." I never thought of checking Kimmel's whereabouts yesterday afternoon. Was he telling the truth?

"Believe it. Now, what do you know about a hunting accident?"

I let out a breath. Emily's trouble made it easier to think. "You killed a man and arranged the evidence to implicate Billie and Emily. You've controlled their lives for nearly fifty years."

Kimmel crossed his arms. His cold eyes bored into

mine before he burst into laughter. "Your gullibility is astounding. I should write this down." He snorted with delight.

"You deny it?"

"My wife has been suffering from depression for years. She's seen a shrink, attempted suicide, and has been in a psychiatric hospital. She's cost me a lot of money over the years. I won't save her a second time."

I balled my hands, ready to strike. Blood pounded in my head, and I bent my knees slightly, ready to draw blood. But Kimmel had a height and weight advantage on me. I was no match for him. "Monster," I said. "You should be shot."

He withdrew a leather-covered bar with a handgrip from his suit jacket. "Hit me, and I'll knock you out."

I stared at the cudgel, knowing Kimmel would not hesitate to use it. "You forgot to deny the killing and the blackmail. Emily's emotional state is probably your doing."

He ignored my remark. "Relax, Rohling. Since she tried to off herself, the therapist suggested she find a purpose. Get involved with a group. She joined the Historical Society and got the idea for putting together a few camp exhibits. With Virginia's building contractor connections, the Chamber of Commerce got involved, and that meant dozens of jobs for this sorry town. Even the wife's cornball idea of a reunion has worked out. Tourists for miles around will come to see the attraction."

"Playsets," I muttered.

Kimmel peered at me, bemused. "You're losing it, Rohling."

"Your secret is about to come out," I said and then

retreated down the hallway to the lobby. Kimmel just gave me a direct threat. Part of the plan, but its execution left me shaken. Perhaps the safest course meant staying in my room. That could be a trap as well. The specter of Drosselmeyer's death lurked in the back of my mind. An accidental death? It had to be if Kimmel's alibi was true. And what about Emily's emotional state? Her turmoil could only have come from Kimmel's abuse.

Footsteps, muted by the carpet, approached from behind. I whirled about not sure what to expect. Kathy Zoeller jumped back. "Sorry, Mr. Rohling, I didn't mean to startle you."

"Quite all right," I said, letting out a long breath. "I hoped to find you."

"I didn't see you at the reunion this morning."

"I was outside...stretching my legs. Guess I lost track of time."

"It's okay." She gave me an endearing little-girl smile. "Miss Emily told me how your letter created a stir and that you won't be attending the rest of the conference."

"That's more or less true," I admitted. "But I'd still like to conclude our taping session. If you're amenable."

She broke into a bright smile. "Yes! We can finish here in the lobby." Kathy assembled her equipment on a coffee table between two armchairs.

"Miss Zoeller...Kathy, there is something you should know before we get started. It may affect your decision to finish our interview."

"Just a sec. I want to get everything on tape." She set the hanging microphone before me, flipped on the power, and adjusted the volume. "All set. What happened after our last session?" She rolled her index finger and pointed to her machine.

I leaned back, caught off guard by the question. "Paul Drosselmeyer died. His death is still a shock. I met him during our time at Camp Conrad. I find his passing…disturbing."

"Mrs. Powell said he has been ailing for quite some time. His death was an accident."

"That remains to be seen. The authorities will do an autopsy."

Kathy leaned forward, her voice low. "With what happened to Mr. Novak in the prison camp, are you thinking…there could be a connection with Mr. Drosselmeyer's death?"

A shot of pure energy focused my thoughts. If this girl ever breathed the possibility of foul play, she could face real danger. I grabbed her arms, pinning them to the table. "Listen to me." My words came low and urgent. "Paul died from his own carelessness. His air ran out, and he didn't have a new tank. An accident—that's all it was!"

She stared at my hands. "Mr. Rohling, you're hurting me."

"Oh, God." I released her and rubbed my temple. "Kathy, I am so sorry. You must understand. Mrs. Powell has every right to bar me from the rest of the conference. I'm a fraud. The letter I showed you was a forgery. I made it look real. But it's a fake. Like me. Please, forget what I said about Novak. And forgive me."

She sat appraising me for several seconds. Finally, she reached for the recorder but did not stop the machine. "You're not fooling me, Mr. Rohling. Something happened in that camp that is still haunting you. And you have a secret you're not sharing. Mr. Novak's killer is alive, isn't he?"

I nodded, refusing to meet her eyes.

"And is he here?"

I lick dry lips. "Yes, but I have no proof."

She drew her hand from the switch. "This recording will force the listener to ask questions. Seek out answers."

"Please. I beg of you. Don't make these tapes public. It's—it's not safe."

"Don't worry. I'll make copies and keep one in a secure place. But completing the oral history is important. Your story demands it."

"This is a dangerous game."

"We're not accusing anyone of a crime. Brian Novak's story is an intriguing real-life mystery stretching back fifty years. Everyone looking into the story will see it differently. In a sense, you've already accomplished your goal. Mr. Novak will be remembered for years to come."

"I see your point. But the risk to you—"

"Great! All I need is Mr. Novak's history and the experiences you shared."

For the next forty minutes, I related how Novak and I first met, soldiering in the Afrika Korps, the surrender, and our journey to Kansas. "It's hard to realize I saw him only a week before leaving for the Henning farm," I concluded.

"There were other hangings. Some questionable deaths. But nothing ruled as murder at Camp Conrad," she said.

"A convenience for the Americans to deem a POW death a suicide."

"A different time," she mused. Kathy turned off the recorder and disconnected mic cords. "Thank you, Mr. Rohling. A great interview. What will you do for the rest of the day?"

"Wait for my son to return from Salina. This is a working vacation for him."

"We talked yesterday about meeting with Bill Henning. Are you still interested?"

My mouth fell open. "Of course, I'd very much like to see him."

"Let's do that. I'm meeting with some friends for lunch. After that, you and I can drive out to the museum grounds and visit with Mr. Henning."

"You have your own car?"

"A clunker, but it gets me around."

"Where shall we meet?"

Kathy considered. "How about here? My friends like to chatter. Let's say one thirty. Two at the latest."

"I'll be waiting."

Chapter Twenty-Six

Conrad, Kansas
November 19, 1945
Dear Henry,

My parents just got the word. Josh is coming home
aboard a Liberty ship and should be with us by New
Year's. We're all excited about his return. It's been a
long time since I've seen my older brother. Having our
family together again will be a blessing.

I understand your disgust with those awful death
camps. The newspapers give some horrible details,
much more than the radio. I don't think I could watch
such terrible things. The feeling here is that the war is
over, and we should get all our boys home. There are
even posters that say "Let's Move On!"

I hope you will be able to leave camp soon. While
your guards didn't treat you well toward the end, I'd
say the people who hired you saw you as friends. That
bond will last a lifetime.

Remember your promise,
Emily

****

Camp McCoy, Wisconsin
December 19, 1945
Dearest Emily,

Great to hear about your brother returning. My
only caution is not to press him on his time overseas.

Some of his experiences may shock you. Be patient and understanding as he readjusts to a quieter life in the countryside.

I have my own good news. In two days, a group of us will board a train for Baltimore. There, we will leave for France. Once we arrive in Le Havre, we should get back home in a matter of days, depending on the train schedule and the condition of the tracks. I bought American cigarettes, a new topcoat, and changed the rest of my wages into American dollars. No more phony prison camp money. Now, I'm counting down the hours. It has been an eye-opening experience in America, but I can't wait to see my family again.

When I next write to you, I will be in Berlin. My parents have not written to me in months, so I worry. I imagine Berlin has felt the wrath of the Allies. I start this homeward journey fearing what I will find at its end.

Wish me well, Emily. Before you reply, wait until I write again. I can then give you a proper address.

Henry

****

Reins, France
March 8, 1946
Dear Emily,
Betrayed!

The ruthless victors of this war are working former German POWs and "displaced persons," an interesting term for captured Germans after the war. We've been drafted to rebuild France. Though we are no longer prisoners of war, we are not free, and we are not protected under the Geneva Convention rules. Rumor is there are "DP" Germans in England as well. My money is gone. French soldiers in Le Havre rummaged through my pockets, taking my old watch and all my money. Any resistance we gave was met with more of our possessions being taken away.

For the past three months, I've been working in a quarry, cutting stone blocks for buildings and paving. The guards are a sullen and mistrustful lot, seldom speaking to us, except to warn about trying to escape. They've already shot some who tried. Any escapees captured are forced to search for the thousands of landmines scattered throughout the country. Quarry work is dangerous enough.

So we labor and wonder how long this will go on. Don't write yet. The guards move us every week, and they never tell us where.

I'll write when I can.

Henry

****

Lyon, France
April 19, 1946
Dear Emily,

We are in southeast France, repaving roads that were crushed by tanks, both American and German. New buildings are going up. American officers and even enlisted men swagger about, sometimes with a French girl on their arm. Our victors lack discipline. But I have no complaints. Today, a group of DPs passed over the road we were repairing herded by French guards. They marched to Lyon to remove landmines. I will be here for a while.

Please write. I miss you.

Henry

****

Conrad, Kansas
July 1, 1946
Dear Henry,

There is so much to tell! Josh returned January fourth. He is much older and muscular now. And he's quiet. No longer the brash boy who would take me tadpole hunting or pushed me on the tire swing that used to hang from the tree in the front yard.

Early this summer, he helped Daddy with fieldwork but fell to the ground covering his ears when the tractor backfired. He shook even after we hurried him to the house. Mom wanted to take him to the doctor, but Josh refused to go. "It's my problem. I'll deal with it," he said. Then he went back outside. We didn't know what to do. Some of the boys who came back seem the same, but others seem angry and restless. Yesterday, I saw a young man, missing both hands, pushing a cart at the grocery store. Some of the customers stared at him in horror, forgetting to let him through the crowded aisles.

Daddy may hire another man to take the load off Josh. He thinks my brother will come around in time. Mom and I are not so sure.

I hope you get home soon.

Emily

****

Paris, France
October 22, 1946
Dear Emily,

Your last letter has caught up with me since my relocation. I'm now in Paris, planting trees and gardens around some of the government buildings. The rubble has long been removed, and many new roads are completed, but the city remains stark and barren. My crew plant saplings along the thoroughfares in addition to the gardens. There is a water shortage, though, and the needs of people come first. For now, the trees will have to depend on the rain to survive.

My supervisor is a sergeant from Minneapolis. His uncle runs a small tavern downtown. He chuckled when I told him how guards in my old POW camp found homebrew in our prison camp. Sergeant Irving said rail service between Paris and Berlin has opened again. One boxcar of DPs is allowed per trip. If I was interested, he could see about getting me on the train. "Be patient," he said, "and keep planting those trees."

This news has galvanized me. I hope it will happen soon.

Take care of your brother. Keep him away from startling noises.

Henry

****

I hoped to meet Reinhardt during the noon break, but he was nowhere to be seen. Probably in his room dining on some delicacy. Maybe I'd catch up to him at the museum later this afternoon. Reinhardt could verify a theory I formed linking his secret orders with Novak. Would he verify my hunch? The man liked to boast about his power. I hoped pride would overtake caution, and he would gleefully admit the truth.

At one fifteen, I returned to the lobby to find Kathy reading a paperback. "Good afternoon, Mr. Rohling," she said, putting the book away. "Ready?"

I nodded.

"Great. We can get an early start and beat the crowd."

"You lead the way." I followed as she hustled to her car.

I did not expect the ride to be so short. The downtown business district covered only four blocks of older buildings. Many probably stood while I lived at camp. From there, we turned north, passing a mushroom-shaped water tower, a high school, and retail stores set far back from the street. At the edge of town, she pulled into a gravel lot where a collection of cars and work trucks parked. A guard tower stood between two gates flanked by a double row of chain-linked fencing, not barbed wired. A huge banner hung over the entrance gate: WELCOME TO CAMP CONRAD. Someone had an ironic sense of humor.

Beyond the gate, four structures in varying stages of construction stood at the corners of an asphalt quadrangle, about two-thirds the size of a soccer field. None looked familiar except the barracks.

Kathy helped me out of my too-low seat and swept her arm past the guard tower. "Here it is. In three weeks, the exterior work will be finished. Then work can begin on the interior exhibits. Mrs. Powell hopes Camp Conrad's grand opening will be Thanksgiving."

Thanksgiving at a German POW camp? Better let that one pass. "I don't recall the prison being so close to town."

She looked peeved. Did I offend her? "Well…the museum planners wanted the buildings close to restaurants and motels in town. The Bullseye Megastore is a big sponsor of the museum."

I could imagine my son's response to that, but I had a more pressing question. "What became of the original prison?"

"Not much is left. Two or three rotting buildings and a concrete bathhouse on the verge of collapse. Nobody goes there, except for high school kids out to party. The land is privately owned but abandoned."

"Pity." The news saddened me. Fifty years ago, thousands of prisoners lived there, and a few hundred garrisoned GIs. Now the grounds were barely a memory.

"The museum isn't much now," Kathy said, oblivious to my thoughts, "but it will look great when it's finished."

"I'm sure it will."

"Let's find Mr. Henning. I'm anxious for you two to meet."

"Any ideas where to look?" I asked.

She pointed to the barracks. "Wherever it's the loudest."

"A sound plan," I agreed. We slipped through the partially opened gate and headed across the tarmac. The whirr of an electric motor revved, and the screech of saw blades biting wood blasted the air.

Builders had already completed much of the exterior in white clapboard trimmed in green. Plastic sheeting covered tall, narrow window spaces. As we stepped inside, saw blades ground to a stop. The smell of fresh-cut lumber permeated the air, and sawdust crunched underfoot, making the concrete floor slippery. Three men in denim uniforms, tool belts, goggles, and filters assembled wooden bunks. One held a heavy plank while another set it in place with an electric screwdriver. A third man, stocky, with little hair, measured a length of wood and drew a cutting line. A flip of the switch kicked on the saw which created a powerful electric hum. All glanced up when we stepped in front of the work lights.

The balding man lifted clear goggles over his spectacles and pushed the filter to his neck, revealing gray stubble. "We weren't expecting visitors for another half hour. Can I help you?"

"We're part of the reunion group," Kathy said, "but we came early. Is Bill Henning around?"

"That would be me." The balding man turned off the saw.

Her eyes with flashed anticipation. "I'm Kathy Zoeller, and this is Mr. Henry Rohling."

"Rohling?" Henning peered at me through his glasses. "I'll be, it is you." He stepped around the saw, stripping off his work gloves and held out a massive hand. "It's been fifty years. How the hell are you?"

"I've been well. And please, call me Henry." We shook hands then. His fingers were calloused and rough, the knuckles scarred from many past accidents. "I don't suppose you've been called Billie for some time," I said.

"Not since my first barfight." He chuckled at my bemusement. "Call me Bill. Let's go outside to talk." He gave quick instructions to the other men, and we exited the building.

"Doing well?" I asked.

"My fingers are stiff. Can't climb a ladder anymore. But I'm still working."

I nodded. "Those bunks you're building are exactly how I remembered them. Skinny and uncomfortable."

"Sis found some old photographs from another camp. I drew up some specs based on those pictures." Thick in the chest, Bill Henning stood stoop-shouldered, but still seemed strong enough to lift and tote all day. His wrinkled forehead and perpetual squint indicated, however, a lifetime of worry.

"Can I record your conversation?" Kathy produced a microcassette recorder from a pouch around her waist. "It's for the oral history project."

Henning eyed the recorder but shrugged. "I guess so."

"Fine." I wanted to talk in private but could see no way to say no.

"I can tell you a bit about each of the buildings." He pointed to the gate tower. "We have a dozen Camp Conrad pictures detailing the tower scaffolding and machine-gun nest, and we didn't vary from the original design, unlike the dining hall." He swept his hand across the asphalt to a blue and white structure with the words MESS HALL painted in bold Gothic script. "Since the historical society is using that building on their brochure, we dressed up the building for visitor appeal. Food served there will be catered by the German restaurants around the area."

"Will the seating inside be the same as it was fifty years ago?" I asked. Those rough wooden benches made sitting for any length of time uncomfortable.

"The benches will be upholstered, plus there'll be live music on weekends."

"What are the buildings near the gate?" I asked.

Henning brushed sawdust from his chin. "Housed together on the left is the theater and museum. Film students from Kansas State are working on a documentary to show there. Sis and Mrs. Powell spent a lot of time gathering photos for the movie project. To the right is a gift shop."

I held my breath. Would Kathy notice Bill's mention of Emily?

"I don't understand." She held her recorder higher. "Is Miss Emily your sister?"

"Big sister. Been close since we were kids."

She turned to me, surprised and maybe a little hurt. "So you and Miss Emily knew each other from way back? And you never told me?"

My cheeks burned. "It's...difficult to explain." A lame excuse, but I refused to say more.

Henning smiled knowingly. "Not so complicated when you think about it. I was twelve at the time. Sis was eighteen and feeling confined. Henry was twenty-three, a trim young man at a time when most of our boys were off fighting. When he and the other POWs worked for Pop, it changed my sister's world. Once, I heard Pop talking to Mom late one night. He worried about Henry and Emily running off to marry. Mom knew better."

Her eyes widened. "You two were...involved?"

"We knew each other." My voice held an edge. I cast Henning a stern look, but he seemed not to notice.

"There were good reasons why Uncle Sam discouraged fraternization with American girls." Henning winked at me, taking an all-knowing tone. "German soldiers were chick-magnets."

"Get out!" She giggled.

I wanted to snap at Henning, but that would only draw attention to my discomfort.

"It happened all over the county," he said. "Whenever my sister's friends came around, they talked about driving out to the camp to catch sight of 'those German boys.' " Henning's grin faded. "Those were

325

simpler times."

Kathy bit her lip, pointing her recorder to Henning. "Didn't Mr. Kimmel work in the Labor Program? I thought that's how he met Miss Emily."

Henning frowned, glancing at the parking lot. "You'll have to ask Oskar about that. Say, I better get back to work."

I grabbed his elbow. "A word, please, before you go. It's important." I hoped to dismiss my interviewer without being harsh. "Kathy, I have an old and sensitive issue to discuss with Mr. Henning. It's best you not be present."

"Does it have to do with Miss Emily?" she asked.

"No." I lied.

"Will you tell me about it…later?"

"If things work out, I can." Never mind what would happen if I made a mistake.

"Okay, I'll be waiting in the car until the others arrive." She gave me the same look a child would if she didn't get her way.

"There's one more thing I have to ask."

She raised an eyebrow. "Yes, Mr. Rohling?"

"I wish to borrow your tape recorder."

"Why not?" With sullen eyes and a set jaw, she retrieved the machine and replaced the cassette with a new one. "There are three buttons you need to know." Kathy demonstrated how the recorder worked, then slapped the machine in my hand. "Remember to ask the person for permission to record while the tape is running. It's common courtesy."

"Got it. And thank you." I pocketed the recorder. "I'll talk to you soon."

Henning had already wandered back to the

barracks. I hustled after him. "Glad you waited for me. Emily told me how Kimmel manipulated the two of you."

"Why did she…?" Henning retreated a step, then stepped forward to grip my arm. "Henry, you have to keep this to yourself."

"I already told Kimmel I knew about his game."

Sweat glistened off his forehead. "Be careful. The man is dangerous."

"Agreed, but I'm hoping he's clumsy as well. Can you watch my back at least while he is around?"

"I've got a job to do, Henry. The best suggestion I got is to stay with a crowd. Don't wander about alone. Especially if you don't know where he is."

"I'll try. In the meantime, I have one more person I need to talk to. A Nazi who still dreams of the Reich."

Henning gave me a sideways glance. "You need to find a better class of friends."

"It's necessary. The more I know, the better I can shake Kimmel's tree."

Henning scratched his whiskers. "Let me get this straight. Do you plan to reveal Kimmel by provoking him? What if he attacks you?"

"That's the idea. I want him to."

"To succeed, you'll have to survive."

I cleared my throat. "Of course."

"What then?"

"Kimmel is bound to confess." I produced the tape player. "This machine will record his words."

"Your plan could use some work."

"You got a better one?

"Hell, no. Kimmel's got Sis and me hogtied. I've run out of ideas a long time ago."

"You could break the knot by informing the authorities about the blackmail."

"I've considered coming clean. Each time I drive to the police station, I turn away. If I go to jail, who will protect Sis? I rushed her to the hospital after Oskar drove her to taking those sleeping pills."

"He told me Emily tried to take her own life."

Henning smirked. "That's the story he likes to tell. Two years ago, Sis tried to leave him, but he threatened her. Said he would destroy me. That pushed her over the edge. Oskar might as well have forced those pills down her throat. Did you know he bought her a new rifle? I think he plans to kill her and dress it up like a suicide."

The thought left me queasy. "All the more reason to act now."

"I'll think about it," he said.

"If I fail, that may be your only action left."

Henning produced a rag and wiped his brow. "Hell of a plan, Henry," he said ruefully. "Do you enjoy living on the edge?"

"I'm terrified, but I can't back out now."

He gazed over my shoulder. "It's showtime. Visitors are coming. Sis and Oskar will be here soon. Good luck, Henry." Henning reentered the barracks.

Outside the gate, a van pulled into the parking lot, followed by a convoy of cars and pickups. Clusters of people stepped beneath the welcome sign and trekked across the asphalt. Emily and Mrs. Powell walked together with the rest of the conference attendees following behind. Kathy caught my eye and waved. Reinhardt and Stecklein lagged behind the others.

I didn't see Kimmel. Needles prickled my back. He

could be anywhere.

A few minutes later, we assembled on the tarmac. Mrs. Powell paced in front of us, raising her hand for silence. "Attention, please! I want you to divide into two groups for the tour. One will follow Mrs. Kimmel; the other will be headed by me."

Kathy called my name and lifted her hand in a questioning gesture. I pointed to Reinhardt, making circles with my finger. She shrugged and joined the crowd who followed Emily to the mess hall. Reinhardt and Stecklein poked along, following Mrs. Powell's group to the theater. I met both men outside the auditorium doors. "Colonel, I didn't think you were interested in museums."

"I despise them," he said. "Nothing but roadside attractions. Few of the wartime museums mention the *Rheinwiesenlager* concentration camps. Now that the American troops are gone, the truth will come out." The rest of Mrs. Powell's group entered the building, leaving Reinhardt, Stecklein, and me alone under the August sun.

The US concentration camps for *Wehrmacht* soldiers and displaced persons continued to be a controversial subject, especially among American historians. Some Germans called the 1945 POW camps along the Rhine American Death Camps. Depending on the nationality of the historian, those who died there numbered less than five thousand or more than a million. The true number of those lost? Only the ground knew.

Stecklein fanned himself with a Camp Conrad souvenir cap that many of the former prisoners wore today. "For all their talk about German prisoners being brothers, the Americans have forgotten how vindictive they were to Deutsch prisoners in Europe."

"But they don't hold a candle to the Russian horde." Reinhardt produced a handkerchief and mopped the back of his neck. "Half of Europe shrouded in darkness for decades thanks to the conspirators at Yalta. Yet the German people bore the blame. If it wasn't for Churchill, the Americans could have helped us to push Russia beyond the Urals. The world today would be a different place."

I had heard variations of this tiresome argument many times and wanted to turn the conversation in a different direction. "Victors write the histories, but at least the voice of a few German soldiers will be heard."

Reinhardt chuckled. "I gave my little fräulein an earful. It will be interesting to know what she will keep in."

"I talked about going to Britain and cooking for a crew of roadbuilders," said Stecklein. "The Tommies assumed I was a kitchen chief." Stecklein shifted his feet. "I was a prisoner in peacetime longer than during the war."

"Go rest inside, Sergeant," Reinhardt told him. "You need to sit. I'll be along soon. I think Herr Rohling has more questions." His eyes shifted to me. "Am I correct?"

"A few," I said.

Stecklein bowed. "Thank you, sir." He trudged up to the theater door, using the ramp rather than climbing the three steps. "You should rest as well, Colonel," he said, before maneuvering his bulk inside.

Reinhardt leveled me with an intense gaze. "How can I help you, Private?"

"Since our talk yesterday, I've learned a few more things about the camp. How Private Novak was murdered is still a puzzle, but I've assembled some of the pieces. All I ask is for you to confirm what I surmised."

Reinhardt took a deep breath. "We could discuss this on the way home. Much more comfortable on a plane, wouldn't you agree?"

"This can't wait."

His head drooped for a moment. "Ask your questions, then."

I retrieved the recorder from my pocket and pushed the record button. "Do I have your permission to record this conversation?"

He brushed the air with his hand. "It matters little to me."

The tiny wheels spun inside the case. I held the recorder for him to see.

"Since our conversation, someone stole the letter I received from Novak. And Sergeant Drosselmeyer died. That wasn't an accident. Were you with anyone after the conference yesterday?"

Reinhardt's eyes narrowed. "I find that question offensive, Private. As I already explained to the police, Alfred and I sampled a number of dark ales in the hotel tavern before the banquet."

I pursed my lips. No doubt the police verified their stories. Another mark for Drosselmeyer's death to be an accident.

"We were supposed to meet." I plunged on, knowing if Reinhardt pretended ignorance, I would be left with nothing. "He mentioned secret orders. That could only have come from you."

"I don't know what you're referring to." Reinhardt looked the picture of innocence.

"You admitted some of your lower officers saw truth in Novak's warnings. For this reason you could not convict him in your trial."

"Get to your point, Rohling. This heat is bothersome, and I'm not partial to the sun."

"Not much left to tell. You wanted to teach Novak a fatal lesson, but your kangaroo trial wouldn't yield the result you wanted. The usual tactic of shaming him into suicide seemed unlikely to work either. You had only one card left to play."

"You give me much credit, Rohling. So, tell me. What could this final option be?"

"The farm laborers returned to camp hours after the shooting. None of them knew Novak, except me. One of them could be your angel of death. After you determined the time and place for the hanging, you chose your likeliest killer and offered him a reward he couldn't resist."

A faint smile played across Reinhardt's face. "I must admit. I didn't think Kimmel had the guts to kill Novak. But when I offered him a spot in the officers' quarters, he jumped at the chance."

"But Kimmel wasn't an officer."

"I told the Amis we needed him to maintain the quarters. As it turned out, he continued to work outside the camp. Quite all right by me. The man is distasteful."

"And you didn't make Stecklein aware of the plan?"

Reinhardt considered for a moment. "Alfred and I have always been friends. We served together in North Afrika. He is a plodding and regimented soldier. Not an original thinker. I wanted an honest reaction from him. When he reported the hanging to my office, I knew the plan succeeded."

"You underestimated the man. He explained to me how a prisoner could hide in the bathhouse. That helped me to unravel the puzzle."

"Alfred is deliberate and careful. Not stupid. I lost his trust for months after the trial for keeping him in the dark. He accused me of playing him for a fool. To this day, I ask myself; has he forgiven me?"

I despised this man who orchestrated the death of my friend. Yet a profound calm came over me. I held the proof that Brian Novak did not die from his own hand. This tape also sealed the fate of Oskar Kimmel. Justice, long overdue, could be served.

"These days, I treasure the few friends I have," Reinhardt said. "I don't want to die alone." Reinhardt stared at some distant object, as if watching his own death angel approaching.

His story still seemed incomplete. What did I miss?

"Why are you telling me about Novak and Kimmel now?" I asked. "I'm recording your words. Aren't you afraid of what would happen if the police heard this tape? We're talking about murder."

"Like you, I want to set the record straight," he said. "There is little time left for me, and I wish to die with dignity. At least as much dignity as a man with AIDS can muster. At the proper hour, I will end my turmoil."

I found myself taking a step back. Acquired Immuno-Deficiency Syndrome. The twentieth-century equivalent of leprosy. Prisoners with AIDS could be confined to a segregated unit until the disease took its course. I wanted Novak's killer to pay, but to linger in an isolated cell? Dying alone? Reinhardt already received his death sentence. "How…advanced is your…condition?"

"I've had two episodes of pneumonia this year. Doing the simplest activities wears me out. My life wavers with every ailment."

"Wasn't it risky coming to America? You could get sick here."

He nodded. "When I left the hospital in April, I found the reunion invitation in my box. It felt like a calling. A chance to resolve past indiscretions, to explain what happened. If I can't find forgiveness, I can at least express contrition."

"Did you tell all this to your interviewer?"

"I told her how I was HIV-positive for years before getting AIDS. But I refrained from talking about Novak or Kimmel. You saved me the trouble of dictating the story. Do with it however you see fit. I do have one condition."

"What is that?"

"Wait until I've made my exit. Four months at most. Will you?"

The colonel could linger behind bars for a year or more.

"Yes, Colonel."

I cringed at my decision. By agreeing to Reinhardt's terms, I would keep Kimmel free.

The tape was worthless.

"You're an honorable man, Herr Rohling." Reinhardt mopped his brow again. "If you will excuse me, I need to escape this sun." He pulled himself up the steps and entered the theater.

I stood alone in the heat, switched off the recording, and rewound the tape. Melancholy settled on me like a shroud. Novak's hanging, Drosselmeyer's death, Kimmel's guilt without punishment, and Reinhardt's quest for consolation squeezed the breath out of me. I leaned against the auditorium wall, finding relief in the meager shade beneath the eves.

I could still use the tape by taunting Kimmel with it. He could not ignore the threat.

Across the parade ground, Emily's tour group exited the mess hall and strolled to the barracks. Kathy saw me and hustled to my location. "You shouldn't be in this heat, Mr. Rohling. Miss Emily says it's cooler inside the theater."

"I just taped an officer from the camp. He told me how Brian Novak died. It's sensitive material that must be protected."

"Can I hear it?"

"Not now," I said. "Too many people about. Could you take the cassette out?"

"Sure. I can help you."

I handed her the player. "We should make copies and keep them separate and safe."

"Let's see if the recording is good." Kathy pushed the play button.

ROHLING: Do I have your permission to record this conversation?

She advanced the tape.

ROHLING: That wasn't an accident. Were you with anyone after the conference yesterday?

REINHARDT: I find that question offensive, private. As I already explained to the police, Alfred and I sampled a number of dark ales in the hotel tavern before the banquet."

"This is exciting." Kathy clutched the recorder in her hand.

ROHLING: We were supposed to meet. He mentioned secret orders. That could only have come from you.

I reached for the recorder. "We don't need to hear the full recording. Put it away."

"Wait a sec." She pulled her hand out of my reach. "I want to hear more."

ROHLING: You admitted some of your lower officers saw truth in Novak's warnings. For this reason you could not convict him in your trial."

REINHARDT: Get to your point, Rohling. This heat is bothersome, and I'm not partial to the sun.

"Stop it. Now!" I commanded. Her reckless behavior created danger. For both of us.

ROHLING: You wanted to teach Novak a fatal lesson, but your kangaroo trial would not yield the result you wanted. The usual tactic of shaming him into suicide seemed unlikely to work either.

I grabbed for the recorder, but Kathy danced back, holding the machine high. I caught her arm, pulling it down. The cassette player flipped from her fingers. I could care less if it broke. Only the tape mattered.

It skittered across the asphalt, stopping at the feet of Virginia Powell. Incredibly, the recording continued to play. Mrs. Powell retrieved the device, listening.

REINHARDT:...I must admit. I didn't think Kimmel had the guts to kill Novak. But when I offered him a spot in the officers' quarters, he jumped at the chance."

The director switched off the tape and placed it in

her handbag.

"I'll hold onto this for now," she said.

"Thank you, Mrs. Powell, but…" Kathy held out her hand.

The director ignored Kathy, centering her attention on me. "Mr. Rohling, the hotel has just called. Your son has been in an accident."

Horst? Injured? Dizziness hit me. The world tilted, but I managed to stay on my feet. "Wh-where is he?"

"The ambulance is taking your son to a hospital in Salina. We need to leave now."

I held a hand to my temple. How bad was he? I had to see him.

"I'm coming along." Kathy held my arm. Thank God she stood by me.

"No. You're staying here." The director's eyes radiated a cold hardness I'd never seen before.

"Mr. Rohling, I can take you there." A defiant child. And protective. I nodded my thanks, too overwhelmed to speak.

Mrs. Powell appraised her from head to toe as if assessing an opponent. "Since you insist, Miss Zoeller, we'll take your car. I only hope we get there in time."

Chapter Twenty-Seven

Berlin, Germany
November 21, 1946
Dear Emily,

I am with my parents. They are well, except their home and just about every other house in the neighborhood has burned to the ground. I'm overwhelmed by the devastation here. I'll get to that. But first, my journey from Paris.

The crowded boxcar reeked of unwashed bodies and urine when I boarded. For much of that thousand-kilometer trip, I stood shoulder to shoulder with other returning displaced persons. While we got four or five relief stops during the passage, some of the weaker men couldn't hold their bowels, and the stench grew worse with each hour. With every stop, armed French soldiers would herd us out and surround our group, not allowing us to find any privacy to relieve ourselves. After a few minutes, the soldiers pushed us back aboard again. They ignored any inquiry about food and water. We allowed what room we could for the wounded men to sit. That small concession could not be made for the last third of the journey. Even the weakest German prisoner was forced to stand as more men squeezed inside.

Still, we journeyed home. What would we find when we reach Berlin? Would there be people to greet us? A band to celebrate our return? No one knew. With anticipation and dread, we waited as the train hurtled eastward. Whatever happened, my three years and eight months of captivity would soon be over.

I stood by the thick wooden slats that formed the walls of our boxcar. The wind chilled me through my worn coat. Outside, a pale sprinkling of snow had settled over the fields and villages we passed through. Bombs had damaged many of the towns, but I was most surprised by the destruction of farmhouses or craters in the middle of fields. Could a lone farmer working his land have been a target for Allied aircraft? How many tending their crops met such a fate? Cold sweat flowed down my back. Mama and Papa. Were they still alive?

At last, we entered the outskirts of Berlin. Tremendous forces had blasted businesses, government buildings, apartments, and homes. Parks, statues, fountains—all gone. Even as the train slowed, it became clear; amid the devastation, the city teemed with life. The people had survived.

Ahead, an ear-splitting bang, and the train came to a jarring halt. Station workers threw open the heavy boxcar doors. Men rushed to escape their reeking confines; many sprawled headlong onto the platform with others falling on top of them. Somehow, I sidestepped the melee and staggered to the depot wall breathing in untainted air. Cracks like strange spiderwebs spread across the station's outer facade. Other nearby structures showed entire rooms where walls had collapsed. Jagged craters took the place of some buildings. The air smelled of death.

I needed to find my way home. As chilly as it was now, nightfall temperatures would be even colder. The general direction seemed clear enough, but the lack of street signs would make my journey harder.

Cleared roads made the walk easy at first. Once, a US Army jeep roared past me. Two American officers held German girls in their arms. I stood frozen, my mouth agape. One of the young women glanced back at me. Waving, she bent to kiss her American friend on the cheek. Then they turned a corner, leaving me in a cloud of rock dust. I shook my head. The victors had seized our women as well as our land.

As I trudged homeward, I marveled at the number of people about. Work gangs of women cleaned brick or leveled the ground. Many wore strips of clothing around their faces. Those who didn't held strained expressions. Layers of worn, patched clothing, hardly more than rags covered their backs. Yet they also had a look of grim determination. Children dug through mounds of refuse, looking for anything of value. Occasionally, some of the women would disappear inside huts of stone or wood. I realized that beneath these structures were cellars where much of the population still lived. What few men I saw tramped with little purpose, bewildered by their surroundings. Upon rueful self-examination, I realized I was one of those baffled wanderers.

My parents lived some five kilometers from Berlin's central train station. Usually, a trolley would have gotten me home, but it would be a year or more before this wounded city would offer bus service. I'm no stranger to walking, yet each step I took drew greater effort. During my time in America, I assumed my health and vitality would keep me free of injuries. The last eighteen months, however, was a time of strenuous work with few comforts. A fall in a quarry left me with a swollen knee that never fully healed. It hurt now and felt like it would bend backwards if I stepped wrong. A sense of weariness hung over me; how much farther could I go before I had to stop for the night? The dormant grass was an inviting place to lie.

Stretch out. Close your eyes. End your journey later.

"No!"

A woman in a gray shawl stared at me. Did I speak aloud? I slapped my cold cheeks to awaken my senses and pressed on. Though bombs had shattered many structures, an apartment building here, a cobblestone path there, meant home was only minutes away. Anticipation and anxiety played at my thoughts. I trudged faster; discomfort and pain no longer mattered.

Ahead of me, a cabin-like shape marked where my parents' home once stood. The structure showed Papa's handiwork. I rapped on the rough-hewn door and took several paces back, so I didn't appear threatening. For nearly a minute, nothing stirred. I held my breath. Had strangers taken over my parents' home? I'd come too far to leave. If necessary, I would break down the door to learn the answer. *Lord, please don't let it come to that.*

The lock jiggled, and an old couple peered at me with curiosity and fear. They didn't know me. But I knew them.

"Mama? Papa? I've come home."

"Heinrich? Is it you?" Mama's eyes brightened with recognition.

Papa held out his hand. "Come inside, son."

I've been here three days. There is so much more to tell, but the evening is waning. I must get this letter posted first thing tomorrow. I think of you often, and I wonder when I will see you again. Be grateful for your untouched country and never take things like food, water, or a safe home for granted. Decisions by indifferent men can turn cities into powdered stone. Now we must restore our land. I can't sit idle and watch others do the work. With a few of Papa's tools, I'm going out after breakfast tomorrow to join a work gang.

Keeping you in my thoughts,

Henry

****

Berlin, Germany

December 5, 1946

Dear Emily,

My parents have told me much of what has happened to Germany in the last two years: the nightly fire-bombings from British aircraft and the murderous assault and occupation by Russian troops before the Americans and British moved in two months later. The brutal attacks on our women and children still keep me awake at night. Yet it is German women who are rebuilding homes and repairing the buildings left standing. And it is German women who care for the infirm, the very young, and the weary, confused veterans trickling home. Life is still a struggle here. Too many children are dying of disease or starvation. But there is a formidable strength in these women who survived a terrible war and a savage peace. Men will be the hands and feet restoring Germany, but women will be the backbone, keeping them strong.

After the bombs and the pillaging of our cities, the Americans, British, and French swaggered in as conquerors. At first, they did little to help the war's survivors. Now, at least the Americans are less stingy with their lumber, nails, and cement. As ties between East and West continue to strain, the Amis no longer see us as villains. More like a buffer between two bickering victors. We must shape this responsibility to our own advantage.

This is my wish. For the German people to claim their own future.

With love,
Henry

****

Conrad, Kansas
January 25, 1947
Dear Henry,

I am so glad you made it home! Your experience sounded appalling, but you found your parents, and they are alive and well. A family reunited—that is fantastic news!

Life is quiet, here. Daddy listens to the news on the radio, but distant events make little difference in our daily routine. Josh has had fewer fright spells since the harvest. Mother encourages him and me to go into town together on Saturdays. I think she wants my brother to find a special girl. I feel like a matchmaker. But it's good to see him relax and laugh once in a while. He is skittish about going out unless we double date. You said it was okay if I date, but I still feel guilty doing it. One show we saw was about three soldiers coming home from the war. Josh stayed silent for the rest of the evening after seeing that show. As his self-appointed social secretary, I'm only letting him see comedies from now on!

My younger brother Billie has grown some five

inches since you last saw him. Dad is teaching him how to drive the tractor now. Working for Daddy will cut into his hunting.

I cannot imagine how difficult life must be there. Your description of the city paints a dire picture—so much to make right again. All the more reason to return to America as soon as opportunity permits. You can live in a land unspoiled by war. I know you want to do what you can—and you should—but it will take the work of a great many. Let others finish the job you started. Come back; we can share our lives together without worries.

But no matter what happens you'll always be in my heart.

Emily

****

Berlin, Germany
March 12, 1947
Dear Emily,

It is a wonderful feeling to be home again and to know my parents are safe. For days after my return, we shared stories about the war. One tale stands out in my mind. It was my third day back. Over a meal of mushrooms and spaetzles, Papa recounted the time he couldn't reach the air raid shelters before the iron doors slammed shut. Mama was safe inside. Or what passed for safe. But Papa, along with dozens of others, remained outside, unable to find refuge. "Bombs fell with an awful whistle that ended in an ear-splitting blast. The air filled with explosions, and bricks and glass flew like shrapnel. Men and women screamed in terror. There was no escape," he said.

My fork fell from nerveless fingers, clattering to

the plate. "Couldn't you get away?"

Papa shook his head. "Fires penned us in on all sides. Since the buildings were the targets, I ran to an open area, but the air grew hot, and the rising wind blew inward, feeding the flames. I dropped to my knees on the blistering pavement to find breathable air. A young woman rushed past me, propelled by the fierce gale stoking the firestorm. I reached out, but the howling wind tore her from my grasp. One second, she held my hand—then she vanished, her thin wail swallowed by the maelstrom. Then there were the bodies stuck to the melted tarmac." He rubbed his eyes with a trembling hand. "I can't say any more."

Mama reached for my father's arm. "It took months for his burns to heal," she said. "We lost many friends from the bombings. Being in a shelter didn't guarantee survival, either. Some flooded from broken water mains or filled with choking smoke. Some shelters became ovens, cooking the people inside."

My jaw dropped at the calm way my parents discussed death. "Did you try moving to the country?"

Papa blew out a breath. "Many did. But when the British pilots noticed a gathering of refugees, they would attack. Besides, we were not about to leave our home. This was all we had."

I leaned forward, trying to keep the urgency out of my voice. "Was it always the British?"

Mama jumped in to answer. "In the beginning, the Americans only attacked military targets during the day. Folks agreed they fought a brave war. Then we heard about Dresden."

"What happened?"

Papa's voice filled with simmering anger. "Huge

formations of British and American bombers firebombed the city. For days afterward, American pilots attacked the survivors, machine-gunning anyone within their sights—old men, women, and children. They even shot zoo animals."

My insides twisted at the thought of civilians being attacked. "Surely, Ami pilots wouldn't gun down innocent women and children."

Papa chuckled without humor. "That's the talk. One thing is undeniable. Many who knew the truth died or disappeared, overtaken by the Russians soon afterward."

Mama took plates to the sink. "Let's hear no more of the war. Heinrich, tell us about your time in America."

With embarrassment and guilt, I told them about how I worked for your father, a bit about Wisconsin, and my trip home. My slight discomforts could not compare to the horror my parents faced. Sleep didn't come that night. They endured so much while I lived an easy life in America. I could not leave them to an uncertain future. That would be disloyal. A betrayal to them and to my country.

Please understand, Emily; I want so much to return to America and live with you in a quiet corner of the world, but leaving home in its time of need leaves me with a bitter taste. I can make only one choice. To stay here and mend my country.

I've re-read your letters many times, imagining my escape from this dreadful landscape and living an idyllic life with few responsibilities. I made that plan; come back to America. Flee to the land of the victors.

Americans talk about how Germans supported the

lies told by Nazi handlers. But Americans believed lies told by their own government. Nazis were evil; all Germans were Nazis, therefore, all Germans were evil. To break the spirit of the German, their cities had to be destroyed. The German people will see their error and turn on their masters.

But that didn't happen. Every exploded bomb made our people more steadfast. It proved the German leaders correct; the British and the Americans were barbarians, fighting a war against women and children. Before the war ended, your war planners carved Europe like a Christmas goose. And we were branded the villains.

I'm not sure if I'm angry or disappointed. At any rate, I will not turn my back on my countrymen. Or rather, the redoubtable women who have worked to hold Berlin together. I'm a foreman of a crew of men and women constructing apartment buildings. The Americans are slow in getting materials to us, and they even post guards around their refuse dumps. But we are making progress. I intend to keep working until this city regains its former glitter as a place where people will marvel at. It will take years. Maybe a lifetime. When I'm old and stooped, I want to point to a house or an office tower or a park and say, "I built that!" It sounds selfish, but I'd like to think honorable as well.

I'm sorry, Emily. I know this feels like I'm turning my back on you. Please forgive me. I hope you continue to go out and enjoy the company of your friends. Don't let time pass you by. Find that special one you deserve.

This will be my last letter to you, but that does not mean I will forget those tender weeks together. Here, the reality is finding food and staying warm. Rebuilding is a daunting task. I cannot remain idle.

Good-bye, Emily. The man you choose to marry will be lucky, indeed.

Henry

****

The three of us left the museum grounds and walked to Kathy's vehicle. Mrs. Powell sat behind Kathy, insisting I also sit in the back seat. *Why the odd arrangement*? "Did the hotel tell you anything about my son?" I asked Mrs. Powell.

She didn't answer.

From the museum's access road, we soon approached Highway 81. Kathy stopped the car, waiting for a break in southbound traffic. "A lot of people going to Salina today," she said.

Mrs. Powell pointed left. "I want you to head north, Miss Zoeller."

"That's the wrong direction." Kathy glanced back, but the director waved for her to look ahead.

"What about Horst?" I asked.

"What about him?" she snapped.

"He's hurt. You said so." My fingers trembled. Nothing made sense. A thought flared like a warning bell. "Is my son really hurt?"

Powell gave me a smirk. "He's fine as far as I know." She tapped Kathy on the shoulder. "Get moving. Time is wasting."

"Way too strange." Kathy muttered a few more words but complied with the director's order. Seconds later, she accelerated to speed on the four-lane highway.

Truth dawned on me. "This has nothing to do with my son. Where are you taking us?"

"A familiar place," Powell said.

The Republican River loomed ahead. On both sides of us, fields of corn shone under the August sun. Long ago, I walked along the banks of the river watching the wildlife and chewing out a boy for hunting.

"This doesn't feel right." Kathy's voice held concern, but not panic. "At the next turn-off, we're going back to the museum."

"You'll do what I tell you." From her purse, Virginia Powell produced a small, snub-nosed revolver and nudged the barrel against Kathy's neck. I jumped. Powell gave me a sideways glance. "Forget it, Mr. Rohling. You'll never get to me before I pull the trigger."

"What?" Kathy's arms twitched; the car swerved as we drove onto the bridge. A driver behind us blared his disapproval.

"Steady, Miss Zoeller," Powell said, her voice cool and conversational. "I can't imagine the number of dead and injured if you caused a pile-up. But then, you'd be past caring."

The poor girl sobbed but kept the wheel straight as we passed the river.

"Very good." Powell leaned back in her seat. "A mile past the river, you will turn right on a gravel road."

"That...goes to the old POW camp." Kathy's breath caught as she forced the words.

"Very observant, young lady." Powell smiled. "Sorry, no prizes for correct answers."

Why would the director have used Horst as a pretext for going to an old abandoned camp? I wanted to see it, but not like this. Her weapon filled me with unease and dread. Kathy said the place was deserted.

Unless Powell made a mistake, we had no hope of escape. In the meantime, we should remain patient and wait for an opening.

"I've always wanted to see the old camp," I said, masking my anxiety.

"And you shall, Mr. Rohling," she said.

We drove in silence for the next minute, then slowed and turned east amid a grove of weather-beaten oaks. The director pointed ahead. "The camp is about three miles away."

"Yes, ma'am." Kathy's words were barely audible.

To call the dirt path a gravel road gave it undue justice. Rutted and bumpy with several sharp dips. Probably impassable on rainy days. Nearly five kilometers later, the lane widened into an open area littered with beer cans and liquor bottles.

"Pull in here, behind that truck."

We parked behind a pale white pickup. If Powell was concerned about the presence of others, she showed no sign. She leveled the pistol at Kathy. "Come 'round to the driver's side, Mr. Rohling." She tapped Kathy's shoulder. "Come out slowly, Ms. Zoeller."

Kathy muttered an acknowledgment and got out.

"I'll take those keys now." Powell held out her hand. Metal jingled as Powell deposited car keys in a handbag.

I did as requested, stepping past the pickup, which contained a shovel, rake, and bags of lye. Kathy and I led the way through a thick stand of cottonwoods and sycamores with Powell close behind us. The thin trunks rose straight and tall, and closer to one another than I thought possible. Each tree seemed to be seeking its share of sunlight. "Turn more to the left, about ten o'clock," Powell directed.

"How far are we going?" I asked.

"Half a mile. Maybe less."

We startled some blackbirds, which scolded us as we passed. Twigs and branches, hidden by a layer of leaves, snapped beneath our feet. Our canopy of shade made the walk comfortable, though not relaxing. A whiff of skunk had me scanning our surroundings. As we progressed, the trees grew farther apart, some hammered by high winds. A clearing opened before us.

Powell motioned with her gun hand. "Cross to the other side."

Tufts of tallgrass grew in the small glade along with scattered piles of wood ash from old bonfires and more cans and bottles. Atop a rotting stump sat a massive cassette player with damaged speakers. Kathy pointed to a bullet-ridden sign leaning against a tree. Amid the holes, the faded paint read PROPERTY, U.S. ARMY. KEEP OUT.

"We're almost there." Powell motioned ahead. "Keep moving."

Past the clearing, the trunks grew close together again. So many trees made it impossible to see far in any direction. Ahead loomed the vague outline of a block-shaped building, possibly a warehouse. A few steps farther, I came across the remains of a canvas shoe filled with ants. Leaf rot filled the air.

As we proceeded, details of the dingy structure emerged. Graffiti interrupted the scarred whitewashed exterior with gaudy purple and green splashes. Powell directed us to go left. Along the west wall, two doorways stood about twelve meters apart. Atop the cement, someone had repaired the weather-damaged roof with ruffled tin. I knew this place—Camp Conrad's old bathhouse.

"Take the first door," Powell ordered.

Kathy stepped in before me. I halted at the entrance, assaulted by the stench of stale urine, old cigarettes, and mouse droppings. Litter, broken glass, and dead leaves lay scattered on the concrete floor. In one corner lay a pile of trash bags with small chewed holes near the floor. We entered the *toilette* side, but all the stools and sinks were gone. Graffiti adorned the interior walls as well. I wondered if the thrill-seekers who came here knew what this place was.

"Get inside." Powell pushed me from behind. Once we stood in the bathhouse, she circled us, holding her weapon with both hands.

Kathy shuffled to my side, scrunching her nose. "It stinks in here."

I glimpsed a shadow through the doorway leading to the shower room, then a muffled cough. "We've got bigger problems," I said to Kathy. "Kimmel is here."

Kathy breathed out a quiet moan.

Kimmel approached from behind Powell, nibbling her neck. He watched me from the corner of his eye. "Glad you could make it, Rohling." He ran his tongue around Powell's ear.

She made a low groan. "Later, tiger. I can't concentrate when you do that."

"I'll hold you to it." Kimmel plucked the gun from Powell's hand. "What's the girl doing here? You were supposed to get Emily."

Powell stepped away, frowning. "Miss Zoeller insisted on coming. I couldn't get rid of her."

"That's no excuse. Now she's a loose end."

"You got that right. Reinhardt spilled his guts. Now Rohling and Miss Zoeller know the truth. There's even a tape of Reinhardt pinning you with the hanging."

Kimmel muttered a curse. "Any idea where this tape is?"

"Not to worry." Powell produced the small player. "I'm keeping it safe."

"How did you get that?"

She scowled, one hand on her hip. "Can't we talk about this later?"

"I want to know now."

While Powell launched into her explanation, I leaned my head to Kathy, keeping my voice low. "Run when I tap your arm. Get help."

"What?" She looked more scared than confused. Scared was good. It would give her speed.

"Stay in the trees. Find a farmhouse. Call for help."

"I can't leave you."

"Not to worry. I'll distract them and give you a few extra seconds."

Our whispers got Kimmel's attention. He waved Powell to silence and took a step forward, keeping out of my reach. "It's not polite to talk in class." He steadied his aim on me. "Now you'll have to go to detention."

"Of course." I blocked Kathy from stepping forward. "There's still one thing that bothers me." I tried to sound conversational, but it came off flat. Still, if I could sidetrack Kimmel, Kathy would cover more ground before the hounds give chase.

"Okay, Rohling. I'll play. What bothers you?"

"Drosselmeyer's death. I thought you killed him. But you didn't."

"I told you that."

"Agreed." I held out a wavering palm. "Hear me out. I accused Stecklein next, and then Reinhardt. But they had alibis as well."

"Get to the point."

"So it had to be a person with key card access to each room who could move about the reunion with little attention. Am I correct, Mrs. Powell?"

Powell threw back her head. "How did you know?"

I tapped Kathy's arm. *Go.*

She bolted for the open door, her footsteps diminishing amid the wind in the trees.

For two long seconds, Kimmel and Powell gazed at me. I stepped back to the outside door, my legs straddling the frame.

"Get out of the way!" Kimmel rushed at me, ramming a fist in my stomach and raking his pistol across my temple. My head rang; warm blood flowed down my cheek. The world tilted and spun, pulling me toward a dark hole. I wanted to lie down and surrender, but I refused that option. Kathy needed time. Every second gave her a better chance to find help. Incredibly, I stood upright.

"No." I moaned the word.

"Fine." Kimmel drew back a pace and leveled the barrel. "Say goodnight, Henry."

I crumpled to the floor. Darkness closed in. From far away, one voice called to another. "Take the pistol. Don't let her get away." Like a vintage TV set, my senses dwindled to a tiny bright dot that faded to nothing.

****

My head throbbed when I awoke. I sat upright on

the floor inside the old shower room, staring at the place where Novak had died. Kimmel grunted as he tied my arms behind me. The rough wood of a supporting timber ran down the center of my back. He yanked on my wrists again. I groaned with pain, but they wouldn't come any closer together. My mouth was dry with grit and a not-quite-dead beetle. I spat out the disgusting bug.

"Awake, I see." He regained his feet and stepped around in my line of sight.

"Why didn't you kill me?" I asked.

"Dragging your sorry ass to the hole I dug takes time." He dropped the rope meant to tie my ankles. Instead, he snatched a thin-barreled rifle leaning against the cement wall. "Got to find that partner of yours and put an end to this." Kimmel stepped to the dressing room side.

"Is that the gun you bought for Emily?" I asked.

He stopped short at the door. "Why do you ask?"

I ignored the question. "What do you plan to do with it?"

"What do you think?" Kimmel spat the words, then rushed out of the building.

I sat alone, a dull ache already in my back and shoulders and promising to get worse. A wave of nausea rose in my stomach, but I fought back the urge to be sick. The queasiness ebbed, leaving me lightheaded. I had to get free. If Kathy could evade Powell and Kimmel, then she could seek help.

Gaining my feet proved impossible. I do a lot of walking but lacked the strength in my legs to pull myself to a standing position. At one point, I jammed my back against the pole to squirm upward. In struggling to gain my feet, the wood popped behind my back.

The timber had a flaw. Could I break it?

If it broke, would the rafters crumple on top of me?

Could I take the punishment and still rid myself of these bonds?

Don't think.

I brought in my knees, lifting my back a few centimeters from the floor, then launched myself backward against the pole. *Snap!* I flopped to the cement. Spiking pain shot up my spine. I wondered if the sound came from my tailbone breaking. Once the agony lessened, I pushed with my shoulders. A soft grinding, more felt than heard, came from within the wood.

Progress.

Thumping my tailbone against concrete didn't appeal to me. I needed a strategy that wouldn't leave me gasping.

Slowly at first, but with growing intensity, I shifted my shoulders from side to side hoping to weaken the wood. The rubbing and chafing scratched my wrists and forearms. Blood oozed from small cuts. Still, I rocked from side to side, sensing the wood bowing to my effort. Sweat ran down my face in the baking cement oven. Each time I swayed, I drove fine splinters into my wrists and forearms. The ache in my shoulders grew to a sharp stabbing pain. How much longer could I endure this punishment?

Left. Right. Flesh. Wood. Live. Die.

To relieve my shoulders, I sometimes hurled myself back against the roof support. Not as efficient as throwing my weight from side to side, but easier on the body. One lurch produced a long screech ending in a crack that sent a tingle up my back. My fingertips, slick with blood, found a fissure running higher than I could reach.

This chilled me. A weakened support could bring the ceiling down on top of me. No other choice. I licked my lips and continued my attack.

With each minute, my thoughts drifted to Kathy. Was she still free? Would she lose direction amid the trees? No shots echoed outside, but what if Kimmel or Powell took her captive? I only hoped she used the trees to her advantage and outdistanced her older pursuers. The sooner they realized this, the sooner they would want to get back, finish their business, and get away.

That meant killing me.

Think positive.

If Kathy could reach safety and call for help, then all this would be over.

Another wild lurch to the side and a jagged length of timber fell to the floor. The fissure behind me split with a resounding crack. The pole separated from the roof and toppled, throwing me to my side. Above me, the ceiling groaned.

Fearing the roof would fall, I squirmed along the broken timber, sliding my bonds over the end of the shattered wood. Without thinking, I rolled to the *toilette* doorway. Grit, debris, and the remains of an old bird's nest fluttered down from the sagging beams. The cement partition would serve as a haven. I wriggled over the threshold and huddled beneath the frame. Behind me, the rafters and a section of roof crashed to the floor. The shock barely rattled the cement walls. Inside the shower room lay a heap of massive beams, splintered lumber, wooden shingles, and swirling dust. Three sheets of tin lay scattered. One ruffled sheet lay atop a pile of broken boards, its rusty edge extending out by a few centimeters. I gazed at the warped metal like an Afrikaner on patrol would a canteen of water. Still, the lumber beneath held possibilities. I could use the wood's sharp edges to cut my ropes. I swallowed what little spit I could muster and began crawling to the heap.

Midway there, I breathed in some debris. Curled on my side, I wheezed for precious air in between choking spasms that left me writhing on the floor. My strength was nearly gone, and I still needed to cut myself free. Inhaling with care, I crept beneath the tin.

I don't recall how I got my back against those fractured timbers. At times, my mind wandered, and I imagined watching my squirming efforts from above. I do remember giving a silent cheer when my wrists met a sharp edge. With clumsy strokes, I drew the cord tight and rubbed my bonds against the wood.

Scraping the plastic-coated cords was inefficient and chewed up my reserves of strength, but I couldn't angle my wrists to saw in the same spot. Giving in to curiosity, I ran a fingertip along the cord's surface. Only a few wispy strands of plastic. A long way to go. It felt like the end. All my effort had gone for nothing. I leaned against the fallen pile of lumber and surrendered to the inevitable.

The mass shifted behind my back. Above me, the battered tin slid forward, exposing jagged, rusty teeth. Still out of reach, but a desperate idea took hold. I slammed backward, grunting and cursing because the tin scarcely moved.

Tired and needing a rest, I slumped against a rafter. The heavy board fell to the side, allowing the tin to slide forward. I drew my ankles in, and the next instant, the metallic edge scraped the floor with an awful screech. Inside my tin shanty, I now had a herculean challenge—to pivot and use the metal edge to cut my bonds.

So close, but even the smallest movements set my teeth on edge. Shifting my body around took an act of sheer will. Numb fingers made the job of scraping the cord even harder. It had to be done. Nothing beyond that mattered.

Every move in turning around depended on a slippery equation: how much pain could I take for each gain achieved? In the end, my wrists rested on either side of the rusted tin. Sharp points prickled my back as I leaned against the metal, but it didn't move. Those little stings were a joyous foretaste of freedom. Biting my lip, I pinched the rope between fingers caked with blood and began to saw.

I soon learned that cutting at an angle brought immediate results. In two minutes, I breached the plastic coating and split the inner strands of fibers. A minute later, the first cord parted. One more to go. A little more concentration, then I could get away from Novak's death chamber. Kimmel had murdered to gain status within the Nazi cult. This old building was part of a forgotten age. How ironic that Americans boasted about their openness while scrubbing clean their history. Were the POW camps a shining testament of treating the enemy as brothers? Or was it an example of willful myopia when untimely deaths occurred? I admitted harboring ill thoughts against my American hosts. Rude and ungrateful. Look where it got me.

Outside, faint voices approached—Kimmel and Powell. Returning to finish the job.

I froze, like prey caught in a vice.

Once, Della and I toured the Nile on holiday. Aboard a canopied tourist boat, we watched a crocodile clamp its jaws on a gazelle. The poor beast stood immobilized, allowing the giant reptile to drag it beneath the water. For one frigid second, I knew the essence of that fear. But I had gone too far to give up now. The singing agony in my wrists didn't matter; I rolled backward under my tin shelter.

"What the hell happened here?" Kimmel's voice grew louder. "Half the room caved in!"

Powell answered. "Looks like Samson brought down the temple."

"I have to see this." Heavy footsteps crunched glass and sand in the dressing room. "What a mess. Ginny! You should see this place." His voice boomed inside the cement room. "Rohling saved us the trouble of burying him."

"Could he still be alive?" Powell's voice came from farther away.

"Hard to say. People lived for hours buried up to their heads in Oklahoma City. Hard to believe that was four months ago." A board landed nearby. "Henry! We can dig you out. No reason to linger all night and die."

I remained silent.

"He might be too far gone." Powell sounded tense. I imagined her tugging on Kimmel's arm. "Come on. We need to head out while there's still time. We've looked too long for—"

"Quiet! Not another word." Kimmel raised his

voice again. "Henry. We found your friend. Kate, wasn't it? No, wait—Kathy. She didn't suffer. But you're probably thirsty and can't move, bones cracked, blood draining from your body. We can end your suffering."

Kathy dead? Was it true? I clenched my fists and blew out a heated breath.

"Did you hear something?" Kimmel kicked scattered debris. "Ginny, help me find him. He's still alive. I can feel it."

"Forget it, Oskar. There's no time. We need to leave now."

Kimmel grunted. Rubble fell to the floor, and heavy lumber shifted. "There's too much to sift through, but I got one more idea." Moments later, a match struck.

"Are you nuts? With all these trees around here? A fire could spread for miles."

"So what? A blaze will be a nice little diversion." He scratched another match. Three more followed. Kimmel mumbled an obscenity. "I can't get the stuff to catch fire."

"Oskar—"

"Don't start on me! Get back to the truck. There's a jerry can in the back. Might be some old gas in it. Bring along any rags or paper. I'll look for some dry grass. Get moving." Light steps hustled away. Kimmel's footfalls were more deliberate when he exited.

I waited for only a few seconds before scuttling back to sawing the last cord. The scraping seemed loud in my confined space, but time for escape had all but run out. No more caution. I'll grieve for Kathy later. If I lived.

The other rope parted, easing the pain in my shoulders. I crawled to the *toilette* doorframe and pulled myself to my feet.

I should escape, find safety and seek help. Heading in an unexpected direction would increase my chances for survival. But I wanted vengeance, for Novak, for Drosselmeyer, for Kathy.

End this here.

Taking careful steps, I retrieved a stout piece of lumber. Standing out of sight, I waited for Kimmel or Powell to enter. If Kimmel came in the dressing room side and lit his fire, then I would go around and clobber him from behind.

No more fear. This prey would become the hunter.

Chapter Twenty-Eight

I stood at the *toilette* entrance, standing against the outside wall, flexing my fingers and rubbing circulation back into scraped wrists. I placed the board I retrieved within easy reach. Plenty of time to grab it when either Kimmel or Virginia Powell returned. For now, I savored the freedom of standing and stretching my limbs.

Kimmel's heavy footsteps approached the dressing room side and stepped into the collapsed shower room. I remained silent and out of sight. He threw a scattering of branches and leaves on the rubble. He made no sound, and I imagined him listening or scrutinizing the wreckage.

Tin roofing scraped across the concrete floor. "I've found the rope, Rohling. You've been hiding the whole time." His footsteps retreated back outside. Grass rustled. Was he creeping closer to my door? I sensed his approach, coming closer, about to barge through the entry. I could smell his rage, his single-minded goal to annihilate me. And I stood poised. Ready to strike with a killing blow. I already imagined his body sprawled on the cement floor.

But he didn't enter.

His shadow lingered in the doorway, one arm holding the rifle, but he did not step through the door. Some premonition must have warned him. Slowly, his dark form retreated. My plan had failed.

No time to wait.

I jumped outside and spotted him looking straight at me. Lunging forward, I swung the two-by-four in a wide arc as Kimmel brought up his rifle. The wood caught the gun-barrel just short of his fingers. His weapon spun away like a slow-moving whirligig.

"Aww!" Kimmel glared at me, holding his bleeding fingers.

I stepped forward to deliver the final blow.

He ducked his head and charged, his blitz catching me by surprise. Kimmel drove me to the ground, sending my own weapon smacking the bathhouse. We rolled over and sprang to our feet, facing each other empty-handed.

I tingled with adrenaline. No more verbal jabs. No more taunts. Only one man would walk away. Kimmel had a weight and height advantage over me. He could wear me down at his leisure. My only course was to strike his weakest spot. And soon.

He attacked, jabbing my temple, re-opening the cut. My head throbbed with each beat of my heart. I gave him a headbutt that left us both reeling, but I managed to bend back his lacerated fingers almost to the breaking point before he tore his hand away. He screamed and retreated.

Pity. That could have ended it.

We circled. Watching and appraising each other. Drops of blood fell from his right hand. My head thumped like a kettledrum. I watched his eyes hoping they would give away his next move. I should have been watching his feet.

He feinted with a haymaker to my head, then slid

his foot around my ankle and pulled, tripping me. I twisted away, getting to my knees and landed a sharp punch to his side. Kimmel fell against me. I toppled on my back with him pinning me to the ground.

Flailing and windmill blows earned me a malevolent grin. Kimmel leaned over me, his face close to mine. "We could have been friends, Rohling." His voice matter-of-fact. Thoughtful. "Comrades. Like your buddy Novak."

He held my neck, bearing down with his upper body. I strained to push his hands away, but I couldn't. Slowly, his clawed finger squeezed my throat.

Impossible to breathe. In a few seconds, panic gave way to lighted-headed detachment. I was about to die, and I could do nothing about it. I noted with faint disdain Kimmel's soiled clothes, his ruffled hair, his lack of expression, and that unsightly bulge in his pants pocket. That couldn't be his pistol. Virginia Powell took it. A souvenir from the reunion, no doubt.

The edges of my vision drew inward like staring through a wide tunnel. That bulge in Kimmel's pocket—his truncheon.

Get it!

I stretched with my left hand, feeling for his pocket. My fingers could only get past the opening. Jackknifing my body, I thrust my fingers farther, stroking the smooth leatherwork. Where was the handle? How could I grab it?

Oblivion. Only seconds away.

Almost…

My finger closed around the ruffled handgrip, and I pulled the short baton clear.

With all my waning strength, I hit Kimmel.

He fell over sideways with a grunt. I huddled on my side, coughing and taking in great lungfuls of wonderful, intoxicating air. Kimmel rolled over, holding his head. I crawled to the rifle. With difficulty, I regained my feet. Kimmel staggered to a standing position. One hand covered his face. Blood flowed from a deep cut over his right eye. I pointed the rifle at his chest. Could I be merciful? Did Kimmel offer mercy to Kathy? Virginia Powell still lurked out there, and I was alone. Compassion was no longer an option. To survive, Kimmel had to die.

Movement behind me. Powell returning?

My fingers tightened on the trigger.

"Henry! Don't!"

Emily's voice. Terrified.

"Why?" I asked. A stupid question. Even more unwise, I took my eyes off Kimmel.

Emily stood at my side, her eyes wide with horror. Nearby, Bill Henning mopped his neck. Horst came last with Powell's gun sticking out of his belt. He kept a hand on her shoulder.

What happened next flashed by in mere seconds, yet I remember each detail vividly. A hand yanked the rifle from my grasp, stinging my fingers. Kimmel backed away with the weapon, aiming at my head. Looking down the long, narrow barrel, I knew he meant to kill me.

"*Down!*"

In the next instant, a force knocked me to the ground, a ball of fire enveloped Kimmel, and an ear-splitting explosion rocked the countryside.

Emily had screamed the word and fell, shielding me with her body. Horst and Bill also dropped, whether from the blast or Emily's warning, I didn't know. It was then I dared look at the shooter.

Pieces of the rifle lay smoldering around the blackened remains of Oskar Kimmel's head and shoulders. The blast had obliterated his face. I hadn't seen a corpse like that since the war. With a cry, Powell rushed forward and knelt over Kimmel's body. Emily turned to look, but I shielded her from the sight. "He's dead. You don't want to see it."

I had questions, but there was no time to ask.

"Hands up!"

Four men in blue-gray uniforms with belts holding pouches and radios surrounded us with handguns drawn. All of us froze while deputies relieved Horst of the pistol and searched us for other weapons. An uncomfortable silence lingered as the uniformed officers examined our identification. As I pocketed my wallet, the senior officer, wearing a western-style hat bearing a badge, stepped forward. "Horst Rohling, I'm Sheriff Dale Rank. What happened here?"

"This lady..." My son pointed to the crying woman. "She and the *leere flasche*...dead man...tried to abduct my papa. The rifle misfired, killing him instead."

More questions followed. I remained silent, letting Emily, Horst, and Bill answer them. Each response brought forth new queries. Ten minutes later, Rank stopped the exchange. "Okay, this is getting way too complicated. Let's take this downtown where each of you can make a statement. Sorry to separate you, but it would be best for the investigation. Depending what we find out, you will be back home or at your hotel this evening."

I wondered how that would go for Bill and Emily.

"Are you hurt?" Bill asked Emily, looking her over.

"I'm fine." Emily sighed.

We left the bathhouse, each of us walking to county vehicles with a different officer. Rank ambled beside me as we traversed the woods. "Mr. Rohling, it looks like you took a beating. Do you need hospital treatment?"

"I've had better days. But no," I said.

"It's no trouble. The young lady who called in the emergency mentioned you by name. She's at the hospital now, being looked after. Family is with her."

I halted. "Kathy? Is she all right?"

Rank grinned. "The ER doc said she's in good condition. Although she took a tumble down the banks of the Republican and sprained an ankle. She managed to swim the river and find help. The hospital is keeping her overnight for observation."

Tears came to my eyes. "I thought she died."

"She was concerned for you too. Call the hospital as soon as you can. I bet she'd like to hear you're okay."

"I'll do that."

In a few minutes, we reached a group of cars marked *Sheriff*. Virginia Powell sat handcuffed in the back seat of Sheriff Rank's vehicle. Horst would follow in his rental car.

"Before we go," I asked Rank, "there is a question I must ask my son."

"Sure," he said. "But you're staying with me."

Horst sat buckling his seatbelt when I reached him. He rolled down his window. "Anything wrong, Papa?"

"I never had a chance to ask you. How did you find me?"

"When I got back from Salina, I learned the museum site sat on the north end of town. I searched for you there. Mrs. Kimmel and Mr. Henning helped me look as well. Before long, we discovered you, Miss Zoeller, Mrs. Powell, and Mr. Kimmel were missing. We knew we had to act fast, and the old prison seemed like the first place to look."

"Mrs. Powell had a gun. How did you get it?" I asked.

"Oh, that. When we got here, your director had her hands full with a petrol can. Emily rushed her, and I kept the gun she carried. I'm glad we got to you in time."

"Thank you," I said. "I could have pulled that trigger."

It took hours answering repeated inquiries and correcting hasty assumptions. After an early public statement by Sheriff Rank, the "Kimmel and Powell affair" attracted TV crews from Wichita, Topeka, and Kansas City. But when Bill disclosed the long-ago shooting and Kimmel's blackmail scheme, Rank blocked any further updates. Deputies whisked us behind closed doors, away from microphones and cameras. One officer said Horst and I were free to go, but not to reveal Bill's confession. It would complicate the inquiry. Horst wanted to return to the hotel, but I refused to leave. I didn't want to abandon my friends. After some mutterings about my stubbornness, my son agreed to stay with me. "All right, Papa. We'll see this through together."

Connie, one of the office workers, gave us bottles

of water before she left for the day.

It seemed unjust, subjecting Emily and Bill to charges for an accident so long ago. Not after Kimmel held them under his thumb for decades. Of course, Horst informed me murder was no "accident."

"A life had been lost. That demands an investigation," Horst said. "But in this case, you have to ask. Did a crime occur? If so, where is the evidence?"

While we waited, I called the hospital with the help of a deputy and soon Kathy's mother allowed my interviewer to answer the phone.

"Are you okay?" I asked.

"Oh yes. I'm getting the royal treatment here." She seemed ecstatic. In the background a TV blared.

"You deserve it. Thank you for…everything." A stray tear rolled down my cheek. "I had no idea I was putting you in danger."

"I'm glad all turned out well. Reporters have been interviewing me since I got here. All three of the local stations will talk about us at ten o'clock. That's just a few minutes away. You should watch it."

"I'm still at the constable station—I mean the sheriff's office. Still sorting things out."

"Hope you're not in any trouble."

"No. Just tying up loose ends."

"That's good," Kathy said. "What time are you going back to the airport tomorrow?"

"I'm not going back. There are more reasons to stay here than go home."

Kathy paused. "Does that mean what I think it means?"

"I suppose lost opportunities do come around again."

A quiet chuckle at the other end of the line. "Good for you, Mr. Rohling."

I sighed, not really wishing to end the conversation. "Good luck with putting Novak's story together. Now you have a solution to your mystery."

"Part of me wishes the mystery still existed. It lends a certain flair to the story. Silly, huh."

I groaned to myself. Young people. "I, for one, am glad it's over."

"You're right." A voice murmured in the background. "Mr. Rohling, the news is about to come on. Got to go."

"Take care, Kathy," I said.

"Bye." And then she was gone.

****

Around midnight Emily's interrogator allowed her to join Horst and me. "Bill will be out soon," she said. "The county attorney will likely not file charges. The sheriff told me pursuing the case would be like looking for a crime to fit the confession. 'If a body ever turned up,' he said, 'there'd be little forensic evidence to go on.' "

"That's great!" I kissed her on the cheek.

"Will the county release this information to the public?" Horst asked. "It will create a scandal for you and Mr. Henning."

"Sheriff Rank said no further action will be taken. And no statement about the confession."

A nagging question bothered me. "Thank you for shielding me from that blast," I said. "But how did you know that explosion would happen?"

"Oskar bought that rifle for me as a gift, but I don't hunt. Bill wondered if he had a darker purpose, so I decided never to fire the gun. Instead, I plugged the barrels with an epoxy resin in case he tried anything. Then I saw you pointing the rifle at Oskar."

"You saved my life."

"I wish I could have saved his." She covered her face then, sobbing quietly. Emily had been strong all night, but now that the worst lay behind, I think she realized that, while Kimmel was a monster, he was also her husband.

I led her to the bench where I sat earlier. For several minutes we didn't speak; her crying subsided as she leaned against my side. I was drained as well. For years, I grew dependent on Horst, allowing—no, insisting—that he control my life. He took Della's place, and I accepted that. A convenient way to keep him close and allow me to stay in my cocoon and dream about my wife's memory.

I didn't feel that way now. A new resolve stirred within me. These last two days had been frustrating and terrifying, uplifting and redeeming. I would not leave Emily again. Horst had his career. Caroline had her family. Johann had his evening pursuits. Della would always reside in my heart, but marrying the past was a denial of the future. Time to risk living again.

"Emily? Are you awake?"

She nodded.

"I'm staying."

"You can't. What about your family?"

"My children can take care of themselves."

"They'll miss you, Henry."

"They can write to me. It worked for us."

"I still have those letters."

"I've got yours as well."

"Are you sure about this?"

"Positive," I said. "How does an October wedding sound?"

A small gasp. "That's too soon."

"Not for me. Cold feet already?"

Her poke in the chest made me wince. "You know what I mean."

"Whatever you decide. I'll be patient."

"A Valentine's Day wedding would be nice. Meanwhile, you'll need a visa."

"I agree."

"And a place to live," she said.

"Not with you?" I gave her a smirk.

Another jab, this time harder. "Think again, Mr. Rohling."

"I'm thinking of how to frame my questions better."

"You'll get used to it." There was a smile in her voice. "You'll need to speak to your son."

"He thinks I'm forgetful."

"Oh, I don't know. I've seen him peering at you. He's awestruck. You two should talk."

"There are things I want to tell him," I said.

"He'll listen. You're a wonder to him."

"Not a needy old man?"

"Could be that's how you see yourself."

I closed my eyes and pressed her against me, unable to say anything further.

"You okay?"

"No," I sniffled. "Truth hurts."

"You're a tough bird, Henry. You'll make it."

I grinned through the tears. "With your help."

"Tomorrow, I'll take you to the POW cemetery."

"I'm looking forward to seeing Novak's grave. But I thought...with Kimmel's death...you'd rather stay home."

"I wouldn't miss this chance for the world. Besides, someone has to drive the van."

"It will be good to have you there." I rested my cheek against her head, not wishing to talk further. Instead, I leaned back enjoying a peacefulness I hadn't felt in years.

****

The van left the Wheatland Hotel at eight the next morning. Plenty of time for Horst and the other veterans to catch the Kansas City flight to Berlin that afternoon. On the way, we would stop at Fort Riley, home of a formidable army unit, a restored cabin for a Civil War general, and a small German-Italian POW gravesite. Many of the veterans soon dozed, having eaten at the hotel's breakfast offerings. I remained awake, watching the fields and pastures pass my window. A few things had changed in fifty years: travel was faster, cars were sleeker, roads were wider and smoother, but the land remained the same. Horst stirred beside me.

"Sorry, Papa. I know you wanted to talk last night, but I was too tired. It's still hard to believe the depravity of Herr Kimmel. The man must have hated you for years."

"The day we met, he wanted to be my friend," I said, leaning back in my seat. "He craved it. But his character disgusted me, and I shunned him after that. Neediness turned to anger and then a thirst for revenge. It's still unnerving to see how his vengeance entangled Emily and Bill."

"A lonely man," my son said. "With no moral

compass."

I shook my head. "He chose to be lonely. Kimmel married Emily, not out of love, but to deny her to me. But she was never mine in the first place. We loved in a place far removed from war. Yet the war bound us together and tore us apart."

"You could have found happiness in America," Horst said.

"I couldn't leave my country in shambles, and I resented men like Kimmel who fled at the first opportunity. We needed every able-bodied man and woman to rebuild our cities."

"And then you met *Mutta*. Ever had second thoughts?"

I gazed out the van window, imagining the pretty fräulein giving pastries to my work gang. "Times were so different then. During the day she served food to builders and bartered for vegetables stolen from the Americans. She even scrounged for curtains and flowers. Anything to make life a little more beautiful. At night, she rubbed my shoulders with a hot towel. We had a good life together." I glanced at Horst. "No regrets at all."

"It's hard to imagine you and *Mutter* living that way."

"Working together forged our bond. I only wish your mother had lived to see the city become one again."

"I have to tell you. Gretchen and I have been talking about a divorce. But now, I'm not so sure. I should be more open to her. Make an effort to enjoy the things she likes. It's so easy to wander off on different tracks."

I turned to my son. "Don't lose her, Horst. Second chances seldom come around."

"I see that now. I still love her."

"Then tell her that. And show it."

"I'll do that."

"Now, I must tell you a decision I made." I took in a deep breath. "I'm staying here with Emily. We plan to marry as soon as it is proper."

"You're not going back to see the doctor?"

"I'm getting the best medicine here. More than any doctor back home can give me."

Horst remained silent for a moment. "I see your point, Papa. I never thought you would find love again."

"Emily is my second chance."

"You deserve it." He squeezed my knee. "I can't wait to tell Johann and Caroline about the adventure they missed."

"Too bad for them." I grinned. "But I'm glad you came with me. It gave us a chance to understand each other."

"I'm sorry I paid little heed to your concerns."

"There was so much I didn't tell you. You'd have thought me insane." I grinned at the thought.

But Horst didn't return my smile. "I'm serious, Papa. You tried to tell me more than once about your suspicions. I didn't listen. Please accept my apology."

"No apology needed."

"I feel guilty. Looking back, I see all the signs now. And I left you in danger."

"You came through in the end."

"Only with the help of Mrs. Kimmel and Mr. Henning. Hang onto her, Papa. She brings out the best in you."

Some forty minutes later, we pulled off Interstate 70 and stopped at the Fort Riley Visitors Center where we obtained passes to enter the army base. The guard at the main gate allowed us to pass. Minutes later, we drove along well-maintained roads and manicured lawns to a small hilltop not far from several bronze statues. Surrounded by ornamental trees and a waist-high brick wall, the gravesite sat apart from the historical buildings that dotted the landscape. We left the van and soon assembled inside the wrought-iron gate, each of us stood before a small slab headstone. In our hands, we held a wreath provided by Emily.

As senior officer, Colonel Ernst Reinhardt spoke for the group. "With humility, we pay our respects to these young soldiers who died far from home. Each man's story is different, but all were sons who fought for the Fatherland. They were our comrades. Our brothers. We marched and fought together. Celebrated victories and weathered defeats. We still hold you in our hearts. And in time, we will meet again. In peace." I marveled that a man like Reinhardt could put those words together.

After a moment of silence, I placed the wreath on my friend's grave. His small headstone read: B. NOVAK, 1943. Placing a hand on the limestone, I hoped to feel a connection to my friend. A gust of wind ruffled the branches above us, nothing more. "Until we meet again across the river," I whispered.

Horst offered me a handkerchief. "He must have been a good comrade."

I peered at the marker. "Brian and I. There are stories I could tell you."

"We're still two hours from the airport."

"True." I nodded. "Time enough to say how we first met, and our time in the desert."

Horst leaned forward. "You know, Papa, we can plan a fine German wedding for the two of you: a quiet church service followed by celebrating and dancing."

"A honeymoon in Berlin. I think Emily would be thrilled."

"You two seem so comfortable together. I'm looking forward to the family meeting her."

Some of the veterans were boarding the van while others wandered to a bronze officer astride a magnificent horse. Emily motioned for Horst and me to get inside the van. "We'll pick up the rest on the way out."

As we regained our seats, Horst met my eye. "I feel like I know you better. Sorry to leave without you."

"This is not the end," I said. "But a whole new beginning."

A word from the author...

Born and raised in Kingman, Kansas, a small agricultural town not far from Wichita, I grew up in a family with many relatives who loved to tell stories of the Depression and life on the farm. Much of this went into my first novel, *Dust and Roses*.

I went on to Emporia State University where I got a degree in Rehabilitation Counseling. I have worked as a supervisor in sheltered workshops in Great Bend and Hutchinson, as a Rehabilitation Counselor for the State of Kansas, and as an Examiner. After thirty years of running a small business with my wife, Debbie, we are enjoying retirement. And that gives me more time to write stories.

Thank you for purchasing
this publication of The Wild Rose Press, Inc.

For questions or more information
contact us at
info@thewildrosepress.com.

The Wild Rose Press, Inc.
www.thewildrosepress.com

www.ingramcontent.com/pod-product-compliance
Lightning Source LLC
Chambersburg PA
CBHW070807030726
47504CB00003B/729